I0700900

SILENT DEATHFALL

NATALIE TRIUMPHS

Copyright © 2022 Natalie Triumphs

First Printed in 2025

All rights reserved.

No part of this publication may be reproduced, stored in a retrieval system, or transmitted in any form or by any means—electronic, mechanical, photocopying, recording, or otherwise—without the prior written permission of the author, except in the case of brief quotations embodied in critical articles or reviews.

This book is fiction. Though many of the cities and vacation spots in this book, such as Yosemite, do exist, all references to people, places, events and organizations in this book are fictional and any resemblance to real people, places, events and organizations are purely coincidental.

Published by **House of Indigo**

www.houseofindigocollective.com

Ebook ISBN: 978-1-966187-09-7

Paperback ISBN: 978-1-966187-10-3

This book is dedicated to all tree-huggers who love Yosemite National Park, to all survivors of domestic violence and to all independent reporters who defy censorship to expose what Americans most need to know.

Trees have judicial standing and probably grass too. US Supreme Court Justice William O. Douglas, the Free Speech Justice

The American people might have a criminal syndicate running their government. Six-term Democratic Congresswoman and 2008 Green Presidential Candidate Cynthia McKinney

If we stick together as an American people we can bring down the war criminals that are running our country right now. Cindy Sheehan, Vice Presidential Candidate, Founder of Gold Star Mothers for Peace

Children have a lesson adults should learn, to not be ashamed of failing, but to get up and try again. Civil Rights Leader Malcolm X

The tyranny we have imposed on others is now being imposed on us. U.S. Political Prisoner Mumia Abu-Jamal

When the people are afraid of the government, that's tyranny. But when the government is afraid of the people, that's liberty. President Thomas Jefferson, Author of the Declaration of Independence

PROLOGUE

The air was crisp with a scent of pine, the sky was blue and a rush of excitement went through me as my sister, Tatiana, and I hiked down the Panorama Trail from Glacier Point towards Yosemite Valley, my favorite place on Earth. Though the Valley was too low to be viewable from this angle, Half Dome was clearly visible. I was so happy to be vacationing with my sister and brother, I didn't mind the pain in my injured ankle that ached and felt as if it would falter with every step.

My ankle had been badly twisted, maybe sprained, on a hike from Nevada Falls with my brother and sister the day before. I wasn't about to allow physical discomfort to get in the way of my time with Tatiana, the most important person in the world to me. Not wanting to be a burden, I had wrapped my ankle as best as I could and controlled my reaction.

"I'm so glad we're doing this," I marveled to Tatiana. Warmth flooded through me as I thought of how our brother would be waiting for us when we got down to the Valley. I wanted more than anything to rebuild my relationship with both of them. Since they had moved away from home, I had missed them so much. I silently wished we could stay here, hanging out together, forever.

"I'm not. I don't want to be here," Tatiana said, emotionlessly.

"But I thought you wanted to take this trail."

Tatiana seemed to ignore my response.

"You said you'd been looking forward to this since we arrived," I recalled, wondering if I'd done something wrong. "You seemed eager when we caught the bus for the Point."

"I changed my mind," she said angrily.

"I'm sorry. Maybe we can take a bus back to the Valley. We left the car at the Lodge."

"They're on a minimal schedule today. The next one isn't due for hours. And my cell doesn't have a signal here."

"I forgot mine in the room. It only works in limited places in the Valley, anyway. Yours may work better further down the trail. We might be in a dead spot."

"My cell hasn't worked since I arrived at Yosemite. You should have made sure we both had phones with the right carrier."

"I'm sorry."

She rolled her eyes.

Darn. I'm so stupid. Tatiana hates it when I say, "I'm sorry." "Um, we can make the best of it. We should be able to get back in time to eat at either the Lodge or Curry. I think Zinney said he wanted to eat at the Lodge."

"I don't see why we have to eat with him. He left you injured on the Muir Trail yesterday."

"I want him to have a good time here. Besides, he was nicer today."

"Him? Dad taught him to put down women. And you subjected me to living with both of them."

"Would you have preferred CPS take charge of our lives?"

"You were too tight with Mom. I wanted out. And I hated Mom for letting Dad beat her."

"She didn't want to be beaten. Dad threatened to kill everyone if Mom tried to leave him. She took those beatings to protect us and she made sure we got what we needed. Thanks to her, we're alive and safe." *Am I brain-dead?* I knew better than to defend myself or Mom to Tatiana. "Can't we let this go for now?"

"You didn't call the police."

"You saw what happened when we tried to tell anyone. Nobody

believed us. They all thought Dad was a great guy. Everyone we tried to speak to, even that minister, thought we were bad and disrespectful for talking against him. Remember when Mom asked that policeman for help and he told her to be a better wife?"

"That's because Zinney stood by Dad and blamed her for her beatings. You and Mom should have cut off your friendship with Zinney."

"He's our brother. He was there too. He watched the beatings like we did. You and Zinney were safe. After Mom was gone, I took the beatings. We made sure he didn't touch you." *Why do we have to do this here?*

"You should have left when he started beating you," she furiously reproached me.

I had to get out of this argument before she held it against me forever. *How can I make her understand and not be mad at me?* "CPS would have taken us. Remember what happened to Janna, the girl down the street? After CPS got her, she got sex trafficked to Thailand. And Erin, that girl in grammar school who was taken from her parents by CPS, died of a drug overdose in a group home. I didn't want us to go to a group home and be sex trafficked. I'm sorry you had to watch the beatings." *Shoot. I said "sorry," again.*

She glared at me. "Don't minimize what I went through. Dad was a monster and I had to see Mom, and later you, get bruised and bloody. Do you have any idea how much I hated it?"

"I'm really, really—" I didn't want to say sorry again. "I wish I had found a way to make it better for you. I did everything I knew to make sure he didn't take things out on you." Tears welled up in my eyes and I wiped them, not wanting Tatiana to see. I knew any sensitivity on my part made her even angrier.

"You could have figured something out. Getting beaten isn't a fraction as bad as the emotional impact of what I went through. I had to watch and I'm ruined for life."

"What could I have done?"

"You could have run away with me."

"Mom was there for us and we needed to be there for her. After she passed, there was nowhere to go—except to make sure you got into the college of your choice and you did. I was the one who had to stay."

"Yah, yah, yah. You did this and that."

"I know things weren't great back then, but you're doing great in college." I turned away. *I can't let her see me cry.* "At least, you won't have any college debt. I gave you the college money Mom left me. I just want us to be close again, like we used to be."

"You know there is no way I will ever give you back a penny of that money."

"That's fine. I don't want any of it back. Can't we just have a good time, today? Please? It's a beautiful day. Why fight here?"

"Because I want away from everything—including you."

"But you're the one who got away. You're at Berkeley. I love you. You act like you don't even like me at all."

"I don't."

My eyes were filled with water. The tears started rolling down my face. I hated myself for not controlling that. "Look, I did my best. Please. I'm really sorry." *No! Why do I keep saying that? I'm a total idiot.*

"And that's the problem. You're pathetic. Even your clothes are raggedy and out of date."

"I'm getting by."

"On crumbs."

"Just, please, don't be mad at me. I only want you and Zinney to be happy. Mom wanted that too when she was alive."

"You don't get that Zinney isn't your friend. Why do you keep being nice to him? Remember what that guy said when he helped you get down to the Valley yesterday after Zinney injured you?"

"I've done more for you than for Zinney."

"Because Dad hated girls and you wanted to compensate."

"I wasn't compensating. I was afraid Dad was going to kill me and all I cared about was making sure you and Zinney would be safe and okay if I didn't make it. I thought you and Zinney had more of a future than I did. And you do have a future." *There has to be a way to turn this conversation positive. I'm blowing it by defending myself. If only I could find the right words to get her to understand I love her and I'm not a bad person. Maybe I am bad or she wouldn't dislike me.*

"Playing Cinderella again?"

"I'm not Cinderella. I don't expect anyone to save me with a glass slipper. I'm just doing the best I can."

"That's not good enough."

I kept trying to stop the tears that continued to stream down my cheeks but it was useless.

I tried to change the subject. "Look at that blue jay over there. He's beautiful. I'm so glad there are still some blue jays, here."

Tatiana rolled her eyes, again, and took off running. I had pushed her too far by defending myself. *I'm so dumb. I should have just agreed with her on everything.*

I tried to rush to catch up, but my injured ankle hurt too much to go fast and my limp got more pronounced. I was thirsty. I was carrying the backpack with the cameras, binoculars and a few other things. Hers had the water.

Maybe when I catch up with her, she'll be over this and everything will be fine. We aren't just sisters. We are best friends—or at least we used to be.

I clutched my chest, as pain erupted, almost overwhelming me. *Nerves.* I hoped my heart wouldn't misbehave again on the way down the mountain. I had forgotten my nitroglycerin in our room at the Lodge.

My leg ached as I stumbled forward. Dizziness set in and I collapsed, seeing visions of flowers. I knew I was dreaming, but it felt better than being awake.

Fainting wasn't normal for me. I forced myself awake and tried to sit up but couldn't. I had trouble catching a breath and everything was swirling. *It's just a panic attack. It couldn't be a heart attack.* I hadn't had enough money for the daily heart medicine I was told I needed to take, but my stress-related cardiac condition hadn't killed me so far.

Tatiana was right. I hadn't cared about myself for a long time. Maybe I was getting what I deserved. But I always hoped somebody else would care—maybe just a little. My mom did, but she was no longer here. I needed to stop feeling sorry for myself. *Self-pity is disgusting.*

I lay there in a misty haze, wondering if I would die. Nobody would miss me. My life had no value. I had been repeatedly told that during the beatings and I had no reason to believe otherwise. The closest person in the world to me had run off and left me, knowing I was injured. Maybe she was right to do that.

I didn't know how long had passed, but the sky was growing dim, and we had started early in the day. That's when I saw them. Helicopters. Lots of them. There was no sound of engines, weird.

How long had I been out of it? It was close to dark. The copters were flying past me.

Is it a search party coming for me? Maybe my sister really does love me. Of course, she wouldn't just leave me here. Maybe both Tatiana and Zinney are on their way up the mountain, to find me, worried when I didn't make it to the Valley. They know I've always put them first. Tatiana just had to have been saying those mean things for effect. She couldn't have meant them.

Lying down, I was probably invisible from the air. I managed to push myself up, hoping they'd see me.

The helicopters didn't come back. Instead, above me, I next saw planes, also silent, small ones that almost blended in with the sky, following the same route as the copters. All I could hear were the dim sounds of wildlife on the mountain as the copters and planes headed towards the Valley. There was no airport there and yet they were descending.

The sight sent an ominous shiver through me. In all my times at Yosemite, the only flying devices I had observed were a medical helicopter and a rescue helicopter but never more than one at a time.

In the distance, a ghostly grey cloud seemed to settle above the Valley. It couldn't be a sandstorm. They didn't have those in Yosemite. The campfires would be starting soon. I had always loved the smell of campfires. I sniffed, but there was no scent of any fires.

Above me, the sky was blue. Though the Valley itself couldn't be seen from my location, the top of the menacing shroud gave me an eerie feeling.

I worried more and more about my sister. I hoped that she wasn't caught up in whatever that veil over the Valley was. I managed to get up and tried to walk.

I felt my body hit the ground, again.

My eyes didn't want to open, though the ground felt hard. Images of happy times with my sister and brother flashed through my mind—times when we were younger, when we did everything together.

The words the man who helped me on the trail the day before had said, when I kept hoping to catch up to Zinney, grated through my mind. "Forget about that guy. He's not worth it." *How could my brother not be worth it? I love him.*

I found the strength to re-open my eyes. Wolves. They were staring at me. Two of them came closer and clasped my arms in their mouths. A moment later, I felt my legs in the mouths of two other wolves.

I screamed as they dragged me away, maybe to their lair. I prayed to die before they ripped me apart. I didn't want to feel the pain and horror. The dizziness helped. Whether from fear or from my condition, I was barely able to keep my eyes open. Unless this was a dream, this really was going to be the end.

Everything went black.

CHAPTER 1

Fear for my sister crept through the blackness and invaded my dream state. Wolves. If they were with me, they were away from her. But there could be more. *She has to be okay. That's all that matters.*

I don't know how long I was unconscious. I felt someone or something licking my face. Had I just dreamed about the wolves or were they tasting their dinner? I kept worrying about my sister. *Where is she? Is she safe? It's my fault she left. I upset her.*

Immense pain overwhelmed my chest, followed by a sense of peace. All I could see in my mind were clouds.

I heard or imagined my late mother's voice. Before I could grasp what she was saying, the voice was gone—maybe even she knew I was awful.

I opened my eyes. There was a set of human eyes, not my mom's and not wolf eyes, looking at me. I tried to focus.

The eyes, so kind, caring and concerned, immersed me with a feeling of warmth and safety as they searched mine.

Is this an illusion or another dream? Maybe, I want someone to care so much, I'm imagining it. On my other side, I felt something licking my shoulder.

"Back, Everlove," a gentle male voice urged. The feeling of being licked stopped and I felt movement on the other side where the licking had been, but I was still completely unfocused—except on the eyes that seemed to reach into my very soul. I felt a hand softly touch my face as a light aroma of pine permeated my senses.

"What—" My mind was too cloudy to formulate a question. Something was attached to my arm on the same side as those eyes. I touched it with my other hand.

"For a minute, I thought we had lost you. You were extremely dehydrated. I gave you fluids through an IV."

"Is this some kind of hospital?" I asked.

"Stay out of those. They aren't safe anymore," he said matter-of-factly.

"I understand that."

My vision was becoming clearer. Near me sat a guy, a really, really good-looking guy. In that moment, I could have sworn that he was the best-looking guy I had ever seen—especially with those eyes. I couldn't tell if he was my age or maybe in his early twenties. He had light brown hair, blue-green eyes and a warm, friendly smile. He had the kind of face that could land him a starring role on any movie set— well, any movie set where he had the connections to be given a chance.

Embarrassment hit me. I wanted to cover my face. I probably looked a mess and yet his eyes didn't seem bothered.

"Where am I?"

"My humble abode." His eyes seemed to laugh as he smiled.

"You have medical equipment in your humble abode?"

"I do. I used to be an EMT. When I stopped, I made sure I still had whatever I needed to take care of those I cared about. Like I said, hospitals are no longer safe."

With some difficulty, I pulled my eyes away from his and checked out my surroundings. It didn't look like a regular room. The walls were formed of some kind of rock. I froze, seeing two wolves staring at me from the foot of the bed. I turned my head. There were two more on the far side of the guy. One was sitting on the bed, watching me closely with its face inches from mine.

I cringed. "Wolves."

"They won't hurt you."

"Wolves."

"They are the most misunderstood beings in the world. Come here, Everlove."

The wolf at my side got off the bed and moved around it next to the guy.

"Everlove saw you and got the others to help her bring you here."

"You're saying the wolves rescued me?"

"They don't take to just anyone, but they really seem to like you."

"I must smell like dinner."

He laughed. "These four are more likely to find dinner for you to eat."

"They're trained?"

"More or less. My brother is a ranger. When authorities were killing wolves, he managed to rescue part of a litter and bring it here. He and I raised them. Sometimes, they help me find people in need. Though this is the first time they found a beautiful unconscious girl and brought her back here. In fact, this is the first time they have brought anyone into our home."

"Thank you," I said to the wolves, wondering if they could understand me. "And thank you," I addressed the guy.

"If I were still working, I'd be doing this full time."

"I meant for kindly calling me beautiful."

"You must have had some terrible people in your life if you don't know you're a ten thousand out of ten."

"Is that part of your bedside manner, doctor?" The last thing I would have considered myself was anything but plain or worse.

"You really don't like yourself, do you?" He shook his head.

"Nobody does." I couldn't stop the tears again. "I'm sorry. I don't mean to cry and I'm sorry I said, 'I'm sorry.'"

"Did some guy dump you here?"

"My sister left me."

"And so, you came up towards Glacier to forget?"

"She left me on the trail."

"It sounds like she's a very self-centered person."

"She's really great. She goes to Cal and she's an A student."

"Well, she doesn't get an A at keeping her sister safe."

"It's not that. It was probably my fault."

"I doubt that. Let's talk about you. Have you had any previous cardiac issues?"

"Some. Did I have a heart attack?"

"After they brought you here, you went into cardiac arrest. You responded immediately to the CPR."

"Thank you." That's when I realized my chest was in pain and it must have shown on my face.

Apparently noticing my reaction, he responded, "Was it from the jab?"

"Jab? No. I didn't need any more cardiac issues. I refused and tried to talk my sister and brother out of getting them."

"They were jabbed?"

"They thought I was crazy and threatened never to speak to me again. So, instead of being ostracized, I pretended I was. Besides, my dad was insisting on it." *Why am I saying all this to a stranger? And an EMT? Will he dis me, too?*

"Dehydration, depression and other things can trigger a cardiac arrest. Do you take anything for your heart?"

"I can't afford heart medicine and so, no. I was diagnosed a while back but I'm not taking anything for it." I wasn't going to say my dad wouldn't pay for my medicine and after he died, I didn't have insurance and didn't trust government assistance.

"That might be a good thing. Doctors are overprescribing and making cardiac conditions worse."

"I've heard about the statins."

"Never take one of those."

"I don't plan to."

"I put some glutathione, Arterosil and nitric oxide into the IV to help with your heart. I want you to rest for now. When you are hungry, I'll bring you some food."

"The Valley. What was with all the helicopters and little planes?"

"It's a good thing you didn't make it to the Valley. They were spraying again this evening."

"Spraying what?"

"We can talk about this when you've recovered more."

"My sister was ahead of me. My brother is there."

"Let's hope they were not in the open when this evening's spraying happened. Don't worry. I'm sure they're fine. It would have been a lot more dangerous for you with your condition."

But was he just saying that to appease me? I found myself very worried about my family. I wondered if side effects from all their jabs would put them in even more danger than me if they breathed in what was being dropped. The side effects from the jab had become well known, but with each new purported plague, they pushed even deadlier jabs.

I wondered if the spraying was malathion or some other pesticide they used to drop in California at night. The one assurance I felt was that the government wouldn't do anything to hurt the wildlife.

"Let's see if I can guess your name."

"Not likely. It's awful."

"Hi, Awful. I'm Paul."

I started to laugh. My chest hurt more than a little—probably from the chest compressions. "Pleased to meet you, Paul," I squeaked out. "Paul's a nice name. Mine is worse than awful."

"Is that first, middle and last? You aren't one of the Cheneys or Rothschilds, are you? I've told the wolves they aren't allowed to rescue any Rothschilds or Cheneys."

I started to laugh, again, but stopped as my chest felt tight. "Faithful."

"Faithful. That's unique. I've met people named Faith before."

"I'd rather have a name that didn't make me a loyal follower."

"But it fits you. You are loyal to your family. Of course, you could always change it. How about Treasure?"

"That's a silly name."

"Hey, you're the patient and I'm prescribing it for you. Say it to yourself ten times. 'I'm a treasure.' Go ahead."

I laughed.

"I'm serious. Say it. Doctor's orders."

I said it quietly.

"Louder."

"A treasure."

"I'm a treasure," he projected.

"I'm a treasure!"

"I can barely hear you." He raised his hands to encourage me.

"I'm a treasure."

"Eight more times."

With each uttering, I felt more and more alive, almost like I was having a rebirth. "Thank you." *Even if it isn't true.*

"Now you can always change it to something else if you want to. But if you do, make sure you change it to something that makes you feel good. Now, I'm going to let you rest."

"I need to find my brother and sister."

"If you are feeling well enough in the morning, then maybe. You shouldn't go down there alone and especially not at night."

"But I need to make sure they're safe. My sister and I were supposed to meet my brother at the Lodge, I think, for dinner."

"They'd be best staying inside at the Lodge. Besides, if your sister left you there, let her wonder until morning."

"What if she comes back?"

"Does she have access to a car?"

"Yes."

"My brother's a ranger. I'll ask him to keep an eye out for her. He can call down to the desk at the Lodge in case they inquire. Her name is Tatiana?"

"Yes. How did you know?"

"You talked while you were unconscious. In the meantime, you need to de-stress."

Everlove came over and looked at me through her big dark eyes. Paul had said she wouldn't hurt me. Still, I felt a twinge of fear. She could take off most of my arm in one quick meal. But then my arm, now closest to her, was attached to an IV.

I found I couldn't stop looking into her eyes. It was as if her eyes were the window to her essence, and what I saw through them was so beautiful, I almost wanted to cry. I was no longer afraid. Before I could think more clearly, I reached out with my free arm and petted her. She jumped up onto the bed, crossed to the opposite side from the IV, and laid down at my side.

"Everlove, don't overwhelm her," Paul instructed.

"It's okay—as long as she doesn't eat me." I looked at her and put my free arm around her. "Thank you, Everlove, for saving my life."

I needed to get to my brother and sister, but I was so tired. I couldn't keep my eyes open.

In my sleep, I saw visions of my dad telling me I was ugly and then of Paul saying I was beautiful. My dad was more convincing. I woke up to find Everlove's head on my chest. The door, if there was one, was open, and I heard approaching voices.

"They're back," a man's voice said. "In full force."

"Aren't people dying fast enough for them?" That was Paul's voice.

CHAPTER 2

"I guess, when they blew up the Georgia Guidestones, they hoped people would forget. Those were like a confession of their plan." That was a girl's voice. "Why the Valley?"

"Lots of people close together. Tourists will put up with it to enjoy the park." That was the other male voice. "We don't know what they are spraying, but I think it's different each time. A few nights ago, there were a lot of complaints about the odors. The clouds over the Valley looked different last evening and whatever came down was odorless. I suspect they are using different chemicals or changing the density."

My brother and sister are down in the Valley. I have to get up and find them. As I sat up to figure out how to remove the IV, Everlove sat up next to me on my bed and howled.

Paul came in. "Are you okay?"

"I've got to get to my brother and sister."

"Are they down there?" This came from a tall, slender girl about my age who could have been a fashion model. She had shoulder-length dark hair, dazzling eyes and strong cheekbones.

"Autumn, meet—" He held out his hand towards me.

"Well, I was Faithful, but your brother renamed me Treasure."

"I like Treasure," she said. "I'm Autumn. Stay around. You don't know what it's like for a girl living with two brothers and no other girl to defend our sovereign rights."

"Thank you. That's very kind."

I noticed that I was still dressed in the same clothes I had worn on the trail. I was glad that Paul had respected my modesty, though I wouldn't have expected that from a medical professional or even a paramedic.

"I finally get to meet the girl our friends brought in last night," she said to Paul. She looked at me. "Nobody is better at medicine than my brother. He dropped out of medical school because they were pushing pharmaceuticals over caring for patients."

"As an EMT, I would get first crack at patients, before the hospitals messed them up."

"You really helped me. Thank you. If the wolves brought my backpack, maybe I can repay you."

"Forget it. It was my pleasure. Your backpack is here." He pointed to a chair beside a dresser.

"But you probably need—"

"I don't need your money or insurance card," he retorted, looking almost irritated that I was offering.

"I need to go down to the Lodge to make sure my family is okay."

"If they're staying at the Lodge, they should be fine. If you walk down there, alone, you'll definitely not be okay," the girl advised.

I started to pull the IV from my arm. Paul rushed over to help me. "That was your third bag. You should be well hydrated, but you need your strength."

"Remember, I'm a treasure. I'll pull together the strength." But I didn't feel strong.

"Even treasures need some rest. You're lucky. The cardiac arrest didn't do any damage. But that doesn't mean it's safe to go traipsing down a mountain."

"That's my brother. Always protective."

"Grant is going to be making breakfast. Would you like some?" Paul asked.

"I should get going."

"If you wait until the sun is up and the air has settled down, I'll walk with you," Autumn said.

"Sis, that stuff can linger."

"We'll be fine. If you want, we'll each take a dose of selenium and silica before we go."

He shook his head. "We'll talk over breakfast."

"They mostly only spray when it goes dark," Paul told me. "As I said, there could be some lingering residue in the air and I wouldn't play with the dirt. Whatever it is, it can't be healthy. Last night, they were early. They were back again this morning, doing fly-overs—not spaying this time, as far as I could tell. Maybe observation."

"Do I need to get my brother and sister some medical help to counteract the spraying?"

"I have some supplements. Hospitals are death traps." He had made that point the night before.

"Were you outside all night?" I asked Autumn.

"My older brother Grant is a ranger and I was up at the brand-new Glacier Point Ranger Station. It's above the spraying area. So is this place."

"How do the park rangers feel about this?"

"The sane ones don't like it. As for the rest, have you ever heard of mass formation psychosis?" Autumn asked. "It's why so many follow the insanity mouthed by our leaders and go along with narratives against their own consciences."

"How does your brother, the ranger, deal with that?"

"My brother doesn't talk about national topics when he's working. He sometimes asks questions as if he is just mildly curious about things. But many people don't seem to be reasoning anymore." Paul noted.

"A lot of people aren't," I said. "Like my sister and brother." *Why did I say that*? I wanted to bite my tongue.

"Were they jabbed?" Autumn asked.

"Yes." I shook my head. "They said that looking at ingredients in vaccines was conspiracy theory nonsense and Republican. When did the Republicans get the lock on independent thinking?"

"They have their blind spots too. A lot of people who used to have reasoning skills now refuse to look at any facts at all. They don't look at the injury reports from the round of shots that came years ago or the ones that followed those or with current ones."

"I've seen the injury reports. The information is out there for people to see."

"Thousands of healthy athletes dropping dead, doctors dying, pilots dying. That reminds me—" She turned to Paul. "Grant is going to give me another flying lesson later this week."

"He flies?" I asked.

"He's a ranger. He sometimes has to fly a rescue mission."

"Be careful. Just because you and Grant are safe doesn't mean the other airplanes in the sky won't go out of control," Paul advised her.

"Defensive flying. Be on the watch for jabbed pilots," I joked.

"You're normal, aren't you?" Autumn asked me. "You seem like a pureblood."

"Pureblood?"

"As in people who think for themselves. Not the mindless followers, who worship every narrative Deep State throws at them and want to kill anyone who refuses daily jabs or triple masking. Most pincushions, particularly from the latest plandemic, wouldn't risk their lives or inconvenience themselves for relatives."

"I couldn't get any jabs. I didn't need the added myocarditis. A lot of people who got them are still good people. Some, like Steve Kirsch and Jimmy Dore, got the initial jabs and they still really care about others. They've saved a lot of lives through education. I think that, maybe, people become more of what they are, kind or unkind, during these plandemics."

"Don't you two go risking your lives, getting to the Valley," Paul advised. "I should go with you. Make sure you're okay. You might want to wait another day. My brother can go to the Lodge after his shift and explain things to your family."

"Did the clerk speak with them?"

"I don't know. It's been tough getting messages back from the Valley."

"It would be best if I went down there, myself. Besides, I don't want them to think of me as incapable of making the journey down the mountain."

"You had a cardiac arrest. At least, let me drive you."

"I think the fact that I had a cardiac arrest would make them think less of me—if they find out."

"I need to talk with those two," Autumn responded.

"If you have to risk your life to impress your siblings, they don't deserve you." Paul looked angry.

I talk too much, another of my failings. "You saved me. Besides, fresh air and exercise are good for my health."

"Not after what you've been through. If something happens to you on the mountain—"

Autumn turned to Paul. "I'll watch out for her and radio you if we need help. The moment I see any signs, you'll be the next to know. I thought you were making more medicines today."

"Medicines?" I asked.

"Natural ones."

"Can you keep a secret?" Autumn asked.

"We don't want to burden her," Paul said. "If you leave, you'll be blindfolded. This location is confidential."

Everlove was at my side, licking my hand.

"Look at Everlove," Autumn said. "She doesn't take to people like this. If Everlove trusts Treasure, we can too."

"You are too nice," I responded. "I don't meet many people like you. Not anymore."

"That makes it easier for us to recognize normals. They're real people, not cold fake humans," Autumn said. "Do you know about the transhuman agenda?"

"Let's not overwhelm her," Paul discouraged.

"Come." Autumn took my hand. I managed to stand on my feet, which to me was a good sign. I felt a little wobbly but worked to control it so as not to deter Paul from letting me go down the mountain.

I looked around as Autumn led me from chamber to chamber, as touch panels in walls opened doors, and then down a long-curved hallway, also built out of stone, with similar hallways going off to the side. Paul walked alongside me, seemingly watching to see if I fell over, but he also seemed hesitant about the tour. If Autumn noticed his reluctance, she ignored it.

"We're in a cave," I observed.

"You didn't know?" Autumn laughed. "All the conveniences of a house but less conspicuous. You know what the Governor in California has done to houses, don't you?"

"Well, he's a real estate developer. Therefore, he's confiscating what he can."

"She is sharp," Autumn said, turning towards Paul. As the wall at the end of one corridor opened, I saw an inside field of fruit trees, grain fields, vegetables, grape vines, strawberries and other delights. It went on for half a mile or more.

"How did you?"

"The empty chamber was here when we first came. It's a natural cavern. Dad put sunlamps up and he and my brothers tilled the floor into good soil. That lake over there is coming from a natural underground river that runs into and out of the cave."

"You turned connecting caves into a farm and a home?"

"My dad was an architect. He did most of the work. Grant, Paul and I helped. He passed away several years ago."

"I'm sorry about his passing. It sounds like he was an amazing person."

"He was," Paul said.

Autumn looked sad and then lightened up. "There's enough food here to last for a lifetime."

"Well—as long as we keep growing it," Paul said.

"But you can't tell anyone," Autumn noted.

"Breakfast," a male voice announced from behind us. The man I saw as I turned looked perhaps ten years older than Paul.

"Treasure, this is Grant," Paul informed me.

"Hi," I said. "It is nice to meet you."

"My pleasure. Paul, you didn't tell me that your patient was this pretty."

"Thank you. You've all been so complementary."

"A normal," he said, looking at me.

"You can tell that I—"

"I told you. It's easy to tell the difference," Autumn said.

"A lot of jabbed people are nice, too. Many regret getting jabbed," I contended.

"A lot of those who were jabbed, have awakened, worked to reverse the effects, and gotten their humanity back," Paul said. "There are antidotes for those who want to stop the damage."

"There were different batches for different groups of people on the first jabs," Autumn related. "They didn't want to kill everyone off right away."

Paul continued. "The shots from the more recent plandemics are much worse than the original ones."

"So, the effects can be reversed?"

"We think so. A lot received just saline and only thought they were jabbed. Of course, most of those in power made sure they, themselves, got the saline. Many of those who got the real poison still retained or regained their normal personalities," Paul expounded. "The more boosters and jabs, particularly from the latest plandemic, the more danger."

"I hope that happens to my brother and sister—I mean, regaining their old personalities," I blurted. But part of me was wondering if I was falsely blaming the jabs for the way they were now treating me.

"How many of them did they have?" Autumn asked.

"I don't know. They wouldn't talk to me when I refused. So, I lied and pretended I had gotten all of them. If you go down with me, don't tell them otherwise."

Autumn made a sign of zipping her lips.

"Do you like pancakes?" Grant asked.

"I just worry about the glyphosate."

"No glyphosate in these," Grant assured me.

"Then, sure. I'd love some."

I discovered I was really hungry. I thought about how I had heard they usually give liquid diets or awful diets to people who have just had a cardiac arrest. Maybe these were healthy pancakes. I suspected Paul would have advised me to eat something else otherwise. That's when I heard the sound of thunder. Grant went to another room to check the weather and returned. "It's raining. That should clear some of the air."

"Are we close to the surface?"

"The monitors amplify it," Autumn explained. Grant looked a little uneasy, as if she had said too much.

After the pancakes. Grant brought a bowl of sliced peaches to the table and we dug in.

Grant left and returned from checking the weather again. "It's stopped raining, but it's slick out there."

"She looks like she'd fit Mom's hiking boots." Autumn turned to me. "Good for traction." Turning back to Paul, she continued. "We'll be fine."

I returned to the room where I had woken up and picked up my backpack.

As I started to go back to the dining room, I heard Grant ask. "Are you sure you can trust this girl?"

"Don't be a frug. She's nice," Autumn said.

"She's a good kid," Paul told him. There was something endearing about the way he said it. He didn't know me and yet he was standing up for me.

"She might freak out if—well, there were a lot of calls for ambulances and reports of bodies in the Valley last night," Grant warned.

I thought about my sister and brother. *They have to be okay.*

CHAPTER 3

"You two need to play it safe," Paul said. "Autumn, are you sure you want to do this?"

"Rather than hanging out up here with you guys and no female company? Consider this an educational mission."

"Blindfold her when she leaves," Grant insisted.

"I don't think that's necessary," Paul said.

"It's okay," I stated, entering the room. "I know what the government might do if they found this place. I wasn't born yesterday." *I have to get down there.*

Paul nodded. "I have some air quality sensors. I want you to use them. I'd feel better if I went with you."

"Bro, we girls need some girl time," Autumn contended.

"If anyone hassles you."

"I'll beat them up." Autumn pretended to pick someone up and toss him.

"A two-hundred-pound Sumo wrestler?" Paul asked.

"If I see one, I'll trick him into going to the edge of a cliff. Then, I'll trip him."

Paul smiled and shook his head. He gave his sister a hug. "Love you, Sis."

"Same."

He crossed his arms.

"Yeah. I love you too."

"Remember, if there's any trouble, call or radio me."

"Or me," Grant said.

Watching them, I felt a tug on my heartstrings. If only I had a relationship like that with my brother and sister. And now it might never happen. My eyes started to water. I held back the tears as I tried to avoid thinking of the worst.

Paul wrapped my ankle and then put a special boot on it. He put on a hiking boot, I guessed was his mom's, on my other foot. He handed me some nitroglycerine and Losartan Potassium that I put in my backpack. "Do you know about nitro?"

"Yes."

"The Losartan will help regulate your blood pressure. I don't care for traditional medicines but this one can be helpful. The Arterosil, glutathione, berberine, NAC and bergamot will also assist your heart. They're supplements. I put them in your backpack, along with your regular shoes."

"Thank you for saving me, Paul. You've got a beautiful family."

"I think so. It was a pleasure. I hope to see you back here."

On the way out, Autumn and Grant bumped fists. Paul gave Autumn a two-way radio. "If you have any trouble, I'll have it near me. Here is an air quality indicator." He said, handing her a small one with a lanyard to put around her neck.

"Better than most of the big ones." She turned to me. "You've probably noticed that cell phones have spotty coverage on the trails and in the Valley. My cell has an amplifier that works better than most, but it's not great."

"I've had trouble getting a signal. I accidentally left mine in the room. I make a lot of mistakes."

"Stop! Attack yourself again, and I might have to punch you out," Autumn half-teased.

Grant stretched out a scarf he had been holding in his other hand and tied it around my head.

As she removed the blindfold, Autumn said, "It's not that he doesn't trust you. It's that too much is riding on not making a mistake. You're the first person outside of our family who has ever visited the cave."

"I understand. I was just looking at your family and thinking of how I messed up with mine. Somehow, no matter how hard I tried, neither of my siblings like me at all."

"That's their loss. Get a new family."

"These days? Something's changed since I was a little. It's like society has become so cold and robotic. I guess that's what you were talking about."

"Have you been to any freedom events?"

"Aren't they right-wing?"

"Not at all. A lot of liberals attend them. The libs are split, you know. Some crazy, some sane."

"I've seen that. I have always considered myself a leftist but I keep getting called names for opposing war, forced vaxes and masking mandates by leftists who have ostracized me. I spend a lot of time alone. It's really kind of you to accompany me, but you don't have to."

"You kidding? I get to go down and check out the campers, maybe stir up a little trouble."

"Trouble?"

"Fun."

I smiled. "You're my kind of person."

"What about your parents?"

"Mom died a couple years ago. Six months ago, the Tiger Virus jab killed my dad."

"And your brother and sister didn't wake up?"

"When they were younger, they questioned the government, but suddenly they started believing all the narratives. They probably thought I killed him by failing to mask. Masks made me dizzy. My brother would have been glad if I had died instead of Dad. He adored our dad. My sister would be okay if I died. That's what I got from our conversation yesterday before she ran off."

"Jerks. Mass formation psychosis, like I said. At least, we're sane. We should stick together. What was your father like?"

"He had a violent temper he took out on me after Mom died. I made sure everyone else was safe."

"Of course."

"Of course?"

"Fits the pattern. Your siblings were Stockholmed with slightly different outcomes. Instead of canonizing you for saving them, they are abusing you. Definitely, you need a new family."

"Know where I could find one?"

"At a cave on this hill. I've never had a sister and always wanted one."

"I wish I had a sister like you. You are really nice."

Autumn pulled a music player out of her pocket and set it to play loudly so that we had a rhythm to dance to on the way down. She returned the player to her pants pocket, which didn't dampen the sound. Dancing made it an easier trip. Paul had done a great job with the wrap and boot. My ankle almost felt normal.

"Paul was really worried about you," Autumn said. "He thought you needed to rest for a few days. He asked me to talk you into staying."

"I would have liked to stay, but my sister and brother."

Autumn shook her head. "If I didn't know where my family was, I'd be doing whatever it took to find them, but then my family would never deliberately take off and leave me on a mountain." She must have seen that I was holding back tears. "I don't mean to hurt your feelings."

"I'm too sensitive. I get what you and your family have been saying, that I shouldn't be so obsessed with protecting my family. I was as sweet to them as I could be, making sure their needs were met and doing as much as I could to make their wishes come true, and they dumped me like garbage. Maybe I am garbage." *Maybe, I did deserve what they did to me.*

She put her arm around me. "They're the garbage, smelly garbage. I've never gone through anything like that. I don't think I'd be as nice as you. I'd go trash their things, grab their remaining clothes while they are showering and leave them naked."

I laughed. "Thank you. I wouldn't do that, but it's a charming image. My father beating me didn't hurt half as much as what my sister did to me. I didn't slave for him or trust him the way I did her. I stood up to him when he refused things my brother and sister needed. I put the money from my Mom into accounts for them and no matter how many times my dad got rough with me, I didn't give it to him. But my sister says it was worse for her."

"Like watching someone get beheaded is worse than being beheaded. You were their whipping boy."

"Whipping boy?"

"In the old days, kings and princes had whipping boys. They couldn't be punished for their misconduct and so a whipping boy took the blows."

"Did the kings and princes also wind up hating their whipping boys?"

"Did you ever see *Ever After*?"

"The Cinderella movie?"

"Yeah. You're like her but without the slipper and fairy godmother bit."

"And without the prince. My sister said I was acting like Cinderella before she ran off. She thought I was a terrible person because I let myself go."

"A no-win situation—especially for soft-hearted givers."

"You're a giver."

"I'm a giver with a hidden punch. I won't let people abuse me."

"It's always been easier to stand up for others than for myself."

"We'll have to work on that. Mind if I give your sister a few punches?"

I laughed. "But I really don't want her hurt, and she'd hate me afterwards."

"You have to stop caring how she feels. Do you want some hateful, cruel person to love you?"

"No. Just my sister. And my brother." I was tearing up, again.

Autumn put her arm around me. "It will get better. Now let's dance some more. Here's an old Green Day song. 'Don't want to be an Amer-ican idiot?'" she started singing along with the music.

"I love that song," I enthused. We both started dancing again. As I danced, instead of feeling exhausted, I felt better and better. "You've got some good oldies on your player."

"Paul made it for me one day when I was mad at the world. He put all my favorite songs on here."

"You have good taste."

"Thank you. I wonder if there is dancing down the hill?"

"There wasn't any the night before last. At least, I didn't see any."

"Maybe we can do something about that."

I had injured my ankle earlier that day and would have been limited to one-footed dancing without a partner if there had been any dancing that night. I doubted Autumn was the kind to let a minor injury stop her from dancing.

"There weren't any planes the night before last. You're lucky. You may have missed whatever they are dropping."

That didn't ease my worry about my siblings. We were taking the same route I was to take with Tatiana: the Panorama Trail to the John Muir Trail and dropping down from the Vernal Fall Bridge to Happy Isles. It was a long walk and I hoped Tatiana didn't wait for me partway down, getting back late to the Lodge.

In spite of my worries, I laughed with Autumn at older songs like Blue Suede's "Hooked on a Feeling." I felt alive as if all was well with the world, actually enjoying myself, almost forgetting what had brought us together. I hoped I would see her again, sometime.

"I bet that was popular decades ago."

"I heard it made number one on the charts. Can you imagine us singing the lead with Paul and Grant going, 'Ouga-chaka, ouga-chaka' behind us?"

The image made me laugh. "Paul is so nice."

"I guess I won't throw him out with the bath water."

"I meant, it's hard to think of someone so nice, living as a hermit."

"What about me? I live there too?"

"I guess it's like *The Flintstones*."

"That's on my player, too. Seemed appropriate."

"It certainly does. Paul seems so caring. I bet he learned that from your mom. Where is she or should I ask?"

"Officially, she fell off a cliff."

"Oh, no!" And I had gone on and on about my own problems without even inquiring about hers and Paul's. "Officially?"

"I heard a ranger tell Grant that he saw a guy yell at her for not wearing a mask and then push her."

"How awful. Did they arrest him?"

"He got away and the ranger said they didn't have a good description. Masked man with a hat."

"I'm so sorry. When?"

"About a year and a half ago."

"He must have been insane. Most people threw out their masks years ago. Occasionally, I'll see people driving alone in closed cars with masks on."

"Paul, my parents and I never wore them. They made the rangers for a time."

"I couldn't wear a mask. They made me dizzy."

"Odd. I guess you're human, not a plant, and need oxygen to breathe, rather than CO2."

"Your mom. I know what it's like losing a mom you love. Nothing can fix that and I've just been talking about myself."

"It's fine. It actually helps. Paul doesn't know what happened. He thinks she just slipped. He was devastated when she passed, and we didn't want him to remember her with anger about what happened. Of course, he was still angry but only at himself for not going with her. When Grant heard how it happened, he broke his fist trying to put it through a wall. That's why my brothers are so paranoid about me going outside. Paul thinks I'll fall and Grant thinks someone will kill me. That reminds me. When we get below, act as if you're as paranoid as everyone else and vaxed for the latest fake virus. Makes it easier to fit in."

I nodded. "Was your dad gone at that point?"

"He'd passed a couple of years before. Worked himself to death. I talk to my mom at times as if she's still here. I don't know if she's listening. But sometimes I think I see something or hear something moving, and I tell myself, it's her."

"I miss my mom too."

"What happened?"

"They said it was depression. My dad kept beating her. Tatty and Zinney were completely unsympathetic. One day, she just passed out. The autopsy was weird—though I never got to see it. I understand it claimed she was a seventy-five-pound, five-foot-eight Japanese woman. But she was five feet and as far as I know, there is no Japanese in our line."

"She was your mom. It's your right to view the results."

"Dad said I was a minor and as a minor, I had no rights."

"Except when it comes to a sex change operation or injecting poison."

"Yeah. Our state is crazy."

"The whole nation went crazy years ago and half of the population is still crazy. How many are on their fiftieth booster for—is the latest one called the Tiger Virus? I haven't seen any tigers outside the zoo."

"I'll say. But there are still good people in the world. Someday, I'll come back and repay you for your kindness."

"Repay me for having a real adventure for the first time in years?"

"Here it is," I responded to the next song. We sang out the words to "The Flintstones."

"How did you know the words?" Autumn asked me.

"I know all kinds of old show tunes. My mom used to sing them to me. I wish she were watching over me."

"Maybe she is and you just don't know it."

"Just so long as my dad isn't watching over me."

"Hi, girls," two voices said in unison. It was two boys, maybe college-aged, walking down the trail.

Autumn pretended not to hear them.

"We're going the same direction. Have you been down to the Valley yet?" one of the guys asked.

"We're on our way," Autumn said, nonchalantly.

"I understand it's nice. I'm hoping we can get a campsite."

"Maybe we're disturbing them, Jeff," the quieter one advised.

"I hear the campsites aren't what they used to be," I commented.

"Yeah," Autumn agreed. "Lots of bugs and pollution."

Not to mention potentially toxic dust, I thought, but telling what we knew would raise questions and get us called "conspiracy theorists."

"Are you alone?" the more talkative one asked.

"We're expecting our brothers to join us later," Autumn replied, acting disinterested.

"I promise we're on the up and up," the quieter one said. "I'm Eric. If you want us to go on, just tell us. Otherwise, company would be nice."

Autumn and I looked at each other. I nodded to her.

"It's fine," she said, casually.

"I'm Jeff. We're brothers," the talkative one told us. I noticed that the guys had a strong family resemblance to each other, both with slender builds, medium brown hair and green eyes. Jeff was a little taller and maybe a little more muscular. "And you?"

"Nancy and Betty," Autumn said.

"Which one of you is Nancy?"

We each started to react but I held my reaction.

"I'm Nancy and she's Betty," Autumn replied.

"Have you been to the Valley?"

"We're checking it out," Autumn told him.

"We're supposed to meet our brothers and some friends there," I half-lied.

"Maybe we can join your party. I've been told that Yosemite is better if you are with a group," Jeff commented.

"I hear that too," I said. "I mean, who would want to see the most beautiful place on Earth alone?"

"Of course, we should really think about bringing back the firefall," Autumn suggested. "Now that was beautiful, according to my parents."

"I heard someone did that one night. They don't know who. The person shoved dumpsters of burning oak down from Glacier Point," Eric delineated.

"And the rangers are still looking for the culprit," Jeff commented.

"Probably a fairy tale to keep up tourist interest," Autumn said.

The smile in her voice told me she was more than likely the courageous culprit. I liked her more and more. I wished I could stick around and help her do it again.

"Why do you think this trail is so deserted?" Eric asked.

"It's a long walk. Most people prefer trails that don't take so many hours," Jeff answered Eric's question.

"And yet, I hear they have a lottery to get to the top of Half Dome," I remarked.

"My hunch is there won't be much of a lottery soon," Autumn predicted.

"You know something the public doesn't?" Jeff inquired.

"Just a hunch," Autumn said.

"You sound like New York," I told Jeff.

"Had to get out of there. Moved to Iowa."

"How did you like it?" I asked. Their having left New York for Iowa gave me hope that these guys might be okay.

"I didn't like it much at all," Jeff replied.

"Oh," I responded, disappointed.

"There was too little to do. But the government wasn't as bad as New York's."

"I'll say," I noted.

"I heard California's government is pretty bad too," Jeff continued.

"The worst," Autumn interjected.

"So why did you come here?" I asked

"Yosemite," Jeff said. "Why did you come here?"

"Yosemite," I replied. "Also, I'm from California."

"Where abouts?"

"Orange County."

"How is it there?"

"Not as insane as some parts of the state."

"Who did you vote for in the last election?"

I suspected this was about more than learning our vote. The trouble is I had never voted. I wasn't yet old enough.

"We'll never tell," Autumn replied.

"When we get down there, if your friends are late, we can treat you to lunch, dinner, whatever," Jeff offered.

Rather than saying an emphatic "No Way," I told him, "We brought some food."

"And we're on restricted diets," Autumn added.

"How restricted?" Jeff asked.

"Organic macrobiotic."

Jeff cocked his head.

"That means they only eat organically grown, uncooked food. No dairy or meat," Eric told him. I knew she was making it up, but they didn't.

"That's got to be tough."

"We have to do what we have to do," Autumn said.

"Can't you skip your diet, just once?"

"Our mom is very firm," Autumn replied to Jeff. "She even has our blood tested for impurities twice a week."

"Strict mom."

"That's got to be a tough life," Eric said.

"We've learned to live with it," I responded.

I wondered how far this fantasy would go. The boys seemed to be swallowing the whole thing.

I didn't see any other hikers on the way down.

As we rounded the final bend on the trail from Vernal to Happy Isles, I gasped. Scattered across the trail as far as I could see were the lifeless bodies of a black bear, along with squirrels, bobcats, and other small wildlife.

CHAPTER 4

I almost collapsed in shock, wondering if this was a horror movie where the bobcats or the bear would reanimate and jump at us. As I continued looking at the bear, my heart almost broke. For a big creature, he looked so innocent, as if he couldn't harm anyone.

Jeff leaned down.

"Don't touch them. They could be diseased," Eric advised him.

As we continued down the trail, we had to meander through more dead animals: birds, a skunk, a fox, some rats, squirrels, rabbits and chipmunks. I needed to stay strong, but I was starting to feel woozy.

"You alright?" Autumn whispered.

I pulled myself together. "Yes." I swallowed some vomit that was trying to get out. I looked in the river and saw dead fish floating.

"This place doesn't look too healthy. No wonder nobody is walking on the trail," Eric said. "You girls okay?"

"Fine, we're fine," Autumn said, nonchalantly, as if this was an everyday occurrence, though I was sure she was as unnerved as I was.

As we got down the trail to Happy Isles, the museum door was open. "Let's go in and see some animals that are actually supposed to be dead," Jeff suggested.

"It will be more fun than wondering what happened to the other animals," Eric remarked.

"Maybe there's a message inside about the cause of what we saw," Jeff pondered.

"We'll meet you at Curry in three hours," Autumn bowed out.

"Three hours?"

"We have to find our friends," I said.

"And brothers," Autumn added. "We did mention our brothers."

"I remember," Jeff replied.

Heading towards the Lodge, the first place we came to was the Upper Pines Campground. I almost gagged at the sight of people collapsed in the open around their campsites. "Are they sleeping? Please tell me they are sleeping."

"Do they look like they're sleeping? Look, trucks." She pointed to trash pickup trucks coming down the dirt road inside the campground. "Get out of sight." We hid behind some trees and knelt down.

"What does the air quality say?"

"It's safe. But I bet it wasn't when this happened."

Autumn was shooting the scene on her cell as robotic arms picked up body after body and threw them into the trucks, driven by robotic workers. It felt morbid, as if I was a grave-robber, but I pulled out my camera, knowing that the truth needed to get out. I wasn't sure I'd be able to bring myself to show the pictures to anyone or even look at them myself.

"That thing's got a trash compactor," Autumn pointed out.

As it started to take off, I heard a horrendous crushing sound.

"There it goes. No individual graves for those people," she remarked.

"Won't their families ask about them?"

"Too many families are like yours, split over the jabs with those jabbed being totally cold towards the unjabbed."

"Tatiana and Zinney."

"Maybe they were inside. Were you staying at a campground or did you have a room?"

"I footed the bill for a family room at the Lodge."

She pointed to two bikes next to one of the camp sites. "Handy. Not locked."

"Won't the people who own them object?"

"If they can reconstruct themselves from the crusher."

"Good point."

She pulled a wrapped towelette package from her pocket and wiped off the seats, handlebars and other parts. I hoped that was sufficient.

"Let's go," she instructed.

We took off. Nothing could be seen stirring as we rode. We took the bike path and prepared to drop and hide if we saw any officials.

"Listen," she said. The trucks were close to the exit from Upper Pines.

"Let's make sure they don't see us as we cross the road."

"The entrance to Lower Pines is directly across the road from the exit from Upper Pines and they'll probably go there next and then across the river to North Pines if they haven't been there already."

We proceeded cautiously. It was a similar scene at the Lower Pines Campground. I had to stop to throw up. Autumn handed me a wipe. She looked distressed but clearly had more stamina than I did.

As we snuck towards the road that went over Stoneman Bridge towards the Village, we heard heavy vehicles. We slid off our bikes and laid them flat as we hid behind a tree. It didn't look as if any of the robotic drivers and workers were looking our way.

"Radioactive?" I asked.

"Nope. This detects that too."

"How about air quality?"

"More or less safe. It's closer to the higher end of normal but still a ways from the caution zone. Whatever they sprayed must have dissipated quickly after killing the visitors. It may still be in the soil, though.

We got up and continued on. We slowly turned to cross Stoneman Bridge. Nobody could be seen in the Merced River. On the other side of the bridge, we pulled to the side as we approached the former River campgrounds.

"Look, they're digging pits in what were once the best campgrounds," she observed.

We made sure to stay out of sight as we watched robotic workers shovel holes, toss their loads and drag mounds of dirt over the body parts.

"I guess they needed AI workers. The real ones probably couldn't stomach the job," I remarked.

"Don't count on it. Think of all the servicemen shooting brown children in the Middle East."

She aimed her cell phone at the activities in the Lower River Campground.

"You taking more pictures?" I asked.

"And video."

I got some pictures and a little video of the Pines campgrounds on my camera, too.

"I also got some good close-ups."

"What do we do with it? Will anyone believe it's real?'

"My brothers will."

I thought about what would happen to us if we got caught. If Autumn were brave enough to expose this, I needed to find the courage, too.

"Let's go," she said.

"Do you think they have surveillance?"

"If so, they don't know who we are. Let's go back across Stoneman and take the road that goes by Housekeeping to Sentinel Bridge. We don't want to go by the entrance here."

"How about the Swinging Bridge?"

"It's smaller and partially in the open. We could be more easily spotted crossing that."

I nodded. "You're right."

No human bodies were visible in Housekeeping. "If there were bodies here, they've already been rounded up," Autumn noted.

There were dead animals across from the Housekeeping Camp

entrance, though not nearly as many as on the trail. I figured some had been cleaned up with the human remains. My stomach was crawling, and I wanted to throw up again. I hoped the Lodge would be different.

As we got to the Lodge, I saw some movement. I went to our family room and knocked. Nobody answered. I went to the front desk. "I'm looking for Zinney and Tatiana Dover."

"The Dovers checked out. Tatiana, Zinney and—"

"Faithful?"

"Yes. All checked out."

"I'm Faithful." I showed her my ID. "But we were to have it for another two days. Was the checkout automatic or did someone do it in person?"

"I can't tell. The room was paid for in advance. Three keys were issued. It looks like two were returned. It shows a partial refund."

"When did they check out?"

"It looks like late afternoon yesterday, past checkout time. If you're looking to extend your stay, we have a lot of vacancies tonight."

"That's okay. I need to see if my brother and sister left anything."

"Do you still have your key?"

"I do."

"Nobody has checked in yet, but the maid will be cleaning it for the new guests in the next half hour."

"Thank you."

We rushed to the room. All of Zinney's and Tatiana's things were gone. Either somebody was very efficient in packing the correct stuff for my siblings or they packed their bags themselves. My suitcase was still there. I didn't see my phone.

"Do you think it's contaminated?"

Autumn used both the radiation detector and the air quality readings on my case and around the room.

"Nothing. I'd say it's safe. You plan to lug that up the mountain?"

"I need to check for our car. Just because they checked out doesn't mean the car is gone."

Autumn followed me over to the parking space where our van had been parked.

"Gone," I lamented. *Why am I surprised?* I knew they had issues with me, but now I felt so totally alone—except for my new friends, who would likely grow tired of me, soon enough.

CHAPTER 5

"They abandoned you and took the car?"

"Minivan. A rental."

"Who paid for it?"

"I did, but Tatiana used her ID to rent it as she's eighteen. Zinney is twenty, but she refused to let him drive as she likes to go fast and he prefers a snail's pace."

"Remind me never to get in a car driven by Zinney. I'd probably kill him in the first hundred feet. Those lowlifes stranded you. Would you like me to report them as dangerous drivers so they'll get one of those DMV priority re-exams? I hear the DMV likes to take away licenses, and the informants' names are kept confidential."

"They'd just get mad. I'll see if the desk can hold my things for a while."

"I'll call Grant. Maybe he can drive a truck down here to pick us and the suitcase up."

"My sister's cell didn't work at all at the Lodge. Maybe that's why they took mine."

"I have a signal booster and a two-way if it doesn't work. The Lodge is one of the locations where there is better reception—on some phones. Maybe you can get a new phone."

"Where do your brothers park? I didn't see a garage at your cave."

She laughed. "You haven't heard of flying cars sweeping into a clearing and teleporting underground?"

I smiled.

"Grant'll probably use his ranger's truck from the station."

"Of course."

The desk agreed to watch my case and backpack. "If you need your room back, let us know. We've had more vacancies and lots of no shows."

I asked how many vacancies they had.

"Almost three-fourths of the hotel. It's never happened before."

"Maybe people arriving last evening or early this morning," Autumn whispered.

As we started back to the bikes, I remarked, "At least, most of the people at the Lodge seem okay."

"Did you hear what she said about vacancies? I bet a lot of people wanted out of here. I wonder if they saw something that frightened them?" Autumn lifted her hands and plopped them.

"Let's hope my brother and sister are okay."

"They likely figured you'd died somewhere along the trail and left to get a good night's rest elsewhere. Don't take it personally. Kids like that would do as bad or worse to Saint Joan."

"I wonder if they put in a missing ranger's report for me."

She called Grant and spoke with him.

"He can be down here this evening. No ranger's report."

"What should I do?"

"Do you have any family at home?"

"No."

"Is the house in your name?"

"Tatiana is the remainder beneficiary. It was in my mom's name and she wanted to leave it to me, but I insisted on only having a life estate and on Tatiana having all the residual rights. My dad beat Mom pretty badly after that, but she cared more about us than herself. If something happens to me, Tatiana will get it."

"Treasure, you need to slap yourself on the side of the face and run next time you see your sister. Maybe, that's why she left you on the trail."

"I guess I can go back to Orange County."

"Is there anyone to take care of you at the house?"

"No. My dad trashed the place before he died after he found out he wasn't going to get it, and then the guy who was hired to clean it up after Dad died turned out to be a hoarder and added to the mess, turning it into a dumping ground. But it's home. I guess I can catch a bus or something."

"After your cardiac arrest? You're coming with me and letting Paul watch you until there is no more danger. Besides, we have healthy foods that will strengthen you."

"I don't want to inconvenience anyone. Besides, I just climbed down a mountain. If I can do that, I can take care of myself."

"You won't be an inconvenience, and exercise is good for your heart, but you need to be monitored. Also, remember all those athletes who have died of heart attacks since 2021. I owe it to the sane people in the world not to let that happen to you."

"I'm not sure it will sit well with Grant."

"He'll be fine or he'll never hear the end of it. And we can be like sisters. Grant wouldn't throw my sister out."

I smiled. "I could use a sister like you."

"Me too."

I thought about all the vacancies and the disappearance of my sister and brother. They had to be okay. They probably left before whatever hit the tourists. I wasn't going to let myself think otherwise. Besides, Tatiana was well enough to check out and take the car. I was incapacitated a long time before I saw the planes and the wolves—plenty of time for her to get back and for them to decide to take off without me.

"Cheer up. We have a date."

"Our dates probably freaked and ran."

"We'll see."

It was only a five-minute leisurely ride to Curry. When we arrived, the boys were waiting.

"It was like a horror movie," Jeff groaned.

"Without popcorn," Autumn remarked.

"You don't seem upset," Eric observed.

"You should have seen us a couple of hours ago," I said.

"We're strong women," Autumn told them. "Did you see the robots in the trash crusher trucks and the dump site?"

"We saw them do pickups at Lower Pines. What do you think killed all those people?" Eric asked.

"Water, food, poisoned air."

"Will we be next?" I looked up. "What if they spray again tonight before we get under cover?"

"That occurred to me. Maybe we'd better take one of those rooms at the Lodge," Autumn suggested.

"Lodge?"

"They've got a lot of vacancies." I said, "You'd be safer there than in the campgrounds."

"Do you have credit cards?" Autumn asked the guys.

"We both do," Jeff replied.

"This place is dead."

We all looked around in response to Autumn's observation.

"Better place for a party." Autumn always seemed to have the solutions.

"I like that idea," Jeff said.

Eric nodded.

"See that car?" Autumn pointed to a Rolls-Royce.

"We don't steal cars," Eric responded.

"The car will just be moving from a dangerous place to a safer one."

"We'll be more visible along the road," I noted.

"On second thought, let's take bikes."

The bike shop appeared open, or at least the door was open. Eric and Jeff came out a few minutes later with two bikes.

"Nobody was manning it. I left a note with some cash," Eric related.

Autumn shook her head. "Bet someone other than the owner picks it up."

Jeff used his card to get a room while we waited. We had informed our new friends that we would be picked up later.

"Not longer?" Autumn asked when Jeff handed her a key and told her it was for one night.

"I want out of here as soon as we can get a ride. Cemeteries never thrilled me," Eric said.

"If you give us your number, maybe we can arrange a date," Jeff suggested.

"I believe in serendipity," Autumn responded.

"There was a movie about that," Jeff recalled. "It took years for them to find each other again."

"But it was so worth it when they did."

I went back to the office and grabbed my suitcase and backpack as Autumn went to check out the store.

She greeted me with a cloth bag containing some bottles. "Seems the Lodge is short-staffed. I left cash, but since there was nobody there, I guesstimated the bill."

"Want some food?" Jeff asked as we joined them at the room.

"With what we saw today, do you trust the food?" I asked.

"Sealed imported bottles of wine," Autumn replied, pulling them out of the bag and setting them on the table.

"You girls know how to party." Jeff smiled.

Autumn connected her music player by Bluetooth to the TV set and we started dancing. "Bluetooth is generally a bad idea if you want your privacy. I wouldn't do this at home," she whispered to me. She more clearly said, "If we were at Curry, we could raid the sound system and have a huge dance floor."

Jeff nodded, going almost white as she mentioned. Curry "And wind up like the rest of the Curry residents."

"We didn't check the cabins there," I said.

"We did. Just a couple. That was enough," Eric replied.

"Quiet?"

"We got a little closer than that. Their lips were blue."

"Cyanide?" I asked.

"Or a similar poison."

I looked at the French cherry wine as Jeff picked up a bottle from the table.

"This was the only wine they had that couldn't be tampered with and resealed," Autumn told him.

Eric opened a bottle and we passed it around.

We looked at each other after we took a sip. Nobody was dropping. We started dancing to Green Day's "Holiday."

"Will Grant know where we are?" I quietly asked Autumn.

"I texted our location to his private cell. Grant isn't available until seven."

"Not much partying time," Jeff remarked, apparently having eavesdropped.

"I know, but what there is will be awesome!" Autumn exclaimed as he took her hand and started swing dancing her.

After half an hour of partying, there was a knock at the door. "Big brother is early," Jeff griped.

Eric opened the door and was shoved to the floor as an assault rifle was aimed at him. The assailant was wearing a ranger's uniform and swept the focus of the gun from Eric to each of the rest of us. Another person in a ranger's uniform was outside behind him.

CHAPTER 6

"Is partying now illegal?" Jeff asked.

"Shut up. We have a report you four escaped from a state mental hospital in Merced. We're taking you back," the officer in front practically growled.

The ranger's backup came forward with cable ties. Eric, having stood back up, placed his hands over his heart, as if having an attack, and collapsed, rolled and tripped the backup as Jeff threw a bottle of wine at the guy with the gun, hitting him in the forehead.

As the gun-toting ranger was trying to regain his focus, Autumn slugged him as I grabbed the gun.

"You're not going to use that," he said.

"Try me," I replied, working to add venom to my voice. I knew I could come across as fierce when protecting someone else. I had done that when I protected my brother and sister from my dad.

The tripped ranger stood, pulled a handgun out of his back pocket and aimed it at Autumn. "Shoot my partner and I shoot your friend."

A second later that ranger was falling to the floor, rolling in pain. With a wire stuck to him."

"Hi, bro," Autumn calmly said as Grant walked in, followed by

Paul, who slugged the guy I was pointing the gun at, as he started to turn. "You're early."

While Autumn kept her cool, I felt terrified—in spite of trying to look strong.

"If you want, we can go out and come back later," Paul responded.

"No. Now will be fine," Autumn said.

I looked at the guy who had been tased. He was rolling around in obvious pain. The slugged ranger started to get up. Grant pulled out another gun and fired at both of the threatening rangers. The gun didn't make much of a sound, but both collapsed unconscious.

"Tranq darts," he informed us.

Paul took the cable ties that were now on the floor and bound the original rangers' hands and feet. Grant took two washcloths from the bathroom and stuffed them in the mouths of those rangers as Paul pulled some strapping tape out of his back pocket and wrapped long sections around the men's heads, taping their mouths shut.

"You're early? Is that all you have to say?" Grant asked.

Autumn rolled her eyes. "Do the rangers have an APD out after us?"

"They aren't rangers," Grant replied.

Paul pulled a wallet out of the first one's jacket. He showed the ID to Grant.

"FEMA," Grant acknowledged.

"Somehow I don't think we would have made it to that mental hospital," Jeff remarked.

"More likely a lonely section of the road," Grant said.

Our two heroes stuffed the unconscious men in the bathtub and closed the bathroom door.

"You're not going to take them in?" I asked Grant.

"You want to be interrogated by the feds for the next year?" he responded. "How long do you have this room for?"

"Tomorrow at eleven," Jeff said. "We've got a late checkout."

"I suggest we all get out of here now."

"They'll have Jeff's ID information at the hotel check-in. When they find these guys, the feds will look for him."

"I used a wallet I found."

Autumn and I looked a little surprised. Then she shrugged and smiled.

"I didn't trust anyone at the park with my real name after what we saw," Jeff explained.

"Smart," I said.

"What's this stuff you two have been drinking?" Grant asked, picking up the open bottle.

"Cherry wine," Autumn said. "It was totally sealed."

"You two boys do know there are laws against supplying alcohol to minors," Grant stated.

"We're minors, too," Eric told him.

Paul looked at me. "This isn't healthy after what you've been through."

"Right," I said. "It was me that got your sister to drink. Sorry."

"You don't have to cover for me." She turned to her older brother. "You aren't my daddy, Grant."

"Where is your vehicle?" Grant asked the boys.

"Actually, we hitchhiked from Fresno to Glacier Point."

"Where do you live?"

"Arizona," Eric replied.

"I thought you were living in Iowa," I recalled.

"That was before Arizona."

"Okay. You two are going to need transportation home," Grant said. He went into the bathroom and searched the pockets of the two rangers until he found some keys. "One of these keys should operate their car." Before closing the bathroom door, he took the phones belonging to the two men.

I decided to skip the rhetorical question about whether Grant knew how many laws he was breaking. "Does the car need to be decontaminated?" I asked. "Something killed all those people in the park."

"You think the feds are going to poison themselves?" Grant asked. He turned to Paul and threw him the keys. "Disable the tracking and cover any cameras."

Paul nodded, looked at me and Autumn and left the room.

"Aren't you guys supposed to enforce laws?" I finally asked.

"Do you really think the spraying could have happened without official authorization?"

Grant went into the bathroom and brought back several wet hand towels. "Wipe anything you touched."

We wiped down the room.

"I'm glad you two showed up," Eric said.

"I suggest you take the road to Tuolumne and then leave down Tioga Pass. That will get you closer to Nevada. As soon as you can, dump the car. At the latest, dump it by eleven A.M. Don't use your cell phones in the car and avoid Bluetooth."

"You think their backup will be here earlier than eleven when they don't report back?" Eric asked.

One of the phones buzzed with a message. Grant texted back. "That should put them on hold."

"What did you tell them?"

"He had a lead on people with video footage and to wait until they heard further from Mike, the guy whose phone this is."

Grant locked the bathroom door from the inside, confiscated the bottles, and put a "Privacy, please," card over the doorknob. We followed Grant down to a black car with darkened windows. Eric carried my suitcase and backpack.

"Nice car," Grant said.

"When they find their men, they'll do a real search for the car. Get rid of it quickly. You guys need some cash?"

"The wallet was loaded," Jeff said. "I'm not a thief. Some guy, lying on the floor of the general store at Curry, had it lying on the counter. He won't need it anymore. I picked it up with a towel and rinsed it off with peroxide and water before taking it."

"That's still theft," Grant pointed out. "Use cash so the IDs aren't traced to where you're going."

"You're the most understanding ranger I've ever met," Jeff noted.

"These aren't normal times."

As Eric and Jeff drove off, Paul guided me into the back of the ranger's truck. Grant gently shoved his sister into the front passenger seat.

Inside, Paul put a blood pressure cuff over my arm. "Do you have a death wish?"

"I—"

"I know. You don't know the value of your own life."

"Can she stay with us?" Autumn asked, enthusiastically.

"Where is your home?" Grant asked.

"Orange County."

"Her parents are dead and the two nasties have the right to the house."

"Autumn—" Grant's statement was interrupted by his sister.

"They left her for dead and then left Yosemite with the car, deserting her."

"I'd like to monitor her for a while," Paul told him. He turned to me. "And no more alcohol until I give you medical clearance."

I was tempted to point out he was only an EMT, but given he had saved my life, he was better than any regular doctor.

"Will you be in trouble for taking off early?" Autumn asked Grant.

"I wrote in the log that I got a report of an accident in the Valley that I needed to check out. I'm going to have to doctor a report."

"Can you?" I queried.

"We passed a stopped car on the road near Bridalveil. I took down the license plate. The occupants were missing. There are tow trucks at the Village garage. I'm calling it in now."

He pulled out a radio and called the garage. Nobody responded. "I'll have to note that they aren't responding to calls."

"Paul, change the SIM card on Autumn's cell," Grant said. "Also, Treasure's if she has one."

"I thought I left mine in the room, but it wasn't there or in my suitcase when I got back."

Paul pulled the SIM card from Autumn's cell and replaced it. I wondered if Grant thought our new friends had called in the feds and faked their own arrests.

Before I asked, Autumn jumped in, picking up that the feds had tracked her cell phone. "But how?"

"You were probably picked up by one of those fake cell towers that recorded your number. When you texted me your location, that led them to you."

"Brothers to the rescue again," Autumn said. But from the flat way she said it, I suspected she was mostly concerned about a loss of freedom after we got back.

Grant handed Paul a blindfold as he parked. Paul put it in his pocket.

"Paul."

"I've got this."

Back at the cave, the wolves were excited to see us or rather me. I was still surprised that Paul had trusted me enough to show me an entrance. Our four-legged friends jumped up, looking like they wanted to be held.

"You're a bit too heavy for her, Everlove and Esther." Paul turned to me. "Usually, the wolves are eager to see me. I guess they have a new favorite."

"They've got taste," Autumn said. She knelt to her knees. The wolves jumped on her, following up with face licks as she laid back.

Paul and Grant had a private discussion and then Paul spoke to me. "I'm going to have you stay in my mother's room."

"Are you okay with that?"

He looked at Autumn. "My sister has a big mouth."

"She loves you," I said.

Paul picked up my suitcase and backpack and took me to the room. Like the other rooms I had seen in the cave, it had a touch panel in the wall that opened the sliding door. He looked sad as we walked into his late mother's room.

"If it bothers you too much, I can just stay on a couch."

"No. You might be here a while and this is a little larger than the room I had you in originally. I want to monitor you. If you need anything, let me know. We have a lot of supplies here."

"At least, now I have my clothes."

"I'd like to check your case over," he said.

"Sure."

He took it back out and returned a few minutes later. "It's clean—no tracking, hidden mikes or toxic chemicals. We should have checked your suitcase right away. But no harm done."

"Good."

He turned to leave.

"Paul, thank you. Since I lost my mom, nobody, not anyone, has been as kind to me as you and your family." I almost bit my tongue. He'd lost his mom, too, and I was still talking about me.

"Welcome to the family."

"Why are you being so nice?"

"You've given me a chance to practice my profession." I got that that was the easy response. His generosity surpassed his explanation.

I looked around the room. It had a warm feeling to it. I wished I had known his mother. I was sure I would have liked her.

There was an adjoining bathroom and I took advantage of it. After I showered and put on some fresh clothes, I went into the dining room. Paul brought out a couple of plates of fettuccine.

"It looks great."

"It's vegan, not because of political reasons. We don't have a cow. It has no canola oil. A lot of organic premixed foods have that. Very toxic. You probably know it causes brain damage."

"So, I've heard."

He handed me a couple of capsules and a glass of water.

"What's this?"

"Ivermectin. It got the Nobel Prize for human medicine. It will help get rid of any poisons from the Valley. Autumn also took some. The second capsule is zinc."

"I know about that. Thank you."

Grant came in and Paul went back into the kitchen. Grant lowered his voice as he spoke to me. "I hope Paul's right to trust you. You didn't see him after you left. He was pacing and kicking himself for letting you leave before you fully recovered. He kept saying that if something happened to you, he'd feel responsible. It was all I could do to get him not to run and catch you and Autumn."

"He's really a dedicated EMT."

"He's treated pretty girls before. He's never invited them into our home." His tone conveyed a sense of disapproval.

"Thanks for the compliment."

From his look, I got that he didn't understand.

"For implying I'm pretty."

"Your siblings must have really done a number on you."

"That's what Paul and Autumn have been saying."

"You should listen."

Paul came back in with plates for Grant and Autumn, who had just entered the room.

"Can we stay up tonight and watch some old movies?" Autumn asked.

Paul looked at me. "Treasure needs some rest."

"I'm fine," I said. "I think it might relax me."

"Good. You can come into my room and we can have a slumber party," Autumn encouraged.

"Not past midnight."

"Jailer." She sneered at Paul.

After dinner, we went to Autumn's room and she looked through her video collection. I glanced around. It was the room of a girl with multiple interests. Old rock n' roll record covers and pictures of people surfing and climbing El Capitan decked her walls.

"Have you climbed El Capitan?" I inquired.

"Not yet. Maybe we can do that together."

"I've only done rock climbing on walls, never on a real mountain."

"We'll learn together. Paul and Grant have both climbed El Capitan. See that picture over there." She pointed to one of several pictures on her dresser.

I couldn't make out the person in the climbing gear, but it looked as if it could be Paul.

Autumn pulled out a disc of *Men in Black III*. "The online sites generally have trackers that I have to get around, so I prefer my library of discs unless I want to see something new."

As we watched, Paul came in. Autumn gave him a look and he responded, "I like this movie."

"This is girls' night."

"I'll just sit on the floor and watch J save K."

Paul did just that. The warmth and sweetness of their relationship, banter and all, touched me. I kept wishing I had had that kind of relationship with my siblings. What had I done so wrong that Tatiana and Zinney hated me?

I had seen the movie before and it was one of my favorites, but I found myself dozing off before the end.

When I woke up, I was in the bed in the other room, still in my clothes. Had I walked or been carried? I hadn't remembered walking there. I got up and looked around the room, again. Their mother had stored pictures of the kids on top of her dresser, on the walls and in several of her drawers. There was even a picture on the bedside table.

The sheets smelled freshly washed as if someone had taken the time to change them before I wound up in the room.

I felt selfish for wanting a family like this. I knew it wouldn't be long before they'd grow tired of me and I'd have to leave. But that hadn't happened yet. I needed to be happy for what time I had with them—even if it might end in heartache. After all, those who knew me the best, always wound up hating or abandoning me, and I could never figure out why. Still, the thought of getting attached to another family and then losing again sent familiar pangs of pain through me.

I didn't know where my phone was. If I got it back, I'd be able to speak with my brother and sister and know if they were okay. But Tatty, as we had sometimes called my sister, never answered calls from numbers she didn't know and if I left a message on another phone that it was me, she'd assume I was okay and she didn't need to speak with me.

After knocking, Paul looked in to check on me. "If you are going to heal, you need to rest. Would you like me to bring you breakfast?"

"That's okay. I'm not much of an eater." Despite being with a wonderful family, losing my own family stabbed at me. I needed to get off feeling sorry for myself. "The world is being poisoned. We need to fight what is going on before more people die."

I had always tended to jump on bandwagons for causes. It was one of the ways I distracted myself from my own situation. My sister considered it another of my failings.

"We're keeping an eye on it."

"It's great that you are doing that, but those people down below didn't have a chance and if they do it again, more will die. We need a plan." I hoped I wasn't pushing too far or hitting an open wound. Maybe I'd be out of here sooner, rather than later.

"Are you always like this?"

"Like what?" I knew like what. *Pushy. Opinionated.*

"Eager to rush in and save the world. Sometimes, you need to let others handle situations." Everlove entered the room and climbed onto the bed. I sat down and she snuggled up to me. "Everlove agrees you need more rest."

"Now you are seeing my negative side," I said. "You can understand why my brother and sister left me."

"Because you care too much and they were colossal self-aggrandizing fools. You fit in here. You've got the warmth of my mother and the drive of my father. Both are gone and I don't want anything to happen to you."

"I remind you of your mom?"

"She would have done anything for us. She would build us up, telling us we could do anything. And my dad worked himself to death to make things better for us."

"My sister said I was sugary to a pathetic fault. I've got other issues, too. Like I'm strong-willed, impossible, unreasonable, relentless, pushing help on others—even when they don't need it and right now, I'm too focused on myself. You should be tired of my whining by now."

"You are also kind, caring, loving, supportive, self-sacrificing and you don't whine enough. I'll make a deal with you. Stay here for the whole morning and we'll walk to the ranger station together this afternoon."

Autumn came in with a tray of food for me.

"Thank you. You are too kind."

"I'd like to take credit. Paul cooked."

It was pancakes and fruit.

"Still, no glyphosate?"

"No glyphosate."

I had always loved pancakes but hadn't felt safe eating them in years until the cave.

"Do they have eggs?"

"Yes, but not fertilized eggs," he noted.

"Yeah. Paul says using fertilized eggs is like eating a baby chicken," Autumn remarked.

"We keep the two types of hens separated," Paul related.

"That's good of you."

"We can also make them without eggs if you want," Paul offered.

"You could start a restaurant business."

"The government would get its hands on the food and poison it."

"You're probably right."

"I heard you say you were going to walk to the ranger station today. I'm going with you," Autumn firmly declared.

"Have you finished your term paper on Kafka's *Metamorphosis*?"

"Yes. I dropped it off in your room this morning, and I finished my physics homework too."

"You homeschool?"

Paul explained. "I started medical school out of state, but things changed. My father passed away and my mom needed me. Now, I'm doing what my mom would have done with Autumn if she were still alive. What I don't understand is that you are the younger kid in your family. Why were you helping the older kids instead of the other way around? They should have been taking care of you."

"They were eager to get away to college and I wanted to make sure they had a future. College is expensive."

"But did they ever contribute to you?"

"Not financially."

"And I bet not in other ways, either," Paul surmised.

"Their needs were greater than mine and I figured that, someday, maybe they'd be there for me."

"Some kids help out their families, but there should always be a sense of obligation on the part of the receivers. Even when a mother is doing everything for her kid, the kid owes something back."

"I never got to give back to my mother. I guess being there for Zinney and Tatiana was like my tribute to her, and I was hoping that if they saw me giving, it would make them want to give to others in need. Sort of a *Pay it Forward* approach."

"The kid in that movie died. You have too many gifts to end up like that."

"What gifts?"

"Your intellect and your sense of devotion and love. I'll be back," he said. He left the room.

I thought about Paul's relationship with his mom. He clearly missed her and I suspected she was the reason he was so giving. Maybe in helping me, he felt he was helping her. But I wasn't her. I hoped he wouldn't resent me when he got to know me better.

"Wow," Autumn said. "My brother likes you."

"What? No. He's just being kind. He thinks I've got a negative self-concept and is trying to build me up, and well, he's a really nice guy who just wants to help."

"My brother isn't delusional, and he doesn't invent stuff to build people up. He's got a crush on you."

"Thanks, but there is no way on that. I'm sure he's met other girls more capable than me. Besides, he's older than me."

"He's twenty-one."

"How did he get so far in his career and schooling when he is so young?"

"He was homeschooled. He graduated to college at fifteen. He didn't have much time for dating. In fact, I've never seen him interested in a girl before."

"It's the physician-patient thing. He is treating me like a doctor who is trying to encourage a patient."

"I don't think so."

Paul came back with some books. "Have you graduated from high school yet?"

"Actually, I'm supposed to graduate online next month."

"So, you've got the end of this semester left?"

"Yes."

"Those online school platforms are a way for them to keep track of you. They'll likely be checking your location to make sure you're still in the district."

"I know, but what can I do?"

"If you want to graduate with your class, then you need to use a VPN or bounce the signal so that it looks like it's from your home county." He looked thoughtful. "If you want, I'll help tutor you on any tough subjects."

"Thank you. The trouble is, I blew my APs. I was scheduled to take them late. But then, instead of taking them this last week, I skipped them to meet up with my brother and sister."

"Wait," Autumn commented. "You came to Yosemite with your brother and sister while you were supposed to be taking exams?"

"Tatiana's semester ended early."

"And she was your priority," Autumn remarked.

"With the renewed vax insanity, I didn't know if I should take them at all. I knew they'd check if I took the earlier ones and I was hoping they wouldn't check for the late ones. You'd think people would learn."

"They did. People are refusing the vaxes. That's why the mandates are back," Paul pointed out. "Which exams were you going to take?"

"Chemistry, Biology, Latin and Environmental Science."

"Have you taken any AP exams before?" Paul asked.

"Yeah. There were a couple years when they let the mandates slide. I'm an AP Scholar with Distinction."

"You're really smart," Autumn said. "Maybe Treasure should be teaching me."

"I'm sure she can and I bet she'd let you get away with more than I do." He looked at me. "I knew you were smart, but not that smart."

"I helped my sister prepare for college. So, I had to be on top of a lot of stuff. I filled out her Berkeley application for her."

"You got her into Berkeley and she left you for dead on the mountain? So much for helping jerks," Autumn reacted. "You should tell the Dean of Admissions there."

"I wouldn't do that."

"I would."

"What career would you like to pursue?" Paul asked.

"Right now, I'm hoping I even get to pursue a career. After yesterday, I mostly want to help stop FEMA or whoever is poisoning this planet."

"There are also a lot of three-letter agencies, as well as the obvious toxic corporations destroying the environment. They've created massive amounts of aluminum and barium in the rainfall, but the Earth is rebelling. We've had an early summer despite the global cooling."

"That's one of the reasons Tatiana wanted to come up here so early. The weather, and there was an opening at the Lodge."

"I think you need to take it easier on yourself. You are already an AP Scholar with Distinction. What's your average?"

"Five."

"Being an AP Scholar with Distinction, you can probably get into the college of your choice without the additional APs, and you can often get college credit in the same subjects by exam, shortening your time for your degree. I can help you with that. Some universities will even give you units for life experiences. You should avoid over-stressing yourself and instead relax and heal."

"You really do know your way around early graduation."

"But skip Latin. Pig Latin is more fun," Autumn said.

"Autumn is smarter than she's letting on."

"If you don't mind talking about it, what is the history of your cardiac problem?" he asked more solemnly.

"The doctor who diagnosed me believed that stress was the main factor causing it. He didn't expect me to live a week. That was just before my mother died. I'm still alive and if I could get my emotions under control, I think I'd be fine."

"And your sister just deserted you? If I had a sister, I'd be making sure she made it to her hundredth birthday. And I plan to see you do." Autumn smiled.

"Yesterday and the day before didn't help. We need to keep you out of stressful situations," Paul advised.

"I don't want to be protected. I want to be—" I stopped short of saying "cared about."

"I know, "Paul said. "And I want you to know that we care about you."

How did he know what I was about to say? Is he a mind reader? Or am I just that obvious?

"That's the reason we asked you to stay."

I had figured as much. He was just helping me because I was a patient. "I appreciate it. I don't want to be a charity case."

"My sister is happier with you than she's been in years. As stressful as yesterday was, Autumn is handling everything well and I think you're the reason."

"It's true," Autumn affirmed.

I smiled. "Well, she's given me a more positive way of looking at life too."

Something chimed in the next room. "I'll be back," Paul said.

"I bet most people have forgotten the use of Pig Latin," I told Autumn.

"I know. I've tried it on people and they have no idea atwhay iyay amyay ayingsay."

"Iyay etgay atthay."

Paul came back. "That was Grant. Eric and Jeff are back."

"The FEMA car?"

"They brought their dad's SUV. They've got another horror story. This one's more personal."

When we arrived at the ranger station, Eric and Jeff stood up. They were wearing ranger's clothing and looked wet as if they had just showered. Grant turned and stood as we entered.

"I had them shower and change. And I hosed down their vehicle."

"Wolves!" Jeff exclaimed, picking up a metal flashlight as if it were a weapon.

"They're pets," I explained as our four furry friends walked in.

Looking hesitant, the two hikers sat down again.

"They got our parents," Eric choked out.

CHAPTER 7

"I'm so sorry," I said. It was a stupid thing to say, but I couldn't come up with something better.

"We've got to cream those elite loonies for this!" Autumn reacted with an increased determination.

"What happened to them—if you don't mind telling us?" Paul asked.

"I didn't want to tell anyone, long story, but my parents live in Sonora. We weren't on good terms with them. We went there from here to try to make peace—and everyone was dead," Jeff let out a pained expression while making two fists.

Eric was tearing up. "Mom and Dad and my uncle, Tony," he choked out.

"I'm so sorry," I repeated, feeling awkward at not having a more elegant response.

"And you said it wasn't just your family," Grant pointed out. "I heard someone talking on the shortwave radio about a thick cloud that descended over Sonora yesterday. I didn't think they'd do that to a city." He sounded as angry as I felt. "I didn't hear about any drone planes. The guy who reported it on the radio started screaming online and then there was silence. I called an officer I knew in the area to check it out. He never got back to me."

"The planes the night before last were almost invisible," I recalled.

"As far as I could tell—" Eric wiped his eyes, seemingly trying to hide away tears. "Sonora was hit hard yesterday, probably in the morning. There were people reading their morning papers with their breakfast on outdoor tables. Some had keeled over with looks of horror on their faces. It looked as if someone had thrown a bucket of food coloring over their skin. People had dropped dead while walking down the sidewalk, in backyards, all over the place. This time, they didn't clean up like in the Valley. My parents were outside, apparently having slid or fallen off a swinging love seat, clinging to each other. I had so wanted to get them to stop holding our vax and anti-war opinions against us, to talk with them, to be a family again."

I gave him a hug while he broke down into tears. Autumn went over to Jeff and placed her hand on his upper arm.

"Did you take pictures?" Grant asked Jeff. I knew that as a ranger, he had to ask but drilling a guy who had just lost his parents seemed inappropriate—even though Grant was speaking gently.

"We're not that morbid," Eric said, shaking his head.

"It might help us find who did it."

"I know it was FEMA," Eric responded. "The same FEMA that came for us." He was clearly in pain. I wished I could do something for him.

"I took some pictures," Jeff informed Grant. He pulled out his cell.

"Are these the phones you had with you yesterday?"

"But we removed the ID chips," Jeff said. Jeff was more composed, but I could tell he was suffering, just like his brother. "Where do you think they'll hit next?"

"Could be anywhere. People have been getting sick from chemtrails for years. A decade ago, analyses of snow packs and rainwater showed barium, aluminum, lithium, pesticides, herbicides, nanoparticles and other unhealthy stuff that damage health. Then came the heavier trails and people started getting a lot sicker as checkerboard skies started becoming more prevalent. They've hit harder in more isolated communities. But people haven't been dropping dead in large bursts until now. Maybe they thought there were more free thinkers in Sonora. In the Valley, they were spraying but more slowly until the last round, when they killed so many," Grant expounded.

"A town is harder to hide. Park visitors wouldn't be as easily missed," Paul remarked. "They went on vacation and never came back. They could have disappeared anywhere. You know what cell service is like in the Valley. We've had to get special cell phones for good reception."

"They've got to know Sonora will be noticed, but if we can't prove who did what, they'll get away with it," Jeff said.

"I want to stop them. I want to make them pay for what they did to my Mom and Dad," Eric declared.

"We both do," Jeff added.

"We're not leaving the area until we nail these guys," Eric stated.

"FEMA will probably go back to the Lodge to check for witnesses," Paul said. "You can't go there. The agents, last night, didn't have body-cams but they could ID you."

Grant posed the solution. "There's an out-of-the-way abandoned building in the area that they were going to tear down. It still has water. Solar panels were added to it before they decided to demolish it. I don't think that's going to be happening now. The rangers used to use it for a place to stay between shifts, but not anymore."

"Perfect," Jeff noted.

I knew Grant didn't trust anyone enough to invite them to his family's place. He had been very hesitant about me.

"Where do you think they'll hit next?" Jeff repeated his question.

"El Portal is still there. I've heard some reports of early morning fishermen floating down the river. It's got automatic gas pumps and a large motel," Grant reported.

"Remind me not to swim in the Merced again," I said. "You know they'll blame this on global warming, don't you?" Maybe I was being insensitively political. It was a problem I needed to control.

"That's an overused excuse for government misconduct," Paul acknowledged.

"I'll say. Your hair is frizzy. It's global warming," Autumn chimed in. She knew how to lighten things up, or at least she tried.

"My guess is Mariposa," Paul said.

"Should we encourage people, there, to stay indoors and close their windows or evacuate?" I inquired.

"I bet the Lodge had to carry out bodies from rooms that had their patio doors open the evening before last and yesterday morning," Paul commented.

"And they pretended it was just a lot of cancellations," Autumn recalled.

"Liars," I said. I thought about my brother and sister. But while their bags were packed and gone, mine was still there. Our car was gone, while there seemed to be too many cars in the lot for the number of guests. *They must have gotten away*, I tried to reassure myself.

"How about Merced?" Jeff asked. "Should we watch for an upcoming operation there?"

"That's along the main highway. They'll be more careful and slower there, unless they are taking the depop thing to an obvious level," Paul replied.

"You think that's what it is?" Eric asked.

"What do you think?" Paul asked Grant.

"I guess we should have listened more to those statements made by the leaders of the WEF," Jeff commented. "They've been talking depop for a long time."

"We all should have paid attention," Grant agreed. "I even put down my brother a few names when he first brought that up."

"If we think Mariposa will be next, shouldn't we evacuate it?" I asked.

"You think they'll believe us?" Paul responded.

"But we'll just be telling the truth," Eric noted.

"Like with the vaccine. Dr. Malone, Dr. Kory, Dr. McCullough, Dr. Zelenko and the other top experts who saved so many lives were called conspiracy theorists and the government went for their licenses. They turned out to be correct, but that didn't stop the mindless faith in the continuing narratives," Jeff noted. "It was part of our ongoing argument with our parents."

"We have a friend who lives not far off the route to Wawona, the hotel, not the tunnel. He's got a large satellite antenna hidden in the trees, a ham radio, internet and VPNs," Autumn interceded.

Grand looked displeased with Autumn's openness.

"They lost their parents, Grant."

"Let's visit him," Jeff suggested.

On the way to the vehicles, Jeff turned to Autumn. "Grant referred to you as Autumn and Treasure. I thought you said your names were Nancy and Betty."

"Nancy and Betty died from shock when we saw all the bodies yesterday. We were resurrected as Autumn and Treasure."

"Autumn and Treasure are nicer names."

After telling the wolves to go home, Paul joined us in the truck. Our two new friends followed in their dad's older 4Runner.

"They seem like nice guys," I said.

"Very genuine, but I've learned that appearances can also be deceiving," Grant replied. "I wish you would be less trusting, Autumn. Jack's location is on a need-to-know basis. Not everyone who has a problem deserves to be believed."

"Like me?" I asked.

"My family trusts you, but don't ever hurt them."

"I wouldn't."

Autumn put her arm around me. We were in the back seat. "She's my sister."

"The sister I always wanted," I said. A tinge of hurt swept over me, knowing that I would never be that close, again, to Tatiana.

Traveling southwest on Highway 41, we turned off the road onto what didn't seem like any road at all, not even a dirt road.

"Will they be able to follow in that vehicle?" I asked. Grant had to drive around boulders and trees in the way.

"They probably think we're crazy," Paul said, looking in the mirror at our friends following us.

After a bit of a drive, we arrived at a fence. Grant spoke to a tree that I assumed had an intercom. "It's me."

"I know that. Who is following you?"

"Some like-minded informants. FEMA killed their parents."

The section of the fence in front of us opened. We continued, eventually going onto a dirt road that led up to a house, which looked like a fortress under an umbrella of trees.

"This is really hidden," I said.

"In addition to the coverage, he's got shields that deflect any satellite intrusions around the house and over the off-road routes," Paul related.

"Good to see you," an older bearded man said as we exited the truck. "This one is getting prettier every time I see her." He gave Autumn a hug. "And who is this beauty?"

"My new sister, Treasure."

"Perfect name for you."

"Thank you."

Eric and Jeff came up behind us, and Grant introduced them to Jack Taney. "They lost their parents in Sonora."

"Terrible thing. Reports are starting to come in on that. Lots of chatter."

"We're guessing Mariposa might be next. Can we get out a warning?"

"Are you pretty sure about this? Remember the boy who cried wolf."

"Maybe we could get a general advisory out to all isolated communities, including Mariposa," Paul suggested. "Jeff has pictures."

"Let's put them up."

"I also got video and pictures of Yosemite Valley," Autumn said.

Jack took us into his office, which looked almost like a gun shop. "I see you believe in the Second Amendment," Eric commented.

"The *Second's* not about hunting," Jack pointed out.

"Not anymore," Jeff noted.

"Not ever. But under the *Second*, we should have the same weapons the U.S. Government has."

"You have any long-range nukes?" I joked.

"I'm working on that." I assumed he was teasing.

In the basement, Jack had a large computer and monitoring system. With Eric's assistance, Jack mixed Jeff's pictures and Autumn's videos and pictures with an overlay of spoken and written words.

"This could be your community. Drone planes appear in the early morning or evening and poof, the bodies drop. To those responsible, residents and visitors are garbage to be deposited in mass graves. Stay safe. Have someone available who will speak out if you disappear. If you are in an isolated community, get to a more populated zone. Keep your windows closed in the mornings and after dark. And most of all, report on any bodies you see."

The videos, pictures and narrative looked very convincing but so did horror movies. I hoped people heeded the warning.

"If I hadn't seen it personally, I might think this was on a par with fears of Martians and Venusians. Do you think it will work?" I asked.

"We can't rule out that Martians and Venusians aren't running our government," Autumn teased. Or at least, I thought she was joking.

Jack gave me a rundown. "Mass formation psychosis came in strong after the 2016 election, but it had been there to a lesser extent following the 2008 election. Then with the first COVID plandemic, there were even scientists who refused to look at actual science reports and just believed what the government told them as the bodies dropped. Twenty to thirty percent of the population will quickly believe their own eyes. Another thirty to forty percent can be convinced of the truth but will go along with the masses or what the Establishment tells them. Another twenty to thirty percent will steadfastly deny reality as it is happening in front of their eyes. Not only will they be unconvinced. They will attack anyone who points out people who have fallen dead or who question obvious lies. That twenty to thirty percent are dangerous. They'll even kill you to quiet or censor you."

"My sister and brother censored me and so I had to pretend that I got vaxed and kept getting vaxed or they never would have done anything further with me."

"Didn't help much," Autumn said.

"I suspect they had cruel proclivities embedded in their personalities before the jab," Paul surmised.

"Maybe babies were exchanged at birth and you wound up with the wrong family," Autumn added.

I looked at Paul. I had given him a terrible picture of my brother and sister. I had always spoken highly about them, no matter what they did, until I was left on the trail to be taken away by wolves. But had I reacted to the incident with too much negativity? Had I been as bad as they were in giving my new friends a bad impression of what they were like?

"Did you have a fake vax card?" Autumn asked.

"I got an exemption for my heart during the first plandemic, but lied to my family, and later kept lying about the later jabs. Fortunately, my family didn't ask for proof."

"This is quite a secluded place you have here," Eric said, changing the subject.

"It also has a sub-basement in case the elites show up. And if they do, there are some surprises in store." Jack winked at Paul.

"Nice," I said.

"Jack's been advising us to keep under the radar. The government is raiding the homes of people who are likely to expose their narratives," Paul informed us.

"I know. People telling the truth are racists—even if they are Native American or Black," I remarked.

"And Russians or terrorists," Jack noted.

Jack actually looked like he could be a terrorist. Still, from what I had seen, if he was a terrorist and FEMA was a non-terrorist organization, the terrorists were the peacemakers.

"Are you hungry?" Jack asked.

"Cinnamon," Eric sniffed.

"I can make you some cinnamon hot chocolate."

"He makes the best hot chocolate," Autumn related.

"Your parents are gone?" Jack inquired of our new friends. "Where do you boys live?"

"We've mostly been moving around. We were in New York. The government went crazy and so we listened to Jason Bermas and went to Iowa, but the winter was too cold. So, we went to Arizona. We don't like the heat there. We were on our own—though we were under eighteen. It wasn't okay with our dad that we had refused the jab. They took off to California and dumped us. We were going to try to talk our parents into letting us stay with them, but then—"

"Sonora had a poison storm," Jack finished.

"It's amazing how many people dumped relatives to fend for themselves when the first set of mandates rolled out," Grant said.

"They would have said we abandoned them by not going along with the narratives," Jeff contended. "They gave us an ultimatum and we chose our freedom."

"Smart move," Autumn reckoned.

"Leaving you kids is child abuse, just as abandoning parents in nursing homes is elder abuse," Grant pointed out.

"Grant says he knows a place where we can stay," Jeff recalled.

"If you want, you can stay here. Keep me company. Your editing made that video a success."

"Eric used to be a computer whiz," Jeff said.

"Jeff's pretty talented, himself," Eric noted.

"The three of us might make a top team," Jack concluded.

We were about to leave, when more reports came in, including one from Big Sur.

"Hundreds, maybe thousands, dead," Jack read.

CHAPTER 8

Jack continued. "The major news stations have already completely wiped the story. An indy reporter called it a paradise of death and was labeled a 'conspiracy theorist.'"

"Big Sur's along Highway 1. It's a popular community," I said.

"Well, people going through there now will find a lot of closed businesses, not to mention dead bodies," Grant responded.

"They'll clean them up," Jack said. "If they haven't already. And nobody will believe it was anything but people leaving town."

"They're moving fast," Paul noted. "Just because we're up higher than the Valley doesn't mean we can't be nailed. The Valley is four thousand feet above sea level."

"I've got an external contaminant detector. If we stay inside during the fly-overs, we'll be safe." Jack turned to Paul. "How about you guys? This isn't just ordinary chemtrails or some cloud from a chemical fire."

"It's not dioxin. It quickly kills and doesn't seem to leave much, if any, residue after it does its work. We got samples and there were no detectable traces in those samples," Grant noted. "We followed decontamination procedures but if there was any, it wasn't of any known lethal toxins unless they were in what we didn't sample."

"It's got to be some new killer DARPA or the DOD came up with," Paul remarked. "Guess the other ones didn't work well enough."

"Fort Detrick or one of those Ukrainian biolabs?" Jack queried.

"I'll start closing up the house in the evening, but Grant works until dark," Paul said. "The drones and copters. If we didn't see them, we'd have no warning."

"Silent deathfall," Jeff remarked.

I noticed Paul said "house," meaning even his friend Jack didn't know about the cave.

"I'll try to change my hours, or if I can't, I'll find a way to seal up the ranger station to block anything drifting in during the evening."

We continued to watch as more private reports with videos and photos came in of bodies at the beach community. "Of course, they'll call these fake pictures. Only the pictures the government falsifies are real," Jack said.

"Any reports from other states?" Eric asked

"New York. Ithaca," Jack responded.

"That's where Cornell is," I noted.

"Isolated like an island in a sea of trees," Jeff said. "My cousins live in Ithaca, or they did. I told them to get out. I hope they left."

"Of course, in the cities, the people are a little safer than in the Valley where campers are and sleeping outdoors, but a lot of people still got nailed in Sonora, Ithica and Big Sur."

"Bodies were all over sidewalks and in backyards in Sonora," Jeff recalled.

"It probably hit later in the morning there," Jack guessed.

"While we were walking down to the Valley," Eric lamented.

"Would you rather have been under the toxic plume when it hit Sonora?" Autumn asked.

"I would have liked to have seen my parents alive one last time."

"Makes sense that they waited until morning in Sonora, so they'd get the people who normally sleep with closed windows," Paul remarked. "They've mostly been spraying when the sun is down in the Valley. Since workers survived at the Lodge in Yosemite, a massive concentration must have been required to kill, more than a person would get from staying inside a structure. Most of the workers live in the Valley. Did any of the campground hosts survive?"

"There is no word from any of them. They seem to have disappeared. That could be why they added an early morning fly-over yesterday," Grant replied. "It could have been another spraying."

"You believe the killing was intentional." Eric made a fist.

"That's hard to deny at this point," Grant responded.

"Those two FEMA guys you told me about didn't see you, did they, Grant?" Jack asked.

"They were turned away when they were tased and knocked out."

"They were heavily tranquilized. I doubt they'll remember much," Paul said.

"I thought PCP made humans more violent and energetic," I noted.

"It was a different tranquilizer."

"We'll catch you later," Grant said. "I have to get back to the ranger station."

"I hope we'll see you girls again soon." Jeff reached out and put his hands on Autumn's upper arms.

Autumn smiled. "Soon."

"I'm really sorry about your parents," I told Jeff and Eric.

"I just wish we had been able to fix things with them before—" Jeff lamented, unable to finish.

As we walked to the truck, Eric pulled Autumn aside. At first, they both looked serious. Then, I saw her laughing and nodding. She lightly punched him on the shoulder. He looked lighter, happier as they walked back to us. After losing his parents, I was glad she could lighten things up a little for him—even if just for a moment.

"I'm driving," Autumn said.

"You don't have a driver's license," Grant pointed out.

"Yes, I do. And if I get stopped, it will check out as legit, but with a different name and a San Diego address."

"Where did you get that?" Grant asked.

"Jack, of course."

"I'll have to speak with him."

"You'll do no such thing. I'm old enough to drive. I'm a good driver and I want to drive."

"It might be a good time to check out her driving skills," Paul told him.

"The perfect time!" Autumn augmented, throwing her arms around Paul.

I smiled and gave her a thumbs-up.

"I bet she'll turn out to be the best driver here," Eric said. "Stay safe."

"Naturally, with me driving," Autumn said. "You, too."

We said our goodbyes and Paul and I took the back seat while Grant sat up front next to his sister.

"You know if you keep staring at me, your eyes will fall out," she told him.

Grant kept nervously telling her to slow down as she swung past rocks and trees on the way back to the road at a relatively swift pace.

After we were back on Highway 41, I acknowledged, "You really are a good driver. You could win slaloms without any competitors even getting close to you."

"You need to slow down," Grant advised.

"Usually, Paul is the worrywart," she said.

"It's not his truck," Grant pointed out.

"Don't worry. If she scratches it, a coat of paint will be an improvement," Paul teased.

"The paint is good just the way it is," Grant responded.

I was liking this family better and better all the time.

"That SUV behind us pulled out from the side of the road. It has darkened windows like the other night," Autumn said, looking in her rearview mirror.

"Maybe we can switch drivers while still moving," Grant suggested.

"I'll lose them."

She floored the gas, continuing towards the Valley and missing the cutoff to Glacier Point. As she sped up, the SUV behind us increased speed too. The other side of the road had a significant drop-off. Taking the road at high speed always made me a little acrophobic.

"Let's see if it is them," Grant suggested.

She pulled off to the right and the SUV stopped behind us. Grant pulled out his gun and prepared to fire.

Nobody got out of the other car. Grant started to get out to take over the driving.

"Not a chance," Autumn said, taking off and making him reclose his door. The vehicle behind started up again and pulled to the left as if to pass us.

As the darkened window from the other car started to roll down, I suspected a gun was about to emerge. That's the way it often happened in the movies.

A glimpse through the open window told me the passenger was one of the two from the night before. "Definitely them," I said.

Autumn screeched the brakes and shifted towards the center as the other car pulled back but not far enough. She smashed the back passenger side of the truck bed into the passenger's side of the SUV, knocking it towards the far side of the road. It slowed, pulling behind us. Bullets flew out from the other car and I heard the truck's right rear tire losing air.

CHAPTER 9

Autumn spun the truck around. I held on, fearing it would go out of control.

"Duck everyone," she advised, swerving to aim our vehicle towards the front passenger side of the other car. As she did so, the other car swerved to its left in an apparent attempt to miss our truck but miscalculated. She smashed the passenger side of the truck against the passenger side of the SUV, knocking our pursuers further to the left and sending them over the cliff.

The back of the truck started to violently sway as the grazed tire lost its remaining air. Autumn controlled the truck, bringing it to a stop.

"I'm going to report a car went out of control and down the cliff. They'll need a helicopter crew and a tow truck to rescue that car and the occupants. Paul, would you help with the tire?"

Watching how Grant and Autumn had quickly handled the situation gave me a sense that this family might be able to end the danger to Yosemite single-handedly.

Instead of changing the tire, the two guys patched and re-inflated it in less than five minutes.

"I called in the report to the ranger's headquarters in the Valley.

The garage still isn't answering and the helicopter will take an hour to get here. I'll call another gas station closer to Wawona to help," Grant reported when they'd finished.

He opened the driver's door. "Slide over. I'm driving."

"But she saved us," I said. "With all due respect, that was an amazing turn and recovery."

"Regardless, I'm driving."

"Killjoy," Autumn complained, scooting into the passenger seat.

Grant drove us back to the ranger station, where he radioed for additional help for the "out of control car."

The response took him aback. "What do you mean the car is gone?" he paused."I did not file a false or mistaken report. A trucker who was driving by said he saw it go off the cliff. He had to hurry on. He said his name was Sam Dolley…Yes. He gave me his CDL number as N085763 and his DOB as twelve-twelve-two thousand one. I didn't get around to running his information before, but I'll do so now…The license plate was covered with mud but before I had a chance to ask him to clean it, he took off."

We got out of the truck as Grant gave us his theory. "The Feds must have beaten the park rangers to the car, which means the guys probably survived and contacted backup."

"The Feds'll have your license plate," I said.

"After last night, I accidentally pulled it. I'll be sure to put it back on."

"But they'll be looking for a truck like yours," I worried.

"I have access to another truck I can use with a slightly different look. I'll put this one away for now."

"But the ranger logo and lights."

"The logo is an applique and the lights are transferable. I own this truck, but have access to others."

"Nice," I said. "But FEMA has a long arm."

"We'll be monitoring," Paul replied. "I have a scanner back at the cave."

"I've seen some pretty crazy things, but nothing like what is going on now," Grant said.

Grant got another call.

"I see…The CDL is a fake. Maybe he was trying to distract us from something else. I'll file a report of a false report…. Yes, sir."

Grant didn't say he saw the SUV in the calls I heard. He might get away with this—I hoped.

<hr>

Back in the cave, I offered to make dinner.

"You're the cardiac patient. I want you on Arterosil, COQ10, glutathione, NAC, berberine and bergamot. Have you taken any of the supplements I gave you?"

"I've been fine."

"And you want to stay fine. I have a supply of IV glutathione and Arterosil. It will be more effective than the pills. I did some blood samples. You also need vitamin D, zinc and alpha lipoic acid."

"You take this seriously," I said.

"I'm not like those doctors who are okay with patients dying, just to get federal grant money."

I wasn't looking forward to having someone so cute inject something into me. But I trusted him. "As long as there isn't any modRNA in it."

"You kidding? That stuff kills."

He didn't mention any diet restrictions, and I was glad for that. "Hey, do you have more organic almond milk?"

"Tons."

"I make a bang-up drink that tastes like a vanilla bean Frappuccino."

"Go for it! I'll take one, too," Autumn said. Her positive energy and enthusiasm reminded me of the part of me that used to feel alive—until those I loved started acting like they didn't want me.

About ten minutes later, Autumn, Paul and I were sipping ice drinks that tasted like vanilla milkshakes.

"You can make about ten more of those for me," Autumn said.

"For the next course, organic basil garlic mushroom spaghetti," Grant offered, coming into the kitchen to join us.

"You missed the best part, Bro." Autumn stuck out her tongue at him.

"What was that?"

"You'll find out next time you make the board meeting."

"'Board meeting,' huh."

"Autumn didn't tell you, but she sold your stock this morning, Big Brother," Paul chimed in. "You no longer have to attend."

Grant's phone rang.

"Maybe we need to alert all National and State Park-goers," he said into the phone.

Ending the call, he ran his hand over his forehead.

"What?" Paul asked.

"They hit Sequoia."

CHAPTER 10

After dinner, Grant said, "Jack should have had time to get up his latest video. Some tourists who only saw the aftermath in Sequoia posted a video online and Jack picked it up before it was pulled."

"Is your internet wifi or wired?" I asked.

"Never wifi," Paul replied. "We have wired internet here and routers with wires to all the rooms. Jack has wired Internet as well." We went to Paul's den and watched the latest video that Jack had posted.

"*Traveling to a park or beach for camping? Think again.*" Next, it played Autumn's video of Yosemite Valley with the location labeled, followed by videos from Big Sur and Sequoia.

As I watched a video of Sequoia, I reacted. "No!" and started to cry. I couldn't help myself.

Paul and Autumn put their arms around me.

"A toddler. They killed a toddler."

"There were probably some yesterday, too, at—" Autumn stopped herself, maybe seeing I was sobbing harder.

"How could they do that to a child?"

"They're monsters," Paul said. "They have little or no humanity left in them. This isn't much different than the genocides and massacres our government provides the weapons for in the Middle East. It's just a different method."

"The elites think they are above us. The rest of us are useless eaters to them, including the children," I continued, freaking out. This wasn't the first time I had seen the results of our leaders' misconduct. I knew about the funding of genocides around the world.

"We're going to fix this," Paul assured me.

"But we can't bring that little kid back."

"Do you believe in God or an afterlife?" Paul asked.

"I don't know. I wish I knew, but I don't."

"It helps some to believe."

"I need an evidence structure." I had been looking for one for so long, but it was hard to believe when cruel people kept winning and good was never or rarely rewarded.

"Well, how about physics? Energy has to go somewhere. It doesn't just turn into nothing. That's not religion but science."

"I just hope if there is something after life, that kid is happy and loved."

"His parents are with him," Autumn said, looking uncertain if she had said the right thing.

I gave both her and Paul a group hug. "I'm sorry I got worked up." It was hard not to think about the images I'd seen.

"It gets to me, too," Paul said.

"So how was your spaghetti?" Grant asked, rejoining the conversation and trying to change the subject.

"Excellent. You can cook," I responded.

"Wait until you taste mine," Paul countered. "Just as a precaution, we're going to seal off this place tonight. We have an indoor air purification system that can clean and recycle the air for several days. After that, we need to rely on a filter that takes air from outside and cleans it. They might not hit Yosemite again. But we don't want to take any chances."

I nodded.

"Let's watch a video that's really light and fun—like *The Other Woman*," Autumn suggested. "It came out perhaps a decade, decade and a half ago."

"That's the one where the women destroy the guy they're involved with?" Grant asked.

"Three women and one guy. He's a total jerk."

"He deserved it," Paul said. "Let's all watch it."

I knew they needed a release and so did I. Autumn brought the video into the living room player and we all had a great time cheering on the women. Paul looked like he wanted to personally beat up the main guy.

"When I get married, that's it," he said. "I'm into the one woman-one guy thing."

"And I thought you were bi," Autumn teased him.

"Not in this lifetime."

"And I also figured you were mad you didn't get invited to one of Paul Pelosi's sex parties."

"Ha. Ha," he said wryly.

She laughed. "When we first met Eric and Jeff, we pretended we weren't into boys."

"You also told them you were Nancy and Betty. When they came to the ranger station, they didn't know who Autumn and Treasure were," Grant said.

"Well, they were polite enough not to hold it against us at least," I acknowledged.

"Eric asked me out," Autumn informed us with a sheepish smile.

"Ho ho," I said, smiling back. "I thought he seemed really interested in you."

"We'll see. He is kind of cute."

"As long as he remembers that I'm a ranger and have a gun." I wasn't sure Grant was joking.

"I thought Jeff was more your type," Paul said.

"He's fun, but Eric is more the strong, silent type."

When the movie was over, Autumn asked if we wanted to see *Bad Moms* or *First Wives Club* next.

"Maybe Eric is the one who needs protection," Grant commented. "After all, Autumn has a brown belt in Krav Maga."

"Really?"

She nodded.

"Maybe you can teach me."

"When I'm sure you're better. It's a rough sport. In the meantime, you should have a protector accompanying you places," Paul said.

"You mean you, brother?"

"Well, in case she needs medical help."

"You make me sound like an invalid."

"As an EMT, I assure you, you're not an invalid. But it doesn't hurt to play it safe."

"You're really intent on building up my ego. Better watch out. I just might become an egotist."

"I'm not holding my breath on that one."

"I'm going to bed," Grant said.

Paul stayed up with us and watched the other movies.

"The government can detect electronic signals and don't they have detectors for locating people in underground caves? Is there a risk, with flyovers, that they know about this place?"

"We have solar panels and radio towers, but they are camouflaged and away from here to not raise suspicion. The wires are underground. The top of the cave is so thick and has sensor blockers that would defeat even a heat signature," Paul replied. "My dad thought of everything."

"He knew this was coming, well before the first plandemic?"

"He kept warning us. At first, I thought he was paranoid, but he turned out to be right about a lot of things."

"And you've done a nice job of continuing his work," I said. "He'd be proud of how this place looks."

"With help from me," Autumn noted.

"And Grant, too," Paul acknowledged.

"Does Jack know where you live?"

"He's seen the alternate place we were going to take Eric and Jeff to, but no. He hasn't been here. You're the only guest we've had."

"I'm honored."

"Where do you park?"

"We have an underground parking area a mile away."

"Does it connect?"

"It's a long walk but if we have to leave in a hurry, we can take off that way."

"If the wolves hadn't brought me here, I—"

"But they did. And I'm glad you're here, not about the circumstances that brought you here."

"Other than continuing to expose those who did it, is there anything we can do?"

"Stay alive."

"Do you think my brother and sister are in danger?"

"She's in Berkeley, right?"

I nodded.

"And he's in Portland?"

"Yeah. At least, that's where they're living."

"They should be fine. Those two places are brainwash factories. I didn't mean that as a comment on your brother and sister," Autumn remarked.

"I know what you meant. That's actually reassuring in terms of their safety. And I'm glad they left when they did—although it did hurt."

"Well, now you have a new family and we're not going to leave you fallen on a mountain trail," Paul said.

"Thanks." I started to give him a hug and then realized I might be out of line.

"It's okay," he said as if he knew what I was thinking. He gave me a hug, and from the tingling in my stomach, I wished he hadn't. I really liked him. I knew I had no right to think this could go anywhere. I wasn't going to take advantage of a situation with a good Samaritan by making it into something it wasn't. I turned and gave Autumn a hug as well.

"And I don't intend to always live like a hermit. Just until it's safe out there," he said.

"You aren't a hermit. This place is like an underground palace."

"Well, the palace part is small but the garden part is huge."

"It's amazing."

He smiled and then looked more serious. "You need some rest."

"Paul—" Autumn started to object.

"You can talk to her in her room, but I want her to lie down. It was only two days ago that the wolves brought her here and she's lucky they did or she wouldn't have survived."

He escorted me to my door. Autumn followed.

"I'm going to attach an IV," he said, going out and returning to set it up.

"You aren't going to wreck our girls' night."

He smiled as he finished attaching it to my arm and hugged his sister. "Good night, both of you."

When he had gone, Autumn came in and shut the door. "He likes you. He really likes you."

"Nah. He's just being doctorly."

"How many doctors do you know who invite their patients into their mother's bedroom?"

"He thinks I'm going to drop dead, and he doesn't want to have to deal with the body."

"He certainly wouldn't like that."

"I won't drop dead. No matter what happens, I seem to keep surviving."

"You sound as if you would be fine with not surviving."

"At times—" I wasn't going to depress her. I knew I had a depression problem. For some time, I had struggled to keep myself out of the black hole I knew I'd fall into if I let depression take over. "So does it bother you at all that I'm in your mother's room?"

"It's kind of nice to have someone here. It's no longer a shrine to someone who's gone. It was getting weird."

"Have you felt her lately?"

"I dreamed about her last night. I think she likes my new sister."

"What makes you think that?"

"She told me so in my dream. I wonder if she guided you here."

"I think the wolves picked me up with their mouths and dragged me." Everlove was scratching on the door. Autumn let her in and she climbed up on my bed. "I always wanted a pet dog. I never imagined it would be a wolf."

"I think our mothers were alike."

"Paul said something like that. From what I picked up, they both were kind and giving and they put us first."

"It was our fathers who were so different. If kids don't watch out, they are more likely to turn into their fathers, especially when their fathers were the powerhouses. Mine was a good-guy powerhouse. You took after your mom, and your siblings clearly take after your dad."

Feeling guilty about the impression I'd given of Tatty and Zinney, I redirected, while trying to figure out how to make them look better. "Paul?"

"He's more like Mom. Grant and I mostly resemble our father personality-wise. Grant looks a bit like him."

"I wish I had known them."

"Now, enough of the morbid talk. Want to play a game of Scrabble?"

"Sure."

She went to get the game and we played for hours. She was better at it than I was.

"You have to be the smartest girl I know," I told her.

"I took the MENSA test. You need an IQ of 140 to succeed on it and I passed."

"Congratulations. I knew you were a genius."

"You're a genius."

"No. You're a genius."

"You."

"You."

Paul opened the door. "Is this a mutual admiration society or can anyone join?"

"Your sister beat me two out of three games of Scrabble."

"Good work, Autumn. I can tell this lady isn't easy to beat. Any chance you two could get some sleep tonight? Tomorrow could be a long day and somebody wants to go on a date, though you'll probably have to do it in Jack's backyard."

"Hmm. That is a problem. There are no movie theaters worth going to in Jack's backyard."

"You could go for a nature walk," I suggested.

"I like that," Autumn said. She hugged me tight.

As she left, she told Paul, "Next time you do that, I'll stay in here all night."

"Goodnight, Sis."

Paul came over to my bed, disconnected my IV and checked my blood pressure, my heart rate and oxygen level. "You're doing well."

"Rumor has it I've got a great doctor."

"I hear he's a bit awkward and often has his foot in his mouth."

"I heard he is very sure-footed and always says the right thing."

He smiled. "I'll see you in the morning."

"See ya, doc."

***

The next morning, I was awakened by shaking as if I were in the middle of a major earthquake.

I opened my eyes and stood up. It sounded as if I was near an airport or in the middle of a parking garage that had cars coming down the ramps.

Paul was in a den filled with multiple screens, speakers and computers, watching footage of troops. "The military or rather FEMA is moving in. They're all over the area."

"FEMA?"

"They started storming in about half an hour ago, first some jeeps, which didn't make it very far off the road, then ATVs, copters, tanks and troops."

"Would that be National Guard Troops?"

"Doesn't look that way. They're wearing FEMA uniforms, not National Guard uniforms, along with standard officer insignias."

"Will they find us?"

"We're shielded and the main entrances are sealed. The trouble is that Grant is at the ranger station and Autumn went out walking by herself this morning."

"She's out there with FEMA, the same FEMA that was ready to kill us the other night?"

CHAPTER 11

"I need to go out and find her," I said. "She was there for me. I owe her."

"You're staying here. If either of us goes looking for her, it will be me. Grant's looking for her as best he can while pretending to officially welcome the FEMA troops. I'm monitoring the cameras. She's smart enough to stay hidden."

"Where do you think she went?"

"I don't know. The fact that I'm not seeing her on the cameras means she's probably staying out of sight."

"When we were down in the Valley the other day, she was pretty good at hiding."

"She wasn't having to dodge troops and ATVs. As soon as I get an idea of where she is, I'm going out there."

"I will too."

"Not a chance."

"Paul, I'm small, I can hide more easily than you. Besides, you need to monitor the situation from in here."

"No. Doctor's orders."

I would have rushed out then, but I didn't know where the alternate exits were and if they were sealed, they wouldn't be easy to get through. *Maybe, I can convince Paul to let me out.*

"You have a lot of cameras out there."

"We've placed cameras and microphones over much of the mountain."

Men in riot gear and heavily armored all-terrain vehicles were smashing down anything in their way, though mostly following open paths. I was more worried about Autumn than the foliage. I felt a knot in my stomach and a fright I hadn't felt since accepting I might have to die to protect my siblings from my dad and taking blows that were meant for them.

"The good news is, if we can't find her, they probably can't either," Paul tried to reassure me—though his voice projected worry.

"But their tanks could crush her without their noticing."

That's when shots rang out, fired by one or more of the troops in the field. I held my breath.

"Direct kill," I heard a trooper say.

CHAPTER 12

A large figure was lying on the other side of a bush, but I couldn't make it out. One man in riot gear went over to where he had fired and pulled back the bush.

I saw thin brown legs. Everlove was with me but not the other wolves.

"Where are the other wolves?"

"In their room. They were whining to go out, and I knew they'd be targets."

"Smart."

"There." He pointed to what looked like a moving bush on one of the screens. "She's running while everyone is distracted by the dead deer."

"What do you think you are doing?" someone with captain's stripes demanded of the shooter.

"I thought it was a sniper."

"A deer? Are you blind? If you see a real person, capture them. They may lead us to others."

He turned and shouted, "Halt," at a figure moving nearby.

Paul focused the image to see to whom he was speaking.

"I'm a ranger. I heard shots," Grant responded.

"It's handled."

On other cameras, Autumn was slowly edging out of that area, mostly hidden by the foliage and trees and using the distractions to go through more open areas.

"This is still a national park and you aren't allowed to shoot the wildlife. And your tanks are destroying the trees and environment," Grant complained.

"This is a secure area now and we are in charge. We won't be taking the tanks any further down. But our men will continue down the hillside."

"You planning to leave some of the trees intact?"

"We've no need for smart-mouthed rangers."

"We both work for the same federal government."

"When we are set up in the Valley, we'll let you know how much of the park we'll allot to you."

"It's a long way down, and that many men are upsetting the wildlife and vegetation. There are roads you can take."

"If you'd look, they are full of our trucks. We're checking the paths for anything or anyone who could be a terrorist or obstructor."

"There hasn't been much human traffic on this trail in days."

"Good to know. Now, go back to your post."

"Will you be through with this area after this morning?"

"We set our own timetable, and you don't question us."

"I have superiors I have to report to, and they'll want some kind of timetable. DHS is not above the Department of Interior."

"Sir, we want you to go back to your outpost, or we'll have to arrest you for interfering."

"For asking questions?"

"One more word and we'll arrest you."

Grant turned and appeared to trip. He helped himself up and brushed off his slacks. Another camera showed Autumn going behind a tree and crawling under some bushes.

"She's in," Paul said, pressing one of the buttons on his desk. I figured there must be some kind of passage in or near those bushes. I was pretty sure it wasn't the way Autumn had led me out, though I'd been blindfolded, and it certainly wasn't the entrance we'd returned through from the ranger station.

Grant was moving back towards his post, limping.

"Do you think he's hurt?"

"He's a good actor," Paul said.

Paul remotely opened up a door to a passage I hadn't seen before. "All the entrances are independent. If they find one, we can seal it off while keeping the others available to us."

"You think of everything," I noted as he led the way.

"My dad thought of everything. Back in his day, they called him a conspiracy theorist."

"The conspiracy theorists are the ones who will survive this thing."

Going through several corridors and rooms, opening them with wall touch panels, we came upon a tunnel rising upward towards the surface. Autumn rushed to us.

"Did you see me?" she asked excitedly as she and I gave each other a big hug.

"I saw that you almost got Grant killed," Paul scolded.

"Is he alright?"

"I think so. He definitely didn't make any friends." Paul turned back towards the living quarters. "Come on."

Paul texted Grant:

The puppy is alive.

I may have it put to sleep anyway, was the response.

"He's not happy."

"How was I to know the government would be setting up camp?" Autumn defended herself.

"I wonder if they'll be doing the same at Big Sur and Sequoia," I pondered.

"Or Sonora," Autumn reminded us.

"That's a lot of FEMA operations. And Jack said it's happening in other states?" Paul, what do you think they'll do with the Valley?"

"I don't know. Most of their crews are on the Panorama Trail. They may be mopping up survivors."

"When we were walking, I noticed it was hard to see the Valley most of the way to the Vernal Falls Bridge," I said.

"The Four Mile Trail has better visibility but is too narrow in places for them to get their FEMA army down."

"The Valley is visible from the Point," Autumn pointed out.

"Once they get into position, they might hold this area or keep a couple of sentries at the Point, or block the cutoff from 41."

"I thought FEMA was for emergency management," I said.

"It's under DHS and gets more powerful with each new budget. I knew FEMA had commanders and deputies, but from what I could see, it now has its own army. People have been warning about this for years."

I worried about FEMA putting my new family in the middle of a controlled area. "I imagine the road to the Valley is closed past the tunnel with all those troops flooding in."

"I suspect so," Paul replied.

"They would have to do this to the most beautiful place on Earth," I commented sadly.

"I feel that way about Yosemite too," Paul said.

"What about the rangers and personnel in the Valley?"

"Grant says they've been expelled. Some but not all rangers have reported to stations above the Valley."

"Is there something we can do?"

"Whatever we do, we'll need to make sure it doesn't endanger the family," Paul made clear.

"He's very protective. So is Grant," Autumn said, making a face.

"I can understand. You're irreplaceable."

She smiled. "So are you."

"What about the visitors with reservations?"

"Probably cancelled, 'Park's closed due to X, Y, Z' or whatever other reason they give." Paul guessed.

Paul tried calling Jack but got no answer.

Paul texted Grant. "How does it look on the driving range for golf with our golfing buddies?"

"Crowded along the fairway but maybe open to get through later."

I was pretty sure I could read between the lines in their conversation.

"Is there an alternate route to get to Jack's?" I asked.

"By horseback," Paul said.

"You've got horses?"

"You've been holding out on Treasure," Autumn scolded. "We've got some beautiful horses. We've got an underground field where they graze. Paul and I take turns feeding them every morning."

"This place must be well ventilated. I can't even smell them."

"There are a lot of independent chambers with individual oxygen filters and sources. Let's go." Autumn seemed eager.

"She hasn't even had breakfast yet and I need to monitor the situation outside."

"We'll be back before breakfast is done."

"Pancakes?"

"That would be delicious," I replied.

"Don't keep her long. And no more going outside without an escort."

Seven beautiful black horses were grazing in the underground field to which she led me.

"The big ones are the stallions, and the smaller ones are the mares," Autumn said. She picked up some carrots hanging on the wall as we entered the area. "They like carrots, but you have to feed them with your hands open. That protects your fingers, though none of them have ever come close to just biting down."

The horses trotted over to us. One put his muzzle against me and I stroked his nose.

"They're very friendly," I smiled, surprised.

"They are. The one you just petted is Lightning Bolt, though he doesn't have even a streak of white on him. He's the fastest. This one —" She pointed at one next to her. "Is Atlas. He's strong and fast. Libra, the one you're petting now, is the lover. If he were a dog, he'd be a lapdog. They're all fast, but if I were to find a horse to look after me in an emergency, it would be him. Pan is the prankster. He's still an angel."

"What about this female?" I pointed to one of the smaller but still nice-sized horses, who was rubbing her nose against me.

"She's the sweetest of all the horses. She's soft and gentle and yet almost as fast as Lightning Bolt. Her name is Laura, after my mother."

"Your mother was named Laura?"

"That was her middle name. She preferred it to her first name."

"These two, Daphne and Kaliope, are twins. They like to prance together and they actually can keep the beat when I play my music."

"They're all beautiful. I've always loved horses. I'm so glad you invited me to stay."

"To live. It wasn't a temp invitation."

"Well, until you get tired of me."

"And leave me to fend for myself with the boys?"

"You seem to do alright."

"They're nicer to me because you're here. Usually, they're more controlling. 'Don't go out alone.' 'Make sure we know where you are at all times.'"

"It's getting really crazy out there with FEMA."

"I know. I'm tempted to see if I can find their smoke bombs and drive them out of the Valley."

"Or the cyanide sprays," I joked.

"See, that's cool. Most people wouldn't joke about that. They're too busy being proper."

"Your brothers are cool."

"When they aren't trying to keep me in a glass cage."

"I get it. I think, as wonderful as they are, I'd be rebellious if I were in your situation. Paul and I were fighting over who would go outside to find you."

She smiled. "Grant and Paul aren't used to anyone standing up to them. Maybe they'll learn they can't protect everyone."

That had been my problem too. Though I was the youngest sibling, I was always protecting or rather over-protecting, Tatiana and Zinney.

"Have you ridden before?"

"At Irvine Park and at Yosemite."

"Those are mules in the Valley and most of them are trained to follow the leader. You need to ride a real horse. Can you ride bareback or do you need a saddle?"

"I don't know. I've never ridden bareback."

Laura started to kneel down. "I think she wants you to ride her."

Autumn helped me position myself on Laura's back and then got onto Atlas. I wondered if this was safe, but Laura seemed so supportive that I ignored my concerns. I knew we were indoors, lit up by sun lamps, but it felt like outdoors. We rode around the grazing field. "The filters really do work in keeping the air clear."

"That's a biggie. Toxic fumes don't make for healthy living."

"Do the lights ever go out?"

"We have an indoor barn for the horses over there." She pointed to something off to the side.

We rode over to the barn. Upon entering, she turned on the lights and introduced me to some of the horses inside. We picked up some apples and fed them to Atlas and Laura and then went through the structure with a bucket, encouraging other horses to eat.

"With all the microphones and cameras, could Paul have heard what we spoke about on the trail?"

"I know where the microphones are. He couldn't hear anything he shouldn't have when we were talking about the family."

After feeding the horses, we started brushing down Laura's and Atlas's coats.

"Laura has really taken to you."

"She's beautiful and the nicest horse I've ever seen. You have a lot of horses."

"Dad always loved horses. There's enough room for all of them in the barn but we often switch them out so that they all have chances to rest as well as run."

"How long was your dad building this place?"

"Years."

"I wasn't kidding when I called him a prophet."

"He just looked at the signs. Both sides of the political spectrum are heading in the same direction."

"I agree. My family was from the left, but even when I was really young, I could see that the Party had gone against everything for which it claimed to stand."

"My family is liberal too, but not warmongering liberal or censorship liberal. Sane liberal."

"I remember being afraid as a little kid that Hillary would start World War III."

"If she had won, it would have probably been over years ago. But they're all in it together and just when it looks like we might be safe, our government threatens another nuclear war. Sometimes, I think all our leaders want to kill us while they go into their own underground tombs. This place would survive nuclear fallout, but I don't know about a direct hit."

"Now they want to control every aspect of our lives."

"My dad wanted to make sure we had a safe space while not feeling like prisoners. He saw the plandemics coming. I attended a school for a while in Yosemite Valley. Grant wanted to become a ranger and so he stayed close. Paul did college and started medical school out of state so he wouldn't have to be vaxed, but then settled on becoming a paramedic. He was homeschooled and way ahead grade-wise."

"Which is why he accomplished all that by the age of twenty-one."
She nodded.

"I was going to be starting junior college in the Fall."

"And your sister got into Berkeley?"

"I made sure she had the funds for it."

"Nice sister. And you filled out her application?"

"I did. At college time, she suddenly didn't want to take the time to fill it out. I figured she belonged there as smart as she is."

"It certainly isn't the Cal I read about in the history books. After the way your sister treated you, I bet you're glad you won't be getting the Berkeley indoctrination."

"If it were the Berkeley of my parents' time, it would have been okay, but you're right. These days, they are teaching students to follow agendas and censor alternate points of view."

"If the authorities found out they deserted you, CPS might grab you—since you aren't eighteen."

"They won't. I'm pretty self-sufficient. I'd file for emancipation."

"Some have tried and still been grabbed. Seventy percent of sex trafficking comes out of CPS."

"I'm not far from eighteen, anyway."

"But you continued to take beatings after they left."

"At least, with college, they were out of there."

"And they just abandoned you to more cruelty?"

"My dad died from the shot a few months after Tatiana went to Berkeley. I wasn't alone with the beatings too long. He was my brother's hero."

"The person who beat you up," she finished for me. "Great brother. Imagine how he'll treat his wife."

"If he ever gets married."

"If for no other reason, he'll get married just to make someone miserable."

I changed the subject. "I wonder if Yosemite will ever be the same. I used to love wandering through the woods or rafting down the Merced here."

"Did you ever raft down the sections where rafting was forbidden?"

"All the time—well, when I was here."

"Growing up in Yosemite, I sometimes wished for a change of scenery. I wanted to go singing and dancing in a big city."

"Do you feel like a prisoner here?"

"In a way, with my brothers watching over me. They keep telling me what to do to stay safe. I listen and then do what I want. I used to sneak out and take my music down to the campgrounds and get the cooler campers to dance with me."

"That sounds like fun. Maybe we can do it at one of the higher-level campgrounds."

"Most of the people at those campgrounds are complacent and just into nature."

"I haven't heard of them hitting the Bay Area. Maybe we can go there."

"With all those masked retards? Even when COVID was declared over, they were still afraid some evil person would breathe on them."

"Good point. They used to be cool—until all the compliance stuff."

When we got back into the living section, Everlove jumped into my arms, knocking me down. She started licking my face.

"Are you alright?" Autumn asked as she helped me up.

"Just startled."

Esther ran over to Autumn and put her front paws on Autumn's chest and started licking. "You're jealous. You smell the horses on us," Autumn told them, smiling at the attention.

In the dining room, Paul had a fresh stack of pancakes waiting for us.

"The perfect host," I said as we started to devour them.

"I think Everlove has decided that Treasure is her baby," Autumn informed him.

"She's certainly bigger and stronger than me."

"Definitely weight-wise. You're as light as a feather," Paul said.

"Nah. A few more pounds than that."

"So, what would you like to do today, other than go outside?"

"Maybe I can help with your amazing garden. However, I warn you, I've never had a green thumb."

"That's good. Green thumbs aren't healthy."

"I can show you some of the trees I've planted," Autumn suggested.

I listened. The shaking had stopped, along with the thunderous clamor.

"It sounds like most of the tanks and troops are gone."

"And they probably destroyed a lot of nature," Paul lamented.

"Don't they care at all about the beauty here?"

Paul shook his head.

"How much do you know about the U.S. Government?" Autumn teased.

"I know it's the number one polluter in the world, but some things are sacred. On second thought, they regularly destroy ancient artifacts in countries they invade. So, nothing is sacred to them."

"And they aim their bombs at civilian areas to maximize damage," Autumn pointed out.

"Do you have cameras further down?"

"The lines to the ones in the Valley got eaten by bears some time back, and I haven't gotten around to repairing them, but from what I can see, the troops did a lot of damage on the way down."

"How did the tanks survive the grade?"

"The modern ones are designed to do just that. Everything will grow back and most of the trees and bushes appear intact. Still, it's disrespectful. From what I could see, they went partway in the tanks and then stormed down the mountain in large numbers while the tanks were brought back up to do more damage elsewhere."

"How are Jack and our friends faring?" I asked.

"Nobody has been picking up since I spoke with him earlier. It appears the military has blocked off 41 about two miles south of Glacier Point Road. Jack is further south and might not be affected."

"Let's try to reach him, again," Autumn said. "Just to make sure he's safe."

He tried again. Jack was still not answering.

"What if he's in danger?" Autumn asked.

"We'll just have to wait until we hear from him."

"You weren't waiting until you heard from me."

"You're seventeen."

"We can take the horses out on the other side of the road and ride them over to Jack's to check on them."

"You aren't going anywhere."

"Then I'm going to my room and listening to my music."

She left the table.

"I'll go check on her."

As I got to her room, she turned on the music in her room and closed the door from the outside.

"Autumn."

She put her fingers to her lips and motioned toward the path to the horses. I followed.

As she was saddling up Atlas, I tried to convince her to wait. "It could be dangerous out there. They could have men in those woods with guns."

"It's not just Jack. It's Eric and Jeff."

"What can we do?"

"A lot. I'll figure something out."

"Paul's going to be worried."

"I left a note in my room."

"Then he'll be furious."

"I've lived through that before, too."

"He'll probably throw me out."

"I won't let him. You coming?"

I wasn't going to let her go alone.

"The saddles are over there, along with the rest of the tack."

"You use English saddles in Yosemite?"

"I'm a would-be city girl, not a cowgirl. I don't even own a cow."

I saddled Laura and followed Autumn and Atlas through a tunnel to an exit that she opened. We got off the horses and slowly led them outside. As the exit closed, I noticed that it blended in and was completely unnoticeable.

"Where are we?"

"Far enough from the point and from the main part of the cave that we should be okay."

That's when a loud spray of gunshots burst in our direction.

CHAPTER 13

We dismounted and hid with our horses behind a mound of boulders. Autumn motioned for the horses to be still and quiet. They were clearly well-trained. We could see foxes and rabbits lying on the ground in puddles of blood.

"They're using wildlife for the target practice," Autumn rasped.

"What can we do?"

Voices could be heard on the other side of our mound of boulders. "I thought I hit a bear somewhere over here."

Autumn made some maneuvers towards Atlas and he reared up, hitting his hoofs against the boulders. The bulk of the pile fell on the far side. The talking stopped. Autumn and I looked around the side of what was left.

The men appeared unconscious, mostly covered by large rocks and debris.

One of their guns was sticking out of the pile. Autumn pulled it free.

"Should we—" I started to ask about helping them.

"And let them kill us? They're still alive. Their friends will come looking for them."

She nodded her head away from the men and we got on the horses and started riding, quietly at first and then as fast as we could. Autumn seemed to know where she was going.

Autumn was very good at maneuvering and Laura seemed content to follow Atlas's path. Finally, we reached the gate to Jack's place. It opened almost automatically and we rode in.

"That's Grant's truck," Autumn observed.

Paul and Grant came out from inside, along with Jack and Eric. "Do we have to lock you down?" Grant asked.

"We were worried about everyone here," Autumn said.

"And you were going to check on Autumn, not take off with her." Paul sounded disappointed in me.

"Well, I couldn't check on her inside when she was on her way out." I knew my excuse was flimsy.

"We heard shots," Paul remarked.

"They're doing target practice with the wildlife," his sister informed him.

"We heard on the radio they sent for an ambulance for two of their troopers. Seems a pile of rocks fell on them and they are busy looking for that weapon," Grant said, glaring at the item attached to Autumn's saddle.

Paul helped me off my horse and Grant pulled Autumn off hers.

"You're grounded," Grant declared.

"Sir. It was really thoughtful of the girls to care about us," Eric interceded. "Kind of heroic."

"You can't keep a wild animal caged," Jack remarked. He smiled at Autumn.

"But you can tranquilize it," Grant countered.

"Is Jeff okay?" I asked. "I don't see him."

"He's manning the monitors," Jack told us.

"We couldn't reach you," she said. "Where were you?"

"Outside, checking the perimeter and setting up more cameras," Jack replied. "I left my shortwave and phone unmanned for a few hours."

"FEMA will be mostly leaving the point as soon as they find that gun," Grant informed us.

"What do you mean 'mostly,'" I inquired.

"They'll be leaving a lookout," Paul noted.

"Will that be a problem?"

"It shouldn't be. Rangers will be there, too. The trail you took wasn't an easy trail for someone who doesn't do a lot of riding."

"Laura did all the work, following Atlas, and I mostly had a nice ride."

Grant shook his head. "There's too much activity right now at the Point. You girls are going to stay here tonight. I'll see about getting you back in the morning. Anyone but the Rangers is likely to be interrogated if caught near there before they leave."

"A free night," Autumn whispered to me.

Overhearing, Paul responded, "Not quite. I'm staying, too, and the horses as well."

"Paul, how did you get here?"

"Lying under some rescue equipment in the back of Grant's truck. They're allowing rangers through."

"Tomorrow morning, I'll bring three ranger suits to make it easier for you to return. FEMA isn't taking roll of the rangers yet."

"What about Laura and Atlas?"

"They'll come back when it's safe."

Inside, in the basement, Jeff showed me some of what he was seeing on the monitors. When I went back up into the living room, Autumn and Paul were having a serious conversation. "Why don't you just tell her?" Autumn asked.

"It's not that simple."

"Yes, it is."

"What if she doesn't take it well?"

"She's cool. She'll be okay with whatever you tell her."

"If I'm in the way, just tell me," I interrupted their conversation.

"Believe me, you aren't in the way," Paul said.

I felt a little icky inside. Paul probably wanted me to leave so I would stop being a bad influence on his sister, but he didn't want to hurt his patient's feelings. I guessed it was time to go, but I really enjoyed being there. I needed to make it easy on him and just tell him I planned to leave.

"I really should be getting back to OC. My brother or sister might be expecting me to go back there. Maybe, that's where they went when they left." I knew that wasn't true, but it seemed like a good excuse.

"They left you for dead. If they cared enough to go back to OC, they probably would have cared enough to locate you before they took off," Autumn pointed out, blowing away my excuse.

That evening, Jack made us garlic and onion-stuffed potatoes.

"How do you like them?" he asked.

"Interesting. Good."

"Then you'll love my second course." It turned out to be pizza.

I noticed that Eric and Autumn had gone outside. I focused on the food and pretended not to notice so as to not call Paul's attention to it.

However, he did observe. "I hope he's behaving himself with my sister."

"I think Autumn can take care of herself."

"I keep forgetting she's not a little girl anymore. With everything going on, she's got too much courage for her own good."

"You too are really close, aren't you?"

"What I regretted most when I went away to school and started work as a paramedic was being away from her and my mom. Would you like to go outside?"

"They might prefer privacy."

"If we see them, we'll go another direction."

"Okay."

Outside, we sat on the ground and looked up at the night sky. I looked back at the house with its very thick shades blocking out any light from inside. I had a mix of sadness about leaving this new family behind and awe about the magnificence of what I was seeing.

"It's so beautiful up here. You can see a million stars."

"I used to come outside the cave and sit for hours just looking at the stars. Autumn would sometimes come with me and we'd create stories to improve all the myths surrounding the constellations."

A sense of loneliness swept through me, longing to have that kind of relationship with a brother. "I can understand why your parents chose this area."

"Technically, the cave is on federal land. We don't own it, but the feds haven't taken the time to look under the surface."

"Then, you really have to be careful who finds out about it. I'm honored. How about Jack's place?"

"He got a federal grant for this area long ago, but I think they forgot about it. It's not in any of the Rangers' maps."

"There has to be a way to stop what is going on."

"I knew our government was destroying the environment, but I thought this would be one of the last places they'd destroy. I don't want to talk about that now. Thank you for taking care of my sister."

"I thought you'd be mad at me."

"I was worried until you showed up."

"Autumn seems pretty good at taking care of herself."

"I wasn't just worried about Autumn."

"You thought you might lose a patient. Not good for your medical record."

He smiled but his mouth quivered as if he was afraid to give me some news. "Worried that something might happen to the most amazing girl I've ever met."

He was looking straight at me. *He couldn't mean me.*

"I don't expect you to return the sentiment. I just thought I'd say that, well, I don't want anything bad to happen to you. And Autumn isn't the only one who doesn't want you to leave."

A sense of relief settled over me as he touched my cheek and looked into my eyes. His pine scent sought to overtake me but I had to keep my senses.

"It's a really sweet thing to say. You really have been good for my ego. I realize I've gone on and on about my problems and I know you feel I need buttering up."

He shook his head. "I know we haven't known each other long. From the moment the wolves brought you in, I knew. You are more than a patient. I know it's professionally inappropriate for me to say this. I don't feel professional around you. I don't want you to leave, not just now, but ever. I—well, I'm overwhelming you."

This has to be a dream. I'm a nobody. Maybe, I died on the mountain and wanted someone to care so much that I am imagining this in the afterlife. "Me? Wow. I mean wow. Maybe it's this Florence Nightingale Syndrome."

"I'm not Florence Nightingale, and well if you don't feel the same, that's okay. I just wanted you to know."

"I'm—wow." *I have to be careful. There is no way this could last—nothing good in my life ever does.* "What I meant to say is, 'Is this for real?' You aren't going to change your mind tomorrow or when you get to know me bet—"

Before I could finish my sentence, his lips met mine, and it was like the night sky opened up and swallowed me whole. I felt tingly and warm, as if I were floating on a cloud, like I'd imagined heaven to be. Part of me was afraid and another part wanted the kiss to last for the rest of my life.

CHAPTER 14

He released me and then came back for more and more.

"I said it wrong," he murmured. "I don't just want you not to leave. I want to be your guy and for you to be my girl. I know you doubt yourself, but we're alike in so many ways. You really care about others. Most people put themselves first, but you—"

"That's how I see you and Autumn. She's all those things too."

"She's my sister. It's more than just that you care about others. I've never had these feelings for any girl, any woman, before."

"You don't know me that well. I've been told that, when people get to know me, they'll—"

"Don't listen to those people."

"Everything I've ever cared about before has all come crashing down. There is nothing more terrifying than caring about someone only to have them—"

"Betray you? I'm not your brother or sister. I promise you, Treasure. If you allow me to be your guy, I'll never turn on you."

"You barely know me."

"I know you."

I was afraid and yet I wanted so much for this to be true. Paul was the dream I didn't dare dream or even hope for. *Do I dare open the flood-*

gates of my heart? It hurts so much more when you have something that means a lot to you and lose it than to never have known what it was like to have that thing you wanted so much in the first place. But my heart was already surrendering against my attempts to resist, to not risk an unsurvivable heartache.

Another worry occurred to me. I had heard that guys will tell you they love you until they don't. He hadn't actually said he loved me. Maybe it was something lesser. My brain told me to play it cool, but my heart refused to listen to common sense as I blurted out, "I want to stay."

He kissed me again and I felt completely lost in the embrace.

He pulled away. "Are you okay?"

I felt flushed, dizzy, but more alive than ever before. "I'm fine. I'm really fine."

"I'll take you to your room. You need to rest."

"Always the doctor."

"I need you in my life. I'm not taking any chances."

I smiled. "I've never—I mean, I didn't think this could happen to me."

He walked me to the room where Autumn and I would be staying and kissed me again. "I'll see you in the morning. I love you, Treasure."

I knew I was smiling. I was in heaven and I didn't want to return to Earth. He loved me or at least he thought he did. *Do I dare allow myself to trust or dream of a future that may never happen? I don't want another broken heart. I trusted my sister, my best friend, before she dumped me.* I lay down on one of the beds, remembering the kiss, feeling giddy all over again.

At some point, Autumn came into the room and threw herself down on the other bed. "I'm in love."

"You too?" I asked before thinking.

"So, Paul told you how he felt." She sounded excited.

"Do you think it's real? Are you okay with it?"

"Okay? I've got a sister, a real sister for life now. It couldn't be better if I had planned it myself. You're the first girl Paul's been serious about. And no, he's not gay. He just didn't find anyone who appealed to him before."

"Why me? Is he confusing pity for love?"

"Pity? Paul feels anything but pity for you. He admires the way you care about your family despite their awfulness and the way you care about Yosemite and our family."

"Feelings wear off, don't they? Not for me, but for guys."

"If you knew my brother better, you wouldn't say that."

"You're in love too?"

"Well, sort of. I mean I'm crazy about Eric, but I don't know. We'll see."

"I think it's great you have a boyfriend."

"And I think it's great you and my brother are together. But don't go taking his side in arguments."

"And let down my sister?"

My dream started off happy, floating down the Merced, resting my eyes as the sun shone brightly down on me and warmth flooded through my body. Then it switched and I was reliving being beaten by my father. He shouted he was going to cut Tatiana's singing and dancing lessons that had been funded by my mom before her death. There was a fund for both of us, but Tatiana's voice was of opera quality and she could go further with the lessons.

"I'm getting a refund."

"But it isn't your money."

He swung a baseball bat at me, again and again. I lifted my hands, saying, "This is it," knowing my time was up, certain I was going to meet my maker, but it was okay as long as Tatiana and Zinney had the tools and ability to survive.

He stopped short of killing me. Tatiana got to keep her classes and I agreed to eat just the crumbs and nothing else from the dinners I cooked for the family to pay for any shortfall caused by my refusal to end her lessons. I liked being thin, anyway.

My dream turned into a nightmare with Dad returning from the dead to zap Tatiana's dancing out of her as I lay on the floor, starving, kicked in the stomach by him again and again as he often liked to do when he was alive.

This time, as I lay on the floor, Tatiana skipped around me. "I don't like you. I never liked you. I just pretend to be your friend cause you'll give me everything I want all the time."

I woke up, crying. I wondered if that was it. If all she saw in me was someone who would always make sure she got what she wanted. Maybe, she never cared about me at all. But she had hidden the baseball bat after the incident I'd relived in my dream. She had also hidden the knives he'd used to threaten me with. *She didn't want me dead—at least not then.*

"That's a first. Most people are happy when they fall in love." It was Autumn.

"It wasn't that. I was dreaming about my dad and Tatiana."

"Two wonderful people created in the same hell. Are you sure you're related to those creeps? Maybe you were adopted."

"My birthday is tomorrow and she isn't even going to call me."

"Tomorrow? Wow, you don't give us much time to get you birthday presents."

"It's not the presents. I just always loved my sister and my brother and they both are fine with not knowing if I'm dead on my birthday."

"I say we take a road trip to Berkeley so I can beat up your sister."

I smiled. "That would really make her like me," I said facetiously.

"She probably doesn't like anyone she can't use. If there's Karma, she'll wind up with people who use her. You don't seem as concerned about your brother's betrayal."

"He betrayed me long ago. He'd stand there after I was beaten and refuse to take me to a doctor because it would make his dad look bad. He even refused at times when I wasn't sure I was going to survive."

There was a knock at the door. "You're looking for the room on the other side of the house," Autumn called out.

Paul walked in with a plate of food. "What's wrong?"

"Me. I'm really stupid."

"Is this about last night?"

"No. It's about the last seventeen, almost eighteen years."

"She was switched at birth. She's really my twin sister. Sorry, brother. You didn't know you were dating your sister."

"I'm not going there," he said.

"We're going on a road trip," she announced.

"Now?"

"As long as FEMA is still at Glacier."

"That isn't going to last. Jack's been monitoring their radios. Their poison was more lethal than we or they thought."

"Does that mean there is a residue, that we're contaminated?" I asked. I looked at Autumn and hoped she was safe. Then, I thought about myself. I'd just found the love that had always been a distant hope, locked up inside me.

"It could be that there is enough poison that the elites would be in danger if they lived there for long periods of time."

"The animals?" Images from the trail below Vernal flashed through my mind.

"We need to keep them out of the Valley so they don't eat the soil. The rangers will be setting food above the line where the cloud settled. Instead of a resort, FEMA is looking at turning the place into some kind of prison camp in the short term."

"Prison for whom?" I asked.

"Anyone who disagrees with the government, who doesn't want war or mandated medical procedures. NDAA stuff."

"You're saying they poisoned the whole valley?"

"For the time being. They say it's safe enough to set up California Gitmo, but they don't plan to bring a lot of troops in there right away."

"Since when does our government care about the troops?"

"They don't. A lot of those working with FEMA are independent contractors." That was Jack's voice chiming in. "They get uniforms and they make a lot more than the regular troops."

"We're doing a road trip," Autumn announced.

"Good timing."

"I'm coming with you," Paul said.

"This is a girl thing," Autumn objected. "We'll only be gone a day —unless we're having a really great time and forget about you."

"Where will you go?"

"The coast. Not Big Sur or any of the isolated vacation spots they might hit next."

"Big Sur is on Highway One."

"But mostly only the tourists and surfers are traveling up and down Highway One."

"Is this what you want to do?" Paul asked me.

"Sure. It will give me time to think."

"About us?"

I shook my head.

"Your sister?"

I didn't say anything.

"She really hurt you. I don't want to see you hurt again."

"I guess I need some kind of idea of what's going on with her."

"How about you eat some breakfast and then we'll talk. Doctor's orders. I'll be back after you have a chance to get some nutrition into you." He started to close the door, but then stopped. "Treasure, how would you like to go out on the horses this morning?"

"If it's alright with Autumn."

"I'll hang out with Eric and Jeff."

<hr>

An hour later, we were on horseback.

"You ride very well."

"It's Laura. She makes it easy."

"She's a good horse. You've been through a lot the last two days, and I hope I didn't make things worse last night."

"You didn't. I'm still having a hard time believing last night was real."

"It was real for me."

I felt all tingly inside as he said that.

"What if your sister throws you under the bus and runs over you a few times while you're there? It might not hurt to have an EMT handy."

"I don't know that I'm even going to talk to Tatiana. I just want an idea of what is going on with her."

"After all she's done to you?"

"What hurts the most is the betrayal." I looked at Paul. "If you have any doubts about us, now is the time to tell me. It will hurt too much later."

"Not happening. You really don't know how captivating you are. You're so busy worrying about your family, you've never taken the time to take a good look at yourself. Are you having second thoughts?"

"The truth. I've never been in a romantic relationship. I'm a little scared. No—more than that. I'm terrified. I feel like I'm on the edge of a cliff, and I don't know if I can hold on or learn to fly."

"I'll be there to catch you if you let me. Of course, that will be kind of hard if you're two hundred miles away."

"It will be a brief trip."

"I'd rather you let me go with you."

"This is something I need to do for myself."

At a meadow with beautiful wildflowers, we dismounted and walked the horses. Paul put his arm around me. It felt so good to have someone caring about me, wanting to protect me. But it was more than that. It was great that that someone was a person I was crazy about.

I couldn't keep the troops and bodies out of my mind. "We need to find a way to stop FEMA."

"We'll find a way."

"There's a Congresswoman I know in the Bay Area. At one time she had courage."

"Don't count on it."

"Anything's possible."

"This is what my dad prepared us for. If we can stop them, we will. Either way, we have protection—unless we keep galivanting around and getting spotted by armed thugs."

"That's something I plan to avoid in the future."

His lips embraced mine again. "I need you to trust me."

"I do."

"When you get back, we can talk more about the future."

That made me nervous. After all those years of beatings, I never expected to survive. I just wanted my brother and sister to be safe and have their dreams—even though I might not be alive to share them. Now, I had a potential future, but every time, in the past, I had hoped for something positive, it had disappeared from my grasp.

We went back to Jack's.

"You and Autumn will need a fast car," Jack said. He led us to his garage and handed Autumn keys to a Ferrari. "Drive safely or your brother will have my hide."

"A Ferrari. I saw Jack as more the pickup truck type," I said to Paul as he kissed me goodbye.

"He has a couple of those too."

I noticed that Eric and Autumn were smiling and laughing about something. I was glad she had found someone.

We took off racing down the hill towards Oakhurst with Autumn driving, of course. We stopped at a large supermarket. We didn't see anyone. The store was wide open.

"This doesn't look good," I said.

Autumn started grabbing wrapped foods off the shelf. "I can leave some cash."

"I'm worried that they could have doctored it."

"It's sealed."

We started to go towards the front cash register, when I felt the barrel of a gun at my back.

CHAPTER 15

It was a kid. "You're one of them, aren't you?"

"We come in peace," I said.

"Would you like some chocolate pudding?" Autumn offered, holding out a package.

"Where is everyone?" I asked when he didn't respond.

"At a meeting. They're figuring out how to deal with people like you. I might get an award for catching you."

"People like us?"

"You're the ones who poisoned the lake and killed all the fish and then poisoned our drinking water."

"We didn't," I responded. "I promise."

"All right," Autumn said. "I guess he wants us to give him the antidote."

"Antidote?"

"The thing that makes the poison go away."

"You have that?"

"Right here in my boot," I said. I leaned down to reach into my boot as the barrel was lowered, continuing to point at me.

Autumn kicked the gun out of his hand and it went flying across the floor. The kid started to go for it and Autumn grabbed him from behind and held his arms against his sides. He tried to throw her over his shoulder, maybe something he had seen on TV, but failed as I went for the gun. I picked it up and pointed it at the floor.

The kid looked frightened as Autumn let him go. I handed her the gun and tried to assure him, "We're not the bad guys."

"This thing isn't even loaded," Autumn observed.

"Where is the meeting?" I asked.

"I'm not going to tell."

"Maybe we can help. They poisoned Yosemite Valley too. Believe it or not, we're on your side," I said.

"What's your name?" Autumn inquired.

"Calvin."

"Calvin, I'm Treasure and this is Autumn."

"What kind of name is Treasure?"

"I didn't like my old name, and my friends renamed me."

"Maybe I can change my name."

"Maybe."

"Now, where is this meeting? We can drive you there," Autumn offered.

"My mother told me—"

"We'll take you to your mother if she's there."

"She's sick. She may die."

"I'm sorry," I said. The pain of losing my own mother flashed through my thoughts. "Will you let us help?"

He hesitated to speak, maybe deciding about us. "You promise you aren't with the people who poisoned the water? If you are, my uncle will beat you up."

"If we are, he's welcome to beat us up," I told him.

"Speak for yourself," Autumn joked. She turned to the boy, "Take us to your uncle."

With Calvin directing us, we drove to a church building where about two-hundred people were meeting. They turned as we entered.

"Calvin, I told you to stay behind," a man said.

"You must be the uncle," I responded.

"They said they wanted to help. I knew they were lying."

"Do you know who is responsible for poisoning our water and lake?" the uncle asked.

"I think so," Autumn said. "They did worse to Yosemite Valley."

"They?"

"FEMA."

"Why would they?"

"They've now taken over the Valley. Didn't their trucks drive by you yesterday?"

"I thought that was a military operation," another man said.

"Are you a conspiracy theorist?" a woman asked, accusingly.

"Is the poisoning of your water a conspiracy theory?" I reproached her.

"You say they are in the Valley?" a man in the crowd asked.

"They've blocked off Highway 41 before Wawona Tunnel."

"I'm going to give them a piece of my mind," Pete said. Several men stood up.

"They've got guns," I pointed out.

"So do we."

"They also have cyanide clouds or maybe something worse they dropped on the Valley while people were there. We shot video of them burying campers in mass graves."

Autumn tried to pull up the Internet on her phone.

"The Internet's down," a guy in perhaps his mid-twenties said. "I'm Philip."

"Treasure and Autumn."

"Treasure?" Philip asked.

"My friends renamed me."

"Pete," the uncle said.

Autumn went to the videos on her cell. "Can I connect to your computer?"

The guy, who introduced himself as Philip, helped her attach her phone to his laptop with a cord. Another cord connected his computer to a large screen.

She ran the Yosemite Valley videos and pictures. The audience sat there in horror.

"These people are dangerous," Autumn informed them. "Yesterday, they came in with tanks and armed men who were shooting at anything that moved."

"Let's kick their asses," the uncle said to the crowd.

I looked around. We had about two hundred or more backups. But we were up against the government and there could be infiltrators in the group. Our government was known for infiltrating opposition groups, from peace activists to environmental groups.

"With all due respect, even a group this size needs backup."

"We'll get it."

The uncle and several other guys discussed forming a leadership committee to oversee the resistance.

"I need to reach my brother," Autumn said. "Where can we get internet?"

"Maybe in Fresno."

"When do you think you'll have things organized here?" I asked.

"Tonight, tomorrow. Maybe take action tomorrow night or the next morning."

"We'll be back," Autumn told the group.

"Going to Fresno?" the uncle asked.

"I'm going to the Bay Area to track down my sister. She was at Yosemite when it started getting bad. I want to make sure she's okay."

We went to the car and drove up the next hill. There, we pulled out the ham radio we had gotten from Jack. I was concerned that because it wasn't a wired connection, it might not be secure, but Autumn was certain it was.

I told Jack about the poisoning of the water and commented that I hoped hundreds of fish that might show up tomorrow night would survive, my code for telling him about the plans.

Paul was next to Jack. He got on the radio. "We'll do our best to see those fish live to spawn."

"He got it," Autumn said.

We stopped in Fresno to get some additional gas and then took off for the coast.

"Which pass do you prefer?" she asked.

"Altamont is lower than Pacheco, but Livermore is still somewhat radioactive. All those radiation experiments years ago."

"Higher is better, but the towns along 101 are more isolated. Also, Gilroy smells. Garlic."

In the end, we decided to take the Altamont Pass to the Bay Area.

As we drove, another fear washed over me. I recalled a conversation I'd had with Tatiana an evening when I'd traveled to see her sing in a concert not long ago.

"It's all yours and Mom's fault."

"How?"

"Mom shouldn't have had me when she was married to that man or she should have aborted me. And you could have stopped it by getting Mom to euthanize me."

"That's ridiculous. Tatiana, you're older than me and you have made a real difference in the world. It's a better place because you're in it. And I've seen you smiling and happy. You are so special."

"I hate my life."

Families of the performers were going to a post-concert celebration, but Tatiana told me I wasn't welcome at the after-event.

I'd brought flowers. One of the parents offered to give them to her at the celebration but suggested I attend myself. Knowing my presence would upset Tatiana, I lied and said something had come up and I couldn't make it.

"What's wrong?" Autumn asked.

I hadn't realized I was crying. "What if she knew about the deaths and thought I died on the trail and hurt herself. There were times when she said she wished she'd never been born. Why wasn't I more sensitive to her feelings?"

"She sounds like the luckiest girl on Earth, having a sister who loves her so much in spite of all the nastiness she inflicts on you. She said that to hurt you and it worked. It's people with low self-opinions who generally harm themselves. If you put yourself down again, I'll punch you out and I mean it this time."

I hoped she was right about Tatiana being safe.

Tatiana was on the top floor of a three-story apartment complex. The open balcony door was visible from a block away on the back side of the building. A cat was crawling on the rail around it.

"Grant better be taking good care of our wolfies," Autumn said.

"And I hope he keeps them inside. I wouldn't want FEMA to use them for target practice." I cringed, thinking of it.

"So, it's a security building. There's the easy way and the fun way."

"The easy way?"

"Flirt with a guy living in the building. I say we go the fun way. Follow me."

She pulled herself over the perimeter fence and then climbed up from balcony to balcony. I wasn't as tall. So, she assisted me. Finally, we were on Tatiana's balcony. The cat looked surprised but didn't attack.

"Cats eat their owners if they lie still for too long," she mused.

Inside, there was no sign of Tatiana. It was clear Tatiana had cooked lunch or somebody had. I looked around. Bottles of wine and other alcohol lined the cabinets. She wasn't old enough to drink, but apparently, that wasn't stopping her.

"I can't say I'm impressed with her taste in alcohol," Autumn scoffed. Autumn looked at the food in the cupboards and refrigerator. "She doesn't even eat organic."

"Her friends at Berkeley turned her off to organic."

"Why isn't she in a dorm?"

"She's got money."

"Which she wouldn't have if you hadn't made sure her tuition was covered." That's when we heard a key in the lock and voices outside. She had friends with her and I knew she'd be furious to see me there, uninvited.

CHAPTER 16

"Do you want to confront her now?" Autumn asked.

"No. I'd rather wait until she's alone."

We rushed into the bedroom and hid in the closet.

"Is Andrew coming?" a female in the group asked.

"He said he couldn't tonight," Tatiana replied.

The cat started growling at something.

"Muriel, what's gotten into you?" she asked.

"Maybe she's hungry," another female voice suggested.

That was when Autumn slid out of the closet. I waved for her to return. She was peeking out the bedroom door and then quietly exited it. Next, I heard what sounded like the main door opening and closing.

"Who are you?"

"Andrew sent me. He thought I'd enjoy this."

"Andrew?"

"Yes."

"He didn't ask me for permission to invite you," Tatiana griped.

"I'm Winter. Andrew said you were cool."

"Have you played this game before?" someone asked.

"He said you'd show me the ropes."

"Did he send anyone else over?" That was Tatiana's voice.

"Just me. I'm surprised Andrew didn't tell you about me. I thought he had told everyone."

"Are you two an item?" one of the girls asked.

"I'll let Andrew tell you all about us."

I listened through the bedroom door. The girls and a couple of guys started explaining the game to Autumn as she ordered a pizza delivery on the phone. I backed away and quietly closed the door in case they looked towards the bedroom.

"I love pizza," a guy said. "As long as you don't order it from Anthony's."

"What's wrong with Anthony's?" Autumn asked.

"Didn't Andrew tell you? Well, this friend of ours loved Anthony's and ate there all the time. Then suddenly he collapsed after eating a pizza and they found worms crawling in his stomach. Apparently, they were in the dough."

"Yuck. Could you cancel that and order from Romano's instead?" one of the girls asked.

"But I already gave them my card." I wondered where she had lifted the card or maybe Jack had gotten her one under a phony name.

"Please. I don't want worms," the girl reacted.

"Have you girls ever been horseback riding?" Autumn asked.

"It's been a while," another girl said.

"My parents own a stable in Oakland Hills. Maybe sometime I can take you all riding there. The horses are really friendly," Autumn prevaricated.

"I used to take English riding lessons," Tatiana informed her.

"Was that when you were a kid?"

"Sort of. My sister made sure I got years of lessons."

"Nice sister. I bet you two are close," Autumn stated.

"Tatiana doesn't like her sister. Her sister's too weak and pathetic," the girl who had asked Autumn to cancel Anthony's explained.

"Jenny," Tatiana cautioned.

"Well, that's what you said."

"But she got you the riding lessons. Did you pay her back for all she did for you?" Autumn asked.

"It's really none of your business. Andrew never mentioned you to me, and he tells me everything."

"Except what he thinks will make you mad. He says you get mad easily."

"I don't."

"Yes, you do," one of the girls, not Jenny, disagreed.

"You hold grudges over the slightest things. At least, that's what Joe told me," another girl commented.

"Joe?"

"Your ex-boyfriend. He said you always had to have things your own way or you'd get mad."

"Aubrey, if you don't like me, you can leave."

"But we need her to play the game. She always runs the best dungeons," Jenny protested.

"I get the impression nobody who disagrees with you is welcome here," Autumn said.

"Fine. Everyone, leave."

"Tatiana, how about we all calm down?" That was from a guy in the group.

"Barry, I'm done. Everyone, get out."

As I listened, I felt for Tatiana. She was so used to getting everything she wanted that she couldn't handle people disagreeing with her or telling her how they felt about anything.

I heard the door open and people leaving. It sounded like Tatiana was making a call. "Andrew, how could you!" That's all she said. I gathered she hung up on him.

"What are you still doing here?"

"I just wanted to see what it was like for a bitch to squirm. You have the wrong breed of pet."

"Get out!"

"Or what, you'll leave me for dead on a mountain trail because I'm too weak and pathetic?"

"My sister sent you."

"I sent myself. You are a user, a taker, without a shred of decency in you. Tomorrow's your sister's birthday. Do you even know if she's alive?"

"Get out or I'm calling the police."

"And telling them that you didn't like one of your party guests?"

"You aren't a guest. You're an intruder."

"My brother is an officer. Maybe he'll be the one to come check this out. What? You escorting me out?"

"All the way to the street."

That was my cue to exit. I waited a minute and then left the apartment. After watching them take one staircase down, I went to the other stairwell. Both opened onto the street in front. As I opened the bottom door and looked at the door to the one they had taken, I saw Tatiana push Autumn out. Autumn walked past the door to my staircase and pretended not to notice me. A minute later, Tatiana walked the other direction, toward the university, never looking my way. I exited and turned the way Autumn had gone.

"She must be really upset," I said when I caught up with Autumn.

"I know her type. She'll feel angry and then sorry for herself and then maybe something will stick. It's about time someone told her off over her treatment of you. And did you notice, her friends already saw through her?"

"I did notice that they didn't like her much."

"Unless she changes, people will use her, but they won't really like her. Want to go home?"

"I was thinking of sending her a pizza, not from Anthony's."

"As a present for your birthday?"

"I used to do that," I said, almost laughing. "I would give Zinney and Tatiana presents on all my birthdays."

"Of course, you did. And this is where it got you."

"You're right. I did everything totally wrong."

"When you're dealing with cold, selfish witches, sometimes the nice approach is the least effective."

"Do you think she'll ever like me?"

"Not while she believes she's the best thing that has happened to the world."

"I did that to her."

"And someone else will have to undo it."

"Did you really order a pizza from Anthony's?"

"I faked the call."

We didn't say a lot on the way back. I was really sad and had trouble speaking. On top of that, I felt awful for Tatiana. Autumn stopped at an organic food place and picked up some sweet potatoes and cauliflower spaghetti to go.

We ate as we traveled towards Jack's. I knew it would be late before we got back. This time we decided to take the Pacheco Pass. With the lake at our right, a car cut around us, forcing us onto the shoulder, where Autumn had to stop or impact the other car. Two men came toward the car. I recognized them: the FEMA guys from the Lodge. As one approached, Autumn rolled down her window. She pulled something from under a cover behind the seat. It was the gun she'd retrieved the day before on the way to Jack's and it was now pointed directly at the guy.

"Use that and my friend blows your friend's head off." We looked to my side window, where his friend was standing with a gun pointed at my head.

CHAPTER 17

"I guess it's a standoff or not quite. I can get both of you quicker with this than your friend can get her with that," Autumn said boldly.

"Have you used one before?"

Autumn smiled. "Well, you're about to find out or not find out." She tilted her head to me and I noticed her plan. "Sorry, but your friend is covered by my other friend. You'll both be gone in no—"

The guy with the gun on my side turned to see if someone was behind the car, which was the clue she was waiting for. I ducked as she backed up. A bullet rang from the man's gun, right through the windshield as we both ducked.

Another shot was fired through the windshield, exiting through the back window, as she put the car into drive and stepped on the gas. I hoped we didn't wind up off the road down the lake or colliding with a car, as there was no way she could see the road with her head down.

I lifted my head and saw the man who had been on my side, now about to be run over, back up and fall off the edge of the shoulder. Autumn's guy was trying to take aim as she backed up again and went forward again, angling to her left and knocking him out of the way.

She stopped. "Take his car," she hurriedly said.

The other car was still running. With one man on the ground and the other in the lake, I jumped in and took off quickly, hoping to be out of range before the one on the ground started firing. No such luck as a shot made it through the back window, straight through to the front windshield, barely missing me. Another shot hit the exterior of the car. I was surprised the FEMA car wasn't bulletproof.

In the mirror, I could see Autumn sideswiping the man, again, knocking him down a second time as she sped away behind me.

At Santa Nella, we looked for some license plates we could switch with the vehicles. "They left their cell phones in the car," I observed.

"Throw them in the trash," she said. "We can't go far in that thing. They hit the gas tank."

"Bonnie Parker," I glowed. We dropped off the fed car on a deserted road between Interstate 5 and U.S. 99. Then we continued on in the Ferrari. The holes in the windshield and back window raised the wind noise volume.

In Fresno, we stopped at a car glass shop and pounded on the glass door. Someone was inside. "Come back in the morning. "

"We'll be in Tahoe in the morning. You look like a nice gentleman, and I know you'll fix it for us tonight," Autumn replied.

The guy smiled at Autumn and went out to look at the car.

"We're supposed to report gunshots holes in cars, but I don't see any." He winked. "You're lucky. Normally, I don't have this kind of glass. I'll need to replace your back window too. Maybe when you get back from Tahoe, you'll drop in."

"This will be my favorite stop after Tahoe," she responded.

In about half an hour, the glass was fixed. He cut his usual price in half or said he did, and Autumn paid cash. "I owe you half of that," I said.

"Don't worry about it. Next window is on you."

***

We got back to Jack's about two A.M. As we entered the house, Everlove and her friends greeted us with bows and licks. "It's so good to see you again," I told my favorite wolves.

A bouquet of flowers appeared from behind me. I turned. It was Paul. He gave me a big hug. "We were worried."

"We had to get the glass replaced on Jack's car and FEMA might have the license plate."

"It's okay. It's someone else's plate," Jack said.

"FEMA. What happened to the glass?" Paul inquired.

"One of the thugs shot it out after I backed up and then tried to run him over," Autumn said rather matter-of-factly as if she were discussing the weather.

"I was afraid you might be in danger. I should have gone with you."

"It was FEMA that was in danger," Autumn said proudly.

"What about your sister?" he asked me.

"We wrecked one of her parties," I related.

"Ah, poor girl." Paul smiled.

"She'll probably never forgive me."

"She didn't even know you were there. I wrecked the party. Her sister's friends don't like her."

"Good work, Autumn," he congratulated and high-fived her. "We figured you'd be hungry, and so we have some food waiting for you in the kitchen."

"I don't think she's going to like it. It's not her usual food," Grant remarked.

"You're here too," I observed, giving Grant a friendly hug. Paul guided me to the kitchen, followed by the wolves, Jack, Grant and Autumn. The lights went off as we entered and all I could see were lit candles. Everyone, including Jeff and Eric, who were in the kitchen, started singing "Happy Birthday."

I turned to Paul.

"Autumn told us."

"I couldn't let my sister go another year without a proper birthday."

Jack turned the lights on and we all had some cake and mushroom pizza. I laughed and then felt guilty, thinking about Tatiana's party.

"At least it didn't come from Anthony's," I joked.

Paul looked like he had missed something.

"You had to be there," I laughed. "I love you, Autumn."

She gave me a hug. Then Paul turned me towards him and gave me a kiss.

"You two need adult supervision," Jack said to Paul and me. "Champagne?"

"I have something better. It's not the cherry wine you got from Yosemite. This is from Denmark. My dad had cases of the stuff because it was my mom's favorite."

He opened up some Cherry Kijafa.

"This is the best tasting wine I've ever had," I said.

We ate and talked about plans for the future as if nothing was wrong in the world. We were putting off all negatives for at least the celebration. I felt a joyful rush of belonging gushing through me.

Paul guided me outside.

"The stars are still beautiful," I said. We walked a little way and then sat down.

"While you were away, all I could think about was: what if you didn't come back? You could have reconciled with your sister and decided to stay in Berkeley." He touched my cheek and looked into my eyes. I held back a gasp, feeling overwhelmed by the gentle warmth of his touch.

"Even if I did reconcile with her, I would have come back."

"To save the Park."

"And to be with my new family. You are sounding like me, doubting your appeal. I've been afraid you might change your mind about me."

"Never."

"Nobody I ever thought I could count on has stayed in my life. I still have trouble trusting anyone ever will."

"I wish I could have been there long ago to stop all the heartache you went through. To let you know you deserved better."

"Maybe what I went through made me a better person."

"You're the most incredible woman I've ever known. I know you're only eighteen, but you have the kindness and wisdom of an old soul."

"Old soul. Well, I could say the same about you: taking in a stranger and treating me like family."

He started to lean in as if to kiss me again and then pulled back. "I have another birthday present for you and you don't need to take it." He knelt on one knee and pulled out a box.

This couldn't be.

"This was my mother's engagement ring. She wanted me to give it to the girl I intended to spend the rest of my life with."

CHAPTER 18

I opened my mouth in shock. Only a few days before, everything was hopeless and I'd never met Paul and his family. *I have to be dreaming. There is no way my life could change so fast. It can't be real. It's impossible.*

He must have sensed my incredulity. "I won't rush you. If you're not ready, you can wait, or if you feel as I do, you can wear it until you feel comfortable, planning for our future." He sat beside me, caressing my cheek with his free hand as he seemed to search my eyes for my answer.

I opened my mouth, unable to say anything at first. "You want to marry me one day? You really mean that?"

"I really mean that."

I was feeling so much at once that I couldn't get any more words out. I just sat there as he started to look a little dismayed and closed the box.

"I—yes, I'll wear it. I can't believe you feel—about me. I mean, am I hallucinating? Maybe those FEMA guys really did shoot me." I must have sounded stupid and giddy, but his gaze was gentle, warm, steady and his eyes were smiling.

He opened the box back up. "It's real, and I know it seems sudden, but I know what I feel and it's not going to change." The certainty of his tone and the look in his eyes pierced holes through my doubts. The part of my brain that was afraid to trust was shouting as my heart was screaming at my brain to shut up.

I held out my hand and he put the ring on my finger. I could feel it slipping on and yet I had to look to make sure it wasn't just my overactive imagination.

"It fits. That's a good sign."

"I still can't believe—" I was sounding repetitive, school-girlish. "You're amazing. I never thought anyone like you would fall in love with me."

"I never thought I'd meet anyone I would want as much as you. So, we're even," he said, bringing his lips to mine. Then our arms wrapped around each other. I was in heaven again, happier than I had ever been before in my life. I don't know how long the embrace lasted, but suddenly I felt Everlove leaning against me, trying to get into the event. Paul released me and I hugged Everlove.

We went back in. "Let's see it," Autumn said.

I held out my hand.

Grant grinned. Smiling, he smacked Paul on the shoulder and then gave me a hug. "Welcome to the family."

"She's already family," Autumn corrected him. "Do I get to be your Maid of Honor?"

"Absolutely! But not right away."

"I've been waiting for this young man to take an interest in someone." Jack paused and changed the subject. "Now, about the plan. If this militia goes in firing, the FEMA army has them out-gunned and most of that army consists, not of National Guard Troopers from the people but contractors in uniforms, who are earning ten times as much as regular soldiers and are paid for with those disappearing military funds."

I worked to shift my focus back to current events.

"Jack and I went down to Oakhurst this evening," Grant explained. "They're planning to spread out for a sniper operation. They're five hundred strong."

"If they take over the Valley, don't you think the Feds'll just nuke the place?" I asked. "Our government believes in pre-emptive strikes."

"The Governor is in the real estate business. That's too permanent," Paul said.

"They might bring in the real army," Grant warned.

"If they hunt for snipers, will the government raid here?" I asked.

"I don't think so, but we need to be prepared for that," Jack said. "I've got defenses. Do you?"

"Not like you've got," Grant acknowledged.

"An old house in the woods with minimal security is an easy target," Eric pointed out, apparently speaking of our fake hangout.

The next morning, Grant announced that FEMA had left the Point, except for one sentry who was assigned to check the Point to observe the Valley occasionally and what could be seen of the area between. They had fortified their operations at the U.S. 41 Wawona Tunnel and at El Portal on Highway 140, as well as other roads to the Valley. The hotels in El Portal had been closed—except to FEMA.

Most of the rangers who had been kicked out of the Valley were now stationed at the Badger's Pass Rangers Station, not far from the Glacier Point Station.

The horses were already back home and the rest of us returned that morning. When we arrived, Paul covered my eyes with a bandana and led me somewhere. I had thought the secrecy where I was concerned was over. Through my nose, I could tell it was to the field where the horses were grazing. He removed the bandana and Laura was there with a ribbon around her neck. "We took a vote and Laura is your horse."

"Mine?" I threw my arms around Laura. "I've always wanted a horse, and Laura is my favorite horse in the whole world. How can I give you back anything close to what you've given me?"

"You already have," Paul said.

"I'll have to go along with that," Grant chimed in. "I've never seen Paul and Autumn so happy."

"Or me," I acknowledged.

I wondered what I could give to them that they didn't already have. I felt inadequate, unworthy of what I was receiving, like I had to repay them, somehow. I had always found it easier to give presents than to receive them. I remembered being overjoyed when Tatiana or Zinney would light up from seeing a present I gave them, but that wasn't real. They no longer remembered any of the good times with me.

"I didn't see anyone at the turnoff to the Point when we arrived," I said.

"FEMA is setting up operations much closer to the Valley. And there is that roving sentry. Make sure you don't run into him," Grant warned me. "I have to get to work. Happy Birthday, Treasure."

"We'll be up there, later. I want to show Treasure what they've done to the area," Paul said.

In the late morning, Paul, Autumn and I walked to the Point. Grant joined us. He handed us some binoculars. "Don't be too obvious. They're undoubtedly watching the Point from below."

"What made them decide to pull their troops from the Point?" I asked.

"I guess they didn't want to spread themselves too thin."

Looking down, I could see FEMA had set up huge buildings in several of the meadows and had demolished quite a number of trees for their construction.

"Those are prefab buildings," Grant explained. "They put down the sections and then just pulled up the sides. Faster that way."

"All that damage," I lamented.

"Look at the fence around that one section. It's barbed and electrical. We've seen it sparking," Grant said, pointing to an area around one of the buildings.

"And what are those mirrored things in the meadows?" Autumn inquired.

"They make it harder to detect what is going on."

"Hi," Philip said, coming up behind us with Pete. "We have a number of men who will be closing in on them from all directions. We saw what they did to Sonora. We don't want to be next."

"The valley looks like a prison camp," I said.

"Do you guys live around here?" Philip asked.

"There's a house a little way from the Point," Paul responded.

"And you've got a ranger with you," Pete accused.

"None of the rangers like what is going on," Grant related.

"Are you sure we can trust someone who works for the federal government?" Pete asked, eyeing Grant closely.

"You met me yesterday," Grant said. "What's your problem today?"

"You look official, like you fit."

"I work for the National Park Service, not FEMA."

"It's all part of the same—"

"Are you trying to cause trouble?" Autumn asked, putting Pete in his place. "Wreck our chances of fixing things? If you can't work with others, leave it to us to handle."

"Just asking." Pete put his hands up, palms out, and backed away. "We don't need any infiltrators squealing to the enemy."

"If there are any infiltrators, they're with your group," Grant stated, matter-of-factly.

"Let's be civilized," Philip agreed with Autumn. "We're not going to get anywhere if we focus on each other."

"I'm going to be watching the ranger to make sure he doesn't get out of line," Pete advised as Autumn threw up her hands. Paul looked upset, but he didn't react.

"And I'll be watching the enemy," Grant said.

About that time, we saw another ranger approaching the point.

"Brady," Grant informed me.

We left Philip and Pete looking at the Valley to speak with Brady.

"Hi, Autumn, Paul," Brady said as we greeted him there. "And who is this lovely lady?"

"My sister," Autumn said.

"You've been holding out, Grant."

"She means future sister-in-law. She's marrying me," Paul said, firmly.

"No offense."

"None taken," Paul replied.

Brady spoke quietly to all of us. "The other rangers and I don't like what's going on. We're going to send a delegation to meet with our Senator later today."

"The rabid Senator or the sold-out one?" Autumn asked.

"They've probably both sold out. But we're meeting with the one you consider less loony as well as his chief of staff. His staff probably makes all his decisions for him anyway."

"You have my support," Grant offered.

"Who are those yokels?" Brady tilted his head towards Pete and Phillip.

"Some people from Oakhurst. They don't like what they're seeing either," Autumn informed him.

"They figure the same government writes our paycheck," Grant noted.

"Paycheck or none, if FEMA messes up any more of the park, this ranger is going to rebel."

"Don't let the government or FEMA hear you talk like that. You've heard of the NDAA and indefinite detention," Paul warned.

"I know about it. Our government's been doing crazy stuff for a long time."

"The other rangers are pretty cool, but remember, they also get their paychecks from the same government that writes them for the thugs who took over the Valley," Grant noted. "Pete did have a point."

"I would expect you to be more upset. You've been in the area so much of your life," Brady remarked to Grant.

"I am. I hope you have success today."

"Success with what?" Pete asked, coming over to us.

"We're having a meeting today. I have to go." Brady went back to his truck and drove off.

"Ratting us out?" Pete asked.

"They're meeting with one of our Senators to try to end this official-ly," Grant informed him.

"These guys don't follow laws."

"Maybe not. But if the funding is cut, they're gone."

"Did you tell him about our plan?"

"No. The fewer officials who know, the more who can claim to be surprised."

"We'll catch you later," Paul told Grant.

———

After returning to the cave, we rode Atlas, Libra and Laura over to Jack's.

"Those vigilantes seem a bit hot-headed," Paul noted as Jack came out onto the porch. He was decked out in military gear.

"I picked up on that yesterday. Their community has been seriously damaged. They have some ex-SEALS and ex-Green Berets in their group, though. Could be handy," Jack said as we followed him down to the basement.

"Don't you look fancy, Jack," Autumn commented.

"I was once a Navy SEAL."

"You were?" I asked.

"One of the best," Paul noted.

"I know some of the best spots for watching the Valley," Autumn bragged.

"Autumn, you girls are going to be inside with me, monitoring the situation," Paul informed us.

"Paul," Autumn responded, irritatedly.

"I'm not going to lose either of you if anything goes wrong."

"This is for those of us with military experience," Jack said.

"Chauvinist," Autumn grimaced.

"I'm sure there will be women, former Marines and Army. I met some in Oakhurst yesterday," he noted.

"I'll be watching the satellite footage and sending out alerts," Jeff told her.

"I'll be going out, too," Eric said.

"Without me?" Autumn made double fists and placed them on her hips.

"What you four will be doing in surveillance is every bit as important as what we will be doing in the field," Jack assured us.

"But Paul doesn't need me," Autumn countered.

"Yes, I do," Paul said, firmly.

"What if something happens to Eric or to you, Jack?" Autumn asked.

"We'll be fine," Eric assured her. "Don't worry. Just take care of yourself."

I had never operated a gun and didn't know if I could fight my way out of a breadbox. I was content to assist Paul in whatever way I could. Clearly, Autumn was more capable, but I didn't want anything to happen to her. I'd just found my new sister. I admired her rebelliousness but I worried it could put her in danger.

Autumn stomped upstairs, looking ready to kill our team. Paul pulled me aside. "We may have to lock her in."

"I can't do that. She'd hate me."

"I'll do it. Just don't let her out."

I knew she'd hate me if I didn't tell her his plan, but I was worried that she could be hurt or worse. I hated the dilemma.

"This is a crazy way to spend your birthday," Paul said.

"Despite everything, this is the best birthday I've had since I lost my mother."

"I wish I could have met her."

"I wish I could have helped her. I think the saddest thing for her was how Tatiana treated her towards the end. Tatiana refused to speak to her in her last days over some little grudge. I tried to cheer her up, but I couldn't take away the pain."

He shook his head. "And she did the same to you after you repeated your mother's mistake of loving her."

"Loving someone is never a mistake, but betrayal hurts really badly."

"You just need to love the right people." He took me in his arms and kissed my cheek.

Paul and Jack went upstairs to check on Autumn.

Eric pulled me out of my thoughts as he looked at footage from Jack's cameras closer to the highway. "Their militias are slowly moving in trucks towards the Valley." He pointed to the videos of Highway 41. "It looks as if they are riding along the shoulder and stopping at points to be more subtle, like sightseers." He showed me a view of the map on the computer. "They are partially hidden, but with Jack's cameras, I can see men with assault rifles in hand, probably waiting until dark."

As he spoke, a sense of foreboding overwhelmed me, an uneasy feeling that something would go awry.

CHAPTER 19

Eric went upstairs to take Autumn for a walk to calm her down. "If she kills him before tonight, Jack may be on his own," Paul remarked, returning to the basement.

"So, you and your brother are both good at computers?" I asked Jeff.

"Eric's good, but he's burned out on IT. He wants to do documentaries. I always wanted to do something more adventurous and outdoorsy. But now, both our past computer escapades are coming in handy."

"Are you okay with Eric going out there tonight?"

"Not at all. He is an adult." From that, I realized that they had partially lied to Grant the first day when Jeff said they were both minors. Paul shook his head, picking up on that too. "You're pretty outdoorsy. I would have expected you to be there with a rifle in hand."

"Grant has a gun and my dad made sure I knew how to shoot, but I'm not a gun guy. I could probably hold my own in a fist fight."

"I'm worried that this could get bloody," I said. "Eric and Jack are going to be out there. If they catch them, they might try them for conspiracy and treason if any of the troops are killed."

"Eric's not going to shoot anyone," Jeff stated.

"In that uniform, won't Jack be an easy target?"

"They're not going to shoot a military officer," Paul responded.

"If both sides start shooting, it could get bloody and they could be caught in the crossfire. Today, Pete treated the rangers, including Grant, like they were the enemy," I related.

"Remember Ukraine? Anyone who told the truth was put on a kill list. Our government blew up pipelines and bridges and conducted or supported political assassinations. Eventually, our government will come after all the Yosemite resistance and their friends and families if they can identify us." Jeff noted.

"Like a witch hunt," I said.

"Exactly."

"Our best bet is to at least stay away from the fighting," Jeff surmised. "And Eric better stay out of it too."

"But I'm responsible. I told the people of Oakhurst about Yosemite."

"You didn't put the guns in their hands," Paul countered.

"While the militia is distracting them, we'll be uploading," Jack stated, coming into the room.

"What will you be uploading?" I asked.

"You know how cell phones have trouble working in most parts of the Valley? Picture all FEMA's communications going out and all power cut to the Valley."

"But the military has its own satellites and towers," Paul pointed out.

"And there are two hackers here... Eric and I just need to get to one of their computers, plant a virus that will carry it up to their satellite and towers while Jeff breaks in remotely."

"Then you aren't going in guns blazing," I felt relieved.

"That may be what the militia plans, but I don't want to get killed."

"In the dark, they won't know which guys are shooting and which are sabotaging," Paul pointed out.

"Remember, I was a Navy SEAL. I know how to get in and out of places without getting caught."

"I'm liking this plan more and more. Will our cameras stay up when the power is cut?" I asked.

"They aren't dependent on power coming from or through the valley," Paul replied.

"You going to take the Valley's solar panels down too?" Paul asked.

"Absolutely. Those can be re-initialized, later."

"My hero," Autumn cheered, hugging Eric as they entered the room.

"I haven't done anything yet."

"You co-wrote with the program and you have the hard part," Jeff said. "Be careful out there tonight."

"I can go as your lookout." Autumn wasn't asking.

"No!" Paul and Eric replied in unison.

"You need to stay safe so you'll be vertical when I see you, afterwards," Eric told her.

"I'm not so bad horizontal," Autumn teased.

"I didn't hear that," Paul remarked. "And neither did you, Eric."

"You have a dirty mind, Bro," Autumn glared at Paul. "I wasn't talking about what you think I was talking about."

"Good. Keep it that way."

"Between you and Grant, it's like I've got two fathers."

"Feel lucky," Jack told her.

"What time are we going to go?" Eric inquired.

"At dusk," Jack said. "As soon as the program is finished, we'll each carry two flash drives and SD cards with the program and multiple connectors. We look for an open laptop. It will be faster than using the password-busting code I've included on the second drive and card. If one of us is stopped, the other will finish the job. The initiating password is 3."

"That's an easy password," I remarked.

"It's so simple nobody would guess it but it will be fast enough to quickly start up the program to upload the virus. After that, the password changes and keeps changing, both in the computer and the drive."

"How long will it take them to remove the virus?" Paul asked.

"The virus will change every fraction of a second and by the time they figure it out, they'll have to figure it out again, but it will be a hundred steps ahead of them."

We had pizza, again, for lunch. Eric and Autumn seemed happy, but there was a tenseness in their laughter. I could tell they were both worried about how tonight might turn out.

"Do you think Brady and the others had any success with the Senator?" I asked Paul.

"Doubt it. Leaders are good at pretending they care while not really caring at all."

"You and Jack, both, have cameras set up. Do you think FEMA set up their own?"

"I'm sure of it. They haven't set up any near the entrances to our home. As for the rest of their cameras, the program Jeff and Jack put together should wipe out the feed and maybe erase any files they have. That's a good reason for us to stay off the battlefield tonight."

"Battlefield. You make Yosemite sound like Gettysburg."

"It will all depend on what the militia does and on the government's response to what the militia does. The hack is our best shot."

"If they catch Eric and Jack, what will they do?"

"They might hire them. They do that."

"They didn't hire Julian Assange."

"He was just a publisher, not a hacker. He was the equivalent of what the New York Times was once thought to be when they published the Pentagon Papers."

We went outside for a walk. I saw Eric and Autumn strolling around as well. I pretended not to notice when they kissed. I thought about how I'd feel if it were Paul out there tonight.

As Paul and I made our way toward the road, several men with AK-47S and what looked like bazookas rode by. I recognized one of them from the crowd at the church.

"This could get bloody," I fretted.

"I just want to make sure you and Autumn are safe tonight. Grant isn't taking any chances either, but as a ranger, he can be a lookout. As everyone keeps pointing out, he and the destroyers are working for the same government."

I nodded.

"It's going to be an exciting night," Autumn gushed as she and Eric walked up behind us. "And you want me to miss it."

"Yep. I'm a terrible brother."

Back at the cave, Paul pulled out a guitar and the three of us sang popular songs we all knew. After that, Paul made dinner.

"I want to take mine to my room. I'm tired," Autumn said.

"You're not going out," he insisted.

I went in to speak with her.

"Paul probably plans to lock me in my room. I know a way out."

"It's not safe out there," I countered. "I don't want to lose my new sister."

"I'll be fine." She gave me a hug. "Don't tell Paul."

Paul came in. "I don't know what you're planning, but you're not going out."

I followed Paul out of the room and he locked the door. That bothered me. "The rooms can be locked from the outside?"

"It was Autumn's idea to put this lock on her room. Dad did the work. She wanted to make sure nobody got into her stuff when she was out."

"But what if there is an emergency and she's stuck?"

"It's not supposed to be locked when she's in there—except tonight."

"Do you think it will hold?"

"Unless she knows a way out."

"She might. I mean, she's really sharp." I didn't want to betray her, but I also hoped he'd figure out he needed to take extra precautions. He went to the den and was watching the video feeds. "The cameras have infrared sensors that pick up even starlight and magnify it. I've added a number of extra cameras on the lower mountain and close to Curry since you and Autumn went down there."

"That could have been dangerous."

"I kept out of sight and it gave me something to do besides worry while you were gone. The added equipment will help with tracking events tonight."

I went back to Autumn's room. "You okay in there?"

"I'm fine. Just resting," she called through the door. She hadn't left yet. Maybe Paul really had found a way to keep her in. But knowing Autumn, I would have placed my bets on her.

I went back into the den. "That idiot Pete is getting people ready to fire on the troops. Listen."

Pete was telling several men, "We're going down the hillside with guns blazing, scare the daylights out of FEMA."

"You don't scare FEMA," I said, though Pete couldn't hear me. "They'll call in gunships and robotic dogs."

"Stupid. If they get too crazy, the military will be shooting at anything moving, including those working to upload the virus and cutting the power cables." I knew his concern was for our friends.

"What about the backup generators?" I asked.

"Backup generators?"

"You've got to know FEMA has their own generators for areas that have no power."

"I'm sure Eric and Jack have taken that into account. At least I hope they have."

"So, we're just going to sit and watch?"

"Not quite. I have a ham radio with special channels we can use to guide Jack and Eric through any problems I see. He handed me a silver-dollar-sized object on a chain that I guessed was a radio. You can wear this one and listen in." It had a wire that went up to my ear.

I sat next to him and watched. "There's Eric. I think he's waving at the camera. How does he know where it is?"

"I told Jack about the location of a couple of them."

"He's got cable cutters and what's that device?"

"An EMP. Smart."

"What?"

"A miniature electro-magnetic pulse generator to take out the backup generator. He needs to upload the virus first though or he won't have the power to do so."

"Do all the FEMA laptops feed into the main computer?"

"He has to get the right one."

"No! How?" Paul's face went pale.

It was Autumn. She was out and partway down the mountain.

CHAPTER 20

"Does she have a radio?"

"No."

I stood up.

"No! You are not prepared for anything like this."

"I can get a radio to her. I will stay away from the gunfire and get her back up here before it starts."

"Look, I love you too much."

"You have to man this. You're the only one who can. If I don't think I can get to her safely, I'll turn back."

"I don't like it. When I tell you to run, you'll run and you'll go in the direction I tell you to go—even if you haven't gotten to her?"

"Yes. Yes." I kissed him.

"There is a black outfit in the closet. It's Autumn's, but it will stretch in the right places and you can roll up the sleeves and legs and tighten the belt. Also, grab some gloves and my mom's boots."

"Thank you. I slipped the outfit on." Autumn was quite a bit taller than I was, though my bust was bigger. Still, I was able to make it fit.

Paul handed me an extra transmitter and receiver, along with a pair of binoculars. "These have heat sensors, infrared thermal imaging and night vision." He told me where the entrance closest to Autumn was located. I was good at directions and went for it.

I came out under some brush. The ground rolled open and then back into place. It was covered with a dirt-like substance that fit under the bushes. I crawled out slowly and got up. I started running from tree to tree to try to get to where I saw Autumn.

"Three hundred feet to your left but you have to be careful. The ground is a little uneven there." He wasn't kidding. My foot caught in some kind of hole and I had to pull it out. If not for my boot, my foot might have been broken. I continued on but more carefully. I had to go down. I knew the official path was too visible and I had to go off to the side.

My foot caught again, this time on some roots. I fell. I quickly got up.

"Are you alright?"

"Yes," I assured him.

"Look out."

The next thing I knew, there was a knife at my throat.

CHAPTER 21

The blade was cold and the sharp edge was pushing against my neck, ready to Marie Antoinette me.

"Excuse me?" I responded, feeling the blade scratch my skin as I spoke.

"Oh. The girl from the church. Sorry."

I wasn't sure I recognized the guy, but there had been a lot of people there the day before.

"Have you seen my friend?"

"Something is scurrying over there." He pointed off behind a row of bushes. "Watch out for the bears. They're out tonight and that could be one of them."

I ran where he had pointed, hoping it wasn't a bear. Whatever was there was gone.

"She's down below you right now," Paul said. "Be careful. There are some drops." I almost stepped over the edge of a five-foot drop and pulled my foot back. At least, it wasn't a thousand-foot drop. I used my hands to pull myself down and continued on. There was another similar drop and I went down it the same way.

I was a long way above both the valley and the John Muir trail but I kept going. It might take hours before we were in real danger, and I hoped to get to Autumn long before that happened.

"Do you see any sign of Eric?"

"Yes. He's much lower down. I don't see Autumn right now, but from where I last saw her, I think you're headed her way."

"Are there any feds on the trail?"

"Some but they're closer to Vernal Falls. Eric is taking a different route that will bring him closer to Curry."

"Does Autumn know that?"

"Maybe. I don't know what they discussed, but I know he didn't want her to go with him. Just get back up here as fast as you can. How is your breathing? Any chest pains?"

"I'm fine." I wasn't really. I *was* having some chest pains, but they were minor and it could be nerves. I wasn't going to freak him out though. I needed to get to Autumn.

"Did you let Eric know about Autumn?"

"He's going the other way and he needs to keep going. I see her now. There is a ranger on the slope and she's hiding behind a tree. Be careful and watch out. You are close."

"Where is the ranger?"

"About a hundred yards past you and a little to the left."

I hustled closer to the trees and tried to get down to Autumn's level. There were some big steps. I was doing okay until I lost my balance again.

Someone leaned down towards me and the barrel of a gun brushed against the side of my chest.

CHAPTER 22

I put my head in my hands and prayed. Whoever was next to me fell back. I turned. It was a ranger, holding his head. He had dropped his shotgun. Autumn came out from behind a tree, helped me up and started to pull me down the trail.

"Wait," he said. His voice sounded familiar. "You're Grant's sister and future sister-in-law."

Recognition hit me. "Brady?"

"What are you doing down here?"

"It's a nice night and we thought we'd go for a walk."

"It's dangerous. I saw some men with guns."

"That does sound dangerous. We'd better find out who they are," Autumn suggested.

"What if you get shot?" Brady sounded really concerned.

"Who would shoot a girl?" Autumn asked.

"A lunatic."

"I think he's right. We should get back," I encouraged.

"Maybe you should," Autumn replied. "I want to know what's going on."

"I don't recommend that," Brady contended.

"It's great seeing you, Brady," she responded, taking off.

"I'm not letting her walk into the lion's den alone," I stated, starting to follow her as Brady picked up his gun and followed me.

"And Grant would kill me if I let anything happen to his sister or his brother's fiancée." He tried to use his radio, but got nothing. "The fall must have damaged it."

"Sorry."

"I'm sorry about the shotgun. I thought you were one of those militia people."

In a couple of places, Brady helped me down. But I was too slow and I had lost track of Autumn.

"I need to rush," I said.

"This isn't an easy hill to navigate in the dark." He pulled out a flashlight.

"Don't," I advised. "If there are guys with guns, they might aim at us."

He kept it off. "Autumn seems pretty good at navigating this hill in the dark. Most rangers wouldn't do it without a flashlight."

"I guess it will be a new experience for you then."

"Hunting is off season and guns aren't allowed here."

"Good. I like the wildlife here," I said.

"A lot of bears and deer died in the Valley the other day."

"Did you see them?"

"A few and I haven't seen any running around alive."

"Come to think of it, neither have I—seen any running around alive, I meant."

I recalled the deceased wildlife from the other day and shuddered. "Aren't there usually a lot of tourists these days?"

"I guess they blocked their reservations or something. And each time there's a new supposed pandemic, they close the camping on a moment's notice."

He didn't know about the bodies. I wondered about the other rangers. The ones who had been in the Valley had to have known— unless those who knew were dead.

"Autumn is moving pretty fast in a different direction and trouble is coming," Paul said, through my earpiece.

A minute later, gunfire broke out. I saw smoke bombs. "Don't breathe," Brady said, pushing me to the ground behind a bush.

"Autumn, I've got to help Autumn."

"Let's hope she isn't anywhere near that gunfire. He handed me a gas mask and goggles. "Put these on."

"What about you?"

"I've dealt with tear gas before."

I hoped that was all it was. I put them on. Brady was coughing. He pulled his scarf over his mouth. A minute later, he seemed better. The fighting continued. I handed Brady back his mask and goggles.

"Autumn."

"We can't get to her now," he said.

"She's okay. She's off to the side." Paul said. "It looks like she's backtracking to the Four Mile Trail."

"Eric?"

"Who's Eric?" Brady asked.

"My dog."

"Your dog is down there?"

"And I can't leave without him."

"I think he's below the fighting," came Paul's voice.

"Jack?"

"Is Jack another dog?"

"My kitten. They ran after Autumn when she ran down the hill."

"I hate to tell you this, but a kitten is in a lot of danger at night on these hills."

"I have to get to Autumn. Maybe we can find another way. The quick route to Valley, rather than the Muir Trail. That's probably how she went." I started running, feeling out of breath and energy but managing to keep going.

"It's a lot steeper," he said, easily keeping up with me. "One wrong step could end you at night."

"Most of the fighting is in the direction of the Muir Trail." I guessed a significant number of the civilians went that way to try to sneak up from the other side of Curry.

"Listen," he said. "It sounds like there is also a lot of gunfire coming from the Wanona Tunnel area."

I saw the bright light of a major explosion above on the other side of the Valley. "That's the road to Tuolumne or Sonora. What kind of explosion was that?"

"I don't know. I just hope it doesn't start a fire."

"They seem to be coming in from all sides," Paul said. "FEMA is up on our mountain. They were prepared—possibly by a tip."

"Where?"

"Over there," Brady said, pointing at moving figures. "They're coming from below and from above. They're all over the mountain. You need to hide."

"I've got to get to Autumn."

"She's a ways behind Eric, who is close to the Valley now."

I continued rushing towards the Four Mile Trail. There was a dip between some trees and Brady pushed me down.

"Jack?"

"You see your kitten?"

"I thought I did."

"I can't find him," Paul said. "Stay with Brady. Moving is too dangerous."

"Autumn."

"She's a smart girl. We're going to have to trust her."

He obviously felt I was less capable than Autumn. He was right. I wasn't as strong or as agile-footed on this unfamiliar slope at night. I could kick myself for letting her get away from me.

"Brady, can we please keep going? Grant will kill me if anything bad happens to Autumn."

Gunfire erupted a couple of feet from me. I saw several men fall. I couldn't tell which side they were on. Everything was still for a minute.

"Let's go," I whispered to Brady.

I dashed ahead.

"Well, well, well. If it isn't the town crier." It was Pete.

"We need to get out of here before the shooting starts again."

"It's about to start now with you." He aimed his gun at me.

CHAPTER 23

The realization hit me. "You're FEMA. Undercover?"

"You guessed it. Bye."

The sound of a gunshot filled my ears as he fell, killed by Brady's gun.

"Who is that guy? I think I saw him this afternoon."

"He's from Oakhurst. He was claiming to be upset about the poisoned water over there. I guess he set up his local militia guys to get killed."

"They came in by the truckloads."

"You know about the militia? Did you notify someone?"

"I spoke with Grant. He said it was probably an internal FEMA drill and to stay out of it."

"And you still pointed a gun at me?"

"I didn't know it was you. I thought I'd get some answers. Let me get this straight. This guy sent those militia guys into a trap so that FEMA could exterminate dissidents?"

Guilt swept over me. "I told them about the Valley and FEMA. It's my fault."

"I don't know. It looks like they came from all around. FEMA wiped out Sonora a few days ago. The survivors are probably angry too. Either way, the military is likely to move in full force now."

"Autumn." Now I was really worried.

"She's down at the bottom," Paul said.

"Brady, I've got to go down the fast way fast. Can you guide me?"

"What?"

"I'm pretty sure Autumn rushed that way to get around the shooting. I've got to go after her. Do you want to tell Grant you let his sister die?" I didn't know if I could find my way on my own in the dark, but I knew that was low, selfish and manipulative. Maybe my all-out dedication to those I cared about was what drove those I loved away. "I'm sorry. I had no right to say that. You've helped so much already. I'll find my way myself."

"No problem. It's why I became a ranger." He took my hand and we continued. On the faster trail, I could see the lights in the camp. Eric hadn't succeeded in cutting the power yet, or at least not the backup power supply.

As more worry hit me, black filled the sky, not from a power outage but from black helicopters, filling the night above us. Lights burst out as spotlights started searching the mountain. The helicopters were closer to the Muir Trail and I heard machine gun rounds firing.

We started moving quicker. We needed to get off the mountain before they spotted us.

I started to slip over an edge and Brady caught me. Undeterred, I started running.

More helicopters were aiming their lights at whoever or whatever was on both sides of the Wawona Tunnel.

I wondered how many were dead. According to Grant, the militia was five hundred strong. I didn't see much happening on the far side of the Valley at this point. Maybe they saw the helicopters and settled down. If Pete had blown the whistle, he would have done so on the Oakhurst militia that was coming from the southwest. It seemed to take forever, with us dropping every time we saw a light flash in our direction, but we continued until we were close to the bottom.

"Where are Autumn and Eric?"

"I can't see them," Paul replied to me.

"Jack?"

The lights below all went out, including those in the helicopters.

"It's going to be difficult to see them in this dark. That kitten could make a good meal for one of the bears or big cats in the park."

"Over there," I whispered, looking through the binoculars.

Someone was aiming a gun at figures that looked like Autumn and Eric.

CHAPTER 24

I rushed the rest of the way towards my friends, trying to figure out how to rescue them. The sky above suddenly lit up as several helicopters and small planes crashed into the Glacier's face below the point.

Eric and Autumn were still prisoners. They were being escorted across Steadman Bridge in the direction of Ahwahnee Meadow, where the biggest FEMA encampment was.

A blinding flash lit the sky. The FEMA guards dropped their guns and collapsed. Eric and Autumn turned and grabbed the guns. I continued running toward them.

"Tranquilizer darts," Eric said as we reached him and Autumn on their way back toward the path.

"Who are you?" Brady asked.

"A good Samaritan," Eric replied. "Wouldn't you rescue this damsel?" He smiled at Autumn.

"Where's Jack?"

"I don't know. I think he rescued us and then he disappeared."

"The kitten fired that flash and the tranquilizer darts?"

"Didn't you watch *Bowling for Columbine*, where a dog accidentally shot its owner?" I asked.

"Are you with that group of crazies?" Brady asked Eric.

"No."

"Pete turned out to be FEMA. He set up his friends."

"I figured there was an undercover guy somewhere. We need a fast way out," Eric encouraged, turning to Brady.

With Brady's guidance, we started running toward Bridalveil Falls. "This is an easier path, but we'll have to stay away from the shooting on the highway."

"Can you fly a helicopter?" I asked, looking at one on the ground.

"Did you see those things crashing?" Brady asked.

"They were drone copters," Eric pointed out. "Electrically powered and dependent on radar guidance from the system that just crashed. It will have to be flown manually."

I smiled. Either he or Jack must have taken the power and radar out. "But what about the EMP—if that's what you used?"

"It just took out the power around the base camp. I think we're far enough away."

"You sure you're not with the shooters?" Brady asked.

"I haven't shot anyone and we'd better get out of here before those guys wake up."

"I can fly," Brady declared. "But what about the FEMA trooper guarding it?"

Partially hidden by the trees, Eric yelled to the guard in an officious manner, "Over here, trooper. We need your help."

As the sentry ran past us, Eric gave him a knock-out blow to the head.

"He'll be alright?" I asked.

Brady checked the man. "He might have a headache."

We got in. Lucky for us, the helicopter was ready for takeoff. As it lifted with Brady piloting, two men in military uniforms ran towards us. Brady flashed the helicopter spotlight at them and they paused and watched as we ascended from the Valley floor.

"They probably think we're FEMA or they'd be shooting," Eric surmised.

"Where to?" Eric asked.

"Highway 41, the other side of the action," Brady told him.

We could see shooting below us as we passed the tunnel. I felt guilt over the militia who would be injured or killed. "I wish there were something we could do."

"Neither side is going to back down until they're forced to," Eric responded.

"I knew I didn't like Pete," Autumn said.

We continued on. I felt stupid for not figuring out a way to end the fighting.

Brady went a ways down the road and landed the helicopter. Eric set it to lift off again and then jumped out.

"What was that for?" Brady asked. A minute later, the helicopter without a pilot went up and down over the cliff on the other side of the road. We heard the crash below.

"If they discover we took the copter, they'll think we're dead," Eric said.

"Are you a terrorist?"

"A good Samaritan, remember," Eric responded.

We started walking towards the Point. We were stopped by someone in FEMA gear with a very large gun.

"Rangers," Brady said quickly as if we all qualified. "And junior rangers."

"You need to be back at your station. You're lucky I didn't shoot you."

"There was shooting at the tunnel and we were told to check out what was happening so I could report further."

"You reported this?"

Brady picked up his radio as if he were speaking to someone over the broken radio. "I've got that update."

To my surprise, there was a response. "Yes. What's going on down there?" It was Grant's voice.

"It looks like a lot of fighting. I trust FEMA will give us a fuller report in the morning." Brady turned to the FEMA guy. "Would you like to speak to the ranger on call?"

The trooper griped into the radio, "We don't want any of your personnel here. Get them out of the area."

"Glad to comply as soon as we get back," Brady said.

"Can you identify your group?"

"Yes. Ranger Brady." He pointed to his badge. "Also, three junior rangers in training, Autumn, Tres and—"

"Eric."

"Well, get moving," the trooper told us. "And next time, don't get curious. We'll tell you when we need you."

We continued on up 41 toward Glacier Point Road.

"Where are you parked?" I asked Brady.

"At the station, near the Point. We've got a long walk. So, you're a dog?" he asked Eric.

"Arrf."

As we proceeded toward the cutoff, I said, "Not that long. The rescue is here."

Paul was ahead with five saddled horses, including the one he was riding. "Need a lift?" he asked.

"Brady's radio was out and then it was working?"

"Someone sabotaged the equipment, including the radio, at the outpost, probably the militia. It's working again."

"Would you tell me what is going on?" Brady asked.

"Eric is doing surveillance on behalf of an oversight group. Autumn was too curious for her own good and my fiancé went to make sure Autumn didn't get into trouble."

"And Jack?"

"He was supposed to be with Eric." He turned to me. "Jack was captured."

"Darn." Eric's face tightened. "I need to rescue him."

"Nobody is going back down there tonight. We'll have to figure something out in the morning."

"They captured the kitten?"

"You know what FEMA does with kittens," I said, trying to sound less upset than I was.

"They probably cook them for breakfast. But kittens don't usually fire tranquilizer darts."

"Jack's a very talented kitten," Eric boasted.

"I guess he is," Brady said. "What about all the shooting on the mountain?"

"It looked like there were a lot of bodies, mostly militia," Paul related.

"Wait until I see Pete again," Autumn scoffed.

"You won't," Brady said. "I shot him."

"Saved me the trouble," Autumn said.

"Ha! If I see you with a gun, again, you're grounded," Paul said.

She held up the one she'd just confiscated.

"I'll take that," he insisted. She handed it to him and he gave it to Brady.

Partway to the Point, Paul suggested Autumn and I get Eric to his vehicle. "I'll catch up with you girls later."

I knew what he meant. He wanted us to go to Jack's place while he escorted Brady to the station. It would have been riskier going home with the mountain so crowded and Brady couldn't follow the horse trail by truck.

"I think Brady's okay," I told Eric.

"He seemed to really like you."

"He knows I'm with Paul," I said. "I think it's Grant he likes and respects. I was so worried about you. Thank goodness, Jack rescued you. There has to be a way to free him."

It was a long ride, but it was a nice night. I wished that Paul could have joined us on the way, as I felt like a bit of a third party.

As we entered Jack's basement, Jeff was beside himself.

"We're going to have to prepare a rescue for Jack," Eric advised.

"Too late," Jeff responded, barely containing himself.

"I know they captured him."

"He's dead."

CHAPTER 25

"What do you mean?" I asked Jeff.

"He broke and ran and they fired. He dropped. They checked him over and threw him on the pile at Lower Pines Campground as Jack called it."

"Maybe he's just injured," I commented, hoping.

"They checked him."

"Maybe they didn't want to provide medical treatment. We need to find a way back into the Valley."

"Have you seen the hillside?"

"We were there," I said.

"It's covered with militia bodies."

"How about FEMA bodies?" Autumn inquired.

"The militia got a lot of those, too. The National Guard is being mobilized."

"They're turning the National Guard into polluters and killers?" I asked.

"DHS regularly utilizes National Guard troops. Those are lower pay than the contract troops. There is chatter on government frequencies about dropping a nuclear bomb on the place."

"Do you have recordings of that?"

"Yeah."

"We can put that out on the Net," Eric suggested.

"I know the general layout of the area. I want to go back to check on Jack," Jeff stated.

"I'll go down with you," Autumn said.

"Autumn, if anything happens to you, your brother would never forgive me," Jeff noted.

"Or me," I told her.

"I'll go back," Eric said.

"And I'll go with you," Autumn firmly stated.

"You need to stop taking so many chances, Autumn," Eric contended.

"I've got a brown belt. I was about to take those guys when Jack rescued us. You misogynists need to trust us girls. I made it down the mountain. I don't look threatening. Makes it easy to catch them off-guard."

"And the next time you go down the mountain, FEMA will be gone." I turned around as Paul entered the room.

"Jack—" I started to say.

"I know."

"Somebody needs to rescue him. He might still be alive." I paused. "One of my ancestors was told her husband had died on a Civil War battlefield. She risked getting shot to go onto the battlefield to find him. She brought him back alive and they built a statue in her honor."

"If Jack's alive, I want to save him." Eric declared.

"I'm the paramedic. If somebody should rescue him, it should be me."

"Paul, they're not going to let a medical team down there, and you need to monitor the action," I said.

"You want to wind up in Yosemite Gitmo, like Eric and Autumn almost did?" Jeff argued.

"Your sound must have been down," Paul guessed. "Those troopers had orders to shoot them and dump them in the Lower River."

"Then we really owe Jack," Autumn remarked.

We sat around trying to figure out a plan. Grant walked in.

"How did you fake your vax? I know rangers were supposed to be vaxed," Eric inquired.

"I initially got a religious exemption. I know someone who knows someone who later gave me a card. What does that have to do with anything?"

"Wish you could fake military medical credentials," Eric said.

Paul seemed to brighten up. "Brother—"

"We'd need a vehicle."

"If we take the long way to Sonora, my uncle has a garage. Last I saw, Sonora was deserted," Jeff stated.

"Can you get in?"

"He always left the key under loose bricks or above a nearby window."

"Let's go. We need to do this before the satellite is fixed," Eric said.

"We're going, too," Autumn declared. "Military nurses."

"If I refuse, you'll go down on your own?" Paul knew his sister pretty well.

"Absolutely."

"Treasure?"

"I'm with Autumn."

"It will be safer from the Sonora side," Jeff pointed out. "That was the more effective side in the battle."

"The leader of the south side was a FEMA agent," I confirmed.

"There could be infiltrators over there too," Paul said. "I didn't have live footage on that side."

"I was watching. The foreign satellites I was using are still up."

"The military will probably try to piggyback if the virus works like it's supposed to and wipes out their system long-term," Eric predicted.

"How about the contractor satellites?" I asked.

"It looks like they were dumb enough to allow FEMA to connect to those satellites. Eric and Jack's handywork took those down, too."

We took one of Jack's vehicles to Sonora. It took about ten minutes for Eric to find the key.

Inside were a number of vehicles. Eric put his hand to his face, but failed to hide the tears. Autumn went over to him and gave him a hug.

I looked for Jeff, who had gone outside. His eyes were closed and his hands were at the side of his head.

I went over to him. "Jeff."

"We visited him on a vacation when I was little. He showed me how to do oil changes. He was tough and unyielding if I misbehaved but I miss him. I'll be okay."

Back in the garage, Paul patted Jeff on the arm. All our parents were gone. They'd died in different ways, but I knew there was nothing that could be said or done to take the loss away.

"This van will do," Eric said. "It will need a little paint."

"And a military license plate," Grant said.

"We'll have to get that later."

By the time they were finished, the inside and outside of the van looked like a military medical vehicle. Eric put it under heat dryers that were turned up to maximum.

There was a knock at the garage door. We ignored it.

Something smashed through the door. It was a truck, flanked by a group of men holding what I figured were assault rifles, all aimed directly at us.

CHAPTER 26

"You with the local militia?" Grant asked.

"Who wants to know?"

"This is—was—my uncle's garage," Eric said. "He was killed along with my parents, when Sonora was attacked."

"Who is your uncle?"

"Tony Lawrence."

"I knew him. Good man," one of the gun-holders said. "And your parents?"

"Blaine and Maria Lawrence. They moved in recently on the east side of town."

"Can you prove who you are?"

"I have an Iowa driver's license. I'm reaching for it."

Eric pulled his wallet out of his pocket and showed them what was likely his own driver's license. I was tempted to look to see what his real age was.

"So, what are you doing with a military van?"

"That answer depends on who you are," Eric said.

"Sonora Memorial Committee," the questioner replied. "We were in the hills above the Valley last night."

"We saw you," Paul said. "I was near the Point. FEMA almost captured my sister and Eric."

"And who are you?"

"I was a paramedic. We think some of the captives might be alive and we want to get them out."

The two men in the lead lowered their guns and looked at each other. The one who questioned Paul and Eric said, "The plan might work, but it doesn't have a military plate."

"We still need one of those," Eric agreed.

"We might be able to help. I'm Jim. These are Joseph, Miller, Norman and Tim. The two behind are Charlie and Howard."

Eric pointed to each of us as he introduced us.

"I need to get back for my shift," Grant said.

"You're a ranger?"

"I am, and the rangers don't like what is going on any better than the rest of you."

"What do you think they wanted with Sonora?" I asked. "It's a bit of a ways from Yosemite."

"It's a nice, quiet town. They started sending in trucks and somehow the roads kept getting blown up." From the look on Jim's face, I suspected his group had something to do with the roads exploding.

"I noticed it was a rough drive here."

"FEMA wanted to move in here?" Paul asked.

"The National Guard."

"That's state," I noted.

"They have to be working together," Jim said.

"Is this about real estate?" I asked.

"Drive the people out of the state, collect as much as possible at bottom dollar and then make it a high-priced resort," Jim remarked.

"Economic motive," Paul surmised.

"But FEMA, not the state, has a prison camp and mass graves set up in the Valley. They're the ones doing the poisoning." I said.

"The Governor wants all our property," Jim pointed out.

"The Feds may have nationalized the National Guard," Paul

considered. "The National Guard is regularly called in to back up FEMA."

"FEMA, the National Guard." I lamented that they had joined forces against the people.

"It's all under the big umbrella."

"'And we ain't part of it,'" Eric quoted George Carlin.

We were to meet up with Jim on the road to the Valley about five miles outside the ranger station on Highway 120.

"Do you think we can trust them?" I asked Paul. My experience with Pete had me questioning any new alliances.

"I hope so."

We had picked up some medical uniforms for me, Autumn and Paul and a captain's uniform for Eric at a Sonora costume shop. The owner gladly provided them to us. Paul threw them in a wash and dry cycle at a laundromat outside the Sonoma city limits. "You never know what's on them from whatever they dropped."

"Now we need to find a license plate," I said.

"Well, if the locals don't show up, we'll have to find a way to hijack a truck and steal one."

We pulled over to the side at the meeting point and waited. A military jeep drove past us, stopped and backed up. I looked out through a window in the wall separating the driver's area from the back.

A National Guard Trooper got out. "Your ambulance broke down?"

"Something like that," Eric replied.

"You don't have plates."

"Somebody stole them."

"I'd report it, but our communications are down. Even our cells are not working."

"Our commander got a call from the Secretary of Homeland Security saying there were wounded personnel in Yosemite."

"There are a lot of dead personnel, but not as many as the insurgents had."

"The Russians?" Paul asked, acting agendatized.

"Russian sympathizers?" Eric joined in the Russiaphobia.

"Of course," the sergeant said. "Captain," he observed, looking at Eric's uniform. "Sorry, I didn't notice. You're with the Army?"

"This is a joint operation."

"You're telling me, Sir. I don't know whether the DHS, the Governor or the President is calling the shots. FEMA has its own army, that I didn't know existed, ordering around non-FEMA officers with higher ranks. Since when is there a fifth branch of the military?"

"There is a concern some of the FEMA troops might have come in contact with contaminated food or water from what was dropped several days ago," Paul expounded.

"I wasn't here then, but I heard they had to evacuate a lot of sick people and cancel reservations. We were invited in to avoid a major loss of funding."

I wondered what their excuse would be for the prison camps.

"So, I hear," Eric said. "Were you here last night when the attack came?"

"We were." The trooper signaled to the passenger in his jeep. "Maybe we can fix the problem. Dennis, here, used to be a mechanic."

Eric opened the hood and the two men looked in. The hood slammed down hard, knocking both men unconscious, courtesy of Jim and company, who had come out from the trees on the side of the road.

"Now, how about a military escort?" he offered. He placed a set of military license plates on the ambulance.

We didn't ask where he got them.

"And we have an extra jeep." Jim got into the jeep the unconscious men had been using. A military jeep, with more of those we met at the garage, pulled up behind.

"Wait," Paul said, getting out of the ambulance to examine the unconscious men. "This one should be fine. The sergeant is bleeding heavily from the neck area. He's going to need some stitches and he might have a concussion."

"They're thugs," Jim practically growled.

"They're human beings and I'm a real paramedic." Paul grabbed a neck brace and used it to protect the Sergeant's neck while wrapping the neck to stop the blood flow. Autumn and I brought a stretcher out for the man.

"Your paramedic is a thug sympathizer," Jim griped to me.

"Do you really want to be as awful as those creeps who took over the park?" I retorted.

Jim threw up his hands as Eric and Paul placed the stretcher into the back of the ambulance.

As we followed the borrowed jeep with Jim's other one behind, Paul said, "It's getting hard to tell the good guys from the bad guys."

"Most of feds and National Guard out here are just following orders. The militias are out for blood and revenge," Eric pointed out.

"We can't trust either side," I acknowledged.

With the military escort, we were easily let through into the Park and continued on towards Curry. Arriving at Curry, we instead turned left to go over Stoneman Bridge. Paul, carrying his medical bag, and I jumped out, just past the bridge. Eric and Autumn continued towards the little hospital in the Valley to drop off the unconscious patient. One of the jeeps went with the ambulance while the other pulled into the Lower River Campground.

"Who goes there?" we heard a trooper loudly demand answers from our escort.

"We were asked to identify some of the bodies," Jim said. "We think there could be a terrorist among them."

"Good luck with that. They've been crushed together for the most part. You'll have to ID them by blood type."

Jim pulled out a box. "My equipment."

While Jim and the trooper were carrying on their conversation, which was turning into an argument, Paul and I, wearing gloves, were pushing aside dirt and human and other remains, looking for anyone alive on the other side of one of the mounds. I heard coughing. Under the rubble, we found the small body of a little girl, maybe two or three.

CHAPTER 27

We quickly checked to make sure all her limbs had reflexes and were not broken and carefully carried her under Stoneman Bridge as she continued coughing.

Using the Merced River as a wash basin, Paul cleaned her off. The river was pretty fast-moving and I was hoping the water was safe. She seemed to be lightly choking on something that had gotten in her lungs and mouth. He pulled a syringe from his bag and started extracting dirt from her lungs. She continued coughing. I was afraid the troopers would hear it, but Jim was doing a lot of loud talking, questioning the men about a fictitious person.

As soon as she looked stable, Paul, keeping low, went back to try to dig for more bodies while I watched the girl. There were multiple piles. Paul worked to stay on the far side of Jim and the others as he went from pile to pile. Jim went to one of the mounds and started looking as if he were taking samples. I could barely see through the trees from my position near the bridge.

"It's going to be alright," I softly said to the little girl.

"Mommy, Daddy."

"Where are they?"

"Walking. At big hotel."

"When?"

"Long ago. Left me."

I thought about the poison cloud.

"Did they go outside?"

"I think."

"Did you?"

"Someone said, 'Wait.' I wanted find Mommy. I tried to leave. Someone said, 'Poison, dead outside. Can't leave. Didn't know where they went.'"

"Your parents?"

"I don't know. I want my mommy."

From her account, I guessed they had gone out walking the evening the cloud dropped. For the little girl's sake, I hoped her parents were okay. For her size, she seemed very articulate.

"So, you've been at the Ahwanhee?"

"Big men with guns came. I hid. Last night, loud noises. They said, 'Killing people.' I ran out and hid in dirt."

"Where we found you?"

She nodded. "Didn't want be killed."

"Good. We have to be very quiet and sneak out of here when Paul gets back."

"Man?"

"He's a good guy, but the men on the other side of the mound are dangerous—bad."

Paul came back. "I tried to use a stethoscope to hear movement or other sounds. Nothing and no sign of Jack. He would be way down in the pile—if he's here, but this is amplified and still would have picked up a heartbeat."

"The girl crawled into the pile last night," I said.

"We need to get her out of here. Jack was a good friend. But he's not here. Not alive, anyway."

I quietly cried, covering my face with my hand. I couldn't help myself. A fault I couldn't get rid of. I didn't know Jack that well, but the thought of him dying dug deeply into me. From the time I had heard the news, I kept telling myself he'd survived. Paul put his arms around me and the little girl and held us both close for a minute. She seemed really weak.

Paul picked her up and we proceeded through the Upper River Campground toward another bridge leading from Upper River to the Housekeeping Camp.

The stench of death was everywhere.

The names of the River Campgrounds never made sense to me and always seemed backwards. I'd been told, though it was downriver of Lower River, Upper River had about a two-foot higher elevation than the Lower River Campground.

Larger mounds were visible in Upper River. Paul handed the little girl to me and pulled out his stethoscope and another pair of latex gloves to check for life in the Upper River mounds.

"We know they threw him down in Lower River, but it's worth checking," he noted.

A little while later, he came back to us and shook his head. We took the Housekeeping Bridge. The concrete and canvas Housekeeping cabins had been plowed down. We looked around. No signs of life. The little girl cringed at the sight of a dead deer.

"I'm sorry," I whispered to her, holding her head against my body to shield her eyes. It occurred to me we would need to wash her off with clean water fast when we got out of there. There was bound to be some poison left in the soil she had been covered in.

As we got to the Sunset Bridge, the ambulance was back with Eric driving and Autumn next to him. I shook my head.

"No sign of Jack. Just pieces of—" I couldn't finish.

"They put him in whole, didn't they?" Autumn asked.

"From what Jeff saw, they just tossed him onto the mound," Eric replied. "The uniform didn't make them think twice."

"Is your escort still back in Lower River?"

"I think so," Paul said.

"Ours took off after we stopped at the hospital."

"How about we take off before they injure someone else," Paul suggested.

"It looked as if they may have cracked the skull on that trooper. His breathing and heart were normal. But the personnel at the hospital were concerned about possible brain trauma," Eric recounted.

"They ordered a helicopter to fly him to Fresno," Autumn said.

"That one?" I asked, looking up.

"Probably. Who's the little girl?" Eric inquired.

"She was in the first mound we dug through," I said. "She was inside the Ahwahnee when they dropped that stuff. Her parents were outside and she hasn't seen them since."

Eric frowned and put his hands up to his face. As Paul put the girl into the back, Eric whispered to me, "I wonder if she knows."

"She's pretty scared," I whispered back. "And she was likely exposed to poison dust."

"I hope Paul has something to detox her."

"He probably does," I said. "He's well equipped."

"Eric, we need to get out of here," Paul called.

I joined Paul in the back. He had the little girl lying on a stretcher. He was using an antiseptic on her face, head and arms. She reached out to me and held my hand tightly.

"You're a brave little girl," Paul said. "Do you have a name?"

"Help me. Help me."

"I think she's reliving her nightmare," I told Paul.

"We'll help you. We'll take care of you," he assured her.

"Are we going to get through the checkpoint all right?" I asked.

"We'll see," Paul said. He had me work to distract her while he found a good vein for a needle. She didn't seem to react when he stuck it in. He attached it to an IV drip. "She needs some nutrients and fluids." He took a couple of small samples of her blood. "This should be enough to check for toxins and I don't want to overdo it in her condition."

FEMA had set up a checkpoint midway through the tunnel with no way to run if they stopped us and they did.

"You need to pull over."

"There isn't much room," Eric said.

"Now, Captain!"

CHAPTER 28

"Should I run it?" Eric whispered to us as he hesitantly pulled next to the wall.

An officer came over. "We need the ambulance back down in the Valley."

"I have a patient they ordered to be rushed to Fresno."

"I thought they took him out by helicopter."

"This is a different one."

"I'm not arguing with you. This is a priority. Now turn around."

Two jeeps pulled up to the checkpoint. "We have special orders to escort this ambulance to Fresno."

"I have orders," the corporal started to say.

"My passenger has general's stripes and that trumps your orders. Now let us all through."

The jeeps went through and we were waved on. I wondered if our friends had offed a general and stolen his uniform.

We went a few miles past the Glacier turnoff before we all stopped.

"Where did you get that general's outfit?" I asked as all of us but the girl got out and went to the jeep. The general turned towards us.

"Jack," I threw my arms around him. "We thought you were—"

"Greatly exaggerated."

"But how?"

"Ever read Romeo and Juliet? I took a pill that made it hard to detect my senses and dropped as they fired. I looked dead to them and so they threw me into the pile."

"Nice," Autumn said, giving him a hug of her own. "Good thing they didn't use their crusher."

He winced. "As for the uniform, I stole it. It's FEMA and better ranking than the one I had. FEMA never used to have generals, let alone its own army."

"We'd better dump the vehicles before they come tracking us," Jim said.

Eric looked under the hood of the recently acquired jeep and ripped out several wires. "So, it won't be tracked."

A ranger truck approached. Jim went for his gun.

"It's my brother," Paul told him.

"Where would you like a ride? We'll have to make it quick," Grant told our Sonoma friends.

"If the tracking is gone, we'll take the jeeps," Jim replied. "They have too many jeeps to be certain unless they run the plates. You say their computer is down?"

Paul nodded.

"You aren't going back through the Valley," I stated.

"We know an alternate route, longer," Jim said.

After the men left, Jack suggested we drive the ambulance back to his place.

"We might be spotted," Paul noted.

"This vehicle might come in handy later," Eric said. "It has four-wheel drive. If I see a copter, I'll leave the road. If Jim can keep out of sight with the jeep, I can keep the ambulance under cover until we get to the cutoff. Besides, it's a short drive on the road."

"I'll second that," Jack said.

I looked at the little girl. "We need to get her to safety as soon as possible. I'll third it—if it's okay with you, Paul."

"Fourth. You're right, Treasure."

"Then it's decided, we're going for it," Jack said.

"In that case, I'll get back to the station," Grant related.

As we continued on Highway 41 towards Jack's place, some militia men, brandishing some high-powered firearms, sped past us towards the Valley.

"Are they planning another assault?" I asked.

"Who knows?" Paul said. "They probably disbelieve the video I got of Pete and think we were the ones who betrayed them. We're outsiders."

"You got video?"

"It happened right by one of the cameras. I was freaking until Brady shot him."

In a short time, Eric was driving through the woods, hitting Jack's place from a slightly different angle than the one we had taken before. We went inside.

The little girl looked at me with big eyes as I took her into the bathroom. I pulled off her dirty clothing and tossed it in a plastic bag. Then I turned on the shower and started scrubbing her. I hoped I wasn't rubbing too hard.

"Good," she said, apparently not minding.

"It will be easier to speak to you if you have a name."

"Von."

"Yvonne?"

"Yes."

"They call me Treasure."

The shower lasted for about half an hour and I was glad Jack's water heater lasted that long. I dressed her in a long T-shirt. Paul came in and irrigated her nose and taught her to gargle a mixture of water and hydrogen peroxide. Then he gave her something to drink.

"Good," she said.

"I sweetened it," he told me.

"You should shower, too," Paul advised. "Thoroughly. I'm after you."

Jack popped in with several sets of clothes that looked about Yvonne's size. "I'll put these into a fresh wash cycle and she can put them on in the morning."

"We have some of Autumn's toddler clothes at home in storage that can also fit her," Paul said.

When I got out of my shower and put on fresh clothes that appeared in the bathroom. Autumn had carried the little girl to a bed and was telling her the story of Goldilocks.

"Isn't she beautiful?" I asked Autumn.

"If I wanted a little girl, which I don't, it would be her."

Autumn was seventeen. She wasn't ready to have kids. I had just turned eighteen and had been treating my brother and sister as if they were my kids and now it was as if I was, for the moment, getting a second chance with this little girl. Even though I knew I'd be giving her up, it helped to take away the pain of Tatiana's and Zinney's betrayals.

The girl dozed off and I went into the living room. Paul, freshly showered with still damp hair, joined me.

"Jack's showering in one of the other bathrooms. Did you get the poison off?" he asked me.

"I hope so."

"I'm not so worried about the Merced, but there was bound to be some residue in the rubble. I want to test some of your blood for toxins. It may also tell us what they used in the Valley. I've already gotten a sample from Jack."

I nodded and held out my arm. He had me sit down in a chair.

"You really have a full medical bag."

"I've left some medical testing equipment at Jack's in the past. Someone's got to make sure he stays healthy."

"Savior of the world?"

"Not even close, but if I can help those close to me, it matters."

"Do you think the girl will be alright?"

"I want you to drink this." He handed me a glass of clear liquid.

"I hope this is the sweetened stuff." I wasn't wild about drinking something bitter, though I would if I had to.

"It is. It includes Ivermectin, along with some other detoxes. Grant's taking care of the wolves tonight. The horses have plenty of food and water."

"I've been worried about neglecting them."

"They're fine."

I thought about the little girl who had lost her parents. "I think I should be in Yvonne's room when she wakes up."

"There's a second bed in there. I'm going to sleep on the floor so I can keep an eye on her, too."

"A family room?"

"But to be clear, I'm not planning on taking advantage of you—though I'd like to."

"Is that a permanent statement or just until we're married?"

He smiled. "We're going to have a great marriage."

He kissed me. And then again. I found myself getting lost in his lips and had to almost reboot myself when he released me.

Eric and Autumn were going out for a walk as we returned to Yvonne's room. I laid down on the second bed. Paul was looking for a pillow for the floor. I thought about how cold and hard it would be.

"Why don't you join me? I mean, we're fully dressed and you might as well be comfortable." He took off his shoes and lay down beside me. I put my head on his chest and dropped off to sleep.

I was startled as Everlove pushed her way into the room and curled up on my other side. "You came over here by yourself? You're awesome."

***

The next morning, I heard Yvonne crying. Everlove had gone outside. I went over to her bed and held her against me.

"It will be alright. Do you have any aunts, uncles, grandparents?"

She nodded. "Uncle Bill."

"Uncle Bill. Maybe we can find him."

"Uncle Bill."

"We'll see what we can do," Paul said. "We're going to do every-thing we can to find your mommy."

"Would you like breakfast?" I asked. "I know they have pancakes—glyphosate-free."

"Glyfofo."

"Never mind. They're healthy and they pack them with vitamins."

"Vitmins," the girl responded, sourly.

"But they'll taste good."

"And I'll make them really sweet, like you," Paul said, walking out of the room and signaling for me to join him.

"I'm going to give her some penicillin—low dose. There was prob-ably a lot of bacteria in that mound," Paul said as I got out of the room. "I'll watch for any allergic reaction."

I nodded. "It's good to have a doctor in the house." He might just be a paramedic, but he was a better doctor than those who took bribes to vent people and put them on Remdesivir.

As Paul went to make the pancakes, Eric came upstairs. I told him about Bill.

"We'll put out a story going out across the country, asking if anyone named Bill had a sister or brother with their family in Yosemite Valley at the Ahwahnee in the last two weeks. Do you know where the girl was from?"

"I didn't push."

A few minutes later, as I was back with Yvonne, showing her little finger games, Eric came to the room. I went out the door to speak with him.

"The call is out."

"Fast work."

"We didn't mention the little girl. Whoever responds will have to know there was a little girl with her parents and not just some teenager."

"Can Jeff or Jack access the records for the Ahwahnee?"

"For two adults and a young child," Paul suggested, coming into the hallway, overhearing part of the conversation.

"I'll tell him," Eric replied.

"Autumn is warming up the syrup," Paul noted.

"The military has been deleting a lot of records. There may be backup somewhere in the cloud," Eric continued with the prior conversation.

"Didn't we wipe that out?" I asked.

"The virus was for the DHS's operations, not for park or accommodation records."

"Is it still down?"

"Yep. It was a doozy and they were dumb enough to connect to both DHS and the DOD to try to analyze the problem and now the computers from both departments in DC are down and the official cells FEMA handed out to their people aren't working either."

"That could mean years in prison if anyone is caught," I warned.

"I did it locally from their computer with gloves."

I smiled. "Glad you're on our side."

"They are using walking talkies and new cell phones for communication devices now, but there is a lot of confusion."

"Do you have any way of getting word out to Big Sur, Sequoia, and so forth?" I asked. "This might be the time for a peaceful march on those places."

"The people who would want to march might be peaceful, but FEMA sure isn't."

"The National Guard is from the people of California. I can't believe they would turn on their own citizens," I commented.

"They were required to take the jabs from the last three plandemics and most complied. The courts insisted religious exemptions be allowed, but they did their best not to allow them—especially in California," Paul responded.

"And?"

"There is a lot of unhappiness, but you know about the 5G-vaccine interface, don't you?" Eric asked.

"That's not a conspiracy theory," Paul stated.

"I wish it were. The military is the first place they'll power it up to keep the troops in line."

"You're saying the National Guard might shoot unarmed civilians?" I asked.

"They might shoot their own mothers."

"I wonder if Uncle Bill is one of the jabbed and doesn't care about Yvonne's family. I hope that's not the case."

"I don't know about the family, but Yvonne doesn't have any traces of it in her, and that means her mother also wasn't jabbed prior to giving birth or nursing her," Paul disclosed.

"That's a relief," I said. "The kids who are born or nursed with the mRNA will have problems for life."

"You've listened to some good medical advice," Paul praised me.

"McCullough, Kory, Malone, Kheriaty, and Cole, to name a few. With my cardiac issues, that's why I didn't get it and had to lie to my family about not just the jabs for the first plandemic but also for the subsequent ones."

"And why I got an exemption and then a fake card," Grant said, coming in. "The rangers' logs have a link to the Ahwahnee registrations. We have to check cars at night. It looks like a lot of records were erased —probably part of the FEMA cover-up. I've got a drive with possible links to cloud uploads for Jack to sort through. Ours, not FEMA's."

"You won't get in trouble?" I pondered.

He looked at me funny.

"Okay," I said.

Autumn handed me a stack of pancakes with maple syrup on them. "They have some of Paul's detox vitamins in them."

"You eat them too," Paul advised.

"Yes, sir," I agreed.

"Hey. You need to help me give the boys a rough time. Don't be so agreeable," Autumn joked.

"Next suggestion, the answer is 'no.'" I told Paul.

"Oh. Okay. I was going to suggest you go outside today."

I laughed and lightly punched him in the shoulder.

"Ow," he said, pretending to almost collapse.

I took the stack of pancakes into Yvonne's room. "Cakes?" she cried. "Hungry."

"Eat as much as you like. There's more where those came from."

She started to eat but seemed to fill up fast.

"Take your time. You can eat some now and more in a little bit when you're hungry, again. When you've recovered, we have horses."

"Horses, horses."

"I'll make sure you get to ride some before your family picks you up."

"Mommy? Daddy?"

I suspected her parents were dead. "It may take a while. It's hard to find anyone, now."

"Men with guns." She started crying. "Rabbits stiff. Wouldn't move."

"I'm sorry. The people who sent the men with guns did that. Others may be hiding like you did, too."

"Mommy? Daddy?"

"It's possible." I didn't want to share my suspicions until I knew for sure. She'd been through enough. "But we'll take good care of you until your family arrives."

"Horses."

I didn't notice the door being wedged open until Yvonne screamed.

CHAPTER 29

I turned and Everlove ran and jumped onto my bed. Yvonne kept screaming. A second later, Paul and Jack were in the room. I reached out and hugged Yvonne. "You are safe. The wolf is a pet. She's nice."

I reached out to Everlove and she licked me as I put my arms around her. That seemed to calm Yvonne down.

"Everlove, come outside," Paul insisted, guiding her out.

Everlove looked at me. "It's okay, Everlove. I'll see you later."

"We have three other pet wolves too," I said.

"Will eat me?"

"No. They'll protect you. But only go near the pet wolves. The others are dangerous."

"Danger," she said.

She had settled down, but the color that had left her face when she saw Everlove hadn't returned.

"I'll formally introduce you to Everlove. Wolves are really great if they are trained."

"Eat people."

"Not these wolves. They like what we feed them, kind of like a pet dog. They are a type of dog. They saved my life."

"Saved life."

"They do that. They help people."

"Help."

She seemed to be relaxing more.

"Go outside?"

"I'll ask Paul."

"Doctor?"

"He's the best doctor I know."

Paul came back in.

"Doctor, doctor, outside?" she pleaded.

"Sunshine and fresh air are good for you. Can you walk?"

The little girl tried to get up, but she was still weak.

"I'll carry you," he said.

He took her outside. I brought out a cushioned, folding, double-seated chair. He encouraged me to sit next to her on it.

A little while later, Eric came and spoke with us. The three of us stepped aside so the little girl wouldn't hear.

"We found some records for a Benjamin and Angela Sheldon who were at the Ahwahnee with a toddler about the right time."

"Do you have a home address?"

"It's in Sonora. I called Jim and asked him to check if one of the parents had a brother named Bill or any other family. It might not be them. There were some other people there with kids, but they were the only ones with a single toddler in the records we looked at."

"They escaped Sonora, only to be in Yosemite Valley," I lamented. "Do you think they could be hiding out?"

"The first thing they would have done would have been to find their daughter—if they're alive."

Paul shook his head. "That poor little girl."

"Let's hope we can find Uncle Bill," I said. I looked back at Yvonne, hoping somehow her parents had survived, too.

"I didn't mention the little girl to Jim, though he knew we had someone in the back of the van when we left Yosemite," Eric said.

"After what he did to that National Guardsman, I don't fully trust him," Paul pointed out. "I hope that guy's okay."

"He was really nice—until Jim smashed him in the head and neck," I remarked.

"Casualty of war," Eric said. "Good people are always hurt or killed on both sides."

My mind reflected on a story I had heard about a man who had miraculously avoided being on planes that crashed, only to be on flight 99 on September 11. I wondered if people were somehow marked for death—maybe me. The wolves and Paul saved me, but was I supposed to die on that trail? Did Tatiana know it and was that why she was treating me so badly? Maybe, she thought I was cursed and if she stayed with me, the curse would rub off on her.

Jack joined us. "They've taken over South Lake Tahoe and Stateline. No poison but a takeover. Nevada is protesting and there is a standoff between FEMA and the local police, the sheriffs, and the Nevada State Police. The Nevada Department of Public Safety is calling for assistance."

"That's higher elevation," I said. "I wonder why they chose that?"

"Allows them to spread out over two states. Yosemite Valley is four thousand feet."

"So far, they've mostly been hitting the valleys and sea level resorts."

"South Lake Tahoe is also a vacation resort," Paul replied. "And it's somewhat isolated."

"More and more, it's looking like a joint federal, California venture," I said.

"California has gone insane. They don't even have real elections in this state. They haven't for years," Paul commented.

"Grass Valley has a militia that's organizing," Eric informed us. "And there are various groups along the coast doing likewise. Have you ever heard of a place called Asilomar?"

"It's nice. It's in Pacific Grove and a lot of conventions take place there," I recalled. "I have been there a number of times."

"Not anymore."

"Where is the Enterprise when you need it?"

"What?" Paul asked me.

"Enterprise," Jack said. "Didn't you see *Star Trek IV*? It was filmed at the Monterey Bay Aquarium." He turned to Eric. "About ten minutes from Asilomar."

"Wasn't the state running Asilomar?" I asked.

"I guess they plan to put both the state and national park services out of business," Eric said. "We need someone to do a road trip and unite all the resistance—all the sane resistance. The cliffsides were so splattered with blood, it's a wonder there are any males left in Oakhurst."

"Does this mean they killed all the wildlife around the Seventeen Mile Drive?" I asked.

"It looks like a more subtle takeover. They just kicked everyone out of the area and took over. They told them they were expecting a toxic attack from the Russians."

"More humane than what they did here," Paul said

"We do need to organize," I suggested.

"Did I hear something about another road trip?" Autumn asked as she walked up.

"We've got a little girl to take care of now," Paul pointed out.

"Let's bring her. She'll be safer on the road than here, anyway," Autumn advised.

Paul shook his head and threw up his hands as if surrendering. "We will have to make it fast. Grant can watch the wolves and horses. I'd leave Yvonne here with Jeff and Jack, but she might need medical attention."

"That means you're coming?" I asked.

"Once Autumn decides, I know I'm not stopping you girls, and my girl is not going on another road trip without me."

Everlove came over to me. I hugged her. Then she went to the little girl. Yvonne looked terrified at first, but Everlove laid down at her feet, and she started to warm to the wolf.

"Maybe we could bring Everlove," I suggested.

"Cal isn't going to like that. She's his lady. Wolves aren't as fickle as most people. They mate for life."

"Then he'll be extra eager to see her when she returns," I said.

Eric spoke up. "I'll go with you. A pair of wolves might provide additional protection."

"As long as their lives aren't in danger with all those guns we keep seeing among the militia guys," I remarked.

"We'll keep them out of sight in the ambulance and put service harnesses on them. We should repaint it though," Paul recommended.

"Or at least change the license plates," Eric advised.

Paul gave Yvonne a detox treatment and she took a nap. When she woke up, I asked Yvonne if she'd like to see the horses.

"Horses, horses!"

I put her up on Laura's back and walked next to her, making sure she didn't fall as Laura wandered around the yard. After that, I carried Yvonne back in. She still looked tired. "You need more rest."

"Tired of sleeping."

"You need your strength." Paul took more blood tests and gave her another bag of fluids with a natural detox and nutrients.

"I think she's going to be alright," he informed me in the hallway.

"You didn't think that before?"

Yvonne called to me, "Can Everlove sleep in my room?"

"Sure," I said. I was amazed by how quickly she had gotten over her fear of the wolf. Everlove had been running around with the other three wolves and looked like she could use a rest. I brought her in. She seemed protective of the little girl in much the same way she watched over me.

"You're a natural nurse," I told Everlove.

"I heard back from Jim," Eric said as I went downstairs. "Apparently, Benjamin Sheldon's brother William has practiced law in Sonora for twenty years. Benjamin and Angela took their three-year-old daughter Yvonne to Yosemite a couple of weeks ago and were planning to spend a week at the Ahwahnee."

"When can we get her together with her Uncle Bill?"

"That's the problem. He died in Sonora. He wasn't married and didn't have any children."

"How about their parents?"

"Passed, a long time ago."

"Other brothers, sisters?"

"None."

"And Angela, what about her parents?"

"She was an orphan. She never knew her mother or her father."

"So somewhere out there is Yvonne's extended family."

"The mom was dropped off at the orphanage as a baby. She tried to trace her family and was never able to do so."

I thought about the poor girl, alone. It was possible there were some distant cousins out there, but tracking them down at this point in time wasn't going to be easy.

I was lucky. As awful as Tatiana was to me, she was still alive. All I had ever wanted for her was for her to be safe and happy.

I went into Yvonne's room and looked at her. Everlove was lying on the floor and Esther was next to Yvonne on her bed. We had both lost so much, but I had gained so much more than I had lost. I wished I could protect Yvonne from the pain of the losses she didn't know she had suffered. We couldn't be one-hundred percent sure about her parents. *Maybe they did hide—though what kind of parents would just hide when they have a little girl like Yvonne waiting for them?*

I went back outside to talk to Paul. "I can't tell Yvonne she, too, may be an orphan."

"Let's say we're on an adventure while we are waiting to find her parents. Eventually, we may know more and if we don't, it'll allow her to have hope."

I nodded.

"You'll make a good mother."

"So, will Autumn."

"Autumn likes kids, but she's more ready for adventure than motherhood. Both of you deserve the rest of your teen years and your twenties and you especially deserve some nurturing."

"I've been getting more nurturing from you and Autumn than I've had since my mother passed. I love adventure and I want to have fun with Autumn, but I have a strong need for family, too. I guess it comes with losing my own."

"Well, now you've got a family that isn't going anywhere. I'm in it for life." He brought his lips to mine. His kiss still felt like a fantasy, my heart leaping with even more excitement and passion than the last time.

We pulled apart as Autumn rushed to us, calling for Paul. "Something's wrong with Laura. Hurry. I hope she didn't eat poison."

We raced behind the house. Laura was kneeling down and had thrown up. "If it's poison, that's the best thing she could do," Paul related.

He ran inside and got his medical bag and listened to her chest. He took a blood sample and looked at it on a slide.

"You've got to be alright, Laura. You're part of my family," I begged. "You are more than a horse to me, and I couldn't stand to lose anyone else I love."

"I'll be back," Paul said. He hopped on Atlas and raced in the direction of Glacier Point. I got some apples from a tree and tried to feed them to Laura. Something was terribly wrong. She looked hungry but she wasn't eating.

I sat down next to where she was kneeling and buried my head in her side. I started praying that this young horse would be fine. It seemed like an eternity, but it was only half an hour when Paul returned.

He had driven back and brought a machine he connected to an outlet. He placed some kind of sensor on Laura's abdomen. "Well, girl, I'm going to have to make sure you eat healthier from now on. Vitamins and minerals and lots of folic acid."

Noticing he was calm and not upset, I waited for him to turn to me.

"You're getting used to one little girl and now you're going to have another or maybe a little boy."

"She's pregnant?"

He nodded. "Pregnant."

I felt so relieved, but also worried. "She's going to be alright, isn't she?"

"I'm going to see to it. She'll need fresh air, exercise and healthy food. She may have to spend extra time in the cave to stay away from pollutants."

"Have you delivered a colt before?"

"I delivered Laura."

He went into the house and got a bag of food mixed with something else. "Vitamins," he said. "I'm also putting them in her drinking water. No wild exercise for her for a while."

"How far along is she?"

"I would guess that she is several months along. Horses have longer gestation periods than humans. For them, it's about eleven months."

"And your guess is she is several months?"

"I'd say at least four, maybe five. We need to be very careful where we ride her from now on."

There was something very exciting about this. "Is there any danger to Laura?"

"There is always a danger. I have no intention of losing her, though."

"If anyone can keep her safe, you can."

"I've got Grant's truck. Before we go, I'm going to drive her back home, where she'll be safe with filtered air. And Lightning seems very devoted. I'll bring him too."

He was right. I noticed Lightning kneeling nearby, watching the events.

"You're going to be a good father," I said, going over to pet Lightning Bolt. "Paul's going to take good care of your lady and your baby."

Autumn came out.

"You're going to be a grandmother," Paul told her.

"Laura's pregnant?"

She smiled, whirled around and clapped. "I was there when Laura was born and I called her my baby."

"I guess you *are* about to become a grandmother," I repeated Paul's comment.

"How far along is she?"

"Five months is my estimation. She'll start showing in another month. Treasure, she's your horse, too. I guess that makes you a future grandmother as well."

"You old thing," Autumn said to me.

"I'll get you a wheelchair for your birthday in a little over two months," I responded.

"Can we still do the road trip?" Autumn asked.

"We'll be leaving tomorrow morning. I still feel iffy about bringing you girls along."

"We're fine. We both made it down the mountain the other night," Autumn bragged.

"And thanks to Jack, you survived."

"Like I said, I was about to show off my brown belt skills."

"I was reading about Krav Maga. That's a really powerful martial art," I noted.

"The Mossad is always trained in it. They're evil, but that doesn't mean the rest of us can't use the best fighting form."

"Don't be overconfident. That's how people get themselves killed. Remember the Oakhurst militia," Paul warned her.

"Any reactions to the video of Pete's confession to being FEMA?" I asked.

"There was a lot of anger and also disbelief."

"At least we still have Sonoma," Autumn remarked.

"And it looks like groups are getting together elsewhere, too," Paul told her. "If we can unify them, we might be able to drive FEMA out."

"Is Grant going to be monitoring the cameras?" I asked.

"He's taking a few days off work. He reported twisting his ankle. Brady will be manning the station, while Grant watches the live feeds."

"I like Brady. He might turn us in if he knew what we were really up to, but I think his heart is in the right place," I commented.

"He's really cute," Autumn said, enthusiastically.

"I thought you liked Eric," I responded.

"I can still look."

Jack had a covered grassy picnic area out back. We led Laura and Lightning over there and Paul brought over a container of carrots.

"Pregnant women always deserve to be spoiled," Autumn said. "Of course, I'm waiting until I'm fifty."

"Of course," I reacted. I suspected it would be a lot sooner. But Autumn was going to live an exciting life in the meantime—if we all survived this adventure.

Paul and I went into Yvonne's room. Yvonne was sharing a basket of stuffed toys with Esther and Everlove.

"I brought that from home," Paul related. "Autumn used to play with those when she was a little girl. She hasn't looked at them in years and okayed my giving them to Yvonne."

Yvonne looked happy with her new friends. "Wolves are nice. Want a wolf."

"Not all wolves are as nice as the ones we have," I pointed out. "That horse you rode on today, she's going to have a baby."

"Baby horse? Can I have baby?"

"It won't be born for at least six months. If you're still with us then," Paul started to say, then paused and continued. "You'll need your own horse."

I smiled. I was hoping he'd let her stay with us until her real family was found.

"A horse, a horse!" she exclaimed, again.

Our happy mood was broken by the sound of explosions in the direction of the Valley. It wasn't just one. It was a series of blasts. Yvonne looked terrified. I didn't feel safe myself, but I was more worried about her.

"I'd better bring the horses inside."

"Will Jack mind?"

"I don't care."

"Do you think FEMA or the militias are at it again?" I asked.

He shrugged.

We brought the horses into the kitchen and gave them a container of carrots to munch on while we rushed down to the basement.

Jack was looking at the feed from one of his cameras. "Those bastards."

"What?" Paul asked.

"Half Dome." Blown across the picturesque face were the letters F E M A.

CHAPTER 30

That evening, after Grant had picked up Laura, Paul, Autumn and I returned to the cave on the remaining horses while Yvonne napped at Jack's. We brushed the horses and then checked on Grant, who was monitoring the cameras.

"Are you monitoring the horses?" Paul asked.

"Of course. I'm thinking of putting a camera in Autumn's bedroom before she returns."

"Don't you dare," she reacted.

"Yvonne—" Paul started to say.

"I heard. Are we going to adopt her?"

"I don't know if we can do it legally."

"I faked a vaccine certificate. A birth certificate shouldn't be any problem."

"With Jack's help, you faked a vax record," Paul reminded him.

"If Jack could break into the digital vax records, he could break into vital statistics."

"Hmm. I'm with a family that knows no bounds," I chimed in. "I love it."

"I knew you'd fit in," Autumn said.

"I take it I'm driving you three back to Jack's."

"You haven't met Yvonne yet. Got to meet the rest of the family."

"It will be love at first sight," Autumn predicted.

"She's a little bit young for my taste," Grant replied.

"But she's a real charmer," Paul noted. "I mean, if I weren't totally in love with Treasure, then I'd wait for Yvonne to grow up."

"Says the guy who was never interested in romance until about a week ago."

We fed all the horses and made sure Laura was comfortable. We let our four-legged friends know we'd miss them but we'd be back soon. We decided to have Grant take Esther and Valiant back home with him that night. Everlove and Cal would be coming with us.

"Don't worry. Bro. I can handle everything. It's you and your crew, I'm worried about," Grant said.

"Eric has redone the van. It's now 'CHP Emergency Services'."

"California's only state police. What about the license plate?"

"Jack snagged a couple earlier this year from a wrecked CHP vehicle. It should be good at a glance."

"You're counting on their not checking past the obvious."

"Correct. Since the Governor is supporting FEMA's operation, they'll assume we're part of their family."

We returned to Jack's to find he already had service harnesses on Cal and Everlove.

Yvonne was excited Everlove and Cal would be coming. "What bout Esther?"

"She'll greet us when we return."

Cal licked Yvonne's face. She laughed. "Friendly."

"Boys are generally friendlier than girls in the dog kingdom," I said.

"You've noticed," Paul replied.

"I made that observation long ago."

"Horses?" Yvonne asked.

"They won't fit in a medical van. We'll see them when we get back," he explained.

"Horses, horses!" she said excitedly.

"You're going to see the ocean," I told her.

"Ocean?"

"Ocean."

We left Autumn to play cards with Yvonne while Paul and I made dinner and further discussed the plans.

When we returned, Autumn stated, "This girl is a card shark."

"Of course, she is," I replied. I was pretty sure Autumn was working both sides of the game and helping the girl win.

***

After dinner, Paul advised us to get some sleep so we'd be alert on the trip.

"And you?"

"I'll be getting contact details from Jack. Various members of resistance groups have taken to the radio and we're going to follow up."

"If the feds are monitoring them, we'll have to be careful. Then, there is the undercover problem we had with Pete," I warned.

"Jack's been checking the backgrounds on everyone we'll be dealing with and he'll get us any updates we need. We've all got burner phones. We'll have a backup radio with a military scanner in the ambulance."

He kissed me goodnight.

"You'll need sleep, too."

"I'll get some."

I went over to Yvonne's bed and kneeled down to tuck her in. As I started to get up, she said, "Please. Don't leave."

I could see she was afraid of me disappearing like her parents. I wondered if we were doing the right thing taking her on the trip. But part of me felt she'd be safer away from Yosemite than staying. Both sides had guns in the area, and I didn't want her getting caught in the crossfire.

CHAPTER 31

Early morning, we took off, heading straight for the coast. We went past Interstate 5, taking 152 over the Pacheco Pass, and 156 west to southbound Highway 1.

We were to meet a guy named Montrose who regularly played racquetball at the Monterey Sports Center. While we went in, paying the daily fee, Monterey's sea breezes cooled the van through the partially open windows in the overcast weather that was all too common for the area.

Autumn participated in jazzercise and kickboxing classes. A bathing suit had been among Autumn's hand-downs and I gave Yvonne a little swimming lesson, which involved mostly holding her up and getting her to paddle and kick. Paul went into the racquetball court and challenged a guy to racquetball. The guy wasn't Montrose. Paul hung around there, challenging players in the hopes Montrose would show up. Eric went into the handball court after looking around the place.

We had learned Montrose had been running an organized crime syndicate out of Pacific Grove. It was apparently known to all the people in the area. Someone pointed Montrose out to me as he went into the racquetball court. He and Paul played a couple sets and to my surprise, Paul won. I didn't know he was so skilled. Eric came over to watch them as if he were a racquetball enthusiast.

I wanted to limit Yvonne's contact with the syndicate guy. I took her to the equipment section, pulled out a giant ball and helped Yvonne roll around on it. I knew this was good for inner ear development. But it was important she not move too abruptly as her brain was still developing and growing.

Montrose came out of the court. A minute later, Paul and Eric came out. "We're going to meet him at The Aquarium."

"At least, that's still open," I said.

Paul got us some tickets to get inside. Autumn and I stayed with Yvonne, where we could see our guys. We knew it would be best to let Paul and Eric do the talking. At the gift dress shop, we got some jackets with the Aquarium's name on the back for ourselves and Yvonne and picked her up a stuffed dolphin. Then we continued to follow, stopping in front of the humpback whale tank so as not to get too close. Yvonne laughed as she watched the whales. I thought of *Star Trek IV*.

Eric came over to us and said, "'There be whales here.'"

"You've been doing too much LSD," I joked.

"That's because I have found the Nuk-we-are Wessels."

I laughed.

"I think that's my cue." He looked towards Paul as Montrose approached him. Eric joined them.

They talked for quite a while before two jacketed men who were apparently with Montrose came up.

"I think they've got guns under those jackets," Autumn said.

They guided Paul and Eric away. We followed. Montrose didn't seem to pay us any heed if he did recognize us from the gym.

Outside, Paul, Eric and the other men got into a car.

Another car pulled up outside. Putting her new jacket on, Autumn stepped up to the driver's door. "We'll leave the key under your name at the entrance."

"Since when does the Aquarium have valet parking?"

"Since we decided to make it more convenient for you."

She got in the vehicle and followed the men's car up to the corner. There was a lot of traffic in that location, and they were all moving slowly. I carried Yvonne to Autumn's borrowed car while she waited in the line to turn the corner where the men had turned right. We got in. She turned and sped up to follow our guys but not too closely. As she pulled past the ambulance, she handed me the keys. I got out and followed her, following the leaders.

We passed a field where the Monarch butterflies were supposed to return. The lead car pulled into a driveway down the street. We stopped past the driveway and stepped outside our vehicles.

"How much do you want to bet they have surveillance?" I asked.

"Look," she said, pointing to boxes of Bibles and literature on the back seat of the borrowed car. "JWs."

I turned on the van's air conditioning and asked Yvonne to stay in the back. The wolves stayed in the van to protect her. We grabbed a couple of dress jackets from the van and a box of Bibles and literature from the car and knocked on the door.

"We have a free Bible for you," Autumn said as a woman answered the door. "May we come in and talk?"

"We're busy."

"Too busy for the Lord?" Autumn strode past her with the box. "We'll only take a minute."

"What's this?" a man sitting on the couch with our guys asked. It looked as if another man behind the couch had something pointed at our men under a cloth.

"We're giving out Bibles." I pulled Bibles out of the box for each of them. "You do believe in God, don't you?"

"We're Roman Catholic. We have enough Bibles," the man behind the couch said.

"Well, here's another one," I said, handing him a Bible. He took it in the hand, not covered, as Autumn smacked him with the box.

Eric jumped up and threw the other man across the room, grabbing a gun the man tried to pull out, as I kicked a third man in his privates with my boot.

"Now, who are you?" Montrose asked. "I saw you at the gym and the Aquarium."

"We're the people who are going to help you get FEMA out of your city. Or do you want them to stay? I suppose you can move your operations to Seaside," Autumn replied.

Montrose grimaced. "Okay. What do you want?"

"First, direct violence fails and makes FEMA sympathetic. Sabotage is the way to success," Eric stated.

"I can go for that. How do we sabotage?"

"Cut the power lines. Put viruses in their computers and drive them out." Eric shoved his free palm forward as he spoke.

"Feed them their own poison. They're the ones who have messed up our food," one of the men growled, shaking his head in disagreement.

"They have a history of toxic clouds and poisoning water and food. So, expect them to have a lot of antidotes," Paul pointed out.

"We caught them trying to poison the desalination plant." Montrose made a fist.

"What did you do?" Eric asked.

"We shot the men who were doing it and confiscated the poison."

"We are planning to put it in Asilomar's water supply," one of the thugs boasted.

"There are some good people working at Asilomar. We want to make sure they aren't poisoned," Paul pointed out.

"How many?"

"Maybe a dozen or so. Some have gotten word out that they want to stop it as well," Paul advised.

"If FEMA's toys don't work, they won't get very far," Eric contended.

"You're saying you want us to be high-tech saboteurs?" Montrose looked dubious.

"That and water their gas tanks. Cut their power lines or use an EMP device to take out more than just the computer and power systems," Eric continued.

"You plan to do this tonight?" Montrose asked.

"Do you have a computer tech?" Eric inquired.

"We have an accountant. He's kind of meek."

"I can handle the computer, myself, then," Eric told them as he put down the gun he'd confiscated.

The men seemed agreeable, but remembering Pete's betrayal and Jim's violence, we knew we had to be prepared in case of a double-cross or dangerous conduct.

Montrose stayed behind but sent a number of his men with us. In accordance with the plan, we entered Asilomar in the medical van, followed by several of Montrose's men with fake credentials in a regular car under the pretext there was a person who needed to be picked up. I guessed Montrose didn't want to be there if anything went wrong. Paul had tried to get Autumn, Yvonne and me to stay in a nearby hotel but I pointed out FEMA probably had all the motels monitored and they had already killed people.

Once inside, Eric used equipment we'd brought to monitor for significant electronic usages or surges. Jack helped remotely with a foreign Satellite view. He reported normal satellites weren't showing the area and he had had to tap into foreign ones.

Our guys were to go to the door of wherever they suspected FEMA was setting up operations and find a way in. First, we stopped at the front desk of the Administration Building.

"Sadie," Eric whispered to a clerk with a nametag. Jack had learned she was to be our contact.

"Yes?" she whispered back.

"Eric. I misplaced my key. Do you have a master that could work for my room?"

She handed him a key we suspected bypassed the electronic locks.

The monitoring equipment showed the main power usages and surges were in White Caps, one of the various blocks of rooms at the campground. We parked in the underground parking near Guest Inn. Montrose had stolen a number of FEMA outfits and we all slipped them on.

Eric and Paul walked to White Caps. One of Montrose's men, who was on a stretcher in the ambulance, got out with some cable cutters. His job was to wait for the signal before cutting the power. He had obtained a map of Asilomar's electrical system. Autumn and I were to wait with Yvonne and the wolves in the van.

"Do you trust him?" Autumn asked, referring to Montrose's man.

"No," I said.

"Let's follow him."

We had Yvonne get on a cot under a cover like a patient and left her and our four-legged friends as protection for her in the van while we took off in pursuit.

The syndicate guy started to cut the power right away—without waiting for the signal. Autumn had brought a tire iron and knocked him out before he accomplished his sabotage. She picked up the tool and waited for Eric to send a text to the man's burner phone. When it came, she cut one of the wires and threw me the cutters to cut another one. The lights went out.

"I bet this isn't the only betrayal," I worried.

That's when bullets started flying. "This wasn't supposed to involve guns," I reacted.

Eric and Paul were running as bullets were hitting all around. I saw Paul fall and ran over to him. As I ran, something hit my arm.

I was bleeding. Bullets continued to fly in my direction, but that didn't stop me. Paul wasn't moving. They could shoot me, again, for all I cared.

CHAPTER 32

I can't lose him was all I could think. I said a silent prayer, wishing I had vetoed the idea of the trip. *I could have stopped this before it happened.*

Paul was lying very still, as I kneeled down. "Paul," I started to say as he pulled me down flat against his chest. I could tell he was okay. I felt more relieved than ever before in my life.

Paul felt the blood oozing out of my arm. "I need to get you out of here." Bullets blasted out from various directions. Still, he started to pick me up, shielding me with his body.

"No. I need you safe," I whispered. "Autumn—"

"She's out here?"

"Somewhere."

We looked in the direction from which I had come. We didn't see her.

As the barrel of a rifle touched my shoulder, we turned to see two real FEMA agents.

"They're shooting from over there somewhere," I said, pointing to where Montrose's men were firing from.

"You've been hit," the FEMA agent told me.

"I know."

The agent who had spoken was struck by a bullet and fell into the arms of the other agent, who kneeled down. We ran towards the van. I was hoping Autumn had made it back. She wasn't there. Paul pulled out bandages for my arm. Yvonne started to cry as she saw me.

"I'm fine. It's make-up. Stay covered. We don't have time for this. Where's Eric?"

"He is still in the hotel room," Paul said, wrapping my arm. "When the power goes back up, they'll be in for a nasty surprise. That's when the program will wipe out their feed."

"I've got to go back for Autumn," I said.

"I'll go back. You're staying here."

"I'm going with you. I won't comply or compromise on that."

He realized the argument was useless. We proceeded out of and away from the van as something tapped our backs. We turned.

We were looking down the barrels of guns held by two of Montrose's men. "Thanks for the assist," one said coolly.

"We're supposed to be on the same side," I countered.

"There's our side and then the other side."

"Montrose said—"

"Gave us orders to leave no problems behind."

CHAPTER 33

They both fell back, grabbing their throats. Everlove and Cal had wrapped their teeth around the backs of the mobsters' necks. Our wolves pulled them down and jumped on top of them. Paul and I grabbed their weapons and slugged them.

"Good work." It was someone with captain's stripes.

"Thank you. I think the intruders are under control," Paul said.

"I rounded up another one," I heard Eric say from behind me. I turned. He was with Autumn. They were dragging the one she had slugged. "We have a patient in the ambulance. We have to go to the local hospital for an emergency action."

"I can give you an escort," the captain said.

I wasn't too happy about that.

"Are those army wolves?"

"They're good at detecting explosives and they are also service trained," Paul explained.

"Nice."

Two more real FEMA agents came up. "I recognize this guy." He pointed to the one Autumn had knocked out. "He's on a most-wanted list. Where did these guys get these uniforms and guns?"

"They must have taken them off other agents. They were shooting at us and trying to kill as many FEMA personnel as they could," Eric said.

The agents carried the unconscious men away, probably for interrogation.

We got into the van, followed by the captain, and were off to the local hospital. We pulled in and started to unload a stuffed stretcher. Our escort pulled away.

One of the orderlies objected. "These are just sheets."

"We're trying to get rid of excess materials."

"Well, you can't dump them here. Reload."

We put the stretcher back in the van.

After we left, I asked Paul, "Is uniting the areas hit by FEMA ever going to happen? Everyone has their own plan of action and isn't interested in being a team player."

"It isn't going to be easy."

"FEMA is evil but some of the people we're dealing with are equally evil. Will Montrose come after us for revenge?"

"He doesn't know much about where to find us—except that we're from the Yosemite area. And he'll have FEMA to deal with if he goes there."

"I bet his men will rat us out to the authorities."

"Let them. We helped FEMA subdue them. That will wipe out their credibility."

"Guess we won't be coming back here in the near future."

"There's a freedom rally in OC," Eric informed us. "A mass fire wiped out Laguna Beach up to the hills. The fire hydrants didn't work and all highways out were blocked by FEMA. There are over a thousand missing people and children. Nobody is allowed to go in to find them.'"

"Climate change?" I asked sarcastically.

"That's what they'll claim. Now they'll get to rebuild back better."

"Is the state or FEMA behind that?"

"Depends on who gets the land when it's rebuilt," Eric responded.

"That's something the Governor would like to grab for his holdings," Paul remarked.

"I bet we'll meet more sane people there," I said.

We headed south. We took our time traveling as Paul and Eric took shifts driving. The next morning, we drove to the Huntington Beach pier. We had changed out of our government clothes into regular clothes.

"They aren't going to like the official nature of the van," Paul said, as Eric parked on a side road.

Eric pulled out a van cover.

"Good move," Paul noted.

"While we're here, would you like to drop by your home?"

"I'm giving up that life—for now."

There was a crowd of thousands, including a number of famous guest speakers at the event: Dr. Judy Mikovits, Dr. Paul Alexander, Dr. Peter McCullough, Dr. Pierre Kory and Dr. Ryan Cole. They had all been correct from the start of the first plandemic and we knew they were correct about the subsequent ones too. The audience seemed alive and enthusiastic—unlike most people I'd encountered after masking and jabs started rolling out.

I spotted a stand with organic cotton clothing. We picked up quite a few new toddler clothes for Yvonne.

Jack emailed us a flyer with pictures from Yosemite, Sonora, Big Sur and Sequoia with a descriptive note, saying FEMA was killing off communities one by one, dropping poison, and causing death and destruction. We printed out a thousand and walked through the crowd, handing them to participants.

People at the event were very knowledgeable about healthcare, but didn't know what to do about the government. "Our elections don't count," was a concern radiating through the crowd. "Every time we trust a politician, he lets us down."

"And if you question anything, even from the left, you're either a right-wing racist or a Russian," I commented, referencing the propaganda against truth.

Many in the crowd were shocked at the sight of our pictures. The news certainly hadn't carried the information. Even pictures and videos of Laguna Beach had been suppressed. One man had several pix of the city, showing burned bodies. He gave us copies.

Paul was invited to speak on stage.

"We need to find a way to unite the people to stop the aerial poisonings and government-created disasters wiping out our national parks and our communities. Firearms don't work. The Oakhurst militia discovered that the hard way. Hundreds died between Glacier Point and Yosemite Valley. The government has bigger, nastier weapons, along with biological and chemical weapons. Of course, we've all heard the Administration threatening to use nukes in preemptive strikes and they'll have no qualms using them on us."

"What do we do?" someone called out from the audience.

"It's not up to me to tell you. We need everyone to unite and brainstorm solutions before it's too late."

"Is it the feds behind all this damage?" another person called out.

"It's the feds and the state, working together. The National Guardsmen called out by our Governor are from California. They aren't bad people. They are under orders to follow the dictates of FEMA. FEMA is dangerous. It has its own unofficial army that includes mercenaries."

"What if we set up monitoring stations for people to sit and watch what is going on up and down the state. If we televise it live as we march in, will they shoot us?" one of the rally hosts asked.

"They might. Look at the pictures of the mass graves. Think of all the people they dropped poison dust on and then buried in those mass graves," Paul told them. "And think of what happened to those people just south of here? Laguna Beach is valuable land for stealing."

"We do what Gandhi did with the salt marches. We march down the major highways right into the Valley," came another suggestion from the crowd.

"Remember, during COVID, they brought out the tear gas. They'll do it again."

"Then we bring gas masks and protection from their metal pellets that they call rubber bullets." The crowd really seemed motivated.

"Remember the People's Convoy to DC," a person shouted. "They couldn't stop us and millions of Americans came out to greet us in spite of a total news blackout."

By now, the deaths from the jab had gotten up to seventy million, according to one of the speakers. I figured that was an underestimation, as five years before, it was announced the documented jab deaths worldwide had been about twenty million and coroners were speaking extensively about all the children dying from the jab as the Internet censors tried to hide the reality. Morticians were pulling long, hard clots out of arms and legs. I looked at Yvonne. I was so glad she didn't have any mRNA in her. So many kids whose parents had been too trusting of the Establishment had gotten their children injected with death.

A number of people offered to help with organizing. Several attorneys offered to put together actions. The National Parks were for the benefit of the public and there was no emergency authorizing FEMA to take charge. As for places like Sonoma and Big Sur, people worried it could happen in their communities. They did not believe the Laguna Beach fire was natural, but rather part of the same scheme.

Several environmentalists asked if FEMA had followed the National Environmental Policy Act and filed an Environmental Impact Statement for the federal land or an Environmental Impact Report for the non-federal property or held public hearings. A couple researchers checked and found that there had been no public hearings or filings, not even a NONSI, a Notice of No Significant Impact.

An attorney named Evan Long pointed out that NEPA is weak and only requires looking at environmental impact and alternatives but has no teeth. It does not require a specific outcome, but rather just calls for a process. He also pointed out that FEMA could get away with violations, claiming national security or other allowable exceptions or that their actions were non-discretionary. There were multiple potential avenues for legally stopping FEMA, and NEPA was just one of them.

After the rally, we gathered with several legal teams, who agreed to file for injunctions the following day. It was decided to file actions in federal court as a federal issue and national parks were involved. Though it was pointed out that there were also state involvement and attacks on cities within California, several people argued that California courts had been stacked by recent governors with pro-tyranny judges.

We were all concerned about the censorship issue. The vast majority of those present had had no idea whatsoever that all these poisonings and deaths had taken place.

"I like the idea of legal bullets, rather than lead ones," I remarked. "Or do they even use lead bullets anymore?"

"Have you heard of exploding bullets? They hit their target and shwoo," Paul said.

"Those have been around for a while," Eric replied. "There are also dirty bullets with depleted uranium."

Several of the people in the rally promised to help recruit a peaceful resistance. Some from out of state offered to rally up citizens in other areas that had been hit and to drop off flyers around Grand Canyon, Kings Canyon and Yellowstone.

As we drove back to Yosemite, I felt more reassured than before. When we arrived the next morning, things were not well. Jack looked concerned.

"What happened?"

"They rounded up all the rangers they could find and they are in detention in the Valley. Apparently, rangers are now 'Enemies of the State.'"

"Grant?"

"They got him, too."

CHAPTER 34

"Somebody has to care for Yvonne. I say that's you," Paul told me.

"Are you going to let my brother order you around?" Autumn asked. "If you let him start now, it will only get worse. Check out the books on that."

"Sis."

"Don't sis me. We made it down there before, and you are needed for monitoring the situation."

"Yvonne."

"She can stay with you while you watch us," I said. "I was pretty handy at Asilomar. Besides, if she has a medical emergency, it's you she'll need."

He pointed to the bandage on my arm.

"A scratch."

"And who's the expert at Krav Maga?" Autumn asked him.

"And there is your heart."

"I've been fine since you saved me." I wasn't going to mention any of the tightness or chest pains I'd had since, hopefully just from nerves.

"You are still girls."

"Misogynist. He now shows his true colors," Autumn stuck out her tongue at Paul.

"I'm not going to talk the two of you out of it, am I?"

"Nope," Autumn and I said in unison.

"If I'm to be part of this family, you need to trust me to do my part."

"Your part doesn't include dying."

"I was in more danger walking down the hillside with Tatiana," I reminded him. "I'm not going to let them arrest or shoot me. I have a plan."

"Yes?"

"Wasn't there a Congressman at that rally in Huntington Beach?"

"Yes. Representative Reynolds."

"Let's ask him to fly in by helicopter to inspect the place. While he's there, we'll search the camp for the rangers."

"Not bad. I'll call him."

A few minutes later, the Congressman agreed to the event over the phone. He would be arriving in two hours by helicopter.

"It's a good thing he was partway to Northern California when I called," Paul said.

"We need to livestream and video the event as well," I suggested. "Maybe others will get some courage."

"This is a home?" Yvonne asked as we removed the blindfold. This was for her protection so nobody could force her to lead them to the cave.

"It is."

"Why no windows?"

"Well, there are some but they lead to other parts of the home. Here's the best part." I led her down to the grazing area.

"Horses."

I handed her a carrot and showed her how to safely feed a horse.

As Yvonne fed Laura, she started jumping up and down, shouting, "I get Baby. I get Baby." I hoped, through whatever miracle, nothing would ever dampen her spirit. Autumn put her on Atlas and we walked her around the field.

We took Yvonne back to a room Paul had prepared for her.

"Do you sleep here too?"

"I sleep in my own room, but if you want, I can still snuggle up next to you while you are going to sleep."

She looked down.

"Or you can stay in my room if you like."

"I like."

As Paul was manning the surveillance of the park and Yvonne was playing with toys, Autumn and I walked to the ranger station. Paul had given me an amplified cell phone in case I was able to broadcast live. Eric was waiting for us.

Paul and Jack were video recording the events via additional cameras that had been set up near Curry. The Congressman was a large man, very stout and tall. He had a jolly attitude and believed he could change the world for the better.

"They sent out the beauty queens for the reception committee."

"Thank you," I said, while Autumn made light of his comment, pretending to pose for pictures.

The Congressman pinned a flag on each of us and handed us pocket-sized copies of the *Constitution*. Autumn, Eric and I accompanied the Congressman, his three assistants and his two plain-clothes security detail on the flight below.

As we flew into the valley, I said, "Even they couldn't destroy all the beauty of this place."

Apparently, FEMA felt safe turning off any blockers they might have set up as they had taken the rangers into custody, were controlling the whole site and there were no legitimate tourists. That made it easy to livestream. The helicopter had numerous active cameras to capture and send out what our cell cameras didn't.

"This is criminal," the Congressman said. "I spent my honeymoon here and now look what they've done to it."

"I think it can be repaired," I responded, optimistically.

"I'm going to demand an immediate end to these operations." He was clear and firm on the subject and that was what we needed.

The helicopter landed by the Camp Curry amphitheater. Several of FEMA's military guards ran up with guns pointed in our direction.

"Gentleman. You belong in the actual service of our country—not involved in the crimes here," the Congressman stated.

As he spoke, the armed FEMA officers were focused on him. Autumn, Eric and I tried to back away towards the containment area.

"I wouldn't," one of the troopers coldly advised me.

"But I wanted to catch the majesty on my phone," I said, moving my phone around the area.

"I'll have to confiscate that?"

"Do you have anything to say to my live audience?"

"Live?"

"Yes, say 'hi'."

He tried to grab my phone and Autumn screamed and dropped to her knees.

"What did you men do to her?" Reynolds asked.

"I didn't touch her," the trooper said.

"You all need to put down your guns. This is America, and in America, you do not point your guns at a Congressman."

Reynolds tried to take one of the guns and a bullet flew straight into Reynold's chest. He started to react and then collapsed, looking very dead. I thought of Jack's fake death, but I didn't think the Congressman was prepared to pull a Juliet.

CHAPTER 35

The Congressman's three assistants tried to rush the other troopers as his security detail pulled out their weapons. Shots were fired. It appeared the entire detail and all the assistants were lost in the gunfire. Eric, Autumn and I ran while everyone was focused on the bodies of the Congressman and his assistants.

"This was on live video," I heard one of them say as they turned to where we had been. We were hiding under a bench next to what had been the restaurant.

"Find them," someone ordered.

"Live feed."

"If anyone believes it. We'll do a video later about a recruitment production we were doing here."

They looked under the benches in the amphitheater but not the one next to the restaurant.

As they passed, moving towards the base of Glacier and then around the back of the restaurant, we ran.

I heard someone shout, "Over there." Bullets flew in our direction but we kept running until we jumped into the Merced. We swam downriver past housekeeping and got out amongst some trees. Then, we started backtracking towards what we suspected was the containment area in the Ahwahnee Meadow, where Autumn and Eric had thought they were being led before Jack rescued them.

As I snuck past a tree, someone grabbed me. "All of you stop or the girl gets shot."

Autumn and Eric froze. "Which girl?" Autumn asked.

"A wisecracker."

"No. I—" he shoved the gun against me and then fell forward into me as I pushed the gun to the side.

There was a knife in his back. I looked around in front of me and saw Brady coming over to us.

"What are you doing here?" I asked.

"They've got Grant and other rangers."

"We know."

"That man was about to shoot you." He looked as if he felt he might have done something wrong.

"I don't doubt it," I said. "Thank you for another rescue." I was glad I had cut the live video before it could show our escape route. That would have led the enemy straight to us—though I suspected the swim probably destroyed my new cell phone.

Brady picked up the gun. "It's not a lot, but it will have to do." He handed the gun to Eric, stripped the dead trooper and put on the FEMA uniform. "I was late to the station and saw them being picked up, but there was nothing I could do. I came down here to try to rescue them."

"Which containment area is he in?"

"Ahwahnee Meadow."

When I was a little girl, I used to do a meditation. We were to pick a safe space for an imaginary workshop and I picked that meadow. Now, instead of empowering, the meadow was a prison.

En route to that meadow, we paused near the Village Shopping Center. It was still standing. I saw troopers coming out of it with military equipment. They'd turned the general store into a warehouse.

They had painted targets on the fire station across the street and were using it for target practice. It was riddled with bullet holes.

"They better hope there's not a fire in the valley," I said.

"Want some equipment?" Brady asked. "Wait here."

He went into the general store. After a little while, he walked out with a large bag. It contained quite a number of firearms and a radio. He turned it on and we monitored their communications.

"If they think you're one of them, they trust you. Here are some fatigues. They don't have stripes, but they might hesitate to attack you."

We put on the fatigues and continued towards the meadow. There was a sentry moving back and forth in front of a giant pre-fab building with multiple wings. The sentry walked out of sight to the side of the prison.

"I think that fence is electrical," I said.

"Not anymore," Eric replied, discreetly showing me his EMP generator.

Brady pulled out a couple of the guns from his bag as we dashed through the gate towards the building.

"You aren't going to shoot them, are you?" I figured that would bring the whole camp down on us.

"Tranq darts."

As another sentry rounded a corner, he fired. The sentry fell. Another one came around the building, seemingly looking to see where the first one had gone. He dropped to the ground too.

"I'm pretty sure this is a blind spot. I've been monitoring this building and heard them say the cameras they put up around it are malfunctioning and they are trying to fix them.

We rushed towards the fallen guards. In our outfits, it wasn't suspicious if someone saw us. We pulled the men behind a tree and Eric and Autumn put on their clothes.

"You can be the lookout," Autumn suggested.

"Backwards," Eric told her. The lookout needs the uniform.

"You and I are going in," Brady told me.

Inside, a guard said, "Get back to your post."

Brady reached into his shirt and pulled out a paper. "I have orders from the commander. I'm bringing in this disrespectful off-duty ranger. He wants her locked up with the other rangers."

The sentry was about to look at the paper when another trooper walked in.

"Prisoner," Brady said. "Orders and I need to do this quickly and get back to my post. Ranger lockup."

The second trooper took us through a door, through a corridor, and through another door to a holding area and left. There were two guards watching the prisoners.

I had a gun Brady had given me under my shirt. One of the guards opened one of the three cell doors. Inside the cell were Grant and about a dozen other rangers in what looked like less than humane conditions.

"Now, get in there," Brady growled, kicking me. As he did, I turned and put the gun to the head of the guard who had opened the door. Brady asked, "Where did you get that?"

Brady backed up towards the other guard and away from me and the guard I was aiming at. In a quick move, he put the knife to the throat of the guard next to him before that guard could unholster his gun.

Grant rushed out. He looked weak, as if he had been tortured. He was covered with bruises and blood. Grant took the gun and keys from the guard who had opened the door. Brady already had the gun from the one he was holding. Grant released the prisoners in the other two cells.

Brady stuffed handkerchiefs in the guards' mouths while Grant and another ranger tied their hands and legs and tossed them in the cells. Brady gave Grant a tranq gun and we rushed en masse into the corridor.

The trooper who had led us into the containment area turned. "What the?" He was silenced by a tranquilizer dart from a gun Brady was holding. Another trooper started to draw his gun and fell, courtesy of Grant, before he could fire it.

"Let's get out of here," Brady said.

"Can't," Grant told him. He took the keys off the guard and took us through a door to another cell block that reeked of urine and vomit as he opened the door.

"More prisoners," Brady told a guard who stepped through the door. The guard pulled his gun as he stepped out the door and said,

"Move," right before a tranquilizer dart fired by Grant dropped the guard. We went inside and were greeted by another guard.

Pretending to be holding me and Grant at gunpoint, Brady told the new guard, "I don't get it any more than you do, but I'm supposed to bring these prisoners in here."

"I'm going to have to check," the guard said as Brady subtly fired another tranquilizer dart.

Grant opened the door to a cell stuffed with perhaps seventy prisoners.

"I recognize that guy," I said. "He uploaded videos from one of the unofficial wars Congress is funding, showing soldiers and contractors chopping off the legs of children, torturing them and then dumping their bodies."

"Imprisoning journalists fits right in with FEMA's other operations," Grant said. "Recognize him?" He pointed to another man.

"He was a candidate for Governor, years ago, during the recall. The Governor really hates him. And is that a general's uniform that man is wearing?" I asked, pointing to another prisoner. "No respect for the real army."

"I objected to the misuse of military funding for sex trafficking. But that wasn't the reason they put me in here. It was my objection to the use of my troops to overtake a national park that got me indefinite detention. No court-martial or paperwork," the General said, picking up the gun the guard had dropped. He was surrounded by other prisoners in uniform.

"NDAA in action," I realized.

"And we're paying for it in our taxes," the reporter said.

"We all need to get out of here and expose this," Brady responded.

"If we get separated, we'll meet up at the Mariposa Grove," Grant told the group.

A couple of the military prisoner escapees confiscated guns from FEMA troopers we came across as we were rushing from the section. "This is a military operation. Stand down," the General ordered the FEMA troopers. The "stand down" command was followed up with tranquilizer darts. I was glad Brady had stocked up on those at the general store.

As we returned to the compound entrance, the guard who had initially stopped us tried to draw his gun as one of the rangers shot him with a confiscated gun.

"That noise will bring them down on us," Brady said. We ran past Autumn and Eric and headed towards the Ahwahnee. I turned back to see the General leading the majority of prisoners in another direction. We had the rangers, several journalists, and the former candidate with us.

"I know some places to hide," Grant told us.

Sounds of gunfire erupted. Grant opened up a camouflaged door in the outer wall of the hotel and led us down, through a chamber, into a tunnel. "Nobody knows this exists except for the rangers." We came across a ladder and descended into a subbasement with water and sewage pipes. He led the way and we followed.

"Is there an exit?"

"There is. It's close to the hospital."

We came up outside the hospital and rushed around back to find an ambulance.

"Handy how these things just show up," Grant said.

"Are we going to let them get away with this?" Brady asked.

"They just shot a Congressman on live feed. They think they can get away with anything," I told him.

Autumn's expression told me she was ready to take on all of FEMA.

"Later," I told her.

She gritted her teeth.

"Can you drive this out of here?" I asked Brady. He had the most convincing outfit. He drove while Autumn and Eric were pretending to supervise a crowd of bodies under sheets. Grant, I and the other escapees were among those hiding under the sheets. Autumn noticed a vial of blood and poured it over the sheets.

The vehicle slowed. We had to be at a checkpoint. "What are you carrying?"

"Bodies. These guys need to look like they died of natural causes. We're to dump them off the road near Fish Camp."

"I need to check on this." The back door opened.

"We need to get going. We can't delay," Eric said.

"You look familiar."

"Really?" Autumn asked.

I heard something smack against the floor. A minute later we were moving again.

I looked out from under my sheet. One of the National Guardsmen was lying on the floor of the ambulance.

"Brady and Eric tranquilized the remainder of the Guardsmen who were blocking the road," Autumn explained. "When they come to, they'll be in trouble."

"What do we do with him?" I pointed to the FEMA guy in the back of the ambulance.

Up the road, we dropped the sleeping sentry in a clump of trees.

Brady continued on towards the Mariposa Grove of Giant Sequoias. "I don't know if we dare go back," he said.

Jack showed up with tents and supplies. "Hide the ambulance and hang out here.

A few minutes later, the General showed up with his group. "Did you all make it, General Hatfield?" Grant asked.

"A general's rank goes a long way—and it confuses the heck out of FEMA troopers following illegal orders."

"We have help. People are working on lawsuits and peace marches. Though peace marches might be a little dangerous at this point," I advised him.

"I'll say," Eric pointed out. "You saw what they did to Reynolds."

"The world saw it," Paul informed us, rushing in and taking me in his arms.

"Another Guiana. FEMA could be investigated by Congress," Eric added.

"What was this about Congressman Reynolds?" the journalist I had recognized asked.

"They shot him, his security detail and his assistants," Autumn related. "I would have taken them on, but I had to rescue you guys."

A couple of the newsmen who had been prisoners wanted to get back home to do reports. We suggested they take the ambulance we had confiscated. "But be careful. They lock up journalists. Was there a warrant out for you?"

"They just caught us reporting from outside the checkpoint," one of the newsmen said, pointing to himself and one of the other journalists.

"We did really well back there," the General said. "We have an armored tank and several military vehicles. How about you take one of those? The ambulance might open some doors later."

"We've already used ambulances for operations," Paul noted. "They might have them on a list of suspicious vehicles."

"Then definitely take one of the military vehicles and one of those inferior FEMA uniforms we confiscated on the way out."

I smiled. Normally it would be a crime to impersonate a military officer. But that hadn't stopped us so far. This was with the General's consent and as far as most of the public knew, FEMA didn't have its own army.

"General, why did they lock you up?" Paul asked.

"I was asked to bring in the army to back up FEMA here. I not only refused. I sent out a message to my troops telling them assisting would subject them to court-martial when the truth came out."

"The truth will put you in a grave," Autumn said.

"And without the real military, FEMA needed to create a mercenary army devoid of a conscience."

While the rangers, Jack, Eric, Grant, the General, and other former prisoners strategized, Paul, Autumn and I took off for Jack's place.

Paul was pretty quiet on the way back there. Finally, he said, "The two most important women in my life were in deadly danger, and I felt completely impotent sitting around recording and sending out videos. Then, when you cut the feed, I didn't know what happened to you."

"We didn't want the enemy to find us via our videos."

"You should have known I'd be fine," Autumn said.

"I know you think you're next to invincible."

"Didn't you see the red S on my undershirt?" Autumn joked.

"And in the movies, the superhero's sidekick usually survives," I threw in.

"Usually is the keyword."

Back at Jack's, Jeff was showing Yvonne how the computers and videos worked. She seemed very attentive. I wouldn't have put it past her to be a baby genius.

She ran and hugged me when she saw us.

"You're heroes," Jeff said.

"What?" I asked.

"I was looking at some of the independent media and they were talking about how brave you were to get that footage. They are calling for a Congressional investigation."

"Do you think they'll get it?"

"Our government has funded people in Ukraine who have swastikas on their arms and it didn't mean a thing to the members of Congress. After *Collateral Murder*, they went after Assange and Snowden, not the men who shot the reporters and kids in Iraq and laughed about it. So, what do you think?" Jeff pointed out.

"Some of those locked up in the meadow were journalists."

"What about California's involvement? How many people died because of the Governor's plandemic policies and in spite of the deaths, they were still able to rig the elections to keep those mandates going. In short, nobody in office is currently going to care," Jeff noted.

"I think it's time we got this little one home and left the fighting to the big boys," Paul said.

"Misogynist," Autumn teased.

"Because I want to protect my favorite three women?"

"Because you won't recognize we can protect ourselves." She looked at Yvonne. "Well, maybe when she's older."

"I'd personally prefer that you two also wait until you're sixty-five to take any more chances."

"In case you don't remember, it was my brother they were holding prisoner."

"He's my brother, too, and I was sitting in front of a bunch of screens and speakers."

After getting home, we heard from Eric. Paul put his cellphone on speaker. "The General is calling in troops, including those who were relieved of duty for refusing the jab or failing to shoot 'enemy' children. Even though the jab-refusers were invited back, they're still angry. He's planning a military offensive to oust FEMA and arrest the participants."

"Will he be able to do that?" Paul asked.

"As long as he does it quickly. Right now, only a core group of us know what the plan is. He's going to bring in as many troops and tanks as he can before he announces the operation."

"What about other generals? Will the real army be fighting the FEMA army?" I asked.

"It's a possibility. But how many will go up against a four-star general, rather than asking questions?"

"Those who helped enforce the jab mandates," I guessed. "What about other locations?"

"The most active resistance is at Yosemite, but FEMA will likely just move its operations if we kick them out."

"I hate to be the bearer of doom and gloom, but is the General aware he could be court-martialed for this and lose his pension?"

"He's counting on video and social media to help him."

"It didn't help Assange or Manning," I pointed out.

"If they hadn't imprisoned Assange and cut his Internet, he would have exposed the plandemics, the global reset and this, too, years before they happened," Autumn speculated.

"Truth suppression is a top government policy," Paul noted.

"Court-martialing a four-star general is news. What are they going to tell the public? He was a bad man for not wanting to kill a bunch of American campers?" Autumn queried.

"What's our role to be?" Paul asked.

"Getting video out. They'll try to block as much as possible, but Jack plans to get around that. Paul, you will probably put together the best video from your cameras and cell footage."

"And what about me and Treasure?" Autumn inquired.

"You're going to supervise Paul and me."

"What about the rangers?" Paul was concerned about Grant.

"They'll do the follow-up after the military is finished. They'll also provide support. Several of the reporters want to go as embedded news."

"As long as it's a success," I warned. "Yosemite may be salvageable. If it's not, we may all wind up in indefinite detention."

"You two girls aren't alone in considering Yosemite the most beautiful place on Earth. There will be a lot of support for this mission," Eric assured us.

After the call, I decided to get Yvonne some fresh air. Paul and I took her outside.

"I know things have been chaotic since we've met. It won't always be like this," he assured me.

I smiled. "My life was chaotic long before I met you. This is a different kind of chaotic."

"Once we get through this, could you settle for a boring life that's full of nature?"

"I'd like that."

"You need some rest, Treasure. Autumn has already crashed."

"It's daylight."

"You worked through the night and so you need to sleep today."

I was pretty exhausted, but I didn't want to tell Paul. He was already too protective of me. I had mixed feelings about that. My new family was in a precarious situation and I wanted to keep them safe and protect their home.

I hadn't realized how exhausted I was as I laid down and dozed off.

Paul brought me a tray of food. I sat up for dinner, only to discover it was breakfast food. "Breakfast for dinner?"

"You slept through the night," Paul said. "You needed the rest."

"How is everyone?"

"Grant and Autumn are playing with Yvonne. Any military action has been put on hold. There is a hearing on injunctive relief tomorrow."

"Where?"

"It's being heard at the federal district courthouse in Fresno."

"Better Fresno than Sacramento."

"The federal system is better than the state court system. Lifetime appointments are less susceptible to the political climate and big money financiers, giving the federal judges more courage. We had a federal magistrate in the Valley. He disappeared and is supposedly on vacation. That courthouse is closed. The rangers will be joining us in Fresno and we'll be showing video. I'd rather you didn't testify to authenticate your video. Once you go on record, you're more likely subject to attack."

"Is that any worse than the hate my sister feels towards me?"

"FEMA is more deadly. I wish I could do something about your sister. I'd like to go drag her over here to apologize to you."

I hated myself for bringing up my sister again. I sounded pathetic and repetitive, but I couldn't get the pain out of my system. No matter how good my life was here, losing Tatiana kept eating away at me. Chest pains overtook me as I thought about her. I tried to hide them at first. My breathing felt erratic.

Paul knew something was wrong. "I want you to lie down. I'm taking your blood pressure."

He didn't look happy when he saw the results. "Do you know your resting pulse is above 120. I'm going to do some bloodwork on you and put you on an IV."

"It's probably nothing."

"It's stress and it's all related to that jerk you call a sister. I'd like to go over there and pound her head."

I laughed, knowing he was exaggerating his feelings. Paul was the most non-violent man I had ever met.

"I'll be happy to watch my niece." Autumn smiled. I'd worried her too, the last thing I wanted to do.

"She's not your niece," Paul reminded her.

"But you and Treasure are going to adopt her, aren't you?"

"Don't say that to Yvonne. Her goal is to get back to her parents."

"But," Autumn didn't say anymore.

My canine rescuer came into my room. and curled up against me, licking my face.

Paul checked my pulse again. "That's helping."

That afternoon, Autumm pulled out some cartoons of *The Flint-stones* and *Dinosaurs* to show to Yvonne and me while Paul repeatedly checked my blood pressure.

"Just don't show her the series finale of *Dinosaurs*," Paul advised.

"It will teach her not to trust either the government, the media or the corporations," Autumn protested.

"She's three years old. She has a lifetime to learn that," Paul countered.

"I'm afraid she's learned too much already. Children, who have gone through tough ordeals, mature at a different rate than those who have sheltered lives," I said.

"I've seen that with Autumn. She handles it well, but she misses our parents. And you are wiser than most people three times your age. When I first met you, I had to keep reminding myself you were a minor."

"Really, you're too young for me," I teased.

"Cradle robber," Autumn commented, listening in on our conversation."

"I'm the baby!" Yvonne, engrossed in the show, shouted along with Baby Sinclare.

"I think the Baby is the smartest one of the lot," Paul remarked.

"I like Robbie," Autumn said.

After an early dinner, Paul suggested we get rest before the trip.

When I next woke up, Paul was sitting next to me. The blood pressure cuff was on my arm. "You are doing a lot better now," he said. "But you are still not out of the woods."

"No. I'm in a cave in the woods."

"I would advise against you going to the hearing."

"You know I have to be there."

"Jack and Jeff will be watching Yvonne. I can't talk Autumn out of going and Eric wants to accompany her. Your names will be on public record if you testify. I could use my own video and pix."

"Then they'd know you were monitoring the mountain and it might lead them to your home."

"Better that than losing you."

"You won't lose me. I'm feeling a lot better now." I was still hiding the feeling of tightness in my chest. *Nerves*, I told myself. The next day could make or end us.

CHAPTER 36

Before sunrise, Grant, Paul, Brady, Eric, Autumn and I left for Fresno in the ambulance. We had to be at the Robert E. Coyle Federal Courthouse at eight in the morning. Some of the other rangers took additional vehicles, as did a couple of the newsmen.

The judge had shortened the time for the hearing, which was a good sign. The attorneys for our side had worked quickly to serve and file the necessary initiating documents, exhibits, memorandum of points and authorities and proposed order.

Paul made me lie down in the ambulance. He wanted to attach another IV drip.

"Relax. I'm fine," I said.

"That's a matter of perspective. If the wolves hadn't found you that day you collapsed, you wouldn't be here. I felt like a heel for letting you go out after that."

"You couldn't have stopped me. I was worried about my sister and brother."

A new cell phone Paul had gotten me with my old number buzzed. This was the first call on that phone.

I answered. It was Tatiana. I sat up, feeling like I'd won the lottery.

"Hi. It's so good to hear from you. How are you doing?"

"Really well. I got a job offer from this place that is offering me three hundred K to start."

"That's wonderful. I've missed you. I made some new friends after I collapsed on the trail."

"Yeah. I don't have time for that. I met one of your friends and she's a jerk."

"She is really sweet. If you want, I'll take you both out to lunch or dinner."

"Nah. I'm just calling because I need some information from you for my new work form. They want to know the hospital I was born at and the attending physician."

"Usually, they don't ask for an attending physician."

"This one did."

"Also, I can get you references."

"You can email them and the doctor's name to me."

"I will."

"So, I have to go."

"Have a wonderful day. I love you."

"Bye."

Autumn was standing with her arms crossed. "Someone leaves you to die and all you can say is 'Have a wonderful day and I love you?'" She made a face as she spoke.

"What was I supposed to do? Burn bridges? Besides, I do still love her. I always will."

"With someone like that, I'd blow up the bridge and nuke the pieces."

"She called me. That's important."

"I heard Hirohito called FDR before Pearl Harbor."

"Really?"

"I don't know. It sounded good. However, FDR knew when and where the attack would be in advance and let it happen."

"Kind of like 9/11. No. That was different. An inside job."

"You don't believe Arabs who trained at U.S. Government facilities and couldn't fly a plane to save their lives walked through security with box cutters and hijacked a bunch of planes that did impossible and unscientific feats?"

I laughed.

"I'll have lunch with her if you let me demonstrate my Krav Maga."

"She's pretty strong."

"With all that weight?"

I felt bad about Tatiana's dramatic weight gain after she was in college. Tatiana used to be thin.

"Your trouble is you love too much," Paul said.

"Me? What about you with all the IVs and monitoring? Please stop worrying about me."

"I'll work on that if you'll work on putting yourself first."

"Treasure? Probably not happening," Autumn said.

"I'm supposed to do a declaration, aren't I?"

"Do you want me to read the declaration they have for you? We can wait until we get closer."

"Go ahead. Read it."

"*My name is Faithful Dover. I was visiting Yosemite on May 17th this year. I walked from Glacier Point to Yosemite Valley and saw bodies of people and animals at the Upper and Lower Pines Campground. I watched as the bodies were picked up, crushed and dumped in a mass grave in what used to be the Lower River campground.*

"*Later, I witnessed additional events of concern, the most notable being when I was flown into the valley on a helicopter with Congressman Sam Reynolds. After we got off the helicopter, individuals identifying themselves as FEMA shot and killed Congressman Reynolds, his assistants and members of his security detail.*"

"So, I'm skipping much of what I've seen?"

"We're just focusing on two egregious situations to grab their attention. We don't want to explain why you were there during the militia incursion or digging through the piles," Paul noted. "Also, too much information is confusing to judges, most of whom are selected for their lack of comprehension abilities."

I nodded.

"Unless the judge is totally bought off, you should be fine. Eric and Autumn and several of the rangers are submitting declarations which will back yours up and take the heat off of you, we hope."

"If the judge doesn't grant the preliminary injunction, we should string her up. I understand it's a she," Autumn said.

"I have to take off my shoes!" Autumn complained.

"You have to take off your shoes," the marshal insisted.

Autumn reluctantly took them off. She didn't have a driver's license with her, but she did have a fake photo school ID, which worked. I had to use my real license. Grant used his government ID and Paul and Eric used legitimate ones too.

"You turned eighteen a month ago," the deputy said, looking at Eric's license.

Paul gave a knowing nod.

"Why aren't marshals doing security?" I asked Paul.

"They're here. Evan says retired deputies have replaced most marshals on security duties at the federal courthouses.

We went up to the seventh floor, where we met with others in front of District Court Judge Gwen Holloway's courtroom. Autumn and I were wearing dresses and both of us had our hair up to try to look more sophisticated. We both signed numerous copies of our declarations. Declarations from Grant, Paul and Eric were already signed and attached to the paperwork that had already been filed.

Lee Lundon and Evan Long were the lead attorneys calling for the TRO. The government had brought out a team from the Attorney General's office, led by Deputy AG Jack Crooky. Our attorneys presented copies of the additional declarations and photographic evidence to the other side.

Evan advised us that the other side had waited until that morning to hand him the response. It included a newly created FONSI, a Finding of No Significant Impact on the environment.

"What does he call all the dead animals and people?" Paul reacted.

"We are introducing the evidence but necessarily, we are relying on more than NEPA for the injunction."

Lee advised us there would be a four-part balancing test that consisted of (1) the likelihood of success on the merits, (2) the likelihood of irreparable harm from the granting of the order, (3) the balance of equities and hardships, and (4) the public interest. All four of those should balance in our favor if the judge was reputable, but both our attorneys said that this particular judge's husband had invested heavily in defense contracts and too often judges follow personal interests, instead of the law.

Several cases were called before ours. In each of them, the judge gave deference to the government, ruling in its favor. I worried this would be a lost cause.

She called our case, read through the paperwork and looked at the photographs. I crossed my fingers.

Lee argued Yosemite belonged to the people and the government was the caretaker. It was required to maintain it in a way that did not damage it or harm the tourists, the wildlife or the land. Each day FEMA stayed in the Valley, more and more irreparable damage was being done to the park.

Crooky purported we did not have standing.

Lee argued that the rangers and visitors to the Park were directly affected by the actions of FEMA.

Judge Halloway made note of the fact that there had been no public hearings and that the FONSI had only been drafted that morning.

Crooky countered by claiming there had been a virus and FEMA was cleaning it up as an emergency measure. He added, "It was a matter of national security and FEMA's leaving would result in irreparable harm to the nation and to public health."

"What virus?" Evan asked.

"The latest variation of COVID."

Autumn whispered to me. "There was a report last night that the scientist who discovered the Tiger Virus was arrested for pornography. So, they're back to COVID."

"Then why isn't the CDC, rather than FEMA, monitoring the situation?" Evan responded.

The judge asked, "Is there a witness from the CDC, ready to testify to the nature of the virus or health emergency?"

"We can fly someone in," Crooky said.

"But, currently, there is nobody here to substantiate your case. And what virus required the shooting of Congressman Reynolds and his assistants? I have an affidavit from his doctor, stating he was in good health when he flew to Yosemite."

It looked good, but I wasn't holding my breath.

"We believe the video of the incident was doctored."

"Do you have proof of that?" the judge asked.

"We can have a video expert flown in."

"I see. Well, looking at the evidence, your reasons do not seem credible and I'm finding for the Petitioners."

I looked at Autumn. We were both controlling our cheers.

The judge continued. "I expect FEMA to immediately remove its operations from the national parks in question."

"Objection, your honor. I do not believe you have venue or jurisdiction and the Petitioners do not have standing."

"This is a federal district court and FEMA has set up operations in this federal district. It currently has an office in this federal district. Yosemite, where it has set up operations, is in this district and the rangers from Yosemite work in this district. This is the correct court. The rangers and the patrons of the park have a vested interest in the welfare of Yosemite and I rule they have standing."

"It will take some time for FEMA to exit the locations."

"I will give you until tomorrow."

"That is not possible."

"Arrange it."

CHAPTER 37

Outside, we were all hugging each other.

"The other side will likely appeal to the Ninth Circuit. A three-judge panel will make the decision there," Lee informed us. "And we can't count our chickens before they are hatched."

We went out to celebrate. Lee had handled a lot of successful federal actions before, as had Evan. But they warned us FEMA would do whatever it took not to comply with the order.

"At least we have standing and a preliminary injunction to throw them out," Brady said.

"But this is just a first step," Lee pointed out.

"Remember the Oakhurst militia massacre," I said. "Those running FEMA's operation are not sane."

"The militia handled it all wrong," Lee remarked. "They went in there without any authority against a superior force. What did they expect?"

"Part of the trouble was the primary leader of the militia attack was a FEMA agent," I noted.

"That also happened on January 6, 2020. There may have been more federal agents than visitors in the crowd entering the Capitol that day.".

"And the supposed insurgents that day were unarmed," I recalled. "The only one murdered was Ashley Babbitt, a former Marine, who was shot by one of the Capitol Police."

"A policeman who is being protected from prosecution and scrutiny," Lee noted

"I heard the conditions at what they call DC Gitmo were inhumane," I said.

"There was sewage running on the floor of the cells and guards regularly beat and maimed prisoners who were not even arraigned. Some were disfigured or disabled by the guards. The right to a speedy trial, the right to counsel and other rights guaranteed by the *Constitution* were denied to people who were just standing in the general vicinity of the Capitol that day and some people who weren't even there. Eventually, the prosecutions were shown to be an abuse of authority, but there are some who still believe an insurgency occurred."

"And without conscience, members of Congress defamed those poor tortured innocent prisoners over and over again."

"You're well informed, Faithful, or rather Treasure."

"I am actually a liberal from a Democratic background, but I know government oppression when I see it."

"A lot of liberals have joined us in protesting both sides of the aisle."

"One party with two names. The best candidates never make it into office or are attacked by their own parties if they do."

"As well informed as you are, I'm sure you know that voting doesn't count in America," Evan joined in the discussion.

"Not like it does in places like Venezuela, which has the most secure election system in the world. They use thumbprints to open their voting information. The computer prints out their votes according to their instructions and then they put the paper ballot into the box, and the vote is counted that same night."

"In the USA, the Democratic Party tries to say that only whites have identification and Blacks are too stupid to know how to get one. It's a totally racist position," Evan pointed out.

"I know. The DNC puts down Blacks while claiming to support

them. Think of all the Black businesses the DNC destroyed in the supposed BLM riots. What people don't know is it wasn't BLM but the DNC that was responsible for the riots. I saw the DNC take over the BLM rallies and turn them violent."

"A lot of people did, but telling the truth, even if the truth helps Blacks, is called racist or Russian," Lee said.

"This is a crazy world."

"I'd really like to suggest you look into getting a law degree."

"Me?"

"There are alternatives to the braindead law schools that are now churning out graduates who can't pass a dumbed-down version of the exam I took. Someone with your knowledge has an edge in passing the bar. Maybe I can assist."

"I'll think about it."

I looked at Paul. I hoped this wouldn't interfere with our relationship.

"I think I want to become a doctor," Autumn said. "I saw how they discredited the good doctors during COVID and the follow-up plandemics. Those who took bribes to kill patients prospered. I want to join the good doctors, license or no license, like my brother." She looked at Paul.

"Paul is a better doctor than all those who went along with the system," I acknowledged.

"These days, a medical license is a license to murder. The good doctors are mostly losing their licenses," Evan remarked. "Don't tell the bar I said that."

"They need an alternative to the AMA."

"They have the American Association of Physicians and Surgeons. That's an organization that supports quality medicine. Paul, with your medical skills, you should become a doctor as well. You and your sister can open a practice," Lee suggested.

"I'll think about it," he said.

Somehow, I sensed he was happy at Yosemite. I wondered if he thought ambition would change me or his sister. What I most wanted was to be by his side. He was my hero. But I also knew I needed to do more or I'd quickly become boring.

On the way back, I asked Paul. "Do you want to become a regular doctor?"

"At this point, I'd rather become a veterinarian. Some of the vets are worse than doctors when it comes to killing patients without conscience."

"We can still practice together. I do the people and you do the animals," Autumn said.

"Do you want to become an attorney?" he asked me.

"Only if it doesn't take me away from you."

"I don't want to hold back your career."

"Lee said there were alternatives if I wanted to go into law. Right now, I don't want to become as uneducated as Berkeley made my sister."

He nodded.

"I love you and nothing is more important to me than you," I said.

He kissed me. "You're everything I want. And once you're part of the Bar, you can open your office anywhere. The state courts are mostly doing Zoom hearings these days. We can have it all and each other too."

As we passed Fresno and stopped for gas, I heard Brady say, "Holy!"

I got out to look. There were trucks, a dozen of them, unmanned with stacks of robotic dogs.

CHAPTER 38

Eric sent an alert to Jack. "Those could be trouble."

"Especially if they can shoot guns and conduct surveillance," Brady said. "I've heard of those attacking people at the border and elsewhere."

"The General wouldn't have sent for those, would he have?" I asked.

"The first truck was labeled Homeland Security."

"Maybe some of the ranks were tired of imprisoning and killing Americans. They had to call in the robodogs."

"Not a problem," Eric said. "I've got a plan. Quick, catch up with them."

We jumped back in the ambulance as Brady ignored any speeding limits.

"Do you have your EMP generator?" Autumn asked.

"I don't want to disable our vehicle. Pass them."

Brady did just that. Two of the dogs went into action, jumping on our vehicle.

"Autumn, don't!" Eric reacted as she leaned through the window with a gun she'd picked up in the first battle. Before she fired, Brady pulled in front of the trucks as a Hummer passed us going the other way. Brady spun around and the dogs fell off.

The front of the convoy crashed into the Hummer. The line of trucks piled up and exploded as debris blew all over the road behind where our vehicle had spun. On the other side of the road, the General and a couple of his men were getting off the ground.

Autumn took aim at the two robotic dogs that had fallen off the ambulance as their guns turned towards us.

"Stop," Eric called as he rushed to her.

Autumn ignored the request and blasted one as he grabbed her gun.

"They're deactivated," he said. The one not hit wasn't moving, though its gun was still pointed in our direction. He went over to it with a miniature tool kit. "These may be armor-plated, but DHS would want access to reprogram them if necessary." He started to remove a small metal plate on the back side.

"You called for help?" the General asked.

"How did you get here so fast?" Brady responded. "And what caused the explosions?"

"Grenades. We don't want any troop-replacing robotic dogs joining us. That's not bigotry. It's common sense and job protection."

"They may be traveling on other routes too," Brady said.

"We've been picking up the transmissions. We knew about the convoy before we got Jack's call. Thanks for the confirmation. This was the first group and we're prepared to terminate any additional ones they send our way."

On the way back, I asked Eric, who was looking at a tiny disc, "Didn't the EMP destroy what's on that?"

"I can restore it and use it to analyze the programming. It will make it easier to set up a barrier against these things or turn them against FEMA if they dare to send more."

When we got back to Jack's, I figured we'd get some rest. But instead, we had a celebration.

"What are the plans for the military?" I asked.

"More and more of the General's men and women are arriving in the Grove every hour. Their goal now is to enforce the court order."

"Unless it's overturned," Paul warned.

"We need to act before it is," Jack advised.

"Does the federal government actually care about the law? And if they are kicked out, won't they just regroup and return?" I hated being the voice of doom, but it seemed likely.

"Not if the military stays," Jack said.

Yvonne woke up and hugged me. She was becoming more and more relaxed. She still missed her parents, but she spoke about them less and less. That didn't mean she wasn't thinking about them.

"Tomorrow, would you like to go home and ride the horses again?"

"Yes, yes!" she said.

I held her until she fell asleep, again.

I reflected on my call from Tatiana. She only ever called me when she wanted something or for me to be a sounding board and the rest of the time, I never heard from her.

"Real family loves forever. Anyone who would desert a relative was never family in the first place," Paul said as if reading my mind as he and I took a walk outside.

"You should have seen Tatiana when she was a little girl. She was sweet like Yvonne. Where did I go wrong?"

"It wasn't you. I've looked into abuse and when there is an abuser in the family, they generally have more of an impact on children than those who love the kids. Tatiana just picked up more from your dad than from you and your mom. There was nothing you could have done to prevent it."

"I keep feeling that if I had done something different."

"Given her less love? Maybe things would have worked but that isn't who you are."

As much as I would have liked to have gone back in time and changed things, I knew I couldn't have handled that approach—even if being cold had made her gravitate more to me.

"One day, we'll have kids of our own and we'll teach them all about love."

"What about Yvonne? What do you think will happen to her?"

"I'm not going to leave it to CPS to traffic her if her parents are gone. Maybe Lee can help us."

"You mean adopt? Make her our daughter?"

"Or at least her guardians until some family member can be found."

"I love her."

"I love her, too. You are already mothering her. Autumn is acting like an aunt. Yvonne has a ready-made family. Even if she finds a real family, she'll remember the love we give her."

I smiled and kissed him. Kissing him still made me tingle, feeling like I was in heaven. I hoped this sensation never ended.

Paul and I were exhausted, but Autumn and Eric didn't look ready for sleep. They were still out walking in the moonlight.

"It's amazing how everything turned out. You and me, Eric and Autumn," I said.

"Just so long as Eric doesn't hurt my little sister."

I hugged him. "Always the protector."

"Autumn's only seventeen. I'd like her to meet other boys, make sure of what she wants."

I hadn't been with other boys, either—except as friends. I didn't need to meet other guys to know what I wanted.

We took Yvonne, Autumn and Grant back to the cave where Paul planned to monitor the evacuation.

The next day, we watched as tanks and men streamed into the Valley.

"It looks like they're really going to move out," I said. "But why tanks, instead of trucks?"

"That concerns me as well," Paul acknowledged.

Rangers, servicemen and servicewomen drove to the Valley to ask if FEMA needed assistance leaving. Some of the embedded reporters were with them as well.

Autumn and I wanted to see what was happening. We took the Four Mile Trail to the base of Sentinel Rock over Paul's objections.

When we got there, General Hatfield and Brady were arguing with someone who appeared to be in charge. That's when FEMA brought out water cannons and dogs.

"You think you can scare us off?" the General asked.

The next spray wasn't water. The stench was sickening, but I couldn't place it. Men started screaming, "Sulphuric acid."

Several men fell and writhed on the ground in pain as others tried to block the flow and pull the injured back.

Bullets started flying and the General and rangers took refuge behind their vehicles.

The military started using its own tear gas. The situation was a toxic mess.

That's when FEMA countered with gasoline hoses. I could smell the noxious fumes. "One match and the entire place will go up," I whispered to Autumn.

As if hearing me, FEMA followed with flame throwers. Several servicemen caught fire, as well as trees. Yosemite might never be the same again.

It was hard to tell who started the next round of shooting, but at the end, through the clouds, it appeared men from both sides had fallen as fires burned. I prayed the fallen would survive and the flames wouldn't spread. The military, rangers and news crews retreated, carrying their dead and injured.

"Brady and Grant?" I asked, trying to clear my vision.

"They're okay," Autumn said. "The military took the worst of it."

Autumn and I turned to go back up the mountain and were stopped at gunpoint.

CHAPTER 39

It was the National Guardsman whose head and neck had been smashed as he had tried to help Eric with the ambulance. I didn't know how he had gotten back to Yosemite this fast, but we were now in trouble.

"I understand you saved my life," he said to Autumn.

She nodded.

"They said someone had provided some medical treatment to me before you dropped me off. I was told his treatment was what saved my life."

"That was Paul, my brother," she said.

"You weren't really on an official mission, were you?"

"What makes you say that?" she asked.

He tilted his bandaged head to the side.

"We had word a good friend was killed and we wanted to see for ourselves," I explained.

"You were here illegally?"

"Autumn and Paul saved your life. Are you going to get us killed or worse?"

He slowly shook his head. "I need to find out what is going on here. I think we may be on the wrong side."

"You are. FEMA has poisoned the valley and killed a lot of people, including a Congressman. They held a four-star general prisoner along with his troops. FEMA is defying an injunctive order stating they have to leave," I informed him.

"And I have just your word for it?"

"We're telling you the truth. Look at the fires. Video of the murder of the Congressman is online if it hasn't been taken down again. Also, the federal court order for FEMA to leave can be viewed online. We weren't the ones who hurt you. We don't want anyone hurt. Some of the militias are reacting violently because they watched their friends and relatives die. FEMA killed the people living in Sonora and they buried the Yosemite campers they killed in mass graves at the start of the operation. The piles are in what used to be the River Campgrounds. We need all the help we can get."

He seemed to be taking in my long spiel.

"I've seen General Hatfield on the news. He's led a number of military operations and today they were shooting at him."

"The other day, he was a prisoner in Ahwahnee Meadow."

"I can talk to some of the other National Guardsmen."

"It can be dangerous. The leader of the Oakhurst Militia was a FEMA agent. They have infiltrators everywhere," I advised.

"I'll talk to National Guard troopers I know and trust."

"How are you back here so fast?" I asked.

"I pushed to get back. I needed to know what was happening. The little bit I saw fits with what you told me. Until I came here, I never heard of FEMA having its own army. And we hear their troopers are being paid seven times the rate for their ranks."

"And willing to kill Americans for the big bucks," Autumn noted.

"How do we get in touch with you?"

"We're working with the rangers and the real military," I said.

"One of my brothers is a ranger. My other brother is a paramedic."

"He's the one who saved my life?"

"Yes."

"I'm Graham."

"Autumn and Treasure."

I was surprised. I almost expected her to give fake names as she had to Eric and Jeff.

After he let us go, we started back on the path. "We're on the same side. And he is kind of cute." She excitedly told me.

"You said the same thing about Brady."

"I really like Eric, but I am seventeen, going on eighteen. I'm not really ready to settle for one guy for the rest of my life."

"I get it. Until I met Paul, I felt the same way."

Back home, we did a three-way conversation with Jack, the rangers and General Hatfield.

"FEMA says they say they are standing their ground. They've filed an appeal," the General informed us.

"Wouldn't it be a writ?" I asked.

"Injunctive relief is an exception to the final judgment rule. However, they are required to comply, pending the appeal—unless they are granted a stay," Grant explained.

We contacted Lee and Evan and added them to the online meeting.

"There is no stay. I've asked the judge to hold them in contempt. They can be jailed for this."

"People were injured and killed," Paul said.

"And you say FEMA initiated the violence?"

"We just put up the video of their non-compliance."

"I'll seek some additional orders."

"Aren't they responsible to the President?" I asked.

"Have you tried to have an educated conversation with him?" Jack responded.

"Have you?"

"I don't think any of us can," Jack said.

"Who do you think is really running the country?" Brady asked.

"Deep State or Israel," Jack remarked.

"We seek him out," I said. "And get him to listen to us."

"If we could get near to him," Jack commented.

"I can," the General said.

"In the meantime, it's best to avoid violent confrontations," Lee advised. "We may have won yesterday, but, for now, stay out of the Valley. The principle of finality presumes a trial court's decision is valid unless overturned by a higher court. The fact that no stay was granted is a good sign."

Evan added, "If the other side had been granted a stay, we would have demanded a bond for their irreparable damage to the park. But it didn't come to that."

"The Ninth Circuit used to be more predictable. Now, it all depends on factors that aren't on the surface. For instance, do any of the judges regularly take their families to Yosemite or the other areas hit? The Bong Hits for Jesus case depended, not on the law, but on the private concern of the Supreme Court Justices for the future of the principal if they ruled against her," Lee advised.

We cut out of the chat. Paul started pacing. Jack called.

"What if they defy the order for years?" Paul asked.

"It's not this simple," Jack countered.

"What?"

"Local law enforcement and the syndicate threw FEMA out of the Tahoe/Stateline area and then Tahoe and Stateline both suffered a toxic bath. People on both sides of the border started dropping from they don't know what, not a cloud. The hospitals there got wiped too. Now, FEMA's back."

"What about Heavenly?" I asked. It was one of the South Lake Tahoe Ski resorts.

"It's summertime, but people in the resorts there died of unknown causes. Being indoors didn't help but soil samples haven't shown any poisoning at all. We don't know the cause at this point."

"Poison, sound waves, maybe this is about experimentation," Paul surmised. "We managed to get soil samples from Yosemite. There's a mild cyanide residue above the ground in the mounds, but not in the rest of the park. It's apparently more than cyanide that killed everyone but we haven't been able to analyze the deaths. They could have done something more subtle in Tahoe."

"You think they may have killed them with sound waves?" I asked.

"Or something that wouldn't last or stick to the soil," Jack replied.

"Yvonne was exposed after the fact to something that affected her panels and if I hadn't cleaned her blood, she wouldn't have made it. I'm still going to have to detox her regularly," Paul told him. "And whatever she was exposed to, I haven't seen before."

"They don't take any precautions or use any safe approaches. Gulf War Syndrome, resulting from vaccine cocktails. They didn't learn. They later mandated mRNA vaccines for the various plandemics to the forces, only to see jabbed personnel drop dead from heart attacks or crashing military planes. They don't think we'll wake up to them and they don't care what we know."

"Why did they use the visible poison cloud for Yosemite and not Tahoe?" I asked.

"They probably didn't think it through before the first few places they hit. They were hoping Yosemite's poison would dissipate. It would have been far worse for the land if they had dumped glyphosate or DDT."

"I can't help thinking, if the General hadn't been held prisoner, he and his troops might be beside FEMA against us in this," I remarked.

"That's likely true. He probably realized he would have been found dead of natural causes if you hadn't rescued him. But don't expect him to be grateful. The higher the rank, the more desensitized they are to death."

"The important thing is he's on our side," Paul said.

"For now," Jack replied. "If he were threatened with court-martial, he could switch. And don't forget Operation Gladio, where NATO set up covert armies across Europe to commit terrorist acts and false flag attacks. It's still alive and well. I don't think the General was a plant, but you never know."

"That's why we're not giving anyone our home addresses," Paul said.

"And don't think I don't know yours," Jack replied. "Lucky I'm on your side."

I turned to Paul. He kind of shrugged, maybe wondering if it was a bluff or hoping he could trust Jack.

"Do you think we can trust Graham?" I asked. "He's speaking to the National Guard troops to get them to switch sides."

"The feds are good at infiltrating. Pete, January 6, the fake kidnapping of that lockdown governor of Michigan."

"I remember that. Wasn't it feds who orchestrated and ran that whole fake kidnapping bit?" I inquired.

"Yep," Jack replied.

"I couldn't believe Whitmer was re-elected after that."

"Drop boxes and mail-ins."

"Of course."

I went into my room and laid down. Yvonne was sleeping on my bed. It was seeming more and more like home. There was a photobook on a shelf and I looked through it. It felt a little bit like an intrusion, even though this was now my room.

Inside were pictures of Paul's mother with Paul, Grant and Autumn. Many of them were in Yosemite Valley at Mirror Lake, Lower Yosemite Falls, Half Dome, Vernal Falls, and Emerald Lake. One showed Grant chasing Paul across the top of Nevada Falls and their mother chasing them both. They all seemed so happy together.

My mother had brought me, Tatiana and Zinney to Yosemite when we were young. It was her favorite place, too. She would tell me stories about the Firefall. She was the most amazing woman I had ever known, and I wondered how her life and our lives would have been different if my dad hadn't turned out to be so abusive. I kept wishing I could go back and fix things for Tatiana and Zinney.

I laid down and slept beside Yvonne. I hadn't realized I was so exhausted.

Everlove pushed her way into the room, followed by Esther. They both curled up on the bed with me and Yvonne.

Next I knew, I was dreaming about my mother.

"I'm sorry I let you down. I messed up with Tatiana and Zinney," I *apologized.*

"You didn't let me down. I let you down. I left you in a lion's den."

"It's not your fault. You were being beaten."

"She is not your responsibility."

"But I love her—no matter how she treats me. Do you think she will ever love me?"

"She'll have to grow up and get a conscience first. Then, she'll be capable of love. It's not on you to fix her. You did the best you could."

I woke up feeling as if I had spoken to my mom, but did I? I wanted so much to be touched by my mom, my mind could have created the conversation. The message was similar to what others were saying.

I got up and went for a walk. Several cars pulled up alongside me. They weren't FEMA vehicles—at least not official ones. That was a relief. Between the three cars, there were seven guys.

I recognized a couple of them from the audience at the town hall. One of them was Philip. Philip didn't look happy.

"Hi. We're making some inroads. We've got a preliminary injection," I told him.

Next, I saw some FEMA vehicles pulling alongside them and it looked as if a skirmish was about to break out.

A strange terror ripped through my mind. Something inside, I couldn't identify, told me to get as far away as possible.

I ran, tripping over a rock and falling to the ground.

A dark bag went over my head. All I could see was black.

CHAPTER 40

Was I going to be taken to one of the FEMA mounds or to a containment camp? I was roughly placed into a vehicle. If I hadn't passed out, I might have known something about where I was driven.

When I woke up, a blindfold was over my eyes, and I sensed I was in a dark room. I could feel the hardwood of the chair through my clothes.

Ropes prevented me from moving my hands much, but after a struggle, my fingers managed to reach into my pocket. My phone was still there. My last call had been to Paul. I hadn't yet set a password on this phone. I pushed the call button and hoped my fiancé would pick up.

I had GPS tracking off on my phone, but maybe I could get someone to tell me the location.

"Hey, where am I?"

Nobody responded.

I wondered if they were going to kill me. I needed to save my cell signal and battery. "What did you do with the members of the Oakhurst resistance? Are they in dark rooms too?"

I hung up. Maybe if Paul found out where FEMA took the resistance, they'd have a lead on where I was taken. There had been light in the enclosure where we had rescued Grant, but they could have cut the lights. *No. The smell in that compound was rancid.*

Hours seemed to pass. The lights were still out. "I have to go to the bathroom. You don't want me to pee in your chair."

No response. A while later, I heard someone come into the room. A cold metal spoon was put against my lips. I could feel warm liquid. It smelled like a tomato-based soup. I shook my head. I couldn't be sure it wasn't poison.

A glass with some kind of liquid was put against my mouth. Again, I refused, keeping my lips closed and shaking my head.

I could hear whoever was in the room move away. "Please. Where am I?"

There was no answer. I heard the door open and close.

I turned on my phone and tried to call Paul again. I didn't dare put it on speaker but hoped he was listening. "They tried to give me something to eat and drink. I don't know if it was poisoned or drugged. I assume it's FEMA. I saw their trucks. That nice guy Philip was standing there along with other militia men and I ran, like a coward. They were probably taken too." I turned it off.

I tried to stay alert. Maybe I could hear some clues. I heard nothing. I drifted off to sleep.

I worried about Yvonne. She had already lost her parents, probably, and her uncle, for sure. I didn't want to desert her too. It was such a short time ago I hadn't cared if I lived or died. When I collapsed on the trail, I wanted to die, though I wasn't okay with being ripped apart by wolves. At the time, it didn't occur to me the wolves would give me back my life and a reason to live.

Tatiana's last request! I hadn't yet followed through and now I wasn't going to be able to send her what she wanted. I should have done it immediately. Her last request and I was going to let her down. Guilt rushed over me.

At least, I wasn't being beaten or tortured. What did they want with me? Were they going to use me to get to my friends?

I thought about the poem, "The Highwayman." In that, Bess was tied up with a gun pointed at her chest as they waited for the Highwayman to visit her so they could kill him. The only way she could save him was to gain control of the trigger and shoot herself as he was about to approach. But when he thought about it, he returned because he would rather die with her than live without her. I hoped Paul wouldn't be that stupid if using me for bait was what they had in mind.

They knew who had filed affidavits against them. They knew Autumn, Paul and I had done so and they were undoubtedly out for revenge. Would Autumn and Paul be next?

I made another call. "Whatever happens, don't come for me. They aren't mistreating me and if they use me to entrap you, that's the worst that can happen. If they do, stay away."

I couldn't hear what Paul was saying. I knew he could amplify my voice and I was counting on that.

"If anything happens to me, tell Yvonne and Autumn I love them. I will always love you, Paul."

A couple of seconds later, a familiar voice said. "That's all we need. By now, he should have triangulated your location." Someone snatched my cell phone away.

"He?"

"This is payback for Pete and the militia. Soon, you and your gang of traitors will meet the same fate."

CHAPTER 41

"But it was Pete who was with FEMA. He was playing you. He admitted it. There's video."

"You think we believe that doctored video? I've known Pete for years. If he were FEMA, I would have known."

"He *was* FEMA and you should have known it, Philip. Some techie you are."

"We knew him. We don't know you, but we saw your results."

"I didn't tell you to plan a military-style attack. The government has arms you could never hope to parallel."

"You touting the government's ability?"

"No. That's just common sense. We got an injunction to stop them."

"And they didn't stop. How many others will you lead into a trap?"

"I didn't lead you into a trap. Why don't you help us legally fight FEMA? They were the ones who killed your friends."

"FEMA? They knew when and where we were coming. You and your friends betrayed us to them."

"It was Pete."

A hand struck my face.

"Well, at least you and your boyfriend will die together." I heard the door slam and some additional noises. I thought I heard another door in a different location opening and closing, but I couldn't be sure.

"Philip, it was recorded live. There was no way it could be doctored." But he was probably out of the room and not listening.

I had to get free. I struggled with my ropes.

I heard the second door open again. It sounded as if it were in the floor.

"I believe you. I'm sorry," a young voice I recognized said.

"Please, let me go. I have to stop them from harming my friends."

"It's no use. You can't get free and even if you could, you don't have enough time to find the bomb."

"There's a bomb? Please help me."

"I can't."

"Please."

I felt something cut the ropes.

"Run."

"I need to call my friends. I don't want them coming here."

"Calvin, where are you?" Philip's voice sounded distant and muffled. I felt the floor shake a little.

I heard Calvin run and the door he had come through close.

"What did you think you were doing?"

"Just looking."

I heard what sounded like a lock.

I started to pull off what was left of the ropes. That's when I heard it. Something ticking. *A bomb.*

I pulled off my blindfold. I had to find the bomb. If I left and Paul came, well, I couldn't let that happen. Better me than him.

I searched for the source. It was a clock. It wasn't a bomb. I found what I thought was a light switch and tried to turn it on, but the light or electricity was out. I felt around the room. I went to what I thought was the main door to the room and found something weighty attached to it and also to the wall on the side. I thought of movies where opening a door set off a bomb.

I figured they had left the building through the basement. There must be an outside exit from the basement. I felt around for another door. There was a carpet on the floor. I don't know why but I picked it up. There was a trap door underneath. I could feel it. I tried to pull it up. It was locked from the other side. I was trapped. I continued to feel around. *Shouldn't there be a window?* Everything was black.

I felt panicked, but I had to go past the fear to save my friends. I heard footsteps in the house. "Don't come here. Run. It's a trap! A bomb!"

But the footsteps continued. *If I open the door first, I can take the explosion if that is where the bomb is and whoever is approaching the room will be safe.*

Light rushed in as a blacked-out window broke and Paul jumped through it. There really was a bomb attached to the door.

"The door is rigged to explode. They must have exited the place through the basement," I advised Paul.

"I've got her," Paul yelled. He threw his coat over the broken window glass still in place and guided me through, picked me up and carried me away. Brady was waiting outside.

A minute later, we were all rushing away.

"Who was inside?"

"Grant and Jack."

An explosion blew the cabin into burning pieces.

"Grant and Jack!" I freaked.

"Here!" Paul called as I saw them outside running towards us through the smoke.

The cabin was flattened and the flames were shooting up. It was in a large clearing, surrounded by asphalt, an intrusion into nature. If there had been any wind, more than the cabin might be burning. But thankfully, there was no breeze.

"We decided to blow their trap for them with explosives of our own," Jack informed us.

"Was anyone inside?"

"I didn't see anyone," Grant replied.

"Calvin, the kid, was the last one in the room. I think he went out through a door in the floor."

"Well, let's hope he had a good escape route from the basement," Paul stated.

"We can't let a kid die," I said.

Paul shook his head. We sprang back towards the cabin. A secondary explosion knocked us down as it put out most of the remaining fire. There were burning embers and a crater where the cabin had been.

Paul picked me up. "You okay?"

"If he's still there, he's not going to make it," Grant said. "He's already dead or gone."

I didn't want to think of a kid dying. "He untied me. He was probably the one who tried to feed me and give me water. He believed me."

"There was an outside doorway to the basement. We looked down into it for you before we went in. Nobody was there," Grant informed me.

"They think we doctored the video. Even their audio-video guy, Philip, thinks we faked it. They want us all dead."

"Well then, as far as they are concerned, we are dead," Paul said. He was still holding me.

"It's no longer just FEMA we have to worry about."

"In a war, the innocent die. War is always bad," Paul lamented.

"Those were friends of the FEMA guy who tried to shoot you on the mountain?" Brady asked, catching the drift of my worry.

"Yes."

"I'm the one who shot him."

"It's not you they blame."

"Let's get back to Mariposa," Grant said.

"Say 'hi' to Autumn when you see her," Brady requested.

"I will."

After Grant and Brady left, I turned to Paul. "Is Autumn okay?"

"Well, Eric was going to bring her, but he had car trouble on the way."

"On purpose?"

He smiled.

"And they say women are devious."

"She was ready to take on both the whole militia and FEMA."

"I bet she was. Where is Yvonne?"

"With Jeff. He helped triangulate your signal. Your last phone call got us to realize we had to be creative in rescuing you. If they set a trap, it would also get you."

"So, you looked for the darkened window?"

"How many people paint their windows black with thick paint?"

"I love you, Paul."

"Not half as much as I love you."

"What's this not half as much? How do you know how much I love you?"

"You are even more beautiful when you give me a rough time."

I smiled. "I never thought of myself as beautiful until I met you."

"You are loved and not just by me. By Autumn and Yvonne and even Grant."

When we got back to Jack's, Yvonne was having a tea party with Everlove and Esther.

"You, Esther and Everlove are drinking tea?"

"Tea." She showed me the cups filled with imagination.

"May I have a cup?"

Yvonne pretended to pour tea into another cup. I put it to my mouth.

"This is the best tea I've ever had."

"I'm going to kill you!" came across loudly from the living room.

"Hi, Sis. Great to see you," Paul's voice responded.

"Were you in on this obscene crime too?"

Paul didn't answer.

"I hate both of you!"

I rushed out of the room and gave Autumn a warm hug. "I love you, Sis. I didn't even want Paul rescuing me."

"Martyr."

"I'm alive. Unfortunately, he refused to take my advice."

"Fortunately," Paul countered.

"Let's have an 'I hate men party,'" she suggested.

"Yvonne has the most delicious tea. We could drink to it."

We went to see Yvonne.

"By the way, Brady said to say 'Hi' to you. You are so popular with the guys," I said quietly, glad that Eric hadn't followed.

"Kill them all."

"Bullets or poison?"

"Electrocution."

"Well, there are enough electrical devices around."

"Fortunately, no five or six G," she noted.

"That's really good news. They believe 5G was the real COVID."

"I know."

"Why do you want to kill men?" Yvonne asked. Apparently, she heard our discussion as we entered the room.

"Because they are too protective. If they have their way, we'll live to be three hundred."

"Isn't that good?"

"Have you ever seen a three-hundred-year-old woman?" Autumn asked.

"I'm going to be ugly when I'm three-hundred?"

"No, you've got the lifetime beauty gene," Autumn replied.

"She's right," I threw in. "I saw the pictures in your mother's room. You, your brothers and your mom used to have a really good time in Yosemite."

"My dad did too. He's the one who shot those pictures."

"The government has no right to try to extinguish that beauty."

"No. They don't."

Jack came in. "They want us over at the Mariposa Grove for a pow wow. Paul says you've been through enough tonight."

"I'm okay as long as someone watches Yvonne."

"I go?" Yvonne asked.

"Not this time. We worry about you. We don't want anyone to hurt you."

"Someone want hurt me?"

"We're just afraid. When people have something they love, they are often afraid of losing it."

"You love me?"

"Very much," I said.

"I love you, too," Autumn told her.

"You need rest," Paul told me.

"I need to free Yosemite."

After fuming about it, Paul went with us to Mariposa. Yvonne stayed with Jeff.

———

They had built quite a fort while preserving the trees and as much of nature as possible. This was unusual for the army, which often simply plowed things under in their path.

The military personnel had just finished placing their own cameras overlooking the Valley. We looked at the locations on their chart. None of them were located where they could observe us entering the cave or Jack's place. However, the cameras would have caught all or part of the what, when, where and why of my kidnapping if they had been up earlier in the day. The military troops had decided to wire the cameras using long fiber optic cables so as to decrease the possibility of hacking.

General Hatfield pointed out, "Our honor is on the line."

"Have you been in contact with Washington?" Paul asked.

"The President is listening to all the warmongers and contractors now. I don't know that now is the time to tell him to can FEMA."

"Can't you be court-martialed for standing against FEMA?" I inquired.

"Nuremberg."

"It didn't help Chelsea Manning."

"I'm a general and I have tens of thousands of men loyal to me and even more that will assist when they hear my name. Nothing happened to Captain Tulsi Gabbard or General Wesley Clark after they stood with the water protectors against Obama's oil pipeline that threatened the Native Americans' water in North Dakota."

"True," Paul agreed.

"We're waiting for backup and the right moment to take the Valley."

"Timing is everything," Grant remarked.

"We're hearing the National Guard is mixed. Some will follow me and some will follow the looneys down in the Valley. I've said this before, but thank you for the rescue."

"It was our pleasure," I said.

"I'm going to take these two ladies for some rest." Paul pointed at me. "This one just survived a kidnapping and her health is very important to me."

"I guess you can take leave to protect your lady." The General smiled. "But I expect my men to be invited to the wedding."

"We can have it in Yosemite Valley after we throw the thugs out," Paul said. "Or sooner," he whispered to me, "If we don't want to wait."

"I'm still getting used to the idea I'm engaged," I acknowledged.

"Not having second thoughts?"

"Me? Disbelief but not a chance."

"Hi," a familiar face said.

"Graham," I responded. "Good to see you."

"You need to take sick time until your head and neck recover," Paul advised him.

"In an emergency?"

"Recover, so we don't have an emergency with you."

"Hi, Autumn," Brady practically sang. His face betrayed his enthusiasm over seeing her.

"Brady, have you met Graham. He was the National Guardsman that a thug from Sonora smashed and almost killed a little over a week ago," I said.

"Hi. Glad you made it and are on our side. You are on our side, aren't you?" Brady asked.

"I'm not on the side that's shooting at generals and Congressmen. I have over two dozen National Guardsmen with me." He pointed to a large tent with national guardsmen going in and out.

"Good work," Brady told Graham.

"You're a ranger?"

"Yes, sir. If they destroy Yosemite, that will put a lot of us out of work."

"Brady's in it for a lot more altruistic reasons than that," I told Graham.

The two men gently slapped each other shoulders.

"Good seeing you, Autumn." Brady looked as if he wanted to hug her but hesitated with Paul there.

"Likewise, Autumn," Graham said.

"Time for these two to get some R and R," Paul reiterated.

None of the men and women present were wearing masks. The person who was responsible for Paul's mother's death had been a violent masker. As protective as Paul was, I realized that Autumn and Grant were likely correct in withholding the truth from him, though I would have liked to have found out who pushed her. There is no statute of limitations on murder. It could have been a traveler or a local but whoever killed her was under the mass psychosis long after the plandemic.

I pulled Autumn aside. "Is the ranger who saw your mother pushed among the rangers here?"

She pointed to a man who was speaking with Brady. "Paul's got enough to deal with now."

"I wasn't going to say anything to Paul. I wanted to investigate."

"It would be poetic justice if the person was in the Valley when they dropped the cyanide or whatever."

"It would be."

"In addition to tourists, four of the rangers in the Valley disappeared that morning. Their families called and Grant said they didn't know what to tell them."

"How about the truth?" I asked.

"I agree. More public outrage might help. Maybe we could encourage those whose relatives were here and disappeared to sue the Government. With enough suits, maybe they will back down for financial reasons."

"I wonder if the prison camp in the Valley will also be used to lock up anyone opposed to laundering public resources to European Nazis, various wars or a certain Middle Eastern country," I remarked.

"Like the General? "

"Who would have the motive and authority to secretly lock up a four-star general? It wasn't like he was court-martialled."

"The President or someone high up under him or over him."

After Brady moved on from the ranger Autumn had pointed out, I went over to speak with the guy.

"Some time back, you saw someone push a woman off a cliff, killing her."

He frowned. "That was a terrible thing."

"What did the person look like?"

"Mostly, I remember that the person was masked."

"Was the person tall, short, thin, fat?"

"Medium height, slender with muscles, blonde hair, fair complexion."

"About your coloring?"

"Maybe a little darker."

"Did you notice the eye color?"

"No."

"Would you be able to recognize him if you saw him again?"

"Why do you ask?"

"I was wondering if one of the people who was lost in the Valley was the killer."

"In spite of good movie endings, killers rarely come back to the scene of the crime. Without a mask, I wouldn't recognize him. I understand a lot of those bodies were decomposed."

"Thank you for the information. I didn't catch your name."

"Garan."

"Thank you, Garan."

Some people had gone overboard during masking times, beating up unmasked people and trying to run them over with their vehicles. I was among those almost hit by a car. There were repeats of the insanity with some of the later orchestrated viruses. If the killer were in one of the areas hit by FEMA, he might have thought the mask would have protected him, though it wouldn't have. As Autumn had suggested, the person could be in one of the mass graves.

I went back to the General. "We could be taking on the wrong enemies. Which corporations made the most money off the funding you opposed?"

"Well, there are a number."

"Didn't Rockheap just buy a medical company that is currently pushing jabs on military personnel for the new virus? If so, wouldn't it have access to deadly toxins?"

"You saying we need to plan an assault on Rockheap?"

"If we could locate a paper trail and another honest judge, we might be able to find the underlying culprit."

"I'll look into it."

I went over to Brady. "Thank you for being part of my rescue. That's getting to be a habit."

"No problem. Did you tell Autumn I was there?"

"I did. She's upset she wasn't."

"She's got guts. She'd make a great ranger if there are still any parks when this is over."

"Hey," Paul said, walking up.

"I was just planning an illicit meeting with your fiancé," Brady teased.

I laughed.

"I was just planning an illicit breaking of your skull," Paul teased back.

"I may have to take you in for a threat of that nature."

"You two are great," I said, still laughing. "Even at a time like this, you keep your sense of humor."

"We could get all depressed but that wouldn't help anything," Brady pointed out.

Eric was showing Yvonne how to use a keyboard when we returned.

"Before anyone tries any more kidnapping or bombing attempts, I'm taking you, Yvonne and my sister home."

"And then you're locking us up?" Autumn asked.

"You've already proved that's pointless. I may get the wolves to hold you down."

I smiled as Autumn said, "I think Everlove's on my side."

"We'll see."

At home, we watched the original Jack Reacher movie. "Imagine if this whole thing was about getting one person," I said. "Who would that be?"

"The Governor's competition for the next Presidential race? After all, if the Governor owns all the land in the state, he can disenfranchise his opponent by removing his home," Paul pointed out.

"Homeless people can vote by listing a street corner," I noted.

"But homeless politicians generally don't win."

"The candidate could move to another state and run from there."

"After being called a financial disaster—come to think of it, Trump went bankrupt before he was elected. I don't think that's what we're dealing with here. I think it's the Pharma-Military Industrial Complex. They've proven to be more Machiavellian than Machiavelli."

"I think you're right. Years ago, Trump was going to pardon Snowden and Assange. Then he backed down on all his promises and became a vaccine salesman."

"I didn't vote for him, but his promises would have been a reason to do so if I had," he noted.

"I heard he was threatened into not following through with the Assange/Snowden promise. That threat would have been from the PMIC, the Pharma-Military Industrial Complex. More and more. I think we need to infiltrate Rockheap."

"How?" Paul asked.

"They need good computer programmers. Could Jack get some credentials?"

"For me?"

"I was thinking about for himself."

"Because he's unattached?"

"Because he could break into the computer network and maybe ferret out information."

"Locally? From one of their facilities?"

"It might be easier than breaking in remotely. And it's less illegal if he's an employee."

"It's still illegal. He'll need a top degree from MIT."

"Then someone has to break into their records," I suggested.

"My sister's rubbing off on you. You're becoming a schemer."

"Maybe that's the real me. I guess I have a downside when those I love are threatened. Sure you still want to hang out with me?"

"Always."

"Wait. You talking about getting Eric an MIT degree so he can infiltrate something?" Autumn asked, joining the conversation.

"Not Eric. Jack," I replied.

"Oh."

"You sound disappointed."

"I was thinking the two of us could do it together."

"Good reason to use Jack," Paul replied.

"Don't underestimate Eric."

"Jack has been waiting to take down Rockheap for years."

CHAPTER 42

The next morning, Jack dyed his hair black and shaved as he and Jeff prepared to drive to Fresno and fly to Boston.

Paul and Eric planned to monitor things here while they were away.

Jeff was going to help fix the college records and then pretend to be a headhunter who had found the perfect job candidate.

"With all the student techies, you think Jeff can pull this off?" I asked Paul.

"Jeff has incredible skills," Autumn said. "Do our allies in Mariposa know our plans?"

"Rockheap provides a lot of military equipment," Paul responded.

"And you're afraid the General could sell out," I guessed.

"It's hard to know who to trust. I don't even trust all the rangers."

"The rangers?" I asked.

"Nobody is above taking a bribe or selling out."

"I trust you, Autumn and Grant," I told Paul. "There is no way you'd sell out."

"Let's see. If someone offered me a million. Nah," Autumn remarked.

"And you," Paul said.

"Me?"

"You're trustworthy, too."

"I trust Eric and Brady," Autumn said. "Hey Paul, you are worried about me and Treasure getting into trouble, here. How about sending us with Jeff and Jack? We'll be miles away from Yosemite and we can't get into much trouble in a hotel room."

"I know you, Autumn."

"What? Do you think I'm going to blow up the hotel?"

"If it gets you away from here. Okay."

"You leaving?" Yvonne asked as Grant prepared to take me and Autumn to Jack's.

"Just for two or three days. You'll be the lady of the house and Paul and Grant have promised to make sure you have fun."

"Fun."

"It's a requirement," Paul said.

She gave me a big hug.

Massachusetts Institute of Technology was in Cambridge, Massachusetts, close to Harvard. We had reservations at the Parker House Hotel in Boston, the city next door. The hotel was built in the nineteenth century, but the rooms were actually quite nice. Jeff and Jack rented a car. Eric had wanted to come along, but Paul and Grant vetoed the idea. "No boyfriends on this trip."

"You plan to break into the school computer tomorrow and insert a drive. The best way is to do it while everyone is distracted, correct?" Autumn asked as we arrived at the hotel.

"Paul will kill us if we involve you," Jack replied.

"We won't be involved in the hacking. We're just going to ask a bunch of questions to whoever is supposed to be their lead techie. After all, we might decide to go to school there next year."

"That could be helpful," Jeff said. "But if you tell Paul you did it for us—"

"I know. He's very protective."

Eric had helped by researching information on the university's administration and data personnel. His research revealed that Gary Lamb was the main tech for the school data system. He had looked at posts by Gary and reviewed the system being used.

"I'm familiar with that system and I know a backdoor to get around the login. I can easily add the information to the system," Jeff proposed.

Autumn and I went into the records section of the Admin building. There were two clerks in the office, a male and a female, inputting information into two desktops. Autumn frantically implored, "You have to help us. Some guy has been following us and I don't think he's a student."

"The security office is—"

"I don't want to go over there alone. Is there someone here who could help us?" Autumn almost started crying.

"We could call our uncle, Earl Hamilton. Maybe he can come and help us," I suggested.

In checking the information of the school, we had found that Hamilton was a big donor. Jeff had learned that Hamilton was out of town and that he had a brother with three daughters. I hoped the clerks hadn't met the nieces.

"I'll take them," a male clerk said.

"I'd feel better if there were also a female with us. Uncle Earl told us to always be careful," I related.

"But a female clerk doesn't provide enough protection," Autumn said. "I think we should just call Earl."

"We'll both take you, but it better be fast," the female conceded.

They escorted us out. The woman turned the locking mechanism on the door and started to close it.

"I think I left my purse inside," Autumn said, pushing past her back into the office. On the way out, she surreptitiously put tape across the doorjamb and pulled it closed while I questioned the two personnel about how often this sort of thing happened on campus.

"Is it still locked?"

"It is," Autumn said. "I checked it. But my purse isn't here. I must have dropped it when we ran away from that guy."

"Maybe you can help us find it—if he didn't snatch it," I suggested.

As we walked away from the door, I noticed Eric and Jack coming from the other direction towards the office.

"I don't know why you are insisting on MIT," I told Autumn. "This place is so insecure. Just because Uncle Earl is a big donor. When he hears about what happened—"

"So, you are looking into going here?" the woman asked. "My name is Charlene and I highly recommend it. This sort of thing doesn't normally happen here."

"He said merit counts here and going here is better for our career," Autumn countered my comments.

"I'm more likely to make President if we go to Harvard. Look how many past Presidents went to Harvard."

"Girls, would you like to know more about this school? What were your SAT scores?"

"I thought you had stopped looking at those," I said.

"She is 2398 and I'm 2400," Autumn said. "My sister is just mad that she got a lower score."

"I think they misgraded my test. I'm smarter than you."

The Dean walked up and Charlene introduced us.

"I personally think you girls would be well suited for MIT," the Dean said, greeting us.

"Maybe the three of you could personally show us around the campus," Autumn requested.

"We need to get back to the records office," the female clerk said.

"Is it locked?" he asked.

"It is. But what about your purse and the guy who was following you?"

"Someone was following you?" the Dean inquired.

Autumn nodded.

"We have video cameras. Let's go take a look."

Autumn started to faint as I caught her. "I'm so dizzy."

"Oh no," I reacted. "She's diabetic, but we don't like anyone knowing."

"Do you have insulin?" The Dean asked.

"I think I overused it. I need some sugar," Autumn groggily replied.

I noticed Jeff and Jack leaving the building. "I'll get her back to the car. We'll be back later when she's better."

"Do you need some help?" the woman asked.

The Dean had his phone out. "I'll call the paramedics."

"I can help my sister. We don't want this getting out."

"What about that guy?" the woman inquired.

"I think having you with us just now scared him off."

"Your purse?"

"I'll call tomorrow if we don't find it. It's blue and white leather. I've got to get her to the car. Thank you."

As we entered Boston, we noticed a police car was following us.

"You think we were caught?" I asked.

"We also disconnected the university's video system and erased recent video files. There's no evidence," Jeff assured me.

The car continued to follow us. Jeff made some turns and the officers went straight.

"The backdoor worked?"

"One of the clerks didn't log out. Super easy. Now, to get back to the hotel. It's half a mile away. But all these roads are one way, the wrong way. I guess we can turn away from the hotel and maybe we'll go back there after we circle the city. That may be the fastest route."

The turns were more dizzying than Autumn's act. "Now we're five miles away from the hotel... This road goes the right way...Now we have to turn in the wrong direction again."

"Didn't we leave MIT at noon?" Autumn asked.

"It's only seven in the evening," Jack said.

"But it was only a two and a quarter mile drive," Autumn pointed out.

"My phone's mapping system doesn't know how to get back to the hotel either," Jack said. "I've got a device that's hackproof but it's lost, too."

"Finally," Jeff sounded relieved as we arrived at our destination. "I can break into computers but manning the roads in Boston is for a different type of expert. I wonder if the restaurants are still open in the area."

"With these roads, I'm sure a lot of people are eating dinner after midnight," Jack said.

The next morning, as we prepared to go to the airport, Autumn said, "I'll drive."

"We already had the rental company pick up the car," Jack replied. "We're taking a taxi so we don't miss our plane with these one-way roads. The last thing we need is to drive around Attleboro on the way."

"Where to next? Their main headquarters is in Bethesda, Maryland," I noted.

"Did you know Rockheap has been sued multiple times in different locations for toxic waste?" Jeff asked.

"Okay. Are we going to one of those places?"

"They recently purchased a new chemical company in Palmdale."

"We're going back to California?"

"It's miles away from Yosemite."

"Yeah, but Palmdale is in the high desert and very boring," Autumn disparaged.

"You can hang out in the hotel. Stay safe for once. We reserved a multi-room suite at Executive Inn."

"I thought Jack was going to be the candidate," I said as we got to the room.

"We figured Jeff looked more the part. I'll be working things from the room," Jack responded.

Using a new burner phone, I called Rockheap. "I'm Samantha Brown and I'm a recruiter with Top End Tech. I understand you have an opening for a senior project leader and I've got the perfect candidate for you."

"Where did you hear about us?"

"We have access to a lot of job openings that don't make LinkedIn or Indeed. This professional is in demand, but I thought Rockheap would be a better fit."

"Have you worked with us before?"

"Not with your Palmdale office. But I was speaking with Dan, your national director over lunch the other day and he said that I should consider candidates for your office. Of course, that lunch was kind of confidential—if you know what I mean."

"I see. In that case, what's his background?"

"This candidate, Parker Moore, graduated from MIT at the top of his class and was then hired as a professor. He has a double bachelor's degree in chemical engineering and IT, and a masters in IT. He specializes in building websites for scientific projects. One of the other offers he had was from a top government agency analyzing chemical spills."

"Excellent."

"I'll have him bring a list of his positions, but for now, you can contact MIT."

I hung up and turned to Jeff. "You taught at MIT?"

"That's what the records show," Jeff said.

"I'm impressed."

"It's amazing how fake credentials can be much more impressive than the real thing."

"The hiring director is probably checking out that fake headhunting company I hit him with."

"It's not fake on the web," Jack said. "I put up several articles praising their work and recruitment successes last night. Since practically everything real is censored, those articles will appear high on the search."

"Now all I need is to get in the door. If I get access to a high-level computer, I have a flash drive with a program that bypasses their protection and hacks into their servers. It should record what chemicals they are using and if they're involved in operations in Yosemite and other National and State Parks," Jeff explained.

"If you don't take a job, won't you be a suspect?"

"It could be that the job is not up to his standards," Jack said. "They often listen in on phone calls. I'll call him on their phone after he arrives to let him know that there is an offer at Raykillon at high six figures plus an unlimited expense account."

"And the program I'm inserting will erase the traces after it downloads the information."

"So, they won't know who nailed them?" I asked.

"That's the upshot," Jeff related.

"What if they see you?"

"Then, I'm in trouble. "

"I have a robocall program that will tie up their phones with fifty different initiating numbers to distract them after my call. You'll have to act fast, Jeff."

"So other than waiting for a call back for the interview, what can we do?" Autumn asked.

"How about you do a blog, praising your MIT colleague Parker Moore? He received several honors from the university last year, according to their records."

"Did you also fix the California DMV records?" Autumn asked. I knew Jack had faked her out-of-state license.

Jeff pulled out his Parker Moore driver's license and fake Social Security card.

"They won't run his Social until HR finishes his paperwork."

"What about references?"

"We are listing several pro-war Congressmen from out of state. Do you know how hard it is to reach members of Congress for references and how long it takes? Most corporations won't even call when the contacts are that high level."

"You forget Rockheap has lobbyists in Washington."

"And much more important things to speak with members of Congress about than employee references. Most public figures won't say they don't know applicants, as they'll have to check to see if it's the son of a donor. They'll play along."

"Nice."

The burner phone rang. I got into character. "Hello. Top Tier Tech. Samantha Brown."

"We would like to see Parker Moore tomorrow morning at eight A.M."

"Oh, let me look at the file. Yes. I believe Mr. Moore will be available tomorrow morning. He has another interview later in the afternoon and the next day, but tomorrow morning should work out for you."

"It may be an all-day set of interviews."

"Well, if your position looks promising to him, I will recommend he cancel the afternoon appointment. How many people will he be speaking with tomorrow and what are their positions?"

She gave me three names and positions that I wrote down.

"I'll have him there at eight A.M."

After the call, I informed him of what I'd learned. One of the interviews would be with a chemical engineer about various compounds. "I'd refresh my knowledge on the subject, particularly poisonous compounds, if I were you."

"I can research that tonight."

"You'll wear a wire and I'll go online to look up answers to any questions you might not know," Jack told him.

"The IT director for the plant will be the first interviewer."

"I should be able to handle that."

Jeff prepped himself on chemical compounds. It reminded me of the way I had sometimes studied for exams. Sometimes, last-minute cramming was better than keeping up with the assignments all semester.

Jack was prepared to help with answers. Jeff would be wearing a small, invisible hearing aid with a transmitter in his shirt, powerful enough to transmit the discussions to Jack. Jack had sites from MIT, Cal Tech and Johns Hopkins online in prep for answering questions.

"What if they have video that can record him putting the drive into the computer?" I asked.

"He'll have to be subtle."

"I can handle that," Jeff said.

"Fingerprints. If they find out you falsified your ID, they might check the computers for prints. They might check even if they don't catch you."

"Covered," Jack said. He held up a bottle of superglue. "No more prints."

"Let's hope it works," I said to Autumn as we went into our room.

"Do you just want to sit here? Jeff might need help or interference escaping."

"But we don't have a car?" I lamented.

"Leave it to me."

The next morning, about the time Jeff left and Jack was busy preparing the backup and hack in their room, Autumn and I were driven by a guy named Joey to Rockheap.

"So, your brother was poisoned by chemicals while working at Rockheap?" Joey verified.

"Yes. And it's so sweet of you to drive us there," Autumn said.

"Do you have a plan for getting samples?"

"We'll pretend we're from OSHA. That will give us access to everything."

"It's interesting that you say that. My dad is an OSHA inspector."

"Really. Do you have any cards of his?"

"I do. In fact, he left his ID at home and I was going to bring it to him later today."

Autumn had done her homework. The night before, we had taken a taxi over to a local OSHA office and followed one of the workers home. Then we followed a guy about our age coming out of his house and going to a coffee shop. We went in the door with Autumn crying. I asked the guy to help me calm her down, and out came the story about her brother and the guy's offer of help.

As we walked in the door at Rockheap, the first thing I noticed was that everyone was masked. I started subtly taking pictures with my cell phone. It was a long shot, but Laura's killer might be working for Rockheap.

"We need to make sure that all proper precautions are taken with respect to the chemicals they are working with," Joey told the receptionist.

"Clay Crawford?" she asked, looking at the ID Joey handed her.

"That's right. You can call OSHA to check on my credentials. Cindy and Charlotte are my assistants."

"Actually, we have the list of local OSHA personnel. I see your name is on it. You're younger than most of the OSHA agents who have visited us. Most visits last about ten minutes and then the supervisors take the inspectors out to lunch."

"And they got in trouble with the boss for that. This is just routine. If there is a problem, they'll probably send you a letter telling you to take extra precautions. No big deal." As this Rockheap plant was new, I figured they probably hadn't yet met the real Clay Crawford.

OSHA was one organization that often could get around the security precautions at most places during surprise inspections. Supervisors wanted to impress the inspectors with their openness and honesty, relying on distractions and bribes to cover up any threats to the safety of the workers. If Rockheap expected falsified reports after lunches, they could be lax, or they could simply have the dangerous chemicals mislabeled, figuring nobody would check.

The foreman, a guy named Ralph Hawkens, handed Joey six Dodgers' tickets.

"Oh, we love the Dodgers," Autumn said, enthusiastically. "We'll be sure to use these."

I knew that was to put the guy at ease about his bribe and the inspection.

As the three of us walked through the plant, I had baggies and gloves for use in picking up chemicals. "I can't recall the last time anyone checked the chemicals we picked up," Autumn said to Joey within the hearing of Hawkens. "I think they just warehouse them to say OSHA did its research."

"If we came back empty-handed, we couldn't justify our jobs," he replied to her.

Hawkens smiled as Autumn and Joey spoke.

We had picked up supplies the evening before. When some of the chemicals ate through the baggies, Autumn handed me some glass tubes and vials. I had lots of gloves, but I could hardly wait to wash my hands afterwards. I noticed a machine marked, "J35-OP N. Pks."

"Distract him," I whispered to Autumn.

She pretended to trip over nothing. "What is this? I think the floor is uneven." As she and the others were checking it out, I hightailed it over to the machine.

An operator asked what I was doing.

"We're ordered to take a sample. I held out a vial and he helped me fill it."

"Where did you go?" the foreman inquired when I came back.

"Looking for more uneven surfaces."

"It's not problematic enough for a report. I assume you haven't had any injuries from tripping," Autumn said.

"None, and we'll take care of it today."

"Good. So far, you're getting good marks on our report."

As the foreman continued guiding us around, I got a call on my cell from the vice president of Rockheap. "We want permission to run Mr. Moore's biometrics."

"That comes after he's hired—if he likes the position."

"What is this?" the foreman asked.

"This is a private call," I said.

"Private. Aren't you a headhunter?" the vice president asked. I had forgotten to mute the phone when I answered the foreman.

"Yes, but I'm out of the office right now attending to something unrelated."

The foreman looked oddly at me.

"Another inspection that didn't go as well as this one. We have to go," Joey said in response to the foreman's reaction. "We've got another appointment."

"I will call you back when I return to the office," I told the VP.

We hurried towards the door and a security guard blocked our way.

"I'm calling OSHA," Joey said.

"You do that. We'd like to speak to your boss."

I threw one of the vials in the guard's face. As he freaked and went to clear his eyes, Autumn knocked him to the side and we ran. I picked up the pieces of the vial to take with us. As we rushed towards the gate to get to the car, Autumn said, "The license plate."

"I'm not getting my dad into trouble."

We switched direction, ran towards the loading dock and jumped into the cab of a truck, whose driver was walking to the trailer, theoretically to unload boxes.

Joey instantly drove off before the driver could open the back. Another car took off following us.

"Does anything look familiar about those guys chasing us?" I asked.

"Hard to see, but it's them. FEMA," Autumn said.

"What's going on?" Joey asked.

"Lose those guys. They kill witnesses."

"Who are you?"

"We're working with the military and rangers and others to find out who killed thousands of people at Yosemite and at other national parks and resorts," I confessed.

"You faked me out?"

"Check it out. They dropped toxic clouds down and we wanted to get the chemicals. We think Rockheap may have been involved," I expounded.

He cut over a lawn, through an unfenced yard behind a house and onto another street. The FEMA guys followed.

My phone rang. "Top Tech."

"Treasure, where are you?" Jack demanded.

"Being chased by those FEMA killers."

"You're supposed to be at the hotel."

"Well, we spent our day collecting evidence, chemicals for analysis."

Autumn grabbed the phone and held it between us, putting it on speaker.

"Paul's not going to be happy."

"I'll say nice things at your funeral," she told Jack.

"Who will speak at ours?" Joey asked.

"I wonder what's in the back of this truck," Autumn pondered after Joey drove over a curb into another home lot, through garden furniture, and practically smashed the side of a house on the way out. We went through a fence and kept going.

"More chems?" I guessed.

That's when bullets started flying, hitting one of our tires.

CHAPTER 43

"This truck has eighteen tires. We're still moving," Autumn said. "I've got an idea that I've seen in the movies." She opened the passenger window of the cab and started to pull herself out and up.

"Your brother will kill me if something happens to you!" I followed her out onto the top of the cab, preparing to go onto the trailer.

The truck was zig-zagging to avoid being hit by FEMA's bullets. I fell flat on my stomach and held on next to Autumn on the cab's roof. We stayed flat as bullets bounced off the back of the trailer.

Our followers aimed higher, shooting closer to us, almost hitting Autumn. I tried to position myself between Autumn and the shooters, but the next bullet didn't come as a car crashed into the FEMA vehicle from the side. Then the car backed up and hit the FEMA vehicle again.

I heard a couple of shots and I hoped that our rescuer wasn't hit.

"Stop," Autumn yelled towards the driver's window. "We have to go back."

"And get shot?"

"A rescue for our rescuer."

Joey turned the truck around, almost flipping it and almost being hit by an oncoming car.

He raced back and slowed down to let Jeff and us jump inside. The

FEMA car had been knocked over on its side and the occupants were trying to get out through a car cover Jeff had thrown over it. I noticed the car Jeff had been driving had a completely smashed front end.

"Did you blow your cover?" I asked Jeff.

"I don't think so. That wasn't my rental and those men weren't at the meetings. If they saw me there, they still might not guess what I was up to until it's too late."

"Too late for what?" Joey asked.

"For us to get the General and rangers the information on whether Rockheap was responsible for the toxification of Yosemite."

"You do know Rockheap has been sued for toxifying several sites," Joey informed us. "My father filed a report with OSHA on one of their other facilities and was told to stand down. He said the report disappeared."

"Figures," Autumn said.

"What were the chemicals? Does he have a copy of the report?" Jeff asked.

"They kill whistleblowers and witnesses," I pointed out. "We could put together a case for the judge if we could get to a private lab. As private citizens, acting on our own, we're not bound by the Fourth."

"I know a lab," Joey said.

"One that isn't connected to defense, pharma or Homeland Security contractors?"

"My uncle Ronnie has closed down a lot of plants on behalf of plaintiffs. He'll put what you picked up through his lab without mentioning the source. My dad will have to claim his ID was stolen."

"Let's go."

Jack met us over at the lab. He'd gone by Rockheap and picked up the real rental, which had been parked a block away.

Uncle Ronnie was a nice guy. "We'll list this as baby food company D. It might raise some hackles, otherwise. You've got quite a number of chemicals. It could take hours."

In looking through the truck, we found some boxes with more

chemicals, mostly powders but some liquids. We turned those over to Ronnie as well, hoping we hadn't made a mistake.

"Now that we've unloaded the truck, I'll take it elsewhere, like into the artificial lake," Joey said. "See you soon."

"He is rad," Autumn said. "I like him."

Jeff looked at her.

"I'm not going to date him."

"Did you notice all the masked employees?" I asked Autumn.

"That's normal," Ronnie said. "Rockheap has actually been hit with lawsuits over forced masking, and the ones they are requiring are worse than useless. You're lucky they didn't try to shove one of those on you."

"If these chemicals are what I think they are, the workers should have full body suits for their safety."

"When we finish the report, we'll supply it to OSHA and say it was from an anonymous source apparently working for the company as it was brought in on a company truck. We'll provide you with a copy as well."

That meant we had to stay an extra night at the hotel. Jeff, Autumn and I trashed our burner phones but kept the cards. Joey's dad, Clay, had heard from his brother that Joey had helped bring in some materials. We decided to have a pow wow with him for Joey's sake.

I started by showing videos of the Valley the day after the poison cloud had descended.

"You said cyanide but that looks more like white phosphorus."

"I don't think so. I was crawling around in it, thinking one of our friends had been buried and I didn't get any burns."

"If the white powder is anthrax, it would still have nailed you. I doubt it was that. But you may be right. The concentration of cyanide could have partially dissipated but not white phosphorus or anthrax. What do you do if the corruption goes all the way to the top?" he asked.

"Exposing it is the best approach."

"Remember Chelsea Manning, Edward Snowden and Julian Assange?"

"Kind of hard to forget."

After watching the videos and pictures of the shooting of the Congressman, Clay understood. "I knew that Congressman. In fact, I campaigned for him. And they just shot him down like a dog. I'll help in any way I can."

"It's not just Yosemite. They've nailed Sequoia, Big Sur, Sonora and a lot of other places."

"Sonora is a city, not a resort."

"That has us confused too. Also, people dropped from unknown causes in South Lake Tahoe and Stateline," I informed him.

"That could be from the food, water or a number of sources. Have they done bloodwork?"

"I don't know. And I've learned not to trust most doctors. The hospitals there were hit too."

"I can understand."

"Does anyone know if Rockheap was doing operations in Yosemite a year or two ago?" I asked.

"I heard they were planning to set up a plant somewhere in the area but it wasn't that long ago."

"How long ago?" Jack asked.

"About a month ago."

"Sonora or Oakhurst?"

"I don't know. Someone inside Rockheap would know that."

I was hoping Jeff had been able to download something relevant.

"You do know Rockheap has a lot of defense contracts. They made a lot of money off those hundreds of billions supposedly sent to Ukraine," Clay noted.

"We're well aware of that," Jack replied.

"Today was exciting. I'd like to join you for more," Joey said.

"I don't know all that went down, but you need to do high school and college, not risk your life, son."

"Life is dangerous," Autumn said. "It's how we handle danger that determines who we are."

"Do your parents feel the same?" Clay asked.

"My parents are dead," Autumn said.

"I'm sorry. Who has been taking care of you?"

"My brothers. One of them is a ranger and the other is a paramedic."

"The ranger works at Yosemite?"

I noticed this guy was getting a lot of information on Autumn.

"How about you? Have you ever been to Yosemite?" I asked.

"A few times."

"When I was inside, I noticed that everyone at Rockheap was wearing masks."

"And they've already had a judgment against them over forced masking," Clay noted.

"Your brother told me. How about OSHA? When you go out, do you generally wear masks?"

"Not for quite some time. They never did any good and we knew it. The surgical masks and even the M95 masks don't meet the standards for exposure to toxic substances. In the event of toxins, hazard suits are required."

I nodded. It hit me, I was being suspicious of everyone who had been at Yosemite, particularly those who were into masking.

"Yosemite was never in my jurisdiction. I only went there for hikes and vacations."

"Where did you hike in Yosemite?"

"To Half Dome and Upper Yosemite Falls."

"Dad, you said you and Charlie went there about eighteen months ago."

"We were going to go but Charlie got tied up."

"It's sometimes dangerous. A woman fell from the path a while back."

Clay stared at me for a minute. He went quiet and said, "Sometimes you meet some dangerous people in Yosemite. Never trust someone just because of who they are."

"Meaning?"

"There are some dangerous people in the world and sometimes it's hard to know who to trust."

"Can we trust you?" Jeff asked.

"I'd like to think so."

The next morning, Ronnie got back to us. "One of the vials has a unique mixture that has some of the effects of cyanide and cyanide-like traces but it's not cyanide. It's extremely toxic but dissipates fast. Another had SO2. There was a vial of RU-486."

"The abortion pill in liquid form?"

"Population control. At that strength, they could put it in the water or aerosolize it. A lot of side effects."

Another of the vials has a powder that contains traces of cyanide and sulfur mustard, as in mustard gas. There were also vials of LSD and other mind-altering chemicals."

"What do you suppose Rockheap used those chemicals for?"

"Not anything they are licensed to do. There were several chemical compounds we weren't able to break down. The contents of the vial you marked J35-OP N. Pks was something we'd never seen before."

"No depleted uranium?"

"Not in what you brought."

Ronnie had Joey bring us an envelope that confirmed those findings. Still, the J35 chemical breakdown and a number of others were up in the air.

"We're going to be late for our plane," Jack said.

"Sorry, Joey, we have to run," I told him.

"Maybe I'll visit you up at Yosemite."

"That would be great," Autumn said. "I'll show you around."

Jack and Jeff carried the bags and the printout to the car and we headed down Interstate 5 to 405. We drove the rental as fast as we could. "We're definitely not going to be there an hour early," I said.

"If they didn't tell people that, people would be so late, they'd hold up the plane," Autumn replied.

We got off on Century and headed towards the airport.

As we got to the check-in counter, we were told it was too late. "We need to get on this plane," Jeff said, sweetly looking at the ticket girl.

"You need to take the next flight. It was overbooked and your seats are taken."

"And when will that be?"

"We've cut back on our flights. The next one to Fresno will be at six P.M."

"I could drive there faster than that."

"I'm sorry, sir."

"I'll drive," Autumn said.

"We'll need to rent another car," Jeff insisted.

"I want a refund on this flight," Jack demanded.

"I'm sorry. You were told to be here an hour ahead of time."

"I'll call my credit card company. We arrived before take-off."

"Look," I warned, pointing to two men I recognized walking towards us. "FEMA."

CHAPTER 44

I turned back to the clerk. "Thank you! We're looking forward to the flight!"

"But," she started to say as we turned away.

We grabbed our bags and dashed towards the line for the outgoing flights as if we were ready to be scanned or searched. We saw the agents rushing after us. "Hurry so we can make our flight!" I yelled at Jeff, who was behind Autumn.

"She said, they'll hold it for us!" Jack yelled.

I went to an MTA security man. "That man over there running with the other man tried to molest my sister in the restroom. Would you please talk to him?"

"Do you wish to file a report?"

"No. I just don't want him to hassle me, my sister or one of the other passengers again."

He spoke to another man and the two halted the FEMA guys and escorted them to somewhere in the airport while we got into the back of the line. After they were out of sight, we hurriedly rented a car, hoping they would be distracted until we were out of the airport.

As we passed Valencia, Autumn sought out some good music on the radio. As she did so, she passed a news station.

"Wait," Jack said.

"What?"

"Listen."

He had been more fine-tuned to the news than we had been.

"It is not known how many perished in the crash of flight 82 to Fresno. The plane went off course and crashed into Tehachapi Mountain. So far, there are no reports of survivors."

"That was our plane," I said.

"Hopefully, those FEMA guys got on board," Autumn remarked.

"She said the plane was full—full of innocent people," I pointed out.

"Well, it's terrible they perished but if FEMA blew it up, let's hope they got themselves too," Autumn responded.

"Or maybe they just got a bomb on board," Jeff said. "I don't think they'd be stupid enough to stay on a plane they placed a bomb on."

"They didn't say it was a bomb," Jack rebutted our theories. "The radio said it went off course and crashed. Planes have remote programs and have had them since before 9/11. One such program is called the 'Homerun Program.'"

"Whether it was a bomb or a remote takeover, it was aimed for us and if not for my stupid pretense, we were getting on the plane—"

"We'd be dead," Autumn countered. "Besides, they figured out we were flying this morning or they wouldn't have been there."

Jeff stopped at a gas station and I spoke privately to Autumn. "Joey and his dad knew we were going to be on that particular flight."

"But Joey helped save our lives and he got us into Rockheap and to his uncle," Autumn noted.

"How about his dad?" I whispered to Autumn. "Did you see the expression on his face when I mentioned someone fell from the trail?"

"You think he did it?"

"Maybe it's not what we think. It's easy to believe a masked Nazi did it because people under a masking psychosis were frequently committing acts of extreme violence against the unmasked years ago, but what if it had nothing to do with the mask? What if she learned something she wasn't supposed to know?"

"What are you talking about?" Jeff asked, coming up with Jack.

"Just a theory about something that happened long ago."

"I know what you are talking about. Don't let Paul—" Jack advised.

"He's not to know I'm even asking questions."

"What does this have to do with Paul?" Jeff asked.

"Nothing worth repeating," Autumn and I said in unison. We looked at each other. We did think alike.

"We're just speculating about nasty people in the park and well, Paul's over-protective," I added.

Autumn's backup phone buzzed. "We're fine." She covered the mouthpiece. "Speak of the devil."

"You mean angel," I noted.

We could only hear her end of the conversation.

"Right...We missed the flight. We have the analysis. But there are compounds they are still working on. We didn't get them all. One of the ones we missed might be relevant.... Really? Wow. So that's why they tried to kill us if they tried to kill us."

I was waiting to hear what Paul had said.

"Treasure says she loves you too...Sure." She handed the phone to me.

"Hi. I take it something good came up when you saw the records, Jeff and Jack forwarded."

"Lots of contracts between FEMA and Rockheap for chemicals. It calls for a product called J35 to be sent to what it called 'N Pks.' Though I would have expected it to say 'NPS.' Maybe that would have been too obvious."

"Then Jeff was really successful."

"Very much so."

"Did it say what was in it?"

"Just some letters and numbers that didn't relate to any charts. And what trouble did you and Autumn get into?"

"The usual. Car chase, tire shot out, plane crash. Nothing exciting."

"Right. Well, keep it duller on the way back."

"You know us. Trouble seems to follow us." He didn't respond. "We'll try."

"Great work, Jeff and Jack," I congratulated them when the call finished. "The records connect FEMA to Rockheap."

"It's all circumstantial," Jack said. "The connection would explain the crash. As a Federal agency, FEMA had access to the flight list."

I was more than a little iffy approaching Oakhurst. I thought about the kidnapping and bomb. I wondered if they knew my friends and I had survived.

As if she knew what I was thinking, Autumn said, "If one of them touches you, he'll be missing a head two minutes later."

"The boy was nice. He believed me and tried to feed me and give me something to drink."

"He turned out to be a good kid," Autumn acknowledged. "It's too bad he's hanging out with killers."

"With everyone trying to kill us, it's impossible to know where to turn."

"The rangers seem the best of the lot," Jeff noted.

"They do," I agreed.

"Of course, you computer guys are awesome too." Autumn smiled at Jeff.

"Thank you," Jeff said. He stepped on the gas to race through Oakhurst. In almost no time, we were in Fish Camp.

"I wonder if their location for Rockheap's new plant was to be Sonora or Oakhurst and that's why they poisoned the water and people?"

"You think I should take the job?" Jeff joked.

"Life insurance might be expensive," I said.

"But the pay is good."

"Weren't you supposed to return the car in Fresno?" I asked.

"Actually, I rented it for a week and told them I was going to SF to throw off anyone checking on our plans."

"There's GPS on the car, isn't there?"

"There was," Jeff said. He looked in the mirror at me and Autumn in the back seat. "I'm glad I connected with you, that I walked down to the Valley with you that day. If not, I'd be totally oblivious."

"Would that be worse?" I asked.

"When the next wave hits."

We stopped off at the Grove. The General looked as if he were preparing for war. I spoke with Garan. "I have a picture here of a man. I want to know if you've seen him around."

I showed him a picture I'd sneakily taken of Clay. Garan seemed taken aback for a minute.

"You recognize him?"

"I can't be sure. Let me think about it."

"But you reacted instantly."

"I just can't be sure."

I guessed I could give it time to settle in. Had Clay killed Paul's mother? He had seemed a nice man and a devoted father. He wasn't wearing a mask in Palmdale and seemed to know that they didn't do any good. I worried about my obsession with knowing the truth, with finding the killer. If I didn't slow down, Paul would figure out what I was up to and he wouldn't rest until he got answers.

Jeff was filling in the General on what he had heard about a connection between Rockheap and FEMA. As he did, Grant drove up.

"Everything fine back at the fort?" I asked.

"Somebody's missing."

CHAPTER 45

I instantly knew who he meant. "Paul and Eric are looking, but we need a search party."

Autumn was having a happy conversation with Brady. At least, it looked that way. They were both laughing. I waved her over as Grant got Jeff.

The General came over. "What is this about a little girl missing?"

"Somewhere in the woods between here and Glacier or maybe below it."

The General called his men to join the search. At least they didn't know she was an orphan. The last thing we needed was for someone to question her staying with us until we found a relative. But that consideration was not as important as protecting her.

Brady came over and Grant asked him to have the rangers join in the search.

"I've seen you with her. Is the little girl another sister?"

"As a matter of fact. We're very protective of her, especially under the current circumstances," I replied.

Grant pulled up a picture of Yvonne on his phone for Brady.

"Grant, you keep holding out on me. You have three beautiful sisters," Brady said. "Or rather two beautiful sisters and one beautiful future sister-in-law."

Grant smiled. "Looks run in the family. We have to hurry before the bears come out."

"If she's three, she must have been really young when your mother passed."

"Why do you think Paul and Grant have been so protective?" Autumn told Brady, playing along.

"Nothing can happen to her," I said. "She's really special."

"I'm sure she is," Brady agreed.

I didn't think a three-year-old could get too far on foot.

"You live in that old place not far from the Point, correct?" Brady asked as we arrived at the Glacier.

"Paul has thoroughly searched the area immediately around it," Grant stated, rushing off to search himself.

"Where is Paul?" Brady asked me.

"I'm not sure where he is right now. Look, you hang out with Autumn in case Yvonne comes here. I'm going to pursue a wild idea."

I took off, going around bushes, making sure I wasn't seen. In the stable, I got on Libra. He seemed to understand me when I said, "Yvonne's missing."

I was traveling blind, not knowing where she had gone. Still, I was hoping that he would be instinctive enough to take me to where she had wandered and prominent enough that she'd see him. But we could be going the wrong way altogether.

All of a sudden, he reared up and I fell to the ground. As I turned, I saw a bear and I heard her voice. "Bear, nice bear." Yvonne was moving towards the bear to play with it.

CHAPTER 46

"No, Yvonne. Hide."

Hearing my voice, she toddled towards me. "Found bear."

I tried to get up, but my ankle was twisted and I fell. There was a boulder nearby and I pushed Yvonne behind it.

"You pushed me!"

She began to cry. She must have thought I was a monster for pushing her. The bear started approaching me as I crawled away from Yvonne's hiding place to lead it away from her.

Libra hadn't left. He started kicking up his legs at the bear. The bear swatted at Libra's legs. That was when I heard growling, lots of it. The bear backed up. Everlove positioned herself between me and the bear and Esther moved between the bear and Yvonne's boulder. The two male wolves filled in a semi-circle around the bear, growling and preparing for an attack. I didn't know who would win and I didn't want the wolves or Libra hurt, but most of all, I was worried about Yvonne.

I remembered reading that one should stand tall when confronting a bear. I couldn't put weight on my leg, but I managed to pull myself up onto my good leg and stand as tall as I could.

That's when I saw a gun barrel. "I've got it." It was the General, aiming his gun in our general direction.

I didn't know who he was aiming at, the bear or the wolves.

"Don't! Please! They're tame!"

"Tame. They look like they're all attacking."

Brady came running up with a tranquilizer pistol.

"Pet wolves!" I shouted. Brady fired his dart and the bear fell. Everlove came over to me.

A second later, Paul was there, sweeping me up in his arms.

"Yvonne," I pointed as I spoke.

Brady scooped up the little girl. "You're a very brave little girl, but you gave us quite a scare." He looked at me and Paul. "Let's get back to the rangers' station." He radioed Grant to tell him Yvonne was alright as the General contacted his men.

"Thank you so much—all of you," I told my rescuers. "Yvonne. I'm sorry I pushed you behind that rock. I thought the bear might hurt you."

"Bear hurt me?"

"Not all animals are tame," Paul explained.

"You've got a beautiful little sister," Brady said.

"Isn't she?" I reacted before Paul could say anything.

"Oh, Yvonne," he said. "She's a bit young for you."

Brady laughed. "I've got my eye on another sister."

"I wouldn't say that too loudly around Eric," Paul advised.

The wolves and Libra followed us to the rangers' station.

"Where did you get the horse?" Brady asked.

"Paul specializes in training four-legged friends. Give him a week and that bear will be licking everyone."

"I think I've got my hands full," Paul said.

Paul rewrapped my ankle. "I'm sorry I wasn't there to rescue you."

"I had so many rescuers that you were probably better off where you were. Libra and the wolves were awesome. And so were Brady and the General."

"Glad to be of service," the General said, leaving to get into his vehicle with a couple of men to return to Mariposa.

"So, where do you keep Libra? Most of the horses in the Valley died. Is she at Wawona?"

"They do have a stable there, but we don't know where they'll hit next. So, I keep him protected," Paul stated.

"He. Sorry, boy."

"I think he'll survive the misgendering."

"So, the wolves?"

"Wolves are as loving as dogs if they are trained."

"Paul, maybe you could train more animals to help the rangers. It would make our work so much easier. If we get our park back, I bet we can work out a salary for you to do just that."

"I'll consider it."

I smiled. I could see in Paul's eyes that he liked Brady's offer.

"Brady, I wouldn't make a big deal of the wolves," Grant said, joining us. "We wouldn't want people to assume the wrong wolf is tame."

"That could be bad."

As Brady was taking off, Garan came out of the trees, followed by Autumn, and rushed to catch a ride with Brady. Garan called back to Grant, who was standing in the door, holding Yvonne with her head buried in Grant's chest. "I see you found your little sister."

"The love of our lives," Grant shouted back, holding her closely as Autumn ran to the station and threw up her arms in celebration.

"Love you, too," Yvonne said. "Sister?"

"It's a pretend for now. But I'd like to be your sister," I told her.

"Me too," Autumn echoed my sentiments.

Eric and Jack, having heard from Grant that Yvonne had been found, came over to the rangers' station.

Eric gave Autumn a big kiss. "I can't let you go anywhere without me."

She laughed. "We survived. Thank you for looking out for my little sister."

"Sister?"

"That's what we're telling everyone."

"Paul, mind if I borrow your big sister for a little bit?" Eric asked.

"I can drive her home from Jack's later," Grant told Paul.

"Be careful. There are bears out there," he warned.

Paul put me and Yvonne on Libra and walked us back to the grazing pasture. I held Yvonne tightly. "I'm so sorry I pushed you. I couldn't think how else to protect you. I was afraid the bear would hurt you. Please, forgive me."

"Forgive. Bear mean?"

"He's uneducated. He doesn't know better."

"Edu—teach bear."

"That's a future project." Paul grimaced, maybe realizing he might wind up training bears. "For now, if you don't meet an animal at our place, assume it's dangerous."

"Danger."

"One more thing. If you go outside, tell someone in the family and have one of us accompany you. There are some bad people out there."

"Bad people."

"Very bad people. We'll protect you, but we need to be with you to do that," I told her.

It wasn't long before Grant came home with Autumn. We discussed the information that had come out about Rockheap and FEMA. We also discussed our little adventure leaving Rockheap with Joey, as well as the airport.

"It was the same FEMA guys from the hotel?"

"Yep," she said.

"Those FEMA guys backed off for a while until you went to Rockheap."

"Maybe, they think we're dead now—with the plane crash," Autumn hoped.

"If those people on the plane died because of me, I feel awful," I said.

"I feel awful about them, but I'm glad we weren't on that plane," Autumn remarked.

"I'm glad you weren't on it too," Paul said.

"The average person would say we were conspiracy theorists for thinking the plane crash was anything but an accident," I remarked.

"Conspiracy theories generally turn out to be true. The people who keep their eyes closed are always surprised when the truth comes out ten or sixty years later," Autumn said.

"Rockheap has so many ties to the military and DARPA that I'm a little concerned about all the military guys up here." Paul shook his head.

"I know. I've been thinking about that too. Grant, do you trust all the rangers?" I asked.

"They're on the verge of unemployment. Most of us have worked here together for years. We've had each other's backs and been there for each other."

"You said most?"

"Everyone has been with us for more than a year. That's long before FEMA started pulling this stuff."

"Until that ankle heals, I want to keep watch over you," Paul instructed me.

"Me?"

"You've almost been killed too many times. One is too many and it's been way over the limit. Reinjuring your ankle didn't help. Doctor's orders."

"At least it's my favorite doctor."

"What happened with Yvonne?" Autumn asked.

"That was my fault," Grant said. "I was showing her around the ranger station and I got distracted by a call. Next thing I knew, she was gone."

"They kidnapped me to get to you. They figured you'd rescue me and boom. They could do it to anyone," I said.

"They had you in one of those cabins on the way to Wawona. The higher levels have never had the kind of tourism the Valley does and many of the cabins stay vacant. The Mariposa Grove is now seeing more visitors than in a long time, thanks to the military."

"And they're taking good care of it," Grant said. "I was afraid they'd damage the terrain, but they've been very careful."

"Lots of big tents and a fort. That's bound to have an impact on the wildlife," I surmised.

"They've avoided disturbing the trees in setting them up," Grant said.

"Mariposa means butterfly. What about the butterflies?" I asked.

"I don't expect their encampment to be permanent."

I thought about the Valley. "Anyone in the Valley will be in danger from now on. If they can just drop chemicals in there to kill everyone off, how can we trust that it will be safe for camping, rafting and so forth from some future government whim?"

"We'll have to maintain a no-fly zone over Yosemite."

"Will the government go along with it?"

"We'll see. But the rangers are sticking together on that one. They also plan to ban tanks and military vehicles from entering the park."

"The General will love that," I said.

"He'll have to live with it."

"I think this lady needs some sleep," Paul advised.

<hr>

As Yvonne curled up in my bed next to me and fell soundly asleep, Paul laid down a mat on the floor.

"Seriously," I said. "If you feel the need to stay here to protect us, you might as well join us here. It's a large bed. I don't mean anything inappropriate by that."

"I know. After tonight, I think we're all going to be watching Yvonne closely."

"So, to be clear, she's my future sister-in-law? That is the story?"

"Apparently so. I heard that was your idea."

"I didn't want any questions that would bring in CPS."

<hr>

When I woke up, Paul was still holding me. The lights were out but I could feel him against me as I breathed in his pine aroma.

I thought about how wonderful it would be to wake up in his arms every morning. I snuggled up against him. Yvonne was on my other side.

"You awake?" Paul asked.

"Yes."

"I don't know how long it will take to fix things. Would I be too pushy if I suggested we plan a wedding date independent of everything that is going on?"

"When are you thinking about?"

"I'd like to marry you tomorrow, but I also want to make sure you have the kind of wedding every girl dreams about."

"The wedding I'm dreaming about is one where the groom is you. The rest is not that important."

"Autumn's birthday is in early August. How about if we get married a week after her birthday?"

"Autumn will be the maid of honor, of course, and Yvonne will be the flower girl." I hoped that, if she somehow found her real family between now and then, maybe it would give her an excuse to come back for a visit.

"Grant will be my best man. We need someone to give you away. Jack?"

"Jack would be awesome."

I had always thought Tatiana'd be my maid of honor and now I didn't even know if she'd attend.

"How about if we do it on horseback?" I asked.

"Horseback?"

"I know it sounds crazy, but we could include the horses and wolves in the ceremony. Yvonne would love that."

"There is an amphitheater here at Glacier. We could do it there. What interests me is the years that will come after."

I felt a twinge from the past, hoping I wouldn't blow it and wind up alone again. "I'm looking forward to that too."

"I love you and you can count on that to last past forever."

"Wow," I said. It was as if he had read my mind. Maybe in time he'd wipe away my self-doubts—if they weren't confirmed. "If the wolves hadn't found me that day, do you think we would have gotten together?"

"It might have taken a little longer to get you to trust me. But somehow, somewhere, I think I would have found you."

"But would you have felt this way if you hadn't been nursing me back to health?"

"That would have happened the moment we met—no matter how or where we met. You are intelligent, beautiful and compassionate. Compassion is all too rare these days."

"You always know just the right thing to say to make me feel good."

"You want to know a secret?"

"Sure."

"That first day. I was trying to figure out a way to get you to stay. I knew right away you were the one and only woman for me."

"I was crazy about you then, but I didn't think someone as incredible as you would be interested in me."

"Interested? If I hadn't mentioned we were engaged, virtually all the guys at Mariposa would be lining up for a chance with you."

I doubted that. I had considered myself totally unattractive. *Tatiana is beautiful, but me*? "I see them lining up for Autumn."

"If you could see in yourself what others see in you, you'd realize how irresistible you are."

"The only guy I want is you. But what about when I'm a hundred and all wrinkly?"

"I'll love every wrinkle and you'll still be the only woman for me."

He kissed me and I felt as if I were in heaven again. He held me close all night as I dreamed of him.

The next morning, I picked up my phone in the other room and saw a message forwarded from my Boondoggle phone number I had given to Clay. *"I need to speak with you. It's important."*

I could see he had made numerous attempts to reach me. I called him back but there was no answer. I called Ronnie. He was working and didn't know what Clay wanted to reach me about, but he knew his brother had been trying to reach me. Joey wasn't answering either.

"Should I go back to Palmdale?" I asked Paul.

"If you're making any more long trips, I'll be at your side."

"It might be about the chemicals or maybe he found out something else about Rockheap."

"See if he calls you back later today."

Jack, Eric and Jeff were still reviewing the Rockheap files when we went over to Jack's to join them.

"It's a good thing you guys are good at breaking into secure systems," I said.

"I've been doing it since I was seven," Eric boasted. "I accidentally broke into the local fire station database and fire trucks wound up looking for non-existent fires all over the city."

"Did you get caught?"

"Almost, but nobody else was home and the police didn't believe a seven-year-old could do that. They called it a glitch. Security gets tighter each year, but it helps when people walk away with their computers still logged in."

"Who all knows what we did in Massachusetts and Palmdale?" I asked Jack.

"Only our group. We told the General we had found a link between Rockheap and FEMA, but we didn't tell him how we went about finding it."

"Ronnie and Clay know about our sample collection at Rockheap, but they don't know Jeff was even at the plant," I reported.

"I want to keep it that way," Jack said. "The fewer people who know too much, the less likely someone is to spill."

"What's coming up on those files Jeff copied?"

"Weapons contracts. Contracts for special chemicals. One of them is just numbered: 2030."

"As in Agenda 2030?"

"Let's hope not. That's a nasty agenda."

"Part of 2030 involves mass depopulation," I recalled.

"They started that long ago with COVID-19. Look how many

people needlessly died in this state, and the Governor is more popular than ever. He might be President one day."

"Especially with all the election-rigging taking place."

"People are afraid and nobody knows if their vote is counted," Eric said. "Makes it easier for the ballot stuffers to win."

"I know my vote counted," Jack stated. "I hacked into their election system and added in my vote—in case they didn't count the one I did in person."

"Well, we know one vote was legitimate."

I tried to reach Clay again. No answer. I had an uneasy feeling. I called Ronnie. "I was wondering about a compound called 2030."

"It was in the samples we tried to analyze. We couldn't break it down. It needs more thorough analysis."

"We think it could be in use."

"I overnighted 2030 and some other concerning compounds to a friend who works for a lab that is using new techniques for detecting hidden toxins. He got back to me and said he had found something big. He's out of the area, but I may go up to visit him after I leave work today."

"Do you think this is what Clay called me about?"

"I don't know. He didn't come by the lab or go to work today."

"Have you spoken to Joey?"

"No. I tried to call him. But he didn't answer."

I turned to Paul. "I want to go back to Palmdale. Something is going on with Clay and Joey. Also, there is a guy who is doing research into the chemicals we supplied to Ronnie."

"Do you think Clay found something in an OSHA file about Rockheap?" Eric asked.

"I don't know."

"FEMA was trying to kill you down in Palmdale. They may not know you're alive. It might be best for you to stay out of sight," Paul encouraged.

"Unless they check the rental listings," I noted.

"Grant had one of the rangers return the car to LAX," Jeff said.

"Misdirection. Which ranger?" I asked.

"Garan."

"What did you tell him about our activities in So Cal?"

"Just that I had to rent a car, but didn't want to drop it off this close to Yosemite. He didn't ask why I was down there. I guess he minds his own business."

"What about the General? What does he know?"

"Just that we were curious about Rockheap, but for all he knows, we were doing a Wikipedia search."

"Which would have been funded by Rockheap. Nobody who wants accurate information goes there, anymore."

"Grant told Brady you had gone out of town for a family reunion," Paul told Autumn.

"Liar," I replied.

"I don't know if I trust that Brady guy," Eric said

I figured I knew what that was about. Autumn. "What's your issue with Brady?"

"Just a feeling. Remember, Obi-Wan told Luke to trust his feelings."

"I think he was supposed to trust the Force," I said.

"We could have Garan go back to check into the Clay and Joey issue," Jeff suggested.

"Clay called me personally on my Boondoggle phone number that was supposed to forward to my new phone, but I left it in another room and didn't notice until after he had left urgent messages. I don't feel right just sitting here if something is going on in Palmdale."

"Let's borrow a military jeep and go down there," Autumn said. "It's better than finding out second hand."

"What about Clay's brother Ronnie?" Jeff asked. "I'm sure that if something was serious, he'd call."

"I'm also curious about what Ronnie's friend found out about the chemicals we picked up," I said.

"My favorite animal is puppy. What is yours?" Yvonne was watching us while playing with a talking stuffed puppy we had picked up for her in L.A. She hugged the doll.

I smiled. "Wolf," I responded. I turned back to the conversation. "What about Yvonne? She could be in danger—either here or down south."

"She's better off away from Rockheap."

I thought about it. "Okay. Maybe Autumn can—' I looked at her and she shook her head. "Maybe Grant can take a day off to watch her closely."

"Brady is his relief, isn't he?" Eric asked.

"Garan lost his outpost in the Valley and is a floater these days," Paul said. "He could back Grant and Brady up."

"Did Garan used to man the post at Glacier?" I asked.

"He used to work the trails. He sometimes worked in the Badger Pass station."

If Rockheap was involved, maybe the masking was a red herring. "Did you see any mysterious animal deaths or other deaths in the park prior to when they hit the Valley?"

"A lot. It seemed like there were a lot of weird dusty or gaseous mixtures that hit the valley prior to that, but none so deadly. There were dead animals from time to time and it looked as if some had been poisoned. Maybe that was experimentation."

"In other words, someone tied to Rockheap could have been doing experimental dumps in testing the compounds prior to my arrival this Spring and they succeeded in mass extermination either that night or in the early morning, both in the Valley and in Sonoma."

Eric frowned when I mentioned Sonoma. "From the downloads, I saw that Sonoma was one of the potential sites for a new Rockheap facility."

"What about Oakhurst?"

"They were deciding between the two locations."

"And that is how those two towns got tied in with the destruction of the National Parks," I figured.

"Something else has been bothering me. Those robo-operated trash compactors picking up bodies in the pictures weren't the normal trash collectors for the campground. The Park had already been infiltrated when the poison hit. Let's look at the videos," Paul said.

We went back to the videos Autumn and I shot. Jeff zeroed in on a serial number that was barely visible through a windshield. He ran it.

"You aren't going to like this."

"What?"

"It's registered to DARPA."

"And DARPA has been doing biological experiments on people for a long time," I said. "I watched *The Convo Couch* and *The Last American Vagabond* on YouTube before I came to Yosemite."

"Is *The Convo Couch* the show with those cool reporters who do election integrity?"

"That's the one."

"We're dealing with DARPA, Rockheap and FEMA?" Autumn clarified.

"And DHS. FEMA is under DHS," Paul commented.

"While you were gone, I analyzed the disc we retrieved from the dog and wrote a code, containing a signal that deactivates them and wipes out all their programming. We put up blockers broadcasting my code on all routes leading to Yosemite and around the Mariposa Grove," Eric said.

"Is there a tie-in between Rockheap and DARPA?" I asked.

"In the records? You're kidding, right? Thousands of them."

"Then they're all in it together. DARPA and Big Pharma have bought off most of the leaders in Congress and the Executive Branch."

"I would be surprised if someone high up in DARPA isn't the real President behind the charade."

"I have a really bad feeling about Palmdale, like we should be there," I said.

"I trust Treasure's feelings," Paul noted.

"I'll go down there and see what I can find out," Eric volunteered.

"I'll join you," Autumn declared. "Joey and Clay know me."

"Sis," Paul countered. "You died on the plane."

"You've already pointed out that Yvonne needs you and Treasure. One of us needs to go and I say it's me."

I looked at Yvonne. I didn't want to leave her, again, for another trip and it would be too dangerous in Palmdale for her if FEMA caught up with us. We adults could run and talk our way out of it, but putting her through that would be unconscionable.

"FEMA. If they see you," I warned.

"I'll be careful and wear glasses and a hat. Brady is going to get me a taser and dart gun."

"Can he do that?" I asked.

"Only if he recruits her for the rangers," Paul noted.

"I'd make a great ranger," she said.

"I'll hang onto the weapons. I don't want to have to bail you out," Eric told her.

"No faith," she responded. "Either you trust me or you don't."

"I'll see what I can get from the army," Eric responded.

"All we need are you two in an armed gunfight. They have bigger weapons," Paul countered.

"Maybe if we had a cannon," Autumn teased.

"Ha! Ha!" Paul said. "I want Grant's opinion on this."

"Would you rather I went down there with or without your permission?"

Paul turned to Eric for backup.

"It would be better if she went with me than alone."

Paul nodded. "Play it safe and no displaying your weaponry if you have it. I think it would be safer if you didn't."

"I'll keep your sister safe," he assured Paul.

Grant convinced the General to loan him a military vehicle, a BMW, which Grant turned over to Eric. Jeff checked it for bugs and trackers.

As we saw Eric and Autumn off, Paul commented, "Eric's a good, solid guy. I'm pulling for him."

"I'm pulling for Brady," Grant said. "I've known him a lot longer than Eric."

"Why does Autumn have to choose one of them? She's seventeen. Maybe she wants to have fun until she's thirty."

"You're her age. Do you feel the same?"

"I already said 'yes' and I meant it. Neither of Autumn's would-be suiters measure up to you."

"She knows how to stop an argument," Grant said.

We returned to the cave. I had never thought I would become a cave dweller, but this was the most luxurious home I had ever lived in.

During the early afternoon, Yvonne and I played with the wolves. "These four could pass agility tests with top scores," I said.

"Wolves, jump," she commanded as they leaped over a bench. They were good at walking one foot in front of the other on boards and at retrieving whatever she threw to them. Paul had trained them to hold off on eating treats tossed to them. Yvonne had fun putting out snacks and then getting them to "Eat" on command. Their level of self-control was really impressive. I thought about the bear. If anyone could train a bear, it would be Paul.

I insisted on making Paul and Yvonne dinner. Grant was over at Jack's, chatting with Eric. Paul's phone rang. He looked at the number. It was Autumn. He answered, immediately putting it on speaker.

"Hey, how's it going?" he asked.

But it wasn't Autumn on the phone.

"I'm Sergeant Blair of the California Highway Patrol. There was a fiery crash off Interstate 46, between Interstate 5 and US 99. A car careened off the road and down the mountain. We found this phone close to where the car went off the road. Your number was listed as the emergency contact."

CHAPTER 47

"Was anyone hurt?"

"We haven't been able to get close enough to check the condition of the occupants. This phone was thrown clear. This was the emergency contact number. Do you know who was in the car?"

"What kind of vehicle was it?

"A BMW."

"They've got to be alright," I said to Paul, half in shock and half praying.

I went into my room and picked up Yvonne. Paul drove us to the location the officer had provided. Reportedly, the car had caught fire and exploded. Trees, bushes and grass in the immediate area were continuing to burn.

I had Yvonne wait in Paul's Sienna with the doors locked. "Don't let anyone in, not the police, not anyone."

"No one in."

"Right."

It was evening and everything looked a mess amidst the smoke, the red glow from the remains of the vehicle and still burning bushes and trees on the mountainside. We waited until the CHP was able to finish extinguishing the car fire and move in. Small brush fires were still being put out, but there were no nearby houses.

"Stay back," the officer said. A minute later, he called the other officers.

"It looks as if any occupants were thrown out in the explosion."

"No bodies?"

"When the remaining fires die down, we'll do a thorough search of the area. We'll call you if we find anything."

We went back to Paul's minivan. Yvonne was shaking. "What happening?"

"We don't know."

"Fire."

"Yes. Fire."

I tried to reassure Paul, though I didn't feel reassured myself. "Autumn is pretty resilient. And they don't have the VIN yet. It could turn out to be a different car." I knew I was grasping at hope, but I was not going to lose another sister.

"They don't have the VIN, but they had a piece of the license plate and it was a government vehicle."

"There are a lot of government vehicles. Let's believe the best until we hear otherwise."

He looked stiff, almost frozen. "I don't know what I will do if it turns out—" He couldn't finish as he stuffed back a cry.

"She's alive. I don't know how, but somehow, she's alive." I resolved to believe that anything was possible—anything but losing her.

Paul looked at Yvonne in the car. "Let's get a place to stay for the night. We're not far from Paso Robles."

"Why would they drive the car over here? It's not on the way to Palmdale."

"Maybe they were being chased."

I thought about how Autumn had gotten out of past situations. "She's alive. I know she is."

He kissed my forehead. "Thank you for keeping up hope."

"It's more than hope. We'll find her alive. I'm certain of it." But were my convictions nothing more than hope? *No, Autumn did not die in a fiery crash.*

Back at Paso Robles, Paul stopped at a hotel. I knew he was devastated. He was good at holding it in, but I knew his heart was breaking. "I'll get a couple of rooms."

"How about a room with two beds? I don't think any of us wants to be alone tonight."

Some people grieved in private, but I knew from experience that being alone often made things worse. If it hadn't been for Paul and Autumn, I never would have gotten through what my brother and sister did to me.

After we managed to get Yvonne to sleep, Paul and I sat, clutching each other and watching the news. It might not be real news, but it might contain some clues. There was nothing about the crash other than a brief mention that a car had gone off a cliff and exploded, starting a small fire that did minimal damage and was easily contained.

We waited to hear from the CHP. It wasn't long before a call came in from an unknown number. "This may be them," he said. He hesitated and then answered but the caller had already hung up. "Maybe a wrong number or maybe FEMA, trying to find out where we are."

I knew Paul didn't want to hear the worst. He stared at the phone for a minute before calling back the number. I got close enough to hear the call.

"Well, it's about time you called back. We need a ride."

The relief on Paul's face and the feeling of relief I felt at his sister's voice was so real. I put my arms around him and started crying.

"They found your phone."

"I know. I lost it when we jumped out of the car."

"You jumped?"

"FEMA was chasing us. Those guys never give up."

"How did they find you in the BMW?"

"They've got someone inside. They found us at a Starbucks. I knew we should have gotten drinks elsewhere. They tried to take us with them. I beat the heck out of them and stole a briefcase. They chased us and we took a route toward the coast to throw them off but they must have had a GPS on the briefcase. They chased us down 46 and when we knew we wouldn't lose them, we set the car on fire and sent it down the cliff right after a curve to allow us time to jump out, but I lost my phone in the jump and Eric's phone was still in the car. So, I got a burner. What do you think?"

"If you ever scare me like this again, I'll kill you," Paul attested.

"I knew they couldn't kill you. I'm so happy you're safe," I said.

"Where do we pick you up?" Paul asked.

"Remember that DaVinci painting we spoke about?"

"Got it."

We scooped up Yvonne and let her continue sleeping in the back seat of the car as we drove over to the Madonna Inn in San Luis Obispo and went into the coffee shop.

"Would you like some hot chocolate, Yvonne?"

"Yes. Hot chocolate."

Paul ordered some for each of us as we sat at the counter.

"Have you seen the rooms at this place? Each one is individually decorated," a familiar voice said from behind me.

I turned, hugged Autumn and started crying.

"And I thought you'd be happy."

"I am."

"You said you'd keep her safe," Paul admonished Eric.

"Look at her. Not a scratch."

"You don't know what you put us through," Paul said to Autumn.

"Would you rather we had stayed in the car and let FEMA kill us?"

"I'd rather you stay away from FEMA altogether."

The waitress came over with our order. "Can you make that five to-go orders of hot chocolate?" Paul asked.

"Thanks, Bro," Autumn said. "So do you want to see pictures of the rooms?"

"I want to go home," Paul emphasized.

"Killjoy."

"You've said that before." Paul was lightening up.

"I think that was Grant I said that to."

A few minutes later, we were in the car travelling. "Did they catch up to you in Palmdale?" Paul asked.

"We never made it. They caught up to us in Fresno," Eric said. "We couldn't lead them home and we didn't want to lead them to our new informants. So, we headed out to the coast."

"On a windy mountain road."

"It wasn't the best plan, but it appears to have worked. The CHP thinks we're dead and if our deaths are reported, then we're safe."

"I'll make sure to give the CHP all your details and have your social security numbers canceled," Paul said.

"Isn't he cute?" Autumn said to me. "I think I know what you see in him."

"What happened to the briefcase?" I asked.

"Perished with the car."

"The important thing is you're okay," I said.

"Of course, we have these items," Eric informed us. He pulled photos and a camera out from under his jacket. "The case didn't make it. These did."

"Holy. These are of the makeshift camp at Mariposa Grove."

Paul's eyes widened.

"Yep. Someone there is spying for FEMA."

"Well, obviously, I didn't take these pictures. I'm in them," the General said. We were having a private discussion with Eric, Autumn, Paul, Grant, the General and myself. Yvonne was there but she was distracted with a stuffed Smokey the Bear that Grant had given her. The real Smokey may have died, but kids still liked him.

"We weren't accusing you, but someone here is a plant or an informant," Eric said.

"You may be correct. We should look for who is not in the pictures."

"Brady. I didn't see Brady in the pictures," Eric said.

"A lot of people are not in the pictures," Grant observed.

"Standing up for the rangers?" the General accused.

"I'm simply saying that a lot of military personnel, as well as some of the other rangers, are not in the pictures."

"They know you took the case?"

"But they don't know I managed to open it and that I still have the pictures, and they may not know we're alive. The case would have burned up in the car."

"It's unthinkable that one of my men could betray me. I've known these men through the best and worst of times and they can all be trusted."

"Didn't more troops join you?" Paul inquired.

"Troops who have worked under me before."

"Anyone can go into debt and need a government handout," Eric pointed out.

"How about you?" The General retorted. "How do we know your story is real?"

"Because he helped us rescue you, sir," I said.

"I'll be there," Grant said to someone who had radioed him. "There is trouble near the Wawona Tunnel."

"I'll get the troops together."

"Not that kind of trouble," Grant said. "Brady stopped a teenage boy who was going to tell off the FEMA gang."

"Gutsy," Paul said.

"More than gutsy. He's unarmed. And he says they killed his father."

"Let's go," I said. I looked at Paul and Yvonne. "Why don't you get her home. I'll be there soon."

"You?"

"I've been feeling kind of useless. Maybe I can talk to him."

"Me too," Autumn said. "Grant, will you take us?"

"You are both out of there at the first sign of trouble," Paul said.

"I second that," Grant chimed in.

Brady had driven the boy to the ranger station at Badger Pass. The moment I walked into the office, I recognized him.

"Joey."

"They killed my dad."

CHAPTER 48

"I'm so sorry." I still had those words on automatic. It was how I felt, but the words seemed pathetic, insufficient compared to the loss. Guilt rushed over me. His death was partially or wholly my fault.

"Rockheap or FEMA?" Autumn asked.

"He was trying to reach you all last night about something. He said it was important and he needed to speak with you. Then this morning, he got into his car to go to work and it exploded."

"It had to be someone who had access to explosives," Grant said. "And someone who was okay with killing. I'm also sorry about your dad. I didn't know him, but it's a terrible loss."

"Joey is the guy who helped us the other day," I told Grant. "I wish I hadn't gotten you involved," I said.

"My dad used to say that my actions had consequences. I didn't think they'd cost him his life."

"I was trying to reach you and your dad all day when I saw he had called."

"My phone was in the car when it happened. I want to join the cause. I want to get them for what they did to my dad."

"They almost killed Autumn today too," I said. "Yesterday." I noticed it was well after midnight. "She and Eric were on their way to

Palmdale to find out why your dad called and FEMA saw them. They would have no qualms about killing another teenager."

"Then, train me to stay alive."

"It's not that simple," Grant said.

"Either you let me join you or I'll do it alone."

"What about your mother?"

"She died from that poisoned injection. Fortunately, my dad got a religious exemption and so did I."

"My dad also died from one of those poisoned injections late last year, but he wasn't nice like your dad," I said.

"I'll drive you to Mariposa," Grant told him.

"I don't know," I fretted. "There's an infiltrator there."

"Jack's?" Autumn suggested.

"It will be safer," Eric noted.

"What is this about an infiltrator?" Brady asked.

"FEMA has pictures of the Mariposa Grove encampment someone took," Autumn explained.

Eric looked irritated by Autumn and me sharing the information. I was sure he also didn't like me mentioning Palmdale in front of Brady.

"But don't mention it to anyone until we catch him," Autumn advised Brady. "I know it isn't you."

"Am I a suspect?" Brady asked.

"No, but until we find the infiltrator, everyone is," Grant informed him.

Grant left for a minute and then returned. "Jack said, 'welcome.'"

"I haven't been to Jack's," Brady said.

"For now, keep your eyes open for the infiltrator at Mariposa," Grant told him.

I pulled Grant aside. "I don't know Joey all that well. Shouldn't we verify his information? Clay's brother should have known about the explosion. He claimed not to know why his brother wasn't answering his phone."

I pulled out my phone and called Ronnie.

"I didn't know until tonight. I knew he didn't show up for work today. You say Joey is there?"

"Yes."

"He didn't call me."

"He claims his cell phone was lost, but I would have thought he would have come by to let you know what had happened."

"I've been on an assignment inspecting some dangerous chemicals at a soft drink facility since early morning. The inspection lasted into the night. I didn't get a chance to check on my brother until after I finished. That's when I found out."

"If it's too dangerous, you don't need to continue helping us."

"Sometimes you just have to do the right thing. I haven't told anyone where the samples came from. I marked them with a code. Of course, it wouldn't take a lot of checking for someone to figure it out."

"Do you have any idea who did this to your brother?"

"All I know is, after you left, he was disturbed by something he had to tell you."

"Was it about Rockheap?"

"He didn't say, but he told me it was very important. Joey's a good kid. If he's with you, keep him from going off the deep end. Joey is a bit wild and impulsive, but he loved his dad very much."

"It's good to see you, again, son," Jack said.

Grant had driven us over to his fortress.

"And it's my fault my father's dead." While he blamed himself, I knew I deserved most of the blame.

"Nobody is responsible for someone else's acts of violence," Grant said.

"It's good to see you again, buddy," Jeff told him.

"So, what's the plan?" Joey asked.

"Right now, we're between a couple of powder kegs and hoping, when the final decision comes, FEMA will be forced to move on."

"Final decision?"

"A federal judge granted a preliminary injunction ordering FEMA to leave Yosemite and other state and national parks," I responded. "FEMA refused and filed an appeal with the Ninth Circuit, which is above the judge. Our hope is the Ninth will affirm the lower court decision. In the meantime, military personnel FEMA tried to silence have gathered with the rangers, and they plan to enforce the order when they get enough men. It's a powder keg. FEMA versus the military. If that blows, we could all be caught in the crossfire."

"Where do the rangers stand?"

"Our goal is to protect the Park and to make sure that everything is restored to the way it was before FEMA moved in," Grant informed him.

"Except the food," I said. "Nobody likes the food the company with the current concessions contractor sells here."

"It makes MacDonald's look gourmet," Jack commented. "Enough of this head talk. You've been through enough. And so have you two," he said, looking at Autumn and Eric.

"I'm taking the girls with me," Grant said. "And Autumn will be lucky if Paul doesn't cuff her to her bed."

"For helping?"

"For taking too many chances."

After a lot of hemming and debating, Autumn agreed to go with Grant and me. We assured Joey that FEMA would ultimately pay for what it did.

"I don't know how, but we'll make sure they are tried for murder and or treason," I said, doing my best to sound strong. I didn't want Joey to try anything on his own.

In the truck, Grant informed me that Jack had already done a background check on the boy, his dad and uncle and felt good about what he saw. "You may not know, but some years back, Jack lost a son like you lost a brother and sister. He was about my age."

"Narrative insanity?"

"The boy won't even talk to him. It's sad because parents are always there for their kids and when the kids grow up, those parents assume the kids will at least be friends with them. So many kids, worshipping the narrative, lost their ability to have empathy and dumped their parents in nursing homes to die."

"Jack is a great guy. I hope things work out for him."

"Jack needs the love of a son and that boy could use a father, though no one is replaceable. They might be able to help each other."

"You call him a boy, but he's only a year younger than me," Autumn said.

I hadn't asked. That would make him sixteen. "An awful age to suffer such a loss." I looked at Autumn. She was younger than that when she lost her mother.

When we got home, the sun was coming up. "I think we all need some rest," Paul said. He had prepared some pancakes for us.

Yvonne was already asleep. After munching down a pancake, I went into my room and laid down next to her.

Guilt kept me awake. I got up and saw Paul lying on a mat he had put down outside Autumn's room. I kneeled down and kissed him on the cheek. He pulled me into a full embrace.

"I love how you love my family and little Yvonne. If I could have tried to imagine the perfect woman, she would not have been as perfect as you."

"Better watch out. Flattery will go to my head."

"And it should. If nothing works out here at Yosemite, I wouldn't trade these days with you and the ones ahead of us for anything."

"I hope Joey is alright. I feel responsible. He helped with collecting the samples.

"Autumn feels bad about what happened to his dad as well, but she is always trying to present an upbeat front."

"I know. She's amazing. You're like that too. You keep me positive, not dwelling on the past or things I can't change."

"The one thing that will never change is my love for you."

"Nor mine for you. I know I'm only eighteen, but I've never known this much happiness. It's crazy, in spite of all the tragedy around us, I can't help but be happy that I found the perfect family and someone so awesome. I never allowed myself to even wish for someone like you."

"Who did you wish for?"

"I just wished that one day I would be loved."

"Well, you've got that."

"One day, Yvonne is going to ask about her parents. We need to show we made a diligent effort to find out everything we could about them."

"When FEMA is out of the Park and they run DNA on the mass graves, maybe we'll get the answer."

"As long as it's not an answer that will hurt her."

"If they're not there, they'd better have a good explanation for deserting their daughter."

"I'll say."

He kissed me again. Afterwards, I floated to bed on a cloud and when I laid down to sleep, I could still feel the warmth of his lips and the taste of him as if the kiss had never stopped.

"I want to speak to Joey some more," I told Paul after I woke up. "FEMA catches up with us after we go to Palmdale. A plane we're supposed to be on crashes. An OSHA inspector who is also the father of a boy who helps us is murdered. Autumn and Eric are captured by the same FEMA guys but get away with a suitcase of evidence of infiltration of the Mariposa Grove camp and their car winds up in a fiery crash. I feel like a Jinx or worse."

"FEMA has a lot of agents. Those two seem to be focused on you and Autumn and from what you say, Clay previously filed a report on Rockheap."

"True, but are they keeping tabs on us? We met with Clay a day and a half before he was killed. We could have led FEMA to him."

"The flight schedule. If the infiltrator gave them your names, they might have checked the flights."

"Pacheco? It was the same agents from the Lodge. Only Jack, Eric and Jeff knew we were going to Berkeley." *Could we have a traitor close to us?*

"Maybe they followed you from Oakhurst."

"Right. Pete."

Autumn and I took Atlas and Kaliope over to Jack's to see what was happening.

Eric caught us up. "As far as we can tell, they've been experimenting for some time to use just the right poisons to erase people but not plants or wildlife. In Yosemite and Oakhurst, they got the wrong combination. But look. It's a video a ranger got of Sequoia." The video showed deer and squirrels running around between the bodies. "And Sonora."

"Our parents' two Irish Setters were running around the backyard when we got there," Jeff recalled.

"Where are they now?"

"We turned them over to an animal rescue organization operating near Sonora."

"A lot of those animal rescue organizations kill and maim animals while collecting money in the pretense of helping them."

"You mean like HSUS and PETA? We made sure the organization wasn't affiliated with them."

"Good. PETA has giant walk-in freezers for the carcasses of their kills and they have also been prosecuted in multiple states for slaughtering puppies and kittens and dumping them in shopping mall dumpsters," Autumn said. "My dad demanded a refund of his donations to PETA when he found out about it."

"Did he get one?" I asked.

"No."

Joey was looking through FEMA's photographs of the Grove.

"Do you recognize anyone from those photographs?" I inquired.

"No."

"Makes sense if the infiltrator was taking the pictures."

Grant walked in. "Has anyone compiled a list of people not in the photographs?"

"The photos were pretty extensive. All of us here, except Joey, are in the photographs and he wasn't here then. Most, but not all, of the rangers and military personnel are included," Jeff said.

"Which rangers are not included?"

"As you know, Brady wasn't photographed."

"He's not the infiltrator!" Autumn insisted.

"I don't think he is either," Grant said.

"Also, Douglas Martin and Johnny Monarch were not photographed."

"Douglas is a little weird," Autumn said.

"He's just different," Grant responded. "I don't think it's him."

"So, we are looking at Johnny Monarch as a possibility?" I asked.

"His family has had some financial problems. He could have taken some extra money to help them out."

"How about the National Guard recruits?"

"Graham isn't photographed and neither are Jason Marcos and Tully Bertram. But remember, the National Guard came in after the rangers and military. It makes sense there would be fewer photos of them."

"But some of the National Guardsmen are photographed?"

"Some. But don't forget, the infiltrator could have taken a timed photo that included himself to be excluded as a suspect if we came across the photos," Jeff pointed out.

I tossed up my hands. "In other words, everyone is still a suspect."

"We've got everyone watching everyone else at the camp now—sort of a buddy system, but we only told a few about the photos," Grant related. "We explained that there have been too many attempts on the lives of people and everyone is responsible for keeping his or her buddy safe."

"One more thing. There is a hard-to-read imprint on the photos," Jeff advised Grant.

"Let's see."

Jeff frowned and turned up his hands. He put the photo on the screen, made some color adjustments and magnified some writing. It read, "Benjamin Sheldon."

CHAPTER 49

"Does Paul know?" I asked.

"We just called him," Jack replied.

"Let me get this straight. He's with the bad guys and he left his family to die? What about Angela?"

"We don't know," Jeff responded.

"Does that mean he's the infiltrator?" I continued my inquiry.

"Or working with the infiltrator. He or his lab developed the photographs," Jeff surmised.

"Or perhaps one of the infiltrators has an alternate identity."

"We don't know the National Guardsmen that well," Grant pointed out.

"Do we have any pictures of Benjamin and Angela?"

"I just searched for their names," Jack said. "A lot of the security footage from the Ahwahnee has been erased. Maybe there were photos taken in Sonora."

"High school yearbooks, college yearbooks, anything. Please search," I said.

"That's what we're doing," Eric said. "In the meantime, I'd make sure that anyone who needs to be protected stays out of sight."

We hadn't clued Joey in on the Yvonne situation. I felt it best not to say too much. Yvonne had been at Mariposa. Had everyone, including maybe even her father, seen her with us? Would he eventually take her back after leaving her for dead?

Autumn and I went upstairs. I wanted to discuss the situation with her, but Joey and Jeff followed us up.

"Are you saying a guy who was killed at the Ahwahnee is publishing photos for the men who may have killed my dad?"

"There was a couple we assumed was dead and buried in the rubble. But that is a possibility."

"They could have just used his studio," Autumn said. "If he is alive, I'd be willing to off him for what he did." I knew she wasn't serious and was mouthing off. I sometimes said things like that too. It wasn't a problem unless we later became suspects in an actual killing.

"Here's the question. Is he an infiltrator, say into the National Guard, where we don't have as much verification of identities, or is he simply alive and in the background?" I queried.

"What about the Signature Force?" Autumn asked.

"What?" I inquired.

"This guy named Jason Bermas did videos on Signature Reduction, a secret army of over sixty thousand. They can change their appearance and fingerprints and they have equipment that can monitor nearby conversations indoors as they walk down a street in front of houses. There is a whole federal department that creates fake identities and records for them and they don't have to pay taxes. They operate under the Pentagon, monitoring American citizens."

"For real?" I asked.

"I've heard of them too," Joey said.

"No wonder the real army is rebelling. The Pentagon has its own secret army and now we've learned FEMA is using a formerly secret army of mostly contractors, instead of the National Guard and these secret armies are making incomes that most real servicemen and women could only dream of," I grumbled.

"Let's dig up an old Jason Bermas video. I think he did a lot of his stuff for free online," Autumn told us.

We started watching old videos. Jason Bermas was a producer on *Loose Change*, one of the top documentaries on 9/11/01.

"A lot of the reason people miss things is they look at the face of things, rather than going into the details. For instance, the UL contractor who certified the steel in the World Trade Center said the official theory of the collapse was impossible," Jeff pointed out.

"They also ignore facts they don't want to know about, such as Giuliani and Silverstein predicting in advance the collapse of the buildings or about the gold in the tunnels," I noted.

"Or of BBC talking of the collapse of building seven while it was still standing there in the background of their live videos," Autumn recalled.

"Or of GW Bush saying he saw the first plane hit while in his limo before entering the school."

We looked at Joey.

"Hey, I've studied that information too. You wouldn't believe the stuff my dad discovered at military contractor facilities when he was working for OSHA."

Ronnie called. He wanted us to meet him at a lab in Madera.

"Why Madera?"

"It's out of the way and it could be a little dangerous to do further research too close to L.A. My friend Chase owns the lab and can keep things under wraps. Also, he's got more cutting-edge imaging and analytic instruments than at my lab."

"Okay, we'll be there tonight," I said.

"I want to go, too," Joey insisted. "My dad died for this."

"I agree," Autumn said. "He's got a right to be there."

I went downstairs to tell Jack about the planned meeting. "I think Paul should also be there. He may be a paramedic, but he knows biology and chemistry better than most doctors," I acknowledged.

"In Cuba, they have a great medical school program. If he's okay with travel, he should consider it. They pay students–even foreign students—to go to medical school there," Jack pointed out.

"I've heard they do great international assistance. They were the second to offer help following Katrina, right after Hugo Chavez offered assistance."

"And they sent medical teams to Italy during the COVID plandemic," Autumn recalled as she, Joey and Eric joined us.

"COVID wasn't real?" Joey asked.

"I think there was something real but not what they were telling us," Jeff replied.

"I agree. I had COVID and it was a mild cold," Joey acknowledged.

"Did you get jabbed?" I asked him.

"You kidding? My dad worked for OSHA. He knew how dangerous those jabs were. He had to fight for his own medical exemption."

"I'm willing to bet Benjamin Sheldon hasn't been jabbed either," I said.

Autumn nodded.

"Because he's too smart?" Joey asked.

Not wanting to say that Yvonne had no traces of it in her, I simply nodded too.

"We need to check out Graham. He was assisting FEMA before he joined us," Eric said.

"Paul saved his life and Graham could have turned Autumn and me in the next time we saw him."

"She's right. I don't think Graham is the infiltrator," Autumn agreed with me.

"Well, what about Brady?"

"Why are you focusing on those two?" Autumn asked.

I suspected she was stopping short of saying the word "jealous."

"They both seem like nice guys. That doesn't mean my intuition works perfectly, but I trust them," I said.

"Read any books lately? The villain is always the person you trust the most," Eric countered.

"Aha!" Autumn exclaimed. "Now we know. You, Eric, are the infiltrator."

He threw up his hands.

"She's got you, Eric," Jeff teased.

Grant promised to watch Yvonne and keep her safe

Before taking off, I made sure Yvonne got another ride, this time on Daphne. "Daphne is really sweet," she said. "Like her best."

"You'll have lots more chances to ride her."

"Baby."

"Five months must seem like a long time at your age, but it is a much shorter time for me at eighteen."

Back in the residential quarters, I told Everlove and Esther, "If anyone outside of family comes near Yvonne, consider them dinner."

"Dinner," Yvonne repeated.

"Their job is to protect you," I said.

Yvonne hugged each of the wolves. I remembered how frightened she was of them that first day. There had been so many changes in all our lives in such a short time.

I hugged my future brother-in-law. "Take care of our little girl and of yourself."

"And you take care of my brother and sister and yourself."

"I'll do my best," I said as Paul prepared to drive me over to Jack's to pick up Autumn, Eric and Joey.

"Glyphosate-free," I told Joey as I handed him one of the organic sandwiches I'd made to eat on the way.

"My dad said, if I didn't avoid glyphosate, I wouldn't have normal children. That's when I stopped drinking soft drinks with corn syrup."

"Smart dad," I acknowledged.

"What was your dad like, Treasure?"

"Rotten. He was about as bad as a dad could be. He's gone now, too."

"My dad was great," Autumn said. "We're all orphans. It's tough at first. They say it gets easier. I still miss my parents."

"I miss my mom," I lamented. I looked at Paul who seemed to be avoiding the conversation. I touched his shoulder. He gave me a quick smile.

The lab looked like a hole in a wall from the outside. As we entered, we discovered the bulk of the place was in the basement. "This is really decked out," I said, seeing all the testing equipment and refrigerators full of various kinds of samples.

Ronnie introduced us to Chase, a longtime friend of his. "I can run experiments at Chase's lab that I can't run at my regular work. The preliminary scans of the samples were so interesting that I knew I needed to come up here," Ronnie said. He looked at Joey. "I'm so sorry about your dad. He was a great brother. If you need anything, a place to stay, money for college, or whatever, I'm here for you."

"I know," Joey replied. I could see tears in his eyes.

"I don't know why you didn't come to me right away," Ronny puzzled.

"I wanted to find out why my dad was killed and who killed him. And I thought you'd try to hold me back."

"Well, this may answer that," Chase said.

"If anyone can detect a poisonous substance, it's Chase."

"I expected to find several of these combinations dangerous in large quantities but when I tested them, they turned out to be deadly to human cells in more minute quantities than I would have expected. They contain an almost undetectable toxic chemical I'd never seen before. Look. This is that sample you marked 'J-35 OP N PKS.'" He put a drop in a Petri dish with some cells. "These are human cells." After a few minutes, the cells turned black and dissolved. He did the same with something in another Petri dish. "These are squirrel cells." No reaction was visible.

"But animals died at Yosemite."

"They may have improved upon what they used there. I understand animals did not die at Sequioa. This 2030 compound is even more advanced." He went to that sample. After thirty seconds, the human cells turned black, while there was no reaction in the animal cells. "This is more concentrated, but when I tried to detect the chemical compound causing this reaction, even the computers came up negative. We also found a 2030 plus, where the only difference was that the squirrel cells died. Air further activates the deadly effects of 2030, making it more deadly, before it disintegrates all the toxins."

"Could 2030 plus be what they used at Yosemite?"

"From your description, it seems likely."

"You think they killed my dad over this?"

"This toxin can cost a company millions of dollars or make it millions, maybe billions of dollars," Ronnie explained.

"But why did they kill Clay? They had to know he wasn't a lab tech or the collector. He is older than those of us who went to the plant?"

"Maybe they did a facial recognition on Joey and figured they were working on it together. Clay had enforcement abilities."

"I got my dad killed." Tears ran down Joey's cheeks.

Paul and I each put an arm around him. "It was me," I said.

"No. You're all taking it wrong. They are prepared to kill anyone they consider a threat," Ronnie assured his nephew. "On his next inspection, they might have nailed him. Chase and I are going to take precautions ourselves. I've got the rest of the week off and we'll be staying in Madera until we do further analysis on the mixture."

"They've infiltrated some of the people on our side at Yosemite," Paul advised them. "Joey's safe where he's staying, but there is a mole among the people who plan to help us rid the park of FEMA."

"You sure you want to stay at Yosemite?" Ronnie asked.

"I do. I've got to know who killed my dad."

"2030 wasn't one I picked up in the lab?"

"No. 2030 and 2030 plus were on the truck and labeled."

"2030 was appropriately named," Autumn declared. "The invisible people killer."

"The atomic numbers on some of the compounds you've broken down so far are impossible," Paul said, looking at the preliminary analysis. "Thirty-five-point four?"

"I would have thought so too."

"Is 2030 radioactive?" I asked.

"It should be, but it's not."

"This goes against everything I learned in chemistry," Paul said. "Rockheap created this?"

"I suspect the mass production may have been turned over to Rockheap after the development. DARPA has been experimenting for years with chemical and biological warfare. What do you think caused all those deaths around Fort Detrick and why do you think our government was so protective of the biolabs in Ukraine?" Chase asked.

"Isn't Fort Detrick or Ukraine where COVID was supposed to have originated?" I asked.

"That's one theory."

"Grant said, when he was a prisoner, they were injecting some of the inmates with chemicals," Paul told us. "They were sent elsewhere for the injections and never returned."

"Did they inject Grant with anything?" I worried.

"They hadn't gotten to the rangers yet. If you hadn't saved him—"

"He might have been a guinea pig."

"A dead one."

"Why didn't they just pick a regular federal prison, instead of experimenting on prisoners in the Valley?"

"Too much oversight," Ronnie guessed.

"We only checked two cellblocks in the compound where Grant was held, but we didn't check the rest of the compound where they were held and there were other buildings," I recalled.

"Brady was the one who took us to Grant. I wonder if he was just supposed to lead us to Grant?"

"I don't think Brady is the infiltrator," I countered Eric's intimation. I was getting firmer and firmer about it. I liked Brady, not like Paul, but my intuition told me Brady was a nice person. But that intuition had been wrong before.

Outside, I pulled Autumn away. "Eric is getting more and more jealous."

"I'm not ready to make a commitment. That doesn't mean I'm going to pick Brady. Eric's the one I went to Paso Robles with, the one I had a near-death experience with. I don't know why he is jealous."

I noticed Paul speaking with Eric. Eric came over to Autumn. "I'm sorry, I've been overreacting to Brady. I don't like the way he looks at you."

"The way he looks at me is not as important as the way I look at you."

He smiled. "Sorry. I may have been a little biased. Even if I overreacted, that doesn't mean I'm going to trust him."

She gave Eric a quick kiss. "I haven't done that with Brady."

He smiled, again.

"Let's get back to Yosemite. We'll be back here when they get more results," Paul suggested.

When we got to Jack's, Jeff was monitoring cameras, Grant and Jack had put up their own cameras around the Mariposa Camp.

"The infiltrator is going to mess up and when he does, we're going to catch him."

The next morning, we got word the Ninth Circuit had refused to grant FEMA relief from the lower court decision. "That was fast."

"The General is going back to the Valley to evict FEMA and the remaining National Guardsmen," Grant told us.

"Do you think they'll leave without a fight?" I asked.

"They are already in violation of the law by remaining after the district court's decision."

"What about the rangers?"

"We're rangers, not warriors. After the military finishes its job, we'll go down there."

"Where's Yvonne?" I asked.

"Out walking with Autumn," Paul said.

"Autumn came back."

"Where's Yvonne?" Paul asked her.

"Isn't she here? She ran on ahead of me."

I ran through the cave, calling for Yvonne.

There was no answer.

"At least, it's daytime. The most dangerous animals are out at night," Autumn said.

"She's a toddler and snakes are out during the day," Grant admonished her.

We went out to look at the area where they had been walking. I started calling her. I heard a noise in the bushes. I ran towards it. Yvonne was toddling through, trying to get to me. "Treasure, Treasure, I saw him."

"Who?"

"Daddy."

"Did you talk to him?"

"He said he'd be back for me."

"Did you tell him where we live?" Paul asked.

"No. Promised," she answered.

I pulled Paul aside. "If her dad is alive and working with the enemy, Yvonne could be in danger."

"If he were on the up and up, he wouldn't have left her in the first place or he would have let the rangers know his daughter was missing," Paul concluded.

Autumn and Grant escorted Yvonne back while checking for onlookers. They took a different and more obscure entrance than the closest one to make it more difficult for someone to follow—especially with Paul and me bringing up the rear, observing everything around us.

I was so concerned about her dad being a bad guy, but the worst didn't hit me until we were home. "He can take her back any time he wants. And she'll probably go with him," I whispered to Paul

"I thought about that, too."

"We need to find out if he is dangerous before that happens."

Yvonne was devouring a stack of pancakes. Paul called the rest of us together and declared, "The girl doesn't leave the cave until we get more information on her dad."

We all agreed.

Jack sent us a video from a foreign satellite. We could see the military trucks driving towards the Valley.

"I want to hear what they are saying," Autumn requested.

"If they have a discussion close enough to our cameras, we'll get that," Paul replied.

"Not good enough," Autumn said, almost under her breath.

"I'm going to the station," Grant announced.

"Isn't Brady there today?" she asked.

"Yes."

"Make sure Yvonne stays here. Let her play in the garden," she told me and Paul.

"What are you up to?"

"Me. I need to rest." She went into her room.

"Remember the last time?" Paul asked.

We knocked on her door. No answer. He used an electronic lock pick to open the inside lock on her door.

"Autumn's gone," I observed. "I'm going after her."

"That's my—"

"Bye, Paul." I kissed him. "It's safer now."

"Until the shooting starts."

"I plan to catch her before then. We'll be back. Watch Yvonne."

I ran out the way I assumed Autumn had gone. I was about to race to the Valley and then saw her going toward the rangers' station. I followed. A few minutes later, she came out with Brady. I rushed to join them.

"So, what's the plan?"

Brady answered. "I guess I'll drive partway to the tunnel and then pull off onto the side. Then we'll walk the rest of the way. It will take the General a while to get to the Glacier cutoff."

Wawona was the longest tunnel in California. It was two lanes and over a mile and a quarter long. Approaching from the southwest, the mountain went up on the right side and there was a long drop-off on the left. We figured we were mostly invisible walking up among the trees. As we got to the Wawona Tunnel, which went through the mountain, we moved over it, hidden by the trees.

A long line of military vehicles entered the Tunnel, taking both sides of the road. As cars started to emerge from the other side, it began violently shaking, rocks started falling and debris filled my lungs.

CHAPTER 50

It wasn't an earthquake as it was limited to the tunnel and area around it. The ends of the tunnel collapsed as we were nearly crushed by falling boulders from higher on the mountain.

Brady, Autumn and I had to stabilize each other to avoid falling. When the shaking stopped, it appeared the worst of the damage was the collapse of both ends of the tunnel.

"I didn't hear any explosions," I said.

"They probably did some drilling and booby trapped it to collapse when they pulled a rope or something to make it look natural."

It looked as if fifty or more vehicles had been trapped inside.

"Aren't there escape hatches in the tunnel?"

"How much would you like to bet those are blocked too?" Brady asked. "Did anything about this look natural?"

We moved back towards the side where the vehicles had entered. Men in the vehicles that hadn't made it into the tunnel tried to lift rocks out of the way to release their friends. "If they can just get enough open for them to crawl through, everyone can be saved," Autumn conjectured.

"Not quite," Brady said, pointing to the backs of two military vehicles that had mostly made it into the tunnel only to be directly under the collapse.

"We should help," I encouraged.

Brady grabbed my arm. "We're not supposed to be here."

"Those are our friends, sort of and we have to help. FEMA's on the other side."

From our vantage point, I could see the FEMA and National Guard vehicles coming up the mountain. "I guess those are the National Guardsmen who didn't defect to us."

"I'm with Treasure," Autumn said, joining me in rushing down to the upper end of the tunnel. We joined the men in trying to pull rocks free. Ropes and chains were attached to large sections of the collapse as vehicles backed up, pulling the granite boulders and chunks of concrete away from the crushed cars. Together, we worked to do our best to clear the wreckage, but it took hours to feel like we were accomplishing anything. When we got the vehicles at the opening uncovered, there was nobody in them.

"Help," we heard from somewhere inside the tunnel. We assisted the former occupants of those vehicles out. They were barely harmed. They had apparently jumped out and crawled under less impacted vehicles when the cave-in started and their injuries were mostly limited to scratches and bruises. Men were climbing out, leaving their vehicles behind. Among those who climbed out was the General.

"My driver was killed, and I don't think the soldiers in the front vehicles made it either," he said.

It wasn't long before a path at the Valley end was cleared too. The General went back through the tunnel to meet with the FEMA officials.

Brady, Autumn and I snuck back over the top to watch. I turned and found Paul was behind me. "What about—"

"Grant's watching her. Everything visible is being recorded by either Jack or my setup."

I nodded.

"Will you ever stop risking your neck?"

I wasn't going to blame it on Autumn. She may have been first out, but I didn't suggest turning around.

"Guess I have a death wish."

"Just wait until after we're together for seventy years before you carry out that wish."

I smiled. "Seventy years. I was counting on eighty or ninety."

"Okay, a compromise. One hundred."

"I'll go for that."

We needed to get closer to hear. I pulled out my latest cell and started recording and live-streaming.

"The Ninth Circuit has ruled. You have no choice but to leave."

"We have lots of choices, but our work here is almost finished."

"Does that mean you'll pull out?"

"We'll start pulling out the day after tomorrow. Pulling out all the equipment could take several weeks."

"I wonder what the work is that is almost done?" I queried.

"As destructive as they are, they'll probably burn the place down when they leave," Paul said.

I couldn't hear everything, but I saw our general and a FEMA commander with his fake general's stripes shake hands.

"They captured him for experimentation and he's shaking their hands," I griped.

"Camaraderie among the government aficionados," Paul critiqued.

"Yeah. The General would have needed to attend college to become commissioned prior to becoming a general. He was probably indoctrinated at West Point," I figured.

"What are they, best friends now?" Brady asked.

"Just so long as the General doesn't share information."

"Do you think we can help those men in the front vehicles?"

"When the lovefest is over, maybe they'll pull them out. We need a limited profile," Paul responded.

FEMA used its equipment to clear the fallen section of the Lookout side of the tunnel.

"Look at that pile they pulled from the Lookout side. There's got to be casualties."

A FEMA medical crew pronounced five of the guys up front dead and took away their bodies. The FEMA General ordered his men to assist the military in getting their vehicles out of the tunnel.

I was glad we had kept Paul's and Jack's homes secret from the

General and had not told the General the truth about Yvonne. But he could reveal a lot of other details about us and Jack to FEMA if he was so inclined.

"Does the General have any of our computer or video information?"

"Just copies of the videos and pix we made public, and he knows about the attempt on Autumn and Eric and the FEMA pictures," Paul said.

"I guess you can't trust a man in a uniform," Autumn remarked.

Brady looked at her. "It could be that he's just being diplomatic to convince them to leave without any shots being fired."

"As cozy as they are, I wouldn't be surprised if the General brought that guy back to Mariposa for some R and R," I commented.

"They didn't say they were leaving right away. Maybe our general is going to do a wait-and-see approach before moving into action," Brady noted.

A dozen FEMA soldiers were helping remove vehicles from the tunnel.

"Let's go," Brady suggested.

We retreated to Brady's vehicle and returned to the ranger station.

"Did you get that on video?" Paul asked me.

"The collapse and the pow wow," I said.

"Same," Autumn related.

"Are you going to put that on the Net?"

"I don't know," Paul said. "It made FEMA look like a bunch of cooperative nice guys."

"We could put up the tunnel collapse," I said. "That isn't something likely to happen in the absence of an assist. It's been standing since 1933."

"Do you really expect FEMA to keep its word to leave?" Brady asked.

"Doubt it," Paul said. "Though I would be surprised if some in Congress weren't calling for an investigation into the death of the Congressman."

"You saved us that night, Brady," I remembered. "Thank you."

"You might have done okay without me."

"I don't think so. We were in more than a bit of danger."

"I think we should get him a hero's trophy," Autumn said.

"Thanks for helping the two women in my life. Though I'm not happy you took them to the tunnel today."

"Big brother, notice we're still alive," Autumn said.

"I'm just glad there wasn't any shooting, today," I commented.

"I shot lots of pictures," Autumn noted.

"I like a woman who has a mind of her own," Brady said.

"Thank you." Autumn smiled.

Back at the cave, Yvonne and the wolves were running through the garden and rolling in the grass. Esther was licking Yvonne's face.

"These wolves are recruiting family members," I remarked to Paul.

"They don't take to anyone the way they've taken to you and Yvonne."

"If Yvonne's father is alive, maybe he was just investigating what was going on with those pictures and somehow FEMA got their hands on them."

"Maybe. I've asked Jack to get his picture from online files but so far, the father seems not to have any pictures up. His fingerprint was on his driver's license at the DMV, but for whatever reason, his photo was blurry and so was the print."

"Don't they have a program to fix that?" Autumn asked. "The DMV is doing biometrics. They aren't allowing blurry photos."

"The DMV is picky about photos—unless the government wanted his identity kept secret," Paul noted.

"Do you think he could be part of Signature Reduction?" I asked.

"That's a nasty group," Paul said.

"Maybe he's with one of the better government agencies and had his image protected. I'd like Yvonne to stay as much as you do, but I also want her to be happy. When we picked her up, she kept calling for her mother."

"But not her daddy."

"Maybe she was closer to her mother."

We all went over to Jack's for a conference. While there, Yvonne played with Teach Your Baby to Read cards.

"The military is leaving," Jack said.

"What?" That surprised me. "Aren't they going to wait for FEMA to leave?"

"They worked out a deal."

"And then FEMA will fail to follow through."

"That's probable. They both work for the same master and the General probably didn't want to face a court-martial. This way, he leaves with a win."

"Are all the military going with him?" Paul asked.

"They were kind of rogue in being here. This provides them cover."

"They were kidnapped by FEMA," I pointed out.

"We've still got the rangers," Jack said.

Paul frowned. "There aren't that many of them."

"I know."

"What about the National Guard?" I asked.

"They're military. I imagine they'll leave too."

I looked at the upside. "With the tunnel collapse, FEMA will have a harder time checking on the Point."

"When they want to, they can work fast. They've already shored it up. Don't know how safe it is."

I went upstairs with Autumn and told her, "I want to talk to Graham."

"I'm going too."

"I'll join you," Eric said.

"I think it would be more convincing if just Paul went with us," I contended. "He saved Graham's life."

Eric looked uncomfortable with that. I suspected it was the jealousy thing again. Eric conceded and agreed to watch Yvonne with Jack.

On the way there, I told Autumn, "I like Eric, but he needs to get the jealousy under control. You can't have him doubting your every action."

"It would help if you didn't appear to be interested in every handsome guy you meet," Paul told her.

"I don't," Autumn said. "I like Graham, Brady and Eric. I haven't kissed anyone but Eric, and I have the right to have friends."

"She's got a point," I told Paul. "Maybe you could speak with Eric. The jealousy thing may be sweet at first but if it continues, it could be a red flag for future problems. Eventually, it will drive Autumn away, and I'm sure Eric doesn't want that."

"He is somewhat insecure in your relationship, but at least he hasn't responded to his feelings in an inappropriate way. I will talk to him."

I knew Paul liked Eric. I did too, and I got that Autumn liked him best of the three guys. I thought about what I had learned about domestic violence and other situations. Men often seemed to worship the ground their victims walked on until they had them under their thumb and then the violence started. I didn't trust men in general.

I looked at Paul. He was so sweet, but there were never any guarantees. I wondered if my mother had thought my father was sweet when she married him—until he wasn't. Paul's parents were warm and loving, a good sign. Men often took after their fathers. My brother certainly had. Even my sister picked up my father's cruelty. I didn't know anything about Brady's or Graham's parents, but Eric seemed devastated by the loss of his parents, as did Jeff.

When we arrived, the military was packing up. I went over to Graham. "What are your plans?"

"We're supposed to be under the authority of the Governor. He sent us here to back up FEMA, the group that's killing people."

"Do you think he'll retaliate if you stay?"

"In the end, we have to do the right thing. There are currently thirty of us. If we continue to stand together, it will probably be okay—I hope."

"Some of the Guard is with FEMA."

"And they're violating Nuremberg."

Garan came out of his tent. I walked over to him. "We're discussing plans. FEMA says they'll leave, but after what they've done, I don't believe them."

"We rangers are sticking together. Our retirement depends on it. Economics matter."

"Of course."

Graham and Autumn seemed to be having a serious discussion. Maybe she was gaining some more insight into him.

"Garan, with all the people here this year, have you seen anyone who resembled the person who pushed Grant's mother off that cliff?"

He shook his head. "That picture you showed me the other day looked a bit like the assailant, but it could have been someone who just looked like him. The man was wearing a facemask. It was back when people were willing to kill their own relatives over facemasks during the third pandemic."

Was that what Clay was urgently trying to reach me about? Had he suddenly felt guilty? Was he going to admit to what happened to Paul's mom? If so, could Joey be trusted?

"I heard that little girl you brought here the other night was Grant's little sister."

"After what happened to his mother, Grant's very protective of the family. He's not letting anyone near her." It was a sidestep. "Has anyone else asked about her?"

"Graham was curious."

"Graham?"

"He said that she didn't look like Paul or Grant."

"I think there is a major resemblance. And Grant and Paul have different looks. Grant has dark hair and Paul has light brown hair. I think it relates to which parent they take after."

"I pointed that out to Graham. He didn't seem to accept that."

"Really?"

I looked at Graham. He was relatively young. But appearances could be deceiving. The little girl was only a few years old. Anyone could grab a National Guard uniform. Graham was pretty eager to join the resistance, but he clearly had friends in the National Guard who had joined him—or were they National Guardsmen? In Benjamin's blurry picture, the hair color was close to Graham's but then anyone could use hair dye. Why would the DMV allow such a blurry picture—unless he was tied to FEMA or the Signature Force? I hoped Angela had also survived.

The tie-in between government officials and the trafficking issue crossed my mind. Trafficking victims had claimed that trafficking went up to the highest levels of government. Yvonne might not even be their baby. They might have purchased her. That could explain why Benjamin was willing to desert his daughter.

I thanked Garan for his information and asked him to keep his eyes open for anyone who might try to harm the family.

When we got back to Jack's, I said, "We've got the rangers and about thirty National Guardsmen, but Garan has some questions about Graham. I'm wondering if he is the FEMA informant."

"No way," Autumn declared. "He was telling me about his family. His father is a minister. Did you know that? He taught him to always follow his conscience and that's why Graham went with our side."

"You do know about the sex scandals in the churches?" Eric asked.

"The majority of ministers are good people," I defended. "There are some bad computer experts, but you can't blame the rest on the few who do bad things."

"Which bad things?"

Autumn jumped in. "Mistreat their families. I heard about a computer tech from San Diego, Mark something or other, who beat his wife, caused the death of his mother-in-law and hacked into bank accounts that weren't his and emptied them."

"What happened to him?" I asked.

"Nothing. Prosecutions these days are politically motivated. Nobody cares about real criminals."

"Domestic violence is becoming more and more acceptable in California," Eric pointed out.

"We need to change that," Paul said.

"Definitely," Eric agreed. "I'm glad my dad treated my mom well."

Paul called Lee, one of the attorneys who was handling the action.

"I don't see any evidence FEMA is leaving. The military, which was going to check them, is leaving...Really. I'm putting this on speaker phone."

Paul continued. "You say people are planning to march on Yosemite? They already killed a great many people when this started. There's more. We have some evidence they've been experimenting with various poisons. The final report is not out, but they've come up with a poison that will kill humans but not animal or plant life. Anyone coming here could be in danger."

"Have you seen any evidence they've used that?"

"Animals survived poison drops elsewhere. What was dropped in Yosemite killed wildlife. The trees and plants survived."

"So, it wasn't Agent Orange? You do know glyphosate is related to Agent Orange."

"Agent Orange was in the last century. But rangers have continued to find dead animals that have gone into the Valley. They may have eaten contaminated soil or trash."

I thought about Yvonne. We were lucky she didn't eat any of the dirt and came out of the Ahwanhee after the worst had dissipated. There were so many questions in the air.

"The pets didn't die in Sonoma," Eric told Lee.

"In Oakhurst, they contaminated the water and fish. People eating or drinking the contaminated substances got sick," I recounted.

"It appears that Rockheap may be the source of the poisons," Paul informed her.

"Can you prove it with a chain of custody?"

"No. People could be in danger if we did."

"Then, unless FEMA admits the source or if you can't prove the specific poisons used came from Rockheap, there's not enough evidence to go after them."

"Grant said they injected some of the prisoners with something but didn't get to the rangers before the rescue."

"How about the military?"

"Don't know. But aren't they usually the first ones to get experimental injections?"

"The testimony of the rangers would help make the case. If you could prove what they were using for injections, that would help as well."

"Tomorrow morning, the rangers and National Guard are planning to offer to help FEMA move out and check for evidence as they do so," Paul informed Lee. "Maybe they'll come up with something."

Autumn and I went outside to plan a strategy.

Before we could start, Paul joined us. "We're going to let the rangers and the National Guard take care of this one. They're trained. And I won't go crazy if they run into trouble."

"Crazy is not a word I'd use to describe you," I responded.

"That's because you didn't see me when you were at the tunnel earlier today or when you went down the cliff when the battle was going on or when you were down there trying to rescue Grant."

"They captured Grant and the other rangers and almost injected them. Maybe we should watch from the shadows—just in case they pull something like that again."

"You can watch from the cave."

"If you think I'm going to let my brother and Brady get captured again while I'm twiddling my thumbs that far from the Valley, think again, Bro."

"Autumn."

"And if Autumn's out there, I don't want her to be alone. Think of it this way. We've gotten into really dangerous situations, and we always come out alive."

"Getting killed only happens once."

"Remember when the wolves dragged me in. I didn't just believe I was going to die—part of me didn't care. You and your family gave me a reason to care about living, and I'm going to fight to stay alive, but I won't like myself if I don't do something to help out. What you are doing is so valuable. We never would have convinced the judge and others if you hadn't done your video work. And you guided us with the use of your cameras when we needed guidance. You saved us. Let me feel like I am useful. There is no way you can stop Autumn, and we can watch out for each other."

"I don't like it."

"And I love you for that. I need to do this to feel okay. Keep a tight grip on Yvonne. If she's watching the cameras with you, maybe she'll point out the man she thought was her father."

"I hadn't thought of that," Paul said.

"And it could be she wanted so much for her parents to be okay, she simply imagined she saw him."

"Do you know how to use a gun?"

"I've never used one."

"At least, take a tranquilizer gun. Grant and I can show you how to use it."

"And me? I've used a real gun," Autumn said.

"Talk that over with Grant."

"Passing the buck." She glared.

"My temptation is to say 'yes' as long as you keep the safety on. I'd rather you shot one of them than got shot yourself."

I could see her beaming. She kissed Paul on the cheek. "No wonder you're my favorite brother."

"Avoid all confrontations and stay invisible. This is only for self-defense."

"Got it," Autumn said.

The following morning, Grant worked on my grip of the tranquilizer gun and my aim. It also had a safety. He had me practice against a hanging carpet until he felt I could handle it.

I hugged Yvonne. "No matter what or who you think you see, stay here until I get back. Paul needs you."

She hugged Paul. "Need me?"

"I do. I need you. You'll be right here beside me watching these movies."

"Movies."

Autumn and I raced down the Four-Mile Trail. We wanted to be at the bottom before the boys arrived. At one point, I misstepped and started to slip. Autumn grabbed my hand and steadied me. "Let's take it a little slower," she said.

I was glad when we reached the bottom.

"It looks like they've got the tunnel cleared and functional," Autumn said. "Look, here they come."

"Over there, too," I pointed. I could also see vehicles coming from the road from Tuolumne.

"Grant said there were more rangers and National Guardsmen stationed on the other side. They are also coming up 140."

"Nice. Maybe we won't miss the army. The National Guard still has to answer to the Governor and he doesn't seem to be on our side," I reminded her.

"But they're from us and they won't like taking out their own."

"The mass psychosis is still in effect. It's just changed a little."

"Treasure, don't be a pessimist."

I smiled. "Thanks for always keeping my head on."

"Guillotines are for use on them, not us."

"Do you think Yvonne really saw her dad? His name was on the pictures you recovered."

"Maybe it was someone with the same name or maybe they used his studio after he died. We can worry about it later."

I nodded.

The rangers, along with some National Guardsmen and women, pulled into the Valley with no resistance as far as I could tell. FEMA troopers watched as they approached Curry. I recognized some through my binoculars. "They're the guys who shot the Congressman."

Grant was in a truck a ways back. I radioed him to point that out.

"You think they'll lure them all in and then open fire?" I asked Autumn.

"I don't know. Let's run to get there."

We raced for Curry. As we approached, we saw FEMA troopers shake hands with the men in the front vehicles.

"Democrats?" she quietly asked.

"What?"

"The difference between a Democrat and a Republican is that a Democrat will shake your hand and hug you before he shoots you in the back. The Republican just shoots you in the face without any friendly gestures."

"Let's get close enough to hear," I suggested.

We moved next to what used to be the bike and raft rental shop in the Curry parking lot.

"We appreciate your offer to assist us in tearing down the camp. It should speed up our exit."

"Maybe they really are planning to leave," I whispered to Autumn.

Several of the Rangers and National Guardsmen and women got out of their vehicles and went into the compound in the meadow across from Curry. Grant's and Brady's vehicle was far back behind the first group and not close to entering. Hiding behind trees and bushes and moving only when the FEMA guys weren't looking our way, we crept toward the enclosure. More and more men and women were marched inside. We could see FEMA troopers confiscating their guns.

"Notice nobody is coming out? You think they'll lock them up again?"

"I don't hear anyone complaining yet." Then two men who were entering the door tried to back out, exclaiming, "What the!"

The FEMA agents started to push them in. The men turned and fought. That's when FEMA surrounded all the cars with guns in hand and ordered the occupants to get out and follow the others inside.

CHAPTER 51

"I don't like this," I said.

"Neither do I," Autumn agreed. A couple of FEMA troopers were backed up against where we were hiding. Autumn knocked out one with her gun as I nailed another with a dart. We pulled them back, rather than letting them fall in place.

"Put on their uniforms?" I asked.

"If we're going to get in there, we're going to need their clothes."

We put their outfits over ours and used their caps to cover our hair.

Holding the FEMA guns as an implied threat to anyone approaching us, we did as the others did and encouraged the rangers to go into the facility.

Brady and Grant gave us knowing looks as we ushered them in. I knew they and other rangers had been planning to conceal small guns behind their backs under their jackets and hoped those weren't confiscated.

The rangers and National Guard Troopers were ordered to sit on benches. I wondered if there was going to be a movie and popcorn. No such luck.

The FEMA General we'd seen at the tunnel came into the room, followed by someone brandishing what looked like a large dart gun.

He put it against the arm of one of the rangers and fired some kind of pellet into him.

Grant stood up and started to aim his gun but one of the FEMA troopers pointed his gun right at Grant's neck and said, "I wouldn't try it."

The person who had received the shot looked flustered and then said. "I'm fine."

I was looking for a way to end what was going on, but we were outgunned. I still had my dart gun handy. I backed up, pulling it out. Autumn got in front of me to make my actions less obvious.

A minute later, the FEMA General collapsed. The rangers jumped up and grabbed the FEMA troopers' guns. Gunshots from both sides could be heard. Autumn fired at someone about to aim at Grant. He hit the ground.

Grant grabbed a second gun and started firing both guns at the same time. Another FEMA trooper took aim at Grant but took a nap before he could shoot, thanks to my tranq gun.

Several of the rangers had pulled out hidden guns and were copying Grant, firing multiple weapons at once.

It appeared our side was winning. Our group rushed from the building.

We followed, still clad in our FEMA gear. Outside the building, FEMA was out in full force with guns loaded and aimed. Grant and the other rangers lowered their guns. It didn't look good.

FEMA Troopers marched our people over Stoneman Bridge as Autumn and I each grabbed a vehicle and plowed into the FEMA troopers. This resulted in another fracas with many of the rangers jumping off the bridge while others ran.

I saw a teargas canister in the vehicle I'd driven and tossed it into the crowd. More and more rangers went over the side of the bridge. "Those two," someone yelled, pointing at us.

We started to run but were grabbed. Our caps were pulled off. "Such pretty young girls," a trooper said.

We acted as if we were surrendering as we moved onto the bridge and then, with teargas still in the air, Autumn tripped. "I can't see anything," she cried. A trooper reached down and she twisted his arm and threw him off the bridge.

I kicked the one escorting me in the privates and pulled his gun away. He kept struggling for it, and I was sure I had lost it to him when it went off. The trooper fell dead. I was almost in shock I had killed someone, even though I hadn't meant to.

The other rangers were engaged in fighting. Grant picked me up and threw me over his shoulder as Brady did likewise with Autumn.

Grant tossed me into one of the vehicles as Brady joined us with Autumn. Grant spun it around and drove the wrong way from Curry in the direction of the tunnel. Several FEMA vehicles appeared in the way as he started moving past Bridalveil.

"Hand me that gun behind you," Grant said to Autumn. She complied and he made a quick turn, going off-road into the trees. I was sure they were following. "You two get out," he said.

"Nope," Autumn replied. "We're sticking with you."

He spun around again and fired. It wasn't a regular gun but a flare gun. He fired into the front of an oncoming vehicle and spun around again. We jumped out and he sent ours towards the valley road. We ran for the trail.

"Too obvious," I said.

"Exactly," he agreed. We hid near the bottom of the trail and watched as the FEMA group following us ran up the trail. We bolted across the road towards the Merced and followed the river near the bank until we got to El Portal.

"Now what?"

"Rockheap," I said. "That truck is heading towards the Valley." As it stopped at an automatic gas station, we climbed onto the top and held on. It continued to the Valley.

We watched as we approached the Ahwahnee Meadow, where Grant had been held.

Two men signed for shipments as Autumn got video. We slid off to look at what was happening. Boxes were unloaded onto the ground and the truck took off. The men, who were manning the compound, were taking them inside two at a time. When they went in, we pulled away one of the boxes and looked inside.

"Hypodermic needles," I said. "Filled ones."

I photographed them and then photographed the troopers taking the other boxes into the detention building as Autumn continued her video recording. One of the two came back outside and went to sleep as I tranquilized him.

"You're pretty good at that. How long have you been practicing?" Brady asked.

"My first time was today."

"A natural."

Brady pulled off the trooper's outfit. Grant put it over his. He hustled toward the compound as Autumn and I followed, tranquilizing the entry guard.

In the opposite direction from where we had found Grant during the earlier rescue, I heard someone cry. We moved towards the sound. "NO!!!"

A doctor was injecting something into a man as a guard watched. Other men on the floor looked lifeless.

The man started to relax and then collapsed.

The doctor listened to his chest. "Another cardiac arrest."

"They're not going to help him," I whispered to Grant.

He borrowed my tranq gun and took down both the doctor and the guard. We went over to the man. Grant tried CPR. The man opened his eyes.

"Auschwitz. My dad escaped Auschwitz, and I never thought I'd be in a place that was worse, being tortured by my own government."

"Take it easy. We've got you," Grant told him, but the man fell silent. Grant grabbed his wrist. No heartbeat. He tried CPR again to no avail.

"Look," Autumn whispered. In a cell next to the room, was a pile of dead bodies, some with blue coloring, others looking as if their flesh was eaten off.

"The test experiments for the new chemicals," I said. We heard footsteps and moved out quickly. There was a jeep out front. Grant put another trooper to sleep and Brady took the uniform. We took the jeep and one of the boxes through El Portal.

"What's that?" a FEMA trooper asked as we were stopped entering El Portal.

"The General told us to deliver this to someone in Merced," Grant explained.

The man hesitated and I was sure we were finished, but then he let us through.

We cut off at Mariposa towards Fish Camp, taking an off-route that bypassed Oakhurst. We dropped Brady off at what was left of the Grove encampment. Grant drove us to the Glacier Station."

"What about the chemicals?"

"We need to have them checked out."

"Grant put them in his truck. After I get you home, I'm taking Eric and Joey to Madero."

"We don't get to go?" Autumn asked.

He gave us a look that said "no."

He dropped us off not far from the passage to the garage and sped off.

Paul met us the moment we got inside. He took me in his arms and kissed me. "You said you were just backup."

"They were going to inject them and then take them off to either be shot or captured," Autumn protested as we proceeded towards the living quarters.

"It was a trap. Grant is taking the chemicals they're injecting into prisoners to Madero for analysis."

"Autumn took video and I took pictures," I said.

"They may be useful in court," Autumn pointed out.

"We've already won, and they won't leave," he reasoned.

"Maybe we can get someone to convene a grand jury. What they are doing is murder," I contended.

"All I know is I want to hold you all night."

"Eric will be going to Madero. Brady should be at Badger Pass by now. Maybe I can hang out with him for a while," Autumn said.

"I thought the idea was to make Eric less jealous, not more jealous," I pointed out.

"I was just thinking of hanging out with him."

"I've got an idea. How about if we watch a movie?" I asked.

"Okay. Which one?" Autumn inquired.

"*Russkies.* It's an older one, but given our insane foreign policy, it's relevant again."

"*ET* with a Russian sailor," Autumn said. "Have you seen it, Treasure?"

"No. But I saw you had the disk."

"Yvonne should like it."

Yvonne was asleep on my bed. Esther was curled up next to her. Everlove was on the floor.

"Did she have dinner?"

"No, but she ate snacks—healthy ones," Paul informed me.

"And I would have thought you would have fed her the most unhealthy snacks you could find."

"Well, with Yvonne asleep, how about we watch *Double Jeopardy.* That's where the wife gets to kill the husband twice," Autumn suggested.

"Isn't there a movie where guys are nice to women?" Paul asked.

"The bad guy's usually a man," Autumn said. "Sorry."

"How about *Ishtar*? The CIA gave it bad reviews long ago," Paul urged.

"That might be good. Or how about *Kate and Leopold*?" I suggested.

"I'd like to time-travel through a portal," Autumn said.

"I wouldn't want to. I wouldn't want to accidentally change anything." I looked at Paul

Yvonne started crying as if she were having a nightmare. "What's wrong, honey?" Paul and I both sat down next to her. He kissed her forehead.

"Daddy and Mommy, fighting."

"Fighting?" I asked.

"Daddy hit mommy."

"It was a dream," Autumn said.

Tears were running down Yvonne's cheeks and I wiped them away as more flooded. "It will be alright."

"Mommy crying. He told her stop asking questions. Hit her."

"What happened after he hit her?" I asked, hoping I wasn't making it worse for her.

"She fell."

"Did she get up?" Autumn questioned.

"Don't know. He was mad at me. I ran."

"Then what?" Paul asked.

"Woke up."

"Don't worry," Autumn said. "It was a bad dream. It wasn't real."

Paul kissed her forehead as I kissed her cheek.

I turned to Autumn, thinking about my own dad. "Unless of course it was." I wondered if repressed memories were coming up.

Paul caught my drift and followed up. "You said your parents went out and didn't come back."

"I came back after I ran. I was bad. They were gone—cause I was bad."

"You weren't bad. You are good, very good," I said.

"You are sweet and good. You did the right thing," Paul assured her.

"I ran. They left cause I ran."

"The last time you saw your mom, she was on the floor?" I asked.

"Don't know. Don't want think about it." She started crying again and my heart was breaking for her.

I pulled her close to me. I didn't know if it was right to press, but I knew he might come back for her. "Did your father ever hurt you?"

"No. I don't know. I was bad."

"It's okay," Paul said. "You're safe now."

"I want my mommy."

I found I was crying as well. "We'll keep looking for her," I said. "I lost my mommy too."

Paul took both of us in his arms. "Good men don't hit women. Running was good."

"Whatever happened, I know you," I said. "You are a wonderful girl, a real treasure."

"Like you."

"Better than me."

Paul looked at me and shook his head. "Never cut yourself down, honey."

I held her close until she fell asleep again.

Grant called. We left the room as Paul put it on speakerphone. "I'll be back late. I didn't mention, but the rangers and National Guard all managed to make it out. They went downriver and managed to help each other. They have relocated from the Grove to Badger Pass. Given they got chummy with the other side, we figured the infiltrator may have been military all along. I've suggested they relocate closer to the Valley."

After the call, I turned to Paul. "That puts them closer to us and Jack."

"We'll still have privacy. Badger Pass is about six miles from Glacier and several more miles from Jack's. There's been a rangers' station there for years. There have been times when Badger Pass was crawling with people, and it didn't bother my dad. Glacier used to be very popular with tourists too."

I checked on Yvonne. She was sleeping peacefully. I went to Autumn's room and found she was out. I suspected she was on her way to Jack's or to visit Brady. Paul came in.

"Autumn called. She is at Badger Pass with Brady. The ranger who got the injection is acting very weird."

"Do you want me to watch Yvonne while you check it out?" I asked.

"If you wouldn't mind."

"Of course. Yvonne's gotten enough exposure. We need to protect her while we figure out whether her father is alive and either an infiltrator or abuser."

I laid down beside Yvonne with my cell on the table next to us.

At three in the morning, I noticed I hadn't heard from Paul. I picked up the phone and gave him a call.

"Dean, the ranger who was injected, is acting like he's under mind-control and waiting for instructions."

CHAPTER 52

"Ronnie found the syringes had some powerful hallucinogens, along with fentanyl, sodium pentothal and a few other things, acting together. They also contain some kind of electronic receptors," Paul continued.

"They were going to mind-control the rangers, then? "

"Grant and Eric are on their way back. I took some additional blood samples, and I am running them over to Madero. Grant and Autumn should be back with you soon."

"Be careful."

"I will."

"And watch for those two FEMA hitmen while you're driving. It's really late. You might want to get some rest in Madero before coming back."

"I'll be okay."

"If you can wait until they arrive, I'll go with you so you'll have a co-driver."

"I could use the company."

Autumn arrived and Grant came in a few minutes later and agreed to watch Yvonne. I got ready for the drive, made some sandwiches, and took those along with some drinks to the underground garage. Paul was already there, preparing to get out of the car.

Seeing the dinner I brought, he said, "You think of everything."

I tried to stay awake but dozed on the way to Madero. Paul didn't try to wake me up. The next thing I knew, we were stopping outside the lab. Chase let us in. Ronnie was napping on a cot at the side.

"I guess he really did take time off," I commented.

"His brother may have died for this."

Ronnie woke up. "We didn't have any new information at the time my brother was killed and yet he was trying desperately to reach you."

"You think it might have something to do with something else?"

"Or something he personally discovered or remembered about Rockheap."

"I guess we'll never know," Paul said.

Chase put the blood under a microscope. "Notice these metal receptors in the blood?" He turned on his cell phone and they jumped a little. "If these are inside him, he can be programmed with a cell phone."

"Is there any way to help him?"

"Ivermectin, zinc, NAC and selenium are natural supplements. They may help in the short term. Those were antidotes some used for the various plandemic jabs, which also had reactive metal particles in them.

"I have all four of those back home," Paul said. "I should be back there in a couple of hours."

"Also, lithium may help."

"I have that, too."

"I'll drive," I said. "You need to sleep."

On the way back, we talked about the mind control. "The General was an independent thinker. What if they gave him something that, when activated, would make him cooperative?" Paul pondered.

"Those pictures could have been taken by injected military personnel, all ready to betray the movement on command."

"With mind control, the person who took the pictures might not remember."

"I've been thinking about Yvonne's dad. Do you think he's still alive? If so, what is he doing in Yosemite with all the insanity?"

"Looking for his daughter," Paul surmised.

"Do you believe her dream was just a dream or a memory?"

"I don't know. What do you think?"

"I used to wake up crying when things bothered me. It would be terrible if she really went through what I did."

"It was terrible you went through that. There are a lot of bad men in the world. If her father is alive, before we turn her over to him, we need to make sure there was no violence."

"Her mother fell and she ran. Do you think that was right before the dropping of the poison?"

"If the mother had been inside, Yvonne would have seen her when she came back. She was hiding for days before she wound up in the pile of human debris. Why didn't the mom or dad come back for the daughter if they were alive?"

"Unless they were also hiding out. No. Hiding out or not, their primary concern should have been their daughter." It hit me that I was demonizing them. Did I want Yvonne to stay so much that I would project unjust accusations on her parents? What kind of person was I?

"It will be okay. We'll figure things out."

I knew I needed to relax and let what happens happen.

It was morning when we arrived at Badger Pass. Brady informed us that the only ranger who showed any weird behavior was the one who had been jabbed.

"We'll have to keep an eye on him," Paul said. "The injection particles respond to electronic signals. You should remove all communication devices from him."

"Wifi is everywhere," I said.

Dean, the injected ranger, was almost catatonic, staring off into space. "If they gave the military something, it was a different something or a different concentration," I said. "They weren't catatonic."

"Different people react differently to drugs," Brady noted. "I understand that some people had cool LSD trips while others screamed and jumped off buildings. Also, remember the COVID vaccines. They had different lots, but some people claimed to be fine while others died right after the vaccines and still others died five months or years later of complications."

"Good point, Brady," I said.

"We've been up all night. We'll discuss this later," Paul excused us.

"Tell Autumn, 'good morning,'" Brady requested.

"We will," I assured him.

Autumn was up and eager to go see Eric when we got back. Grant was ready to take off to Badger's Pass.

"Brady said good morning to you," I informed her.

"He did?"

"Be careful. There is a catatonic ranger at Badger who could go out of control."

"I know. It's like a Frankenstein movie," Autumn said.

"He might not be the only one. We don't know what they did to Graham when they treated him at the clinic," Paul advised her.

"He's definitely not catatonic," she declared.

"Chase said that the blood samples from our ranger were different than the contents of the syringes." The thought of all those bodies in the compound had me cringing. I changed the subject. "How did Yvonne sleep?"

"Fine, after I got back. No more nightmares."

"Good."

"I used to have nightmares as a child," Autumn recalled.

"What of?"

"That the President would start bombing Yosemite."

"Almost prophetic."

"Treasure drove all night. As her doctor, I prescribe sleep. Unless she wants breakfast first."

"Pancakes? I deprived myself of them all those years because of glyphosate and yours are awesome. You drove the first part of the night. If you want, I'll cook."

"I'll cook and bring you breakfast after you have a warm shower and hop into bed."

"Sounds wonderful."

If he had been someone else, a statement like his would have had an entirely different meaning.

After showering, I laid down next to Yvonne. She woke up.

"Cakes!" she exclaimed as Paul brought in two stacks.

"You came prepared," I told him.

"And I wasn't even a Boy Scout."

He put two bed trays down for me and Yvonne, and then he started feeding me.

"And what an amazing bedside manner."

"You'll get a lot more of this after we're married."

"Really? Great selling point."

I looked over at Yvonne. "You look beautiful, today."

"Brutiful. Treasure said I'm brutiful."

"Treasure always tells the truth."

***

After breakfast, I fell fast asleep. When I did wake up, it was afternoon. I didn't notice when Yvonne got up. I went into the den where Paul was.

"Is Yvonne here?"

"No. I thought she was still in the bedroom."

I rushed through the garden and fields. "Everlove," I called. "Find Yvonne."

Everlove took off running and I followed. Yvonne was in the grazing pasture talking to Laura and holding out an apple for her to eat.

I gave her a hug. "I'm glad you are having a good time. I worry about you. There are some dangerous people outside."

"I'm inside."

"I know. Do me a really big favor. Next time you go into the tunnels or the fields, let one of us know. I love you and I worry about you."

"Mommy worries bout me, too."

"You said your parents went out and didn't come back?"

"I ran. Mommy was on floor. Daddy real mad. I came back. Gone."

"Did your mother ever get up off the floor?"

"Gone."

"Your daddy hit her?"

She made a fist and imitated someone hitting.

"Did he hit you?"

"No. Hit Mommy."

I planned to call Jack. Maybe her mother wasn't outside at the time of the poisoning. Maybe he carried her off somewhere. If she were still alive, she might be injured and still carefully searching the Ahwahnee for her missing baby.

I forgot about all that when I entered the den.

"Holy shit," Paul was saying. He saw me and Yvonne and said, "Sorry."

"What's happening?"

"The last five Presidents, including President Game Show Host and President Braindead, went on TV and called anyone opposing the FEMA cleanup of the National Parks a terrorist."

"Terrorist?"

"Better than that. We're right-wing Russian racist terrorists, according to four of them."

"Four out of four wrong ain't bad. I got that as a kid when I worked on Bernie's campaign and I later worked on Tulsi's, though I was to the left of both."

"Me too. I'm more of a Kucinich person. He was my parents' hero. My parents were lifelong Democrats."

"Mine too."

"The President is calling for the arrest and detention of anyone standing in the way of FEMA. And the warmonger who lost to Trump the first time concurs."

"Wonderful," I said. "I guess the last person who told the President what to say was a chemical company executive."

"It's insane," he muttered.

"While FEMA's using Yosemite to prepare bioweapons and kill people, including a Congressman, those who support life and nature are terrorists."

"That's about the size of it. And he also had some choice words for the justices who granted the injunctive relief."

"Here he is back again," Paul noted.

"If you support decency and democracy, you will stand with FEMA against the violent racist mob that is trying to undercut the good that our country does."

"Violent terrists?" Yvonne asked.

"That man is a liar. He's bought and paid for by very evil people and so are most of those idiots in government."

"Governmentiots."

"Yes," Paul acknowledged.

Autumn burst in, followed by Grant. "Did you hear what President Lettucehead said?"

"And everyone will go along with it because to get all sell-outs out of Congress, they'd have to unrig the elections." Paul pointed out.

"With voting a disaster in the country, the people don't have a way to get their message across. It's a dictatorship," I said.

Autumn made two fists. "They should be marching in the street as in Europe."

Leaving Grant and Yvonne at the Cave, Paul drove me and Autumn over to Jack's, where we sat around discussing the turn of events. "The President can say whatever he wants, but the order still stands. FEMA is supposed to evacuate," Jack snapped.

"And who is going to enforce it? The military left. And they'll probably side with the President and come back here to clear us out, next," I warned.

"You didn't hear?"

"Hear what?"

"Apparently, a lot of soldiers who left died of a mysterious disease. Supposedly, that's part of what they are cleaning up," Jack imparted.

"The General?"

"Not yet. But I understand he is praising FEMA."

"It's what they injected them with. We saw bodies and a guy screaming and dying from an injection," I recalled.

"And they have other injections that can turn people into Manchurian candidates, controlled by a cell phone," Paul added.

We could hear planes flying nearby. I was a little nervous. Jack picked up on that.

"Don't worry. From the air, we're camouflaged. In addition to the trees, we have reflective coverings that look like water from up above. Down below, we can see through them as if they aren't there."

"Nice," I said.

"I still don't trust them not to drop stuff above here. Make sure everyone stays indoors," Paul said. "If we travel, we do so in hazmat suits." He called Grant with the same instructions and Grant was going to relay them to Brady and the others.

Jack went into the basement and came out. He had boxes full of hazmat suits. "I've seen this coming for a long time."

"You and my dad," Paul reacted.

When it sounded as if the flyovers had stopped, Paul checked the air quality and drove me and Autumn back to the cave. Yvonne was having another tea party with the wolves.

"What's happening with the rangers?" Paul asked Grant.

"Well, they're doubting all the government's prior stories of domestic terrorism now that they've been called terrorists."

"Each President calls the opposition terrorists," Autumn remarked.

"I guess terrorist is the new word for opponent or educated person," I noted.

"That's been true for a long time. Doctors and experts who researched COVID were also called terrorists," Paul said.

"This would be funny if it weren't so tragic," I noted.

"I bet you haven't heard the worst of it." Grant turned on a mainstream news show.

"Americans are calling for the arrest and possible execution of the terrorists interfering with FEMA at Yosemite and other National Parks. Jake, do you think terrorists such as these should get the death penalty?"

"Disappear them under the NDAA. They are a blight on society."

Grant switched news stations. They all seemed to be echoing that sentiment.

"Isn't anyone telling the truth?"

"The indymedia is, but not one person on the broadcast media."

He opened up links to *The Convo Couch*, *Citizens for Legitimate Government* and *The Last American Vagabond*, where the facts of the poisoning and deaths and the killing of the Congressmen were brought out. One presenter asked, *"Is opposing the destruction of human and animal life in our National Parks terrorism or are people being Stockholmed again into believing that war is peace, freedom is slavery and ignorance is strength?"*

"No wonder the truthtellers are censored," I reacted. "If people knew what was going on, they'd take to the streets."

"I don't know," Grant said. "The American people are lazy."

We tried to make the best of things so Yvonne wouldn't be frightened but inside we were on edge, giving an unwanted sharpness to our voices.

"There's nothing more we can do today," Paul said, calmly. "Everyone should get some rest so we'll be prepared to handle whatever the world brings tomorrow."

I was pretty sure that Paul wasn't going to be able to sleep. From the look on Grant's face, I suspected he wouldn't as well.

I looked at little Yvonne, who was worried but somewhat oblivious to much of what was happening. Autumn prepared a warm bath for Yvonne and I shampooed her hair. After, I helped towel-dry the little girl and put on a new nightgown I had picked up for her, we tucked her in. Autumn told her a bedtime story that she had adapted from an old Zorro movie.

As Yvonne dropped off to sleep, I said, "You're going to turn that girl into an anarchist."

"Have you found any other political philosophy that works?"

"Definitely not."

Paul came to the door and looked in on her. "How's she doing?"

"Confused, but she knows she's safe, here."

"I hope it is safe here. Our Presidents are good at drone bombing wedding parties and hospitals."

"What they did in the Middle East, they were bound to do here."

"This is the trouble with pacifism. We have to wait for the government to act and make a mistake."

"And hopefully, they make a big miscalculation that wakes people up," I said.

"Would you like to play Battleship?" Autumn asked.

I laughed. "I never played it, but if there were an appropriate time, now is it."

At some point, I must have fallen asleep on the floor. One minute I was on the floor playing Battleship and the next, I was in bed, next to Yvonne. Paul came in with two stacks of pancakes.

"It's morning already?"

"If you want, you can sleep for a few more hours."

"What time is it?'

"It's still early. About nine A.M."

"Those pancakes look great."

"Can we go outside riding?" Yvonne asked.

"This isn't the best day for that," I replied. "Maybe when things quiet down."

I wondered if it would ever feel safe walking outside again in my favorite place on Earth.

"Grant went over to Badger Pass for a meeting with the other rangers and the remaining National Guardsmen. Autumn insisted on going with him."

"Have any of them left?"

"Not so far. It's a determined group."

"Nature lovers are the toughest type of terrorists," I said.

"Tree huggers and bird watchers. Terrible people," Paul added.

Yvonne looked confused.

"We're joking," I told her.

"Joking."

"You know, some fresh air might be good while it's still available," he noted.

"Perhaps we can all go out for a walk. At the first sign of feds, we go underground. Literally."

Outside, the sky was blue. I didn't notice any chemtrails. I knew that would change if the feds needed them to control us, nature-lovers.

"Has the Supreme Court weighed in on the injunction?" I asked.

"Not yet. It could depend on who has paid them the most money."

"I understand that nobody with any real integrity has been appointed to the Court in well over sixty years. Gorsuch isn't bad, but he's no Douglas."

"Historically, Douglas was the best on the Court," Paul agreed. "More recently, the standard for a nominee has been hating parents and saying he or she is totally unaware of what a woman is."

"Once in a while, a good decision gets through, such as the Bruen case, which had prosecutors going pro-lock-the-Court-up. You would think people would be outraged at the destruction of our parks."

"Most people are too busy sitting at home, playing video games and watching packaged news."

"Remember when we were in OC. There seemed to be a lot of activists who believed that the wishes of the people had been suppressed. Several people said they were certain their votes in the last several elections still haven't been counted."

"It would make a difference if the millions whose votes are not counted got together and stood up," he commented.

"But you don't think that will happen."

"It hasn't happened in a very long time."

After a while, Autumn joined us, and we continued walking.

"What's that?" Autumn asked.

"It sounds like the mountain is shaking," I replied.

Paul shook his head. "It's not an earthquake."

Autumn reminded us, "What happened at the tunnel wasn't a real earthquake."

"They aren't planning to destroy our mountain, are they?" I asked, turning to Paul.

"Probably, but I don't think they have the equipment to completely do that right now."

"Look," I said. In the distance, I saw something in the air.

"We need to get back inside," Paul advised.

After getting back, we looked at the closed-circuit TV of Badger Pass. "Grant set this up so we can keep an eye on what's going on with the rangers and National Guardsmen."

"A lot of dust is being kicked up," I said, looking at the monitors. Helicopters started landing and armed men rushed out, surrounding the ranger headquarters.

CHAPTER 53

"Grant's in there," I said.

"And Brady and Graham," Autumn noted.

"They look ready to gun them down," I worried. "We have to do something."

"There's nothing we can do that Grant and the rangers aren't already doing," Paul advised. I knew he wanted to rush out as much as Autumn and I did, but he seemed to be trying to stop us from acting.

"They need backup," I said.

"The military's left. With all the rangers and National Guardsmen inside, it may be a standoff. Okay, if any of us is going to help, I will."

"I'm going with you. Autumn—" I looked around. I was planning to ask her to stay here with Yvonne.

"Where has she gone?"

"I don't know."

One of the guys who had flown in, used a loudspeaker to say, "This is Special Agent Rogers of the FBI. This can be peaceful. Come out unarmed with your hands up."

A voice came back. "We are acting lawfully and are the law in the Park. We are asking you to leave."

"We are the FBI."

"We are with the National Parks Service."

"We answer to the Attorney General."

"We answer to the Secretary of the Interior."

There was a lot of silence. Over the planted microphones, we could hear the FBI discussing the matter. "The President will have to order the Secretary of the Interior to fire all these guys."

"The Secretary of the Interior has refused and the President has ordered his resignation," another agent said.

"How soon until the second in command can take over the Department?"

"There's a problem. The Secretary is refusing to stand down. He says you are overpowered."

"Overpowered? Against forty rangers?"

"And thirty National Guardsmen," came Grant's voice. Apparently, he was monitoring the conversation as well and was replying over his loudspeaker.

"What's that?" the lead FBI agent asked. "Listen."

We could hear honking and it sounded like a long traffic jam.

Jack called Paul. "Look at the foreign satellite feed."

Paul put up the satellite feed. There were cars and buses full of people on Highway 41, 140, 120 and all other routes leading into Yosemite. Bumper to bumper cars, trucks and buses were headed towards the Valley as well as our way on Glacier Point Road. I worried that another bloodbath was coming.

"We need to act now, sir," one of the FBI agents said. Several of them rushed the ranger station. The rangers did not shoot. We saw a number of rangers being escorted out with their hands on their heads. Among those were Grant and Brady. I suspected that Graham and Garan were in there somewhere. They were ordered to step into heli-copters.

"Those are H-92 Superhawks," Paul informed me.

"Take care of Yvonne," I said as I started to leave.

"Don't go. Please don't leave me," Yvonne started crying. I picked her up and held her. Her parents had left her and now I could disap-pear. I had to choose between helping Grant and staying with Yvonne.

"Please."

I couldn't leave her.

Grant's helicopter was lifting off. I was too late. There was a loud bang and the clanking of metal as the rotor flew off and the helicopter dropped back down from the few feet it had risen.

The FBI agents turned in the direction the shot had come from and prepared to fire as Grant, Brady and other rangers used the distraction to hit and kick the agents, ripping away some of their guns. In some cases, the FBI agents appeared to gain control of the skirmishes. In others, the rangers appeared to be winning.

Vehicles and buses streamed into the area pulling around the helicopters. People and kids surrounded the FBI.

"Look at the indymedia covering this," Jack said. He sent some links that Paul followed. "There must be millions of people inside the park."

"Where did they come from?"

"I guess they were the people whose votes California refused to count in the last couple dozen elections. They decided they wanted their voices heard in saving their national parks," I contended.

As the FBI agents were surrounded by about fifty to one, they surrendered their guns.

"Smart move," I said. "With America watching, the last thing they need is to fire into the crowd."

"The Administration has again lost the narrative," Paul noted.

"Look at the live feeds past the tunnel," Jack said.

On all routes, people and kids were rushing into the Valley and surrounding FEMA. FEMA wasn't quite as professional as the FBI. They fired into the crowd.

As people started falling, other people drove cars, trucks and buses right into the FEMA troopers who fired as they were plowed under.

Undeterred by FEMA's violent reaction or maybe propelled by it, the parade of vehicles swept through the Valley with FEMA eventually laying down their guns.

"We are not terrorists." It was Lee, the attorney, who had gotten us the injunction, speaking at Camp Curry and pointing at the FEMA troopers who had been taken prisoner by the public. "These are the real terrorists." Behind her, a screen showed video of FEMA killing the Congressman and his aids. "We are the people, the children, the voices of real America and we want these agents, and everyone who has authorized them to be in this park, locked up as accessories to murder and for violations of the Nuremberg Code."

Above at Badger's Point, I could see Autumn rushing over to Grant and hugging him. I knew she was the one who fired the shot. From the damage, I wondered where she had gotten a bazooka.

"That girl has courage. She's a real leader," I boasted to Paul.

"That's what I'm afraid of."

"She's got my vote when she runs for office."

"Autumn! Autumn!" Yvonne shouted, jumping up and down.

"She's a hero," I said. "All of those people are heroes."

"Daddy. I see Daddy."

"Where?"

"He's gone."

There were multiple videos going at once. I couldn't tell which one she had been looking at. There were videos of people, National Guardsmen, rangers, kids, FBI agents and FEMA troopers.

When things settled down, we planned to go back over the footage. We needed to look at the feeds right about the time she spoke up.

Paul turned to the MSM broadcasts. There was no mention of what was happening on any channel. Millions of citizens had descended upon a National Park within California's borders and freed it from FEMA and not one mention on the MSM.

The rangers and people locked up the FEMA troopers and FBI agents in one of FEMA's compounds in the Valley. There was a federal district court down there that had been evacuated during the crisis. A federal justice was brought back to arraign the assailants for assault, battery, vandalism, conspiracy to commit murder, murder, animal abuse and destruction of public property.

After dropping Yvonne off at Jack's, Paul, Eric and I joined Grant, Autumn and Brady down in the Valley.

"These trials will take some time," Grant said.

"Do you think they'll get bail?" I asked.

"The January six defendants didn't harm anyone, and they were denied bail. Back then, the government threw out the *Eighth Amendment*. It would be hard for them to demand enforcement of an Amendment they obliterated," Eric remarked.

"We don't want to be like them," I said. "Will all the charges stick?"

"Probably not. The Administration will likely pardon them," Grant replied. "But eventually the MSM will have to acknowledge the FEMA thugs have been arrested if they want to push their rights."

People started tearing down the compounds and facilities FEMA had set up in the valley, leaving only one facility for a jail.

Grant, Paul and I went to the Ahwahnee to see if we could find some record of Benjamin and Angela Sheldon. We went to the room they had occupied. In a closet, we found a largely decomposed body of a woman. I had trouble looking at the body, but Grant had a stronger stomach.

Her purse was in the room and Grant looked at the driver's license picture.

Paul looked more closely while I had to turn away. "It looks like it could be her. Same hair color and about the same height. My guess is that the weight was similar. It looks like her skull was smashed."

"So, it wasn't a dream. She deserves a decent burial," I said.

"There is a cemetery here in the Valley," Grant noted. "I suspect she'd like to be interred there."

I wondered what I would tell her daughter. The girl clearly loved her mother. Would she be better off not knowing?

With millions of people in the park, there was a long celebration that lasted for days. Tents were set up in the campgrounds and people assisted each other with cooking, cleaning and fixing up the campsites. I was glad these people hadn't seen what I had that day I walked down there with Autumn. It would be some time before I would feel comfortable camping in Yosemite.

Grant called in an embalmer who worked to restore Angela's looks to close to those on her driver's license. It had been days, and we hadn't said anything about our discovery to Yvonne. There was no sign of Benjamin. I figured either he skipped or was alive somewhere. I hoped it was a look-alike the little girl had seen.

I brought Yvonne down for a memorial service on behalf of her mother and all who had died in the Valley. Most of the names were unknown. A large wooden memorial was put up to honor those whose names could be located and those who were, for the time, unknown.

We had planned a special memorial for Angela and I was tasked with telling her daughter. We decided it was best to avoid the details while convincing Yvonne that running was what her mother wanted her to do.

"You don't need to do this alone," Paul said. "We've all lost mothers we loved."

I thought about Paul's mother. I guessed I'd never know the truth about that. I hated keeping secrets from him but he was better off not knowing—especially if the murderer was on the loose.

After breakfast, the morning after the Valley memorial for those lost, Paul put a light saddle on Laura.

"Ride?" Yvonne asked.

"Yes, but slowly. Laura is pregnant." We also wanted to make sure Yvonne was safe, but we knew she'd be more concerned about Laura. She was a lot like me, more concerned about others than herself.

After the ride, we went outside. "It's brutiful," she said, looking down at the Valley from the Point.

"It is," I replied.

"That's why my parents loved it so much here," Paul said.

He carefully watched Yvonne as he continued. "You know I lost my parents and Treasure lost hers, a while back."

"They didn't come home?"

"Did your mother ever tell you anything about religion?"

"Religion?"

"Church?"

"Yes. She took me to a church when her friend died. The guy said

God was watching her friend, God would take care of her. She would be happy."

"Do you believe that?"

"Mommy did. She said—" Yvonne paused as if trying to recall. "Dying makes more powerful."

"Really? I never looked at it that way," I responded. "Some believe that those who pass beyond this life watch over their children after they leave: protect them in a way they can't protect them while they're here." I had heard that, but I hadn't had any real reason to believe it. I wanted to believe it. Autumn had claimed to have some contact with her mother.

I knew that a lot of churches, like the International Bible Students, taught that death was a sleep from which all would have a second chance in a perfect world. My mom was from the group that believed that. Many non-Christian religions believed positive things happened after death, such as the belief in past and future lives. I had been raised a Christian, but I was in the "I don't know" category.

"I'd like to believe my parents are watching what I am doing and helping me behind the scenes," Paul said.

I saw tears form in Yvonne's eyes. She knew what we were leading to. I wanted to stop and wait until she was older.

"I want see Mommy again. I want her hold me, say loves me."

"I'm sure that will happen," Paul said. "Sometimes we have to let go so it can happen."

"Don't want Mommy dead."

I was choked up, trying to find the right words, but they wouldn't come.

"I know. Your mommy loves you so much and she always will wherever she is," Paul said.

"Your mommy, my mommy and Paul's mommy may be watching us right now," I said.

"You think she's mad at me for running."

"No. She wanted you to run. I know. I was with someone who hurt me and I did my best to get my brother and sister out of there. My mother did the same for me. You see, when you love someone, their health and safety mean more than your life."

I realized that that was why it had been so hard to let go of Tatiana. Her life meant more to me than my own. When the person you love more than your own life throws you away and is fine with your dying, how do you recover from that? Yvonne's mother had something neither my late mother nor I had. Yvonne loved her in a way that Tatiana and Zinney would never care about me or about my mom. I hadn't realized I was crying, both for myself and for the little girl whose mother I knew loved her too.

Paul was looking at me as if he had read my thoughts. "I swear, I'll never do to you what Tatiana or your brother did. I love you too much."

"If your mother were here, she'd tell you to never let anyone hurt you," I assured her. "If someone ever tries to, you run and get help. She'd be so proud of the fact that you ran."

"Think so?"

"I know so."

Yvonne leaned towards me and I took her in my arms and we both cried. I was crying for her loss and for mine. I looked at Paul, and my tears turned to tears of hope for the happiness that the future might bring.

"Your mommy was so special and her love for you was so great that we are having a remembrance in her honor in a few days. Would you like to be there as the guest of honor?"

"Me. Yes. Will Mommy be there?"

"Not physically, but watching. We'll all talk about her there and she'll know what we say about her."

The next day, we went to Palmdale, where a service was held for Clay.

"Clay wrote a letter to you that couldn't be delivered," Ronnie said. "I wasn't sure you were going to be here, so after it was returned, I sent it care of Grant at Yosemite."

"I don't know if the mail services have resumed in the Valley. Grant may have to pick it up at the post office tomorrow."

Though we decided to have a closed casket service to make it easier for Yvonne, I had decided that it would be best to have a picture of her mother and a basket full of things she loved at the funeral. There was no way a little girl should see her mother's lifeless form. Besides, whatever religion was correct, one thing was clear. Angela was no longer in that body.

"I'll take care of this," Paul told me. "I'll go to their house and search for pictures and bring mementos she'd want Yvonne to have."

"I should help you."

"Yvonne needs you and the house might bring too many memories for her."

"Okay." I kissed him. "I love you."

"I love you forever."

"What if someone at the memorial tries to take Yvonne away from us?"

"It will be a small event with people we trust. We'll ask anyone who remembers her to simply provide flowers or send words of kindness and we won't mention that Yvonne will be there. That way, Yvonne won't be hassled by Social Services or misguided, bad-meaning child advocates."

"I know. According to the FBI, seventy percent of sex traffic victims come out of Child Protective Services."

"I've seen the stats. It's true."

"It's part of the reason I protected my brother and sister. I was able to stop the blows and, at the same time, keep them from being trafficked."

Yvonne and I went to the Glacier Point Ranger Station.

Brady was there. "This little girl gets prettier every time I see her."

"She does, doesn't she?" I responded.

"Paul and Grant will have to fight off the boys when she gets older."

"Autumn, too."

"Yeah. I've seen her in action. Anyone mistreating Yvonne won't have a chance."

"Where is Autumn? I thought she'd be here."

"She went with Grant to try to track down a letter. Do you think I've got a chance with her?"

"I don't know. She's about to turn eighteen and she will probably go through a lot of changes before she decides on someone."

"She loves Yosemite and I'm not planning to leave."

"That could definitely work in your favor." I knew she really liked Eric, too, but she was far from ready to commit to anyone. And if she went away to college, she might find a new slew of guys to choose from.

"Have you seen Graham lately?"

"He was here earlier today. He's going back to Mariposa. That's where his home is. I'm trying to talk him into moving to New York."

"Eliminate the competition? I don't think you have to worry about Graham. She likes him, but I don't think he's top tier with her."

He smiled.

"I'm glad that Grant has a friend like you. He holds it in, but he's been through a lot, too."

"His mom?" he asked.

"Yeah. And his dad. And everything else that happened here."

"I'm lucky my parents are okay."

"Do you know where it was that his mother slipped?"

"Not specifically. I heard it was at one of the observation points on the path to the top of Upper Yosemite Falls."

"Any chance you could show it to me sometime?"

"I can take you there right now."

"Leave the ranger station temporarily unmanned?"

He picked up a hand-held radio. "Garan. I need to leave the station for a little bit. Would you fill in?"

"Sure."

"Garan's in the coffee shop. He should be here in a few. We can leave now."

"Yvonne, you want to see the Falls?"

"See Falls."

As we walked out, I noticed that there was a crowd of people at the Point.

"It may take some work, but Yosemite is coming back," he said.

"Thanks to all the wonderful people like you who saved it."

"And you."

"Me, too," Yvonne said.

Brady drove us in his ranger car down to the parking lot adjacent to Campground Four, which was right by the trail to the top of the falls. He and I initially took turns carrying Yvonne as we hiked up the trail. It was a bit steep in places and had what seemed like a zillion S curves. Brady made sure I didn't slip.

Yvonne was excited. "Want walk."

I held her hand to make sure she didn't slip while Brady seemed to be watching out for me.

"Fun!" Yvonne, who was surprisingly agile and energetic, exclaimed as she started running.

"Not if we break our necks," I warned. It took a while, but we got to an observation point, midway up the trail.

"I could be wrong, but I think this is where Grant said it happened," Brady advised.

Yvonne reached for me. "Waterfall," she said.

It was beautiful. I could see how someone could fall if they got too close to the edge. "Yes, waterfall," I repeated as I took her in my arms, moving further back from the edge.

I heard a thud behind me.

"Daddy!"

"Brady?" I asked as I turned to see what she was looking at. But it wasn't Brady. Brady was lying on the ground. I recognized the man pointing a gun at me.

CHAPTER 54

"Garan?"

"I'll take my daughter now."

He started to reach for me and the girl. I side-stepped, holding onto Yvonne. "She's not going with anyone at gunpoint."

He holstered his gun. "I want my daughter."

"How could you be two pe—you were living a double life?"

"My daughter."

"Which was real? Garan or Benjamin?"

"What do you think?"

"Grant said you've been here for quite a while. Did Angela know? And don't you have another wife as Garan?"

He grabbed at Yvonne. I, again, side-stepped, not wanting to go toward the edge.

He pulled out his gun, again. I turned, placing my body between him and Yvonne so that any bullet would go through me and not her.

Instead of shooting me, he tried to hit me with the gun and I ducked and dodged, moving Yvonne and myself further away from the cliff.

"There was no masked man here that day, was there?"

"She saw me with Angela and said she'd tell my wife. You do know you're not going to make it off this mountain. Now, give me my daughter. I'm sure we both want her to survive."

"You killed her mother. She doesn't belong with you." I stepped further from the cliff, facing away from him as I put down the little girl, whispering, "Run."

I could see Yvonne's face contorting as she understood what her father had done.

Garan kicked me, causing me to fall against a tree as Yvonne was slowly backing up.

"Run!" I shouted as I continued falling to the ground, where a sharp stone gashed into my side. He stepped on my shoulder and reached out for Yvonne, who was starting to lean down for me.

She backed away. "You killed Mommy."

"I didn't mean to."

"You hit her and hit her. I saw you."

Instead of reaching for her, he grabbed me and dragged me towards the cliff. I grabbed his legs and tried to trip him, but he was too agile.

In his boot, he had a knife. I pulled it out but his hand was stronger and he gained control of it and turned it on me, plunging it into my shoulder.

I pulled it out as blood spurted down my blouse. If there was any pain, it was overshadowed by my worry for Yvonne.

I looked over at Brady on the ground. His head was bleeding. I was at the edge of the cliff and Garan was pushing and kicking at me as the knife went flying and I grasped onto a nearby bush.

Yvonne rushed to us and was grabbing at his leg. "Don't hurt her! Please!" she cried.

Garan picked me up, preparing to toss me over when the sound of a gunshot caused him to turn. Brady was waving his gun in the direction of Garan as he tried to get up.

Garan put me down as Brady looked like he was going to collapse and was turning his head back and forth as if everything was a blur. I doubted Brady could even focus in his condition.

Garan pulled out his gun again and aimed at Brady when someone came out of the trees, knocking him down with a kick. It was Autumn, He still had the gun and looked as if he was going to shoot her.

"I wouldn't," Grant said, pointing his gun at Garan.

Garan stood up and pretended to surrender, but using a rock he was holding behind his back, clubbed Grant on the side of his head.

As Grant fell unconscious, Garan picked up Grant's gun and aimed both guns at me and Autumn.

"Daddy, you hurt Treasure. You hurt Grant."

I looked at Brady. He had dropped back with his eyes closed.

If I didn't act, he was going to shoot me anyway. Maybe I could save the others. I started to rush him but slipped on loose dirt and slid toward him. He fired but the bullet went over me.

He bent over me with the fired gun aimed at me. The other gun was still aimed at Autumn.

"Goodbye, Treasure."

As I prepared to die, he was knocked to the ground by something, someone swinging around the trunk of a tree. Paul. Paul had knocked him down, and one gun fell out of Garan's hand, but Garan still had the other gun and was aiming it at Paul.

I got up and tried to stand in front of Paul, but he pushed me out of the way.

I rushed back. I had to save Paul, but he wouldn't let me block him. Grant was unconscious and Brady was mostly unconscious.

"Back, the three of you," Garan said to Paul, Autumn and me. He wanted us to back toward the cliff.

"He can only get one of us," Paul said. "Run."

It looked as if Garan was about to fire as Yvonne started crying. I jumped in front of Paul again but Paul turned around, moving me back and placing himself between me and Garan.

"You killed Mommy!" Yvonne cried.

"Shut up."

"He killed my mommy, too," Autumn said.

"Bad man, bad man!" Yvonne cried. "Hate you!"

He kicked the little girl to the ground near Brady.

"Now back up," he said to those of us standing as he strode

forward. We backed up a little with Paul holding me tight so I couldn't jump in front of him again.

The sound of the bullet echoed through the trees. I wasn't quite sure how it happened. All I knew was that Garan turned as blood spurted out of his back. Autumn advanced quickly and did a side kick and then another kick, sending him over the cliff.

I ran over to Yvonne, who dropped the gun. "I hurt Daddy."

"No. You saved us." I looked at Paul. "How did this thing fire so easily? She's not that strong?"

Paul came over to me and hugged me and Yvonne. "I'm sorry. I should have been here sooner."

"Paul, you saved my life."

"And mine," Autumn said.

"Mine too," Brady said groggily. "I think I've got a concussion. I had fixed my gun so it had a hair trigger. We were up against insane FEMA guys."

"Love you," Paul said, softly as he kissed my cheek.

"I love you, too."

Paul tore the bottom off his shirt and used it as a bandage for the injury to my shoulder.

"Thanks. I forgot about that. Sorry for bleeding on you, honey." I said as I kissed Yvonne's head.

"Love you," Paul said, softly.

"I love you, too. You have two other patients."

Paul tore another piece of his shirt to wrap Brady's head.

Paul checked over Grant. "He's unconscious, but I think he'll be alright. He'll need some X-rays."

Grant opened his eyes. "What happened?"

"You got knocked out, Bro, and missed the action. I need to get you, Treasure and Brady to the hospital."

"I'm fine," Grant said. "What about Garan?"

"Gone," Autumn declared. "Seems he met the same fate as Mom."

"How did you know?" I asked Paul.

"A picture at Benjamin and Angela's place," Paul related.

"I opened the letter from Clay," Grant said. "He saw Garan and Mom. Garan was FEMA then, though working as a ranger. Garan threatened to have Clay put in indefinite detention if he ever talked. Since Clay was government, he figured he'd keep silent. I'm pretty sure Garan killed Clay."

"That was my fault. I showed him a picture of Clay and asked if he had seen him in the park."

"I share any responsibility. I had him drive the rental back to L.A for Eric the morning Clay was killed," Grant confessed.

"Let's get you all to the hospital," Paul encouraged. "And stop blaming yourselves for what Garan did. I was so overcome when Mom died that I didn't question the official story. If anyone is to blame, it's—"

"Stop sounding like me," I murmured, kissing him.

CHAPTER 55

Though some of us were still recovering from our injuries, we decided the memorial for Angela Sheldon would still take place the next day. Brady's concussion had turned out to be a mild one. Grant was lucky and there was no damage, other than a visible bruise and a bump. My injuries were repaired with superglue and stitches. I was told that any scaring would be minor and that I could have any visible remnants removed by plastic surgery if I wanted.

Angela's neighbors had passed away in the attack on Sonora and we couldn't find anyone close to the family still alive there.

Jack and Jeff were able to locate some information on Garan and his connection to the man who was supposed to be his brother. Apparently, they had attended school together and were unrelated. It could be that he convinced the friend he was part of a secret government operation and to say they were brothers. But the friend or fake brother was too dead to talk.

Garan himself had married a rich woman about his age from Oakhurst, who died from eating poisoned trout. I wondered if that was an accident. From the dates on his marriage certificates, we gathered that he had found a beautiful younger woman, Angela, and started a double life, in addition to his double life as a FEMA thug and a ranger.

Garan had said that Paul's mother had seen him with Angela and had threatened to expose him. Grant informed me that Laura had been friends with Garan's real wife from Oakhurst.

Our close group of friends attended the memorial. We had gone through trials of fire, had walked through a valley of death together and would be united in many ways for life. Even Eric and Brady put their differences aside.

Joey finally had the resolution he had sought in connection with his dad's death. He, Ronnie, Jeff, Jack and Lee also joined our family and the toddler we'd all come to love in honoring Angela.

I had asked that nobody, including the minister, actually use the words "death" or "dead." Yvonne clearly knew what had happened to her mother, but there was no need to rub it in.

A large basket on top of the casket was filled with pictures, perfumes, scarves, jewelry and books that Angela had kept in her room. The plan was to put them into a safe place for Yvonne when she became older.

The minister spoke of the love Angela clearly had for her daughter, of how courageous the little girl was and how proud her mother will be when they meet again. Yvonne went over to her mother's picture and cried, "I love you, Mommy. I love you."

"And she loves you too," I assured her.

"She always will," Paul added.

After the service, we went to the Ahwahnee, where a lunch had been prepared. There was a new park service handling the food since the prior contractor had bailed on the place. Yosemite and Asilomar, which had had the same vendor, had both gone all organic under the new one and all food and drinks were being tested before being served. This was the first day they were operating. Food and beverages had been specially brought in from uncontaminated areas and this was to continue until the Valley received full clearance.

Lee asked to speak with Paul and me privately while the luncheon was going on. "The government has offered a one-million-dollar settlement to Angela's daughter when she turns eighteen. I told them of concerns about her safety, given the crimes that had been committed by members of the federal government and they agreed to leave the money in a trust fund to be supervised by my firm."

"My family has considerable holdings and money. We were planning to take care of her out of those," Paul said.

"It will be something extra for her. As for the rest, I've arranged for you to adopt Yvonne, but under the adoption, she has different parentage in accordance with those documents Grant provided us."

Paul explained to me. "A couple who had lost most of their money in the economic non-recovery had filed to adopt out their daughter. They had no close family to assist and were taking a last vacation in Big Sur. We have a report the entire family died but their bodies were dumped in the ocean and it's doubtful they'll ever recover all of them."

"That's awful. I hope the report is wrong and their little girl survived."

"Yvonne is very lucky to be alive. So many others did not make it. It's a lesson that we must never stand down, again," Lee responded.

"Lee, how did you get all those people to march on Yosemite?"

"It wasn't me. It was all the rigged voting and censorship. They were tired of being silenced and called Russians and terrorists."

Lee handed me a file. "I got a judge to sign off on the adoption. With the parents declared dead, nobody will challenge it. If the other girl turns up alive, my firm will make sure she gets a good home."

I gave Lee a hug. "Thank you. You have done so much for us."

"It takes all of us standing together. Never take a back seat. There is more work to be done."

"We'll be there when we're needed."

EPILOGUE

A month and a half later, we had another major celebration at the Ahwahnee. It was Autumn's eighteenth birthday. Her three would-be suitors were in attendance and she was having a great time, as were the rest of us.

"You can't leave the Valley," Brady implored her.

"I've gotten into a really great pre-med program and the university also has a medical school I can attend when I get my BA."

I noticed Eric smiling. "Jack's helping me transfer to an ICS program at the same school," he whispered to me.

"Of course, you're not planning to crowd Autumn."

"It's a good program."

"From what I've seen, you, Jeff and Jack should be teaching that program."

He laughed. "But of course, none of us can leave Yosemite until Monday."

"Monday?"

"I hear there's a big event on Sunday."

"Hmm."

Paul pulled me away. "I don't think this is going to be a small event."

And it wasn't. Right at Glacier Point with family, friends and hundreds of supporters, some of whom had marched into the park to save the place, Paul and I took our vows. Autumn had picked out my wedding dress and I must say she had great taste. It was fluffy and white and really showed off my figure. She was wearing royal blue, as was our flower girl, Yvonne.

Instead of walking down the aisle, I carefully rode Laura over it, followed by Autumn on Atlas and Yvonne on Daphne. Everlove, Esther and their boyfriends trailed us. Paul, Grant and Jack were waiting on Lightning Bolt, Libra and Pan at the Point. The guys dismounted and then assisted us girls off our mounts. Paul walked me towards the Point, where the minister was standing, with the Valley visible below. Paul never let go of my hand during the ceremony.

I hoped our mothers were somehow watching as Paul looked into my eyes and said, "In my life, I never thought I'd experience the love I've found with you. I never thought I'd find someone as perfect for me as you. From the first moment I saw you, I knew you were my future. For the rest of my life, I will love you and only you. You are my love, my hero, my everything, my treasure." With that, he slipped his mother's engagement ring, along with a beautiful wedding band, onto my finger.

I responded. "You are the love I always wished for but never really believed I'd find until suddenly you were there. You didn't simply save my life. You saved my whole being. You showed me who I am and gave me a reason to live and to believe that dreams can come true. Forever isn't long enough. I'll love you for longer than eternity." I put a matching wedding band on his finger.

The minister spoke up: "Paul Patrick Beckett and Faithful Anne Dover, also known as Treasure, I now pronounce you husband and wife. You may—"

I suppose he finished the sentence but Paul was already kissing me. Somewhere in the background, I think I hear cheering. And then I felt small arms go around my legs. Paul and I picked up our little daughter and both hugged her.

As I turned to look at the crowd seated in chairs watching us, I saw a face I hadn't seen since I walked down from the Point months before.

"Tatiana!" I rushed over to my sister. "I wasn't expecting you to make it."

"It wasn't like I had a choice." She tried to raise her arms and I could see she was handcuffed to her chair. "That friend of yours."

I turned to my Maid of Honor. "I love you, Autumn." I turned back to my birth sister. "Tatiana, meet my other sister, the one who has stood by me whenever I needed her. I love you and one day, if you figure out what love is, maybe you'll be like a real sister again. Thank you for coming."

"Which year should I release her?" Autumn asked.

"In about ten. No. You can let her go now." I turned back to Tatiana. "Have a nice life."

After Paul and I cut the cake and had the first piece, Grant and Autumn started handing out slices. I noticed Autumn start to hand one to Tatiana. Instead, the cake made it right onto Tatiana's face.

Part of me wanted to laugh. Instead, I got Tatiana a napkin and a fresh piece of cake. I handed them to her and turned away to avoid showing my difficulty keeping a straight face.

"Faithful." I almost didn't recognize my name. I turned back to see if she needed something. "I'm a bitch. I'm proud of that. I'm sorry I didn't come back and that I didn't talk to you afterwards and also after you objected to the vaccine and the masks. You were there for me. You are the only one who was always there for me. I guess you deserved to be treated better."

My mouth almost dropped. I wanted to check Tatiana's forehead to see if she had a fever. "Thank you." I hugged her. She almost hugged me back. "I've missed you."

"Me too."

Someone had started up music. Paul took my hand.

"Paul, Tatiana. Tatiana, Paul."

"Nice to meet you," he politely said to her. To me, he said, "We've got the first dance."

"See you, Sis." I smiled and gave her another hug before walking off with Paul.

As he guided me to the area people had cleared to turn into a dancefloor, he said, "You've got a great heart. Make sure that everyone you give it to is willing to reciprocate."

I looked back at Tatiana and felt sad that she might never know what it was like to care more about someone than herself—unless she went through a dramatic change.

I turned back to my future. "I have you, Yvonne, Autumn, Grant and my new friends. I'm just glad that Tatiana is speaking to me for the moment, but whatever happens, I've got a real family now and that's everything."

He kissed me, again, and then whirled me around the dancefloor.

***

As Paul, Yvonne and I relaxed on a sailboat off the coast of St Thomas, the boat suddenly started shaking as three swimmers climbed aboard.

"We're here to take your lunch order."

"This is supposed to be a private honeymoon," Paul responded.

"That's why we're here. To make sure you have a really great private honeymoon," Autumn replied.

"We'll see you later," Paul said.

"Not too much later." Eric encouraged, looking out on the horizon.

"Does this thing have a motor?" Autumn asked.

"Got it," Eric replied.

"That way," Brady pointed as the boat sped toward a cove.

"What's going on?"

"Don't you see that plane in the distance?"

"Are they dropping something? Get us out of here," I urged.

"It's not that. I think they are here for you."

"What?"

Inside the cove, we found a staircase and took it up to a street, where a car was waiting. Jack was behind the wheel and drove us to a cottage.

"This is a little more private," Eric commented when we arrived.

"What's really going on?" Paul asked.

"It seems that there is a problem in D.C. and they want your help," Eric explained.

"Our help?"

"Well, all of our help," Autumn continued. "All, except Jack and Yvonne. We've kept their involvement in analyzing what was going on in Yosemite rather secret."

"Hit me with it," Paul said.

"It seems that the General and several of the military personnel who were at Yosemite have gone catatonic and one officer who isn't catatonic managed to get the launch codes to the missiles and threatened to launch them on Sri Lanka."

"Why don't they just change the launch codes?"

"Another problem. Before they discovered what had happened, the codes were changed, the President was locked out and FEMA and DARPA declared they were in charge," Eric explained.

"And this involves us how?" Paul asked.

"World War III?" Autumn responded. "Seems we have to save the world, again."

"For as long as I can remember, our government has been threatening World War III with any country that sneezes without apologizing to Washington's financiers," I recalled. "If they don't like it, let them deactivate their nuclear arsenal."

"They did. Or they think they did."

"Well, that's a good thing. We can all relax and celebrate," Paul concluded.

"There's more," Jack said. "Remember the mind control shots? Ronnie wants you to meet him in D.C. so they can explain to Congress that it was the injections that did that to the military and not an epidemic. DARPA is now working on shots to counter the new Catatonia Virus."

"And of course, the new injections will make everyone brain-dead to match our leaders. Why doesn't the government dismantle DARPA and FEMA?" I asked. "Problem solved."

"Why does the government keep funding foreign Nazis and lunatics in foreign countries at taxpayers' expense while Americans are starving in the streets? I don't think the government is on our side," Autumn contended.

"We were there and saw what the injections did," Jack persisted. "It might not hurt to let them know the cause was just the injections and not a virus."

"Remember what they did to all the truth-tellers during COVID and the following plandemics," Paul pointed out.

"Well, I guess we can broadcast the information from here until it's safe to go back to the States," Jack conceded.

"Or we could go back to Yosemite, where everyone knows what happened to those men—until the latest narrative is all over."

"Now for lunch, what would our favorite newlyweds like to eat?" Autumn asked.

Paul turned to me. "Organic pancakes?"

"Cakes!" Yvonne exclaimed.

"I think Yvonne knows what's important," I observed.

"But Paul. The world could end," Eric warned.

"Not happening on our honeymoon. One stack or two?"

COMMENTARY

Though I never had a sister, I patterned Autumn's personality after that of my best friend April Alyce Higgins, who was always strong, courageous and loyal.

Unlike Treasure's parents, mine were really great people who loved each other very much, a lot like Paul's parents. However, unlike Paul's, my parents lived more normal lives in regular houses.

Domestic violence has a terrible impact on whole families, often resulting in interactions, like the one that takes place at the beginning of the novel. Society is good at blaming survivors for the violence perpetrated on them as if they deserved to be beaten. The courts and police do not protect domestic violence victims and, instead, punish the survivors, who often can't afford food, medicine or housing—even if they were middle class or higher during the marriage.

Survivors who get out are largely discarded as non-human trash with no rights. The vast majority of homeless women got there by leaving domestic violence situations and losing all their property to their abusers in the courtrooms. These homeless women are not druggies, but rather chose to get out of situations where they were beaten, often later wishing they had continued to take the abuse instead of starving to death and not knowing whether their last possessions or their lives will be taken away from them while they sleep.

Even when there is a restraining order in place, it's treated as toilet paper by police and other authorities. Judges routinely assist abusers in getting around these, granting access to the victims, both during a divorce and any time the perpetrator files an Order to Show Cause for bogus reasons. While statistically four or more women are counted as dying daily in the USA from domestic violence, the real number is a dramatically higher multiple of that and this does not include those who died from denial of medical treatment for their injuries. Similarly, children are dying daily while courts remove all rights from protective parents reporting domestic violence on the false legal premise that merely reporting abuse is "alienation," or an equivalent term, a crime worse than murder in the family court injustice system. Police and doctors who can confirm the violence are often prohibited from testifying.

This book is fiction, but if you want to know about what the government is dropping from the sky, open your eyes and see the checkerboards over your head or look at any of the extensive amount of testing that has been done by private labs on the rainwater and snowpacks. Do your own research and come to your own conclusions.

ACKNOWLEDGMENTS

A great many journalists, scholars, researchers, doctors, scientists, friends, former leaders and others, too many to list here, provided me with much of the information necessary to write this book.

I must especially acknowledge my amazing God-daughter Shannon Marie Ream, who is a very positive influence in my life and my friend Tammy Rief, who is a hero and an inspiration to women everywhere. While the political two party illusion has collapsed and American society has become divided being between fact-seekers and research-hating-narrative-pushers from both sides of the political spectrum, Cindy Sheehan, Dennis Kucinich and Cynthia McKinney, and a great many true courageous leaders I've known through the years, have remained steadfast in their quest for truth and peace and have let those of us who seek answers know we are not alone. Craig Pasta Jardula and Fiorella Isabel, the election integrity reporters who used to do the *Convo Couch* (referenced in the book), can now be seen on *Truthwire*. I am also grateful to my wonderful editor, Rosi de Guzman, and my publisher, Jessica Verrill, who made the publication of this book possible.

I wrote both *Silent Deathfall* and *Reset Reset* (soon to be published) in November, 2022 during the now-defunct National Novel Writing Month (NaNoWriMo). While writing this, I attended the California Public Defender's Association Felony Law Seminar in Yosemite National Park, my favorite vacation spot. Yosemite is a national treasure that needs to be preserved and kept free of chemtrails and other environmental pollution.

ALSO BY NATALIE TRIUMPHS

Best Sellers Now Available

Summer Heat: Education: American Gulag Style

#1 Amazon Best Selling Book in Young Adult Schools & Education

#1 Amazon New Release in Teen & Young Adult Politics & Government Fiction

#1 Amazon New Release in Teen & Young Adult Fiction about Parents

After a break-up with her boyfriend, fifteen-year-old Summer Tanner, a survivor of the Family Court Injustice System, finds herself kidnapped and imprisoned in one of America's Gulag Camps, part of a behavior modification system where thousands of teens are taken against their will annually to be "fixed," often returning home in body bags or psychologically damaged for life. There, Summer meets allies, including a new love interest, who, like her, wants to escape and bring an end to America's teen torture programs. But how high up does the corruption of the multi-billion-dollar industry run and how far will the forces in power go to silence Summer and her new friends to keep the truth from coming out?

Taking Down the Deep State: Summer Heat II

#1 Amazon Best Seller Teen & Young Adult Media Studies eBook

#1 Amazon Best Seller Teen & Young Adult Sociology eBook

#1 Amazon New Release in Young Adult Politics & Government

Having escaped their American Gulag Camp, Summer and her friends, now known as the Wilderness Five, return to the States to expose the torture and deaths in the behavior modification programs and close them down. To silence the truth, Deep State retaliates in full force, threatening the lives of the teens, university students and anyone else taking a stand for human rights and against the mistreatment of America's youth. When Americans stand together for rights and justice, even the most powerful forces on Earth cannot defeat them. This book, written in 2017, has predicted numerous real-life events which have taken place in more recent times.

Kakistocracy of the Technocrats

#1 Amazon Best Seller in Young Adult Politics & Government

#1 Amazon Best Seller in Young Adult Fiction Alternative History

As White House researcher for a non-existent department that oversees a demented robotic President, Karissa James finds herself in the middle of a string of murders, fires, earthquakes, embassy bombings, assassination attempts, bribes, wars and an Administration that can best be described as a Kakistocracy.

Everything

#1 Amazon Best Seller in Human Rights Law,

#1 Amazon Best Seller in Young Adult Adventures and Adventurers

#1 Amazon Best Seller in Young Adults Politics and Government

After the deaths of her parents, Meadow Clarkson finds herself woven into the world of child trafficking, false flags, mass disappearances, rogue government agents and secret government operations. Her primary companions are a two-hundred-and-fifty year old talking dog named Everything and Cal, a mysterious guy who keeps appearing in her life, as Meadow fights to save children from capture and slaughter, to protect her canine companion and other dogs from a dog-killing frenzy that has swept the nation and to discover what has happened to curious people who have suddenly disappeared.

Coming Soon:

Everything II: Meadow, her talking Papillion, Everything, Cal and their friends continue their adventure as they work to save the lives of dogs and other animals in a world that will forever be changed by judicial corruption, murders, dognappings and trans-species experimentation. Also coming, the final book in the series is

Everything III: Once again, Meadow, Everything, Cal and their friends fight to expose government corruption so extreme that it threatens the future of humanity.

Reset, Reset: What if World War III was a lie?

ABOUT THE AUTHOR

Natalie Triumphs is a criminal defense and civil rights attorney, private investigator, investigative journalist and best-selling author. She is a strong advocate for the youth rights, for Constitutional rights and for eliminating the NDAA, the Espionage Act and other unconstitutional laws used to target whistleblowers, journalists and truth-tellers. She has fought for protections for domestic violence survivors, for victims of child trafficking and for vulnerable individuals falsely targeted by the criminal justice system. Natalie, who is also an environmentalist and a member of the Environmental Law Section of the California Lawyers Association, grew up camping at Yosemite National Park every summer.

www.ingramcontent.com/pod-product-compliance
Lightning Source LLC
Chambersburg PA
CBHW021335310726
48971CB00001B/135